# Raves for LOKI'S DAUGHTERS

"Ms. Jacobs has masterminded a marvelous tale of love. Ancient rites and determined men and women rule the pages of this humorous and fascinating read." (4 ½ stars)
~ Faith V. Smith for *Romantic Times Magazine*

"This stunningly captivating novel belongs on the keeper shelf."
(Very Highly Recommended)
~ Cindy Penn for WordWeaving

"An excellent story written by Ms. Jacobs, and I look forward to reading more from this author. Four Stars for Loki's Daughters."
~ Natasha for Charlene Smith Reviews

"...an absolutely captivating historical romance. I loved this historical romance so much that I read it again, to quench my appetite for more."
~ S. Wharton, "n2romance" on Amazon.com

"Loki's Daughters by Delle Jacobs is a bold adventure of Vikings and Celts. Written with a deft hand and a fine eye for detail, the story thrusts the readers into the ninth century on a tide swell of love, lust, and revenge."
~ Lisa Jackson, bestselling author

# LOKI'S DAUGHTERS

# Loki's Daughters

## DELLE JACOBS

Montlake
Romance

Text copyright © 2010 Delle Jacobs
All rights reserved.
Printed in the United States of America.

Published by Montlake Romance
P.O. Box 400818
Las Vegas, NV 89140

ISBN-13: 9781612184869
ISBN-10: 1612184863

*For Lady Jan:*

*Always a heroine*

# CHAPTER ONE

———————— ✤ ————————

## CUMBRIA, 9TH CENTURY AD

SHE HAD NOT BEEN TO THE STONE CIRCLE IN A SENNIGHT, AND Arienh yearned to escape to its quiet serenity. But rain had fallen long and hard for six days, and the river lapped threateningly at its banks. In the high mountains, the deluge melted the snow, and if the slopes lost their white coats too quickly, disaster loomed for her narrow valley at their feet.

Arienh paused in the doorway of the little stone cottage, glancing back and forth between the gathering dark clouds and her sister's pale green eyes. Beside the hearth, little Liam sat with his lower lip protruding in an exaggerated pout, for he had already been told he could not go.

"Do you go to move the stones?" Birgit asked.

"Nay. There is no time before the next storm. The stones will have to wait." As if she had no worries at all, Arienh stopped to watch in fascination as Birgit reached into the willow basket beside her and pulled out a skein of brown wool to wind on her shuttle. In the cottage's dim light, Birgit's failing eyes probably could not even see the colors of the patterns she wove, yet her work was always perfect. Arienh shook her head. Birgit could tell the color of her wool just by the texture the dye gave it.

Birgit smiled lightly, her pale eyes brightening at Arienh's unspoken question. "From Mildread's old ram," she said, fingering the brown skein. "He gave the softest wool. I will miss him."

"The ewes will miss him more. I will not be long, but I must climb the low mount near the estuary to look at the mountains. Perhaps I can tell if the snow melts too fast."

Arienh closed the door, hearing the latch click into place. Already the wind had shifted, blowing stiff, cold, and damp from the sea, so she knotted her shawl and strode briskly across the valley. When the slope steepened, the path deteriorated into a slick, muddy rivulet, then ended abruptly. Grabbing a handful of soggy brown bracken, Arienh hoisted herself up past jutting rock faces. If she avoided the mudslides, the climb was not difficult. Yet after a winter's inactivity, her heart raced faster and her breaths came more quickly. It felt good.

A lone, slender ash tree drooped down a branch, and she grasped it and tugged herself up onto the next ledge. Already she longed for the rough weather in her face at the top of her climb, and the view out over the grey, churning Irish Sea and inland to the high peaks with the snow on their slopes that worried her. She looked up to find her next handhold.

Terror slammed into her.

Her gaze slid swiftly up a huge masculine form, past alien boots, legs stout as tree trunks, broad chest, and husky arms, and screeched to a stop at startled blue eyes.

Viking!

Her gasp burst into a shriek. The Viking lunged for her as she twisted away, hurling herself down the way she had come. His steps crashed behind her. Arienh dashed along a ledge, leapt, landed on a mudslide, and skidded down the rock-strewn slope. She scrambled to her feet, clambered over jutting stones to another slide of mud, ignoring bruising rocks and snags that tore at skin and cloth as she hurtled downhill. Behind her the Viking shouted in his heathen tongue.

Arienh hit the valley floor hard, stumbled, lurched to her feet, and ran, dodging around boulders, forcing her legs as fast as they could go. Her lungs burned as she gasped, commanding herself, run faster! Faster!

The Viking caught her hair, yanked her backward. A huge arm ensnared her waist, cutting short her breath. Jerking her dagger from her waist cord, she stabbed backward and felt the sickening give of flesh beneath the blade. The raider dropped his hold, staggered back, astonishment flooding his wide blue eyes.

She stared, stunned. Surely this was not hers but some alien blade that was gripped in her hand, dripping bright blood. Inside herself, she screamed at her legs to flee, but they rooted into the mud like house posts.

The giant man fell to his knees, hands lacing over the bloody wound in his gut. He pitched forward, arms swinging to catch himself, then his blood-slick hands slipped on the boulder before him. His head cracked against it, the sound muffled by a sudden, quiet gasp, cut short.

He was dead. He was, wasn't he? Arienh inched closer.

The Viking moaned. Blood oozed from the side of his head as his eyes rolled open, closed, open. His hand groped toward her. A silent word formed on his lips.

Her scream stuck in her throat as she ran across the rocky valley to the safety of her cottage. She slammed the door behind her and threw the bolt.

Birgit startled at the noise and dropped her shuttle. "Arienh? What?"

"Vikings! They're back!" Arienh leaned against the barred door, gasping for breath, horror still pounding in her chest with the frantic thumping of her heart.

"Vikings! Where? Have they overrun us?"

"No, I saw only one, but there must be others. Up on the mount behind the house."

"Liam," Birgit called to her small son. "Come quickly!"

Already rising, the boy tossed his brassy mop of hair.

"Hurry, Liam. Can we make the cavern, Arienh?"

"I don't think there's time. Oh, Birgit, I did not even raise the alarm. The others will be slaughtered, and it is my fault. I thought only of myself."

From the peg in the stone wall, Arienh lifted the horn her father had made, then grabbed for the bolt across the door.

Birgit's brows lifted high. "You're not going out there."

"I've got to warn the others."

"Arienh, you're no match for Vikings. They'll kill you."

"Bolt the door behind me."

"Check the window first."

"Aye." Arienh rushed to the narrow slit in the stone wall that faced the near slope. If they came, it would be from over the mount, beyond where the Viking lay in the muddy field.

He was surely dead now. But no sign of his comrades.

Yet Vikings never came alone, for one man could not sail a longship. It made no sense.

"Nothing," she said. "Perhaps we can make the cavern."

Standing in the doorway, she blew three long blasts on the horn. The sound brought women and children pouring from their cottages, running toward the rain-soaked cliff behind the village that contained their cavern, the only hope of safety for those who could reach it in time. If any raiders made the mistake of entering the cavern, those who did not fall into the concealed pits would be pelted with stones by the women who had climbed to high ledges.

"Come, Birgit. Hurry."

Birgit threw a shawl over her shoulders and tucked the last of a wedge of cheese into its folds, then grabbed a blanket for Liam as she tugged his hand.

The sky darkened even as Arienh watched, and large globs of cold rain slapped at her face. Arienh took Birgit's hand even though it was not yet so dark that her sister's dim vision could not make out the muddy path. Arienh lifted her nephew onto her hip and, following the stream bank, steered Birgit through muddy rivulets that fed the swollen creek, until they arrived safely at the cavern.

Arienh looked back again across the darkening valley, obscured by rain. Still no alien raiders had come.

"Did you see them?" Mildread asked of Arienh as she reached down her hand to help Liam into the safe haven of the upper cave.

"Only one." Arienh paused for breath and sat, resting her back against dark rock. "I killed him. He's by the stream near our cottage. Perhaps they won't come, now that we're warned."

"Perhaps he was alone," said Mildread, folding her arms with a shudder.

"Perhaps they turned and ran," said Elli. "They are really cowards, my father said."

"They do not know we have no men to fight them," Selma added, nodding. Her pretty blue eyes searched Arienh's face for reassurance that Arienh could not give.

Mildread frowned as she pushed her brown braids back over her shoulder. "Are you sure it was a Viking, Arienh?"

"I know what Vikings look like. It was a Viking."

Old Ferris, his black eyes gleaming like jet beads in the torchlight, clasped his wrinkled hands together. "Then we'll keep watch. Perhaps the rain has merely delayed them."

Selma shuddered. "They will kill us when they find him."

"Nay," said Elli. "The heathens abandon their dead."

Either could be true, and they all knew it. Perhaps it depended upon the importance of the man she had slain.

But only the storm came down upon them. Sheltered within the cavern's lip, they collectively regretted the need to go back out into the soaking rain.

"Perhaps he was alone, lost from his band," Old Ferris suggested. "Perhaps he alone survived a shipwreck in the last storm." Whatever it was, there were no Vikings. The day grew late, and everyone knew Vikings did not come in the dark. They liked to strike swift, hard, unexpectedly, then escape to the sea.

"The Vikings will not come now," Mildread pronounced, as if she had reached the conclusion alone. "But what about the flood, Arienh?"

"Aye, will it flood, Arienh?" The question came from all around her.

In the face of a danger more immediate, she had nearly forgotten the greater one. "I could not tell. I had no time to check the snowpack, so I don't know how fast it is melting, but the river is far too high. We should prepare."

A grim murmur spread through the gathered women. Each one accepted her task, hard work made even harder by the freezing rain, but they could afford no more losses.

Still, Arienh knew them well. If they went to all that trouble to move flocks and fodder from the lower valley, and then the waters receded without event, the entire village would grumble at her. Arienh was used to it. They always expected her to know such things, as if the stones should somehow tell her, for they didn't understand the stones the way she did. But no matter how much they complained, she would do what must be done, or the Celts in this valley would not survive. Sometimes she just had to accept the blame.

"But what if the Vikings come tomorrow?" Selma asked, still wide-eyed with worry.

And well they might. "Then tomorrow we will deal with them. For now, it will be enough to keep watch while we see to the flock."

Elli's eyes glittered a silent demand as she pulled her heavy shawl over her shoulders, took her grandfather's horn from him, and planted herself squarely before Arienh. Arienh studied her friend, knowing what was in her mind. She would be thinking of her father's violent death in his own forge at the hands of a raider while his only child hid behind the ricks of wood. She would be remembering how the red-bearded giant had looked straight at her, then inexplicably turned and left.

Arienh nodded as if Elli had spoken aloud. "We will do what makes most sense. If there are others, they are still here, and if they come, it will be tomorrow, when the storm abates. Take the watch in the lower valley at dawn, Elli," Arienh said, "but stay away from the river and climb the hill where you will be safer. We will all watch until nightfall as we move the flock."

In the unreal calm that followed, Arienh trudged with Birgit and Liam along the valley path toward the lower cottages and their sheepfolds. Old Ferris and Elli gathered disquieted sheep from separate folds to drive to high ground, while other women and children bundled precious necessities to carry uphill to the upper cottages. Even Birgit bundled fodder in her shawl and slung it over her shoulders, for only her eyes were weak.

Repeatedly, Arienh scanned the slope of the distant mount that flanked the estuary until the rain grew so heavy she could not see it. But now that the last light of day was fading, she knew no Viking would roar down its slopes. She searched the turbulent river, knowing no pitch-blackened, dragon-headed longship would dare its roiling ferocity, nor would blood-red sails face the raging sea beyond the estuary. Her fears eased.

Up on the hill beside the stream, the Viking still lay in the mud. Was he dead?

As Arienh adjusted Birgit's bundle of fodder, the sky opened, split by a sword of lightning. New torrents of cold rain soaked the already sodden villagers as bolt after bolt of lightning illuminated the clouds.

Shouts penetrated through the howling wind. Arienh spun around, squinting to search past slanting rain. At the river's sharpest curve where it swung east toward the estuary, the bank crumbled. Sheets of thin mud spread out, fanning out over the flat valley, in moments swirling around their feet, eroding the mud beneath their feet.

With a yelp, Birgit slipped to her knees. Fodder spilled and spread across the surface of the water like a writhing blanket, folding under and back onto the surface. Arienh scooped up Liam onto her hip and gripped Birgit's hand to steady her as, knee-deep in icy water, they forced each treacherous footfall through the flow. Hard, jerking shivers raced through her body as Liam wrapped his lanky arms and legs tightly around her and buried his face into her shoulder.

Collective bellows of the flock blended with the din of the storm as unhappy beasts struggled to high ground. The flock would be safe, but they'd see a new channel cut for the river by morning.

She grasped Mildread's hand, which was extended to help them out of the turbid water.

"Are you all right?" Mildread asked, wrapping her shawl around Liam.

Arienh could only nod, for it almost seemed to be colder out of the water than in. She had strength for little more than shivering as other women herded bedraggled beasts into three abandoned cottages for the night.

She took Birgit's hand and trudged toward home, shivering against the storm that blew through her soaked shawl and kirtle. Her exhausted feet throbbed painfully and slipped beneath her as she walked.

"I am a burden to you," Birgit said, her head bowed to the storm.

How hard it must be for Birgit, who could hardly see where to put her feet. "Nay, Birgit, we need each other." Arienh did not lie, for however hard life might be, it would seem futile without Birgit and Liam. But Birgit, engulfed in all her losses, could not understand that.

By the cottage door, Arienh stopped to strain her gaze out over the dark field. Silhouetted, black against growing darkness, the Viking lay where she had left him in the field, his back to the freezing rain, face to the mud. The flooding stream rose and soon would swallow up his body. Was he dead yet? Like a writhing shadow, the black shape changed, thickening as it rose on hands and knees.

Fear invaded her again. Was he a berserker, to rise and kill in merciless fury even as he died? Cold shudders rushed through her. Arienh gripped her dagger, slogged grimly across the open field, and planted herself between him and her village.

With an agonized groan, the Viking pushed himself up to sit, leaning heavily on his arms. Great jerking shivers from the cold rain racked his body. Mud streamed down his face. The eyes that had been so startlingly blue had deepened, dusky dark in the twilight, wrenched with pain.

She shuddered. He must be as cold as she.

Arienh clenched her jaw, shutting down the surge of pity. He was a Viking, a merciless, brutal killer. She felt nothing for him.

"I wonder what you did to your victims who were as helpless as you are now, Viking? Did you run them through? Or just cut off their hands and feet to watch them bleed?"

With his dark gaze fixed on her, his hand trembled on the buckle of the leather strap at his waist. She sprang back. Only a quick throw of a dagger, and he could have his revenge. The strap fell free, and his long sword clanged to the stony ground. Shaking, he pulled a knife from its scabbard and held it out to her.

"Kill me."

The Celtic words from his heathen mouth startled her. Behind him, lightning split the sky, and in its flash, she saw, not the Viking, but the image of her brother who had died in her arms. As sharp as the brilliant bolt, the torture of Trevor's dying agony stabbed through her anew. A Viking had killed him. Perhaps even this man's kin.

"Finish it," the Viking demanded.

Sudden rage filled her, aching to meet his challenge.

The knife shook in his hand as he swayed dizzily, and his breaths came hard as the dark, metallic daring in his eyes dissolved to anguished need. "Finish it. Or help me."

Help a Viking? Arienh snatched the knife from his hand. Strength shot up from the dark rage in her heart, flooding through her like shafts of iron. Fury lifted her arm, vengeance powered it as it raised high for the downward stroke.

Viking! Hideous, filthy, murdering Viking! She saw the wild-eyed, toothless villain whose ax cut down her father, the red-bearded giant whose sword hacked Trevor to his death, the fiend who raped and brutalized Birgit. Violent tremors coursed through her.

Help him? Dark, sad eyes waited patiently for her blow.

He was Trevor. He was her father. And he was the strange Viking boy who long ago had come from nowhere to save her, then vanished; like the boy, his eyes were the same brilliant blue. Spasms shot down through her arm and wrapped around her chest in a suffocating band.

*Kill him.*

Kill him? It had been easy before, to strike back in fear, but to cut down a wounded man? Even a filthy Northman?

"Nay."

The dagger fell, clattering against a stone. The Viking once more collapsed. A moan faded to silence.

Arienh dropped to her knees beside the wounded man, her gut wrenching, and her hand came within a finger's breadth of touching his before she jerked it back. He was going to die, not quickly, as Trevor had gone, but in slow, merciless agony. In the cold, in the rain, in the mud. In pain, with no one to comfort him.

But horror snatched her back. He was a Viking. How could she pity the vermin? Arienh jumped to her feet and fled across the field.

Once again inside her cottage with the door securely barred, she breathed again, long, precious breaths. She kicked off her soggy boots, pulled on an old brown kirtle, and sat next to Liam by the hearth, wrapped in her blanket.

She squeezed her eyes closed and still she could see the Viking's eyes, agony interlaced with entreaty. Stunningly blue as bright skies that had darkened like a summer storm, they watched her hungrily, as if they were everywhere, following every move she made.

Nay, she could not kill him. How could she have thought she could? His eyes would torment her forever.

Drawing back the rawhide that covered the cottage window, she searched the night's moonless darkness as it deepened with the growing ferocity of the storm. Icy, wind-driven rain slammed past at a vicious slant. She could see nothing, not the Viking, nor the scattered stones of the field where he lay. But she knew without seeing it that the stream rose and spilled over its banks, lapped at his feet. Covered his body.

*He's going to drown.*

She should not care. He was a Viking. Her father's blood was on his hands. Yet...Arienh was drowning in his pain.

"Come away from there, Arienh. You can do nothing."

"It's so horribly cold out there, Birgit. No one should have to die like that."

"It's not your fault. You don't go about pillaging and murdering. In any event, he would have killed you."

Her eyes strained against the darkness, and she shivered at the chill blast of wind whistling through the tiny window slit. In her mind, she saw the frigid mud congealed in the Viking's hair and oozing down his cheeks, sliding into those incredible blue eyes.

"Aye, I know. But he isn't dead."

"Then go back and kill him."

"I can't."

"He's a Viking. The kind that killed our father. They destroy everything they touch. They don't deserve to live."

"Perhaps not. But they don't deserve to die this way."

"If any do, a Viking does."

*He's going to drown.*

"But not of my doing. I can't leave him like that." Arienh yanked on her wet boots and threw her damp shawl over her shoulders.

"Come back!" Birgit shouted. "Don't go, Arienh!"

Arienh shoved up the bolt and yanked open the door. Fierce wind slammed her backward, stopping her breath in her throat. Tightening the shawl around her body, she struggled out into pellets of sleet, across the field. With each step, the mud nearly sucked her boots from her feet.

The spot that compelled her, where the Viking lay, seemed to be as far off as the next valley, but she struggled on against the screeching wind until once again she stood beside the swollen stream.

The Viking was gone.

Buffeted by the howling wind, a shrill scream pierced the storm.

Birgit!

# CHAPTER TWO



The Viking had reached the cottage. But how?

Arienh whirled into the flailing wind and tore across the field, summoning up long-faded strength, whispering urgent prayers. How? The man had not even been able to rise to his feet, much less cross a muddy field.

Memories of bloodied corpses of family and friends slashed apart by godless Vikings rose up like gorge. If he harmed Liam or Birgit, she would flay him alive and cut off little pieces…

She ran faster, faster, slipping, falling, rising to run again. Gasping, she reached the door and shoved, praying he had not thrown the bolt. It yielded to her weight.

Behind the open hearth, the Viking crouched, using the fire like a shield. A dagger flashed in his shaking hand. Brown mud caked his hair and trickled down his forehead, into his eyes in rivulets, and the soft leather of his jerkin and breeches alternately sagged and clung to his skin. Fierce shivers convulsed his body. His eyes, hard and dark like a wounded badger, dared her to attack, yet in an odd way, entreated her.

What did he want? Warmth?

She glanced at Birgit, whose pale green eyes flashed both fire and fear as she huddled Liam behind her in the corner by her raised bed.

"Go to the door, Birgit. Take Liam and go."

"And leave you here? Nay."

Of course she wouldn't. Birgit could not find her way in this dismal night, nor would she ever desert her sister.

"Tell Liam to go." Keeping Birgit and Liam safely behind her, she fixed her gaze on the Viking.

"Nay," said Birgit, her voice icy calm. "There could be more of them out there. Don't go near him, Arienh."

"He's just cold, can't you see?"

"Cold? He'll kill you."

"Then you would be dead already. Nay, he's dying and he knows it. He just wants to be warm." Arienh sidled to her raised bed and pulled off its woolen blanket.

"You don't think he wants revenge? Don't be a fool."

Arienh knew what she must do, and something in the knowledge of it eased her fear. He might kill her, but Viking or not, she could not leave him to die so cold. Yet she must also protect Birgit and Liam. If she could just get him calmed and warm, he might die quietly, but as he was now, he was far too dangerous.

His knife flashed, hard iron reflecting the fire. She flinched in spite of herself. Dangerous eyes studied her, then glanced beyond her shoulder at Birgit and back to Arienh. He leaned forward and set the knife down by the hearth, giving a grim nod of submission.

With her toe, Arienh pushed the knife out of his reach. As she held out the heavy wool blanket, he snatched it and with one hand tugged it over his shoulders.

Arienh flinched, her heart leaping into her throat. She tamped down the fear that quickened again with each sudden move he made.

"We must get you dry," she said calmly. "All the blankets we have cannot help if you are wet. Birgit, bring some rags and Papa's old tunic."

"You are not going to give him Papa's tunic."

"Papa doesn't need it. Hurry, please."

"You have taken leave of your senses, Arienh."

"Just do as I ask."

Beneath the raised bed that had once belonged to her parents, Arienh had stored all the things that had once belonged to a large family, in the bleak hope that the cottage would someday ring again with voices. She pulled out the pallet stuffed with wool, which had been her bed less than a year before. Unrolling the mat, she showed the Viking that she meant it for his use.

Birgit approached, a loathing sneer flaring her nostrils, and dropped the pile of rags and the old linen tunic to the dirt floor beside Arienh.

Kneeling before the man, Arienh raised a rag to his face. At her touch, his wariness softened to wistful sadness. Did he think of a love lost forever? Perhaps there was a sweetheart, a wife, whom he thought never to see again. Then his hungry longing gave way to a sigh and the wisp of a smile.

She dabbed at his cheek. "How did you get here?" she asked.

"Crawled."

"Why?"

Pain flashed across his eyes. "You know."

She did. It was not death, but cold that was unbearable.

"He's addled, Arienh," said Birgit. "Beware."

Arienh ignored her. With gentle strokes, she wiped the mud and water from his face and hair, and away from the swollen knot on the side of his head. Blood came off on the rag, old blood, dark and crusted, along with new, bright red and fresh.

"Let me see it," she said in a low tone.

For a brief moment, he returned a frown of pain but then quietly tilted the side of his head in her direction. She laced her fingers through his dark, wet hair, assessing the hard knot and the broken skin over it. Well, at least his skull was not cracked.

15

She had not noticed the darkness of his hair before. As wet as it was, she could not be sure, but it looked even darker than Mildread's brown braids. It seemed unusual for one of his kind, as did the shadow of a dark beard that bristled on his cheek. Yet in his brilliant blue eyes and enormous, rawboned body, his Viking blood was unquestionable.

"Your clothes must come off," she said.

"Arienh!"

"Be still, Birgit. Take off your jerkin," she told him.

"Nay."

"You must."

"I cannot raise my arm," he said. The Celtic words sounded strange, coming from his foreign tongue.

Of course. Raising his arm would put an unbearable strain on the wound in his gut. "Then lift the one arm from the sleeve. I will help you with the other."

The sleeves were loose, but the wet leather clung to him as she pulled it free of his right arm, then worked the jerkin over his head and down past the left arm. Beneath it lay a blood-soaked linen tunic, with interlaced embroidery in bright yellow and red, the soaked fabric almost transparent against his skin. She lifted it carefully, baring his chest.

He was breathtaking, both in his rugged immensity and form, his body broad-shouldered and lean, with muscles rippling like mountain ridges and sculpted valleys. Even sitting hunched over by her fire, he was intimidating.

She dried frigid skin, quickly covering him again with the woolen blanket. The hard shivers that coursed through his body eased as his skin lost its bluish tinge. As she dabbed gingerly about the wound, he winced but made no sound. It was bad. It must have bled heavily, but now a trickle oozed from the wound, diluted to pale pink by the water from his jerkin.

Through the gaping hole she could see corded tissue the color of raw meat, with a slash cleanly cut in it. Beyond that, she could not tell. Perhaps the blow had not penetrated into his vital organs, but that was unlikely. She knew little about such things, only that people did not normally survive gut wounds.

He would not live. He knew it, and she knew it. Their eyes met with the knowledge.

Guiltily, she looked away. "Best to leave it alone," she said.

Gently, Arienh drew her father's tunic over the Viking's head and onto his arms, then lifted the blanket back into place over his shoulders. A hint of a smile curled at one side of his mouth, and the dark fringe of lashes around his blue eyes merged with a crinkle of lines at their corners, lines that said he was a man who laughed hard and often. She had to work to break away from his fascinating gaze.

Arienh turned to his boots and unbound and pulled each one off, along with the woolen hose. She dried his feet as she had his body, gently, thoroughly, and massaged the puffed and wrinkled skin to warm them.

"Bury me in my clothes, little Celt."

Startled at the deep voice, she glanced again at the blue eyes and once more caught her breath at their brilliance. A shiver coursed over her, feeling like the summer's first warm breeze against skin too long chilled by winter.

Arienh readjusted her composure to renew the strange battle of words. "It is hard enough to get them off. And you want me to put them back on?"

A wry smile formed on his pale lips, seeming to turn both up and down, a sensuous mouth, generously curved, expressive. His intense, masculine beauty tugged at her heart.

She sighed. "Not that you deserve it."

"Perhaps you will take my boots, then?"

He teased her; that was it. Perhaps he expected her to misconstrue his feeble attempt at humor.

"Little good they would do me," she retorted. "I would have to tie the toes about my waist to make them fit. Nay, not the boots, but perhaps that fine linen tunic."

"You would have to mend it."

"Aye, a shame. But it is a fine piece of work." She wondered where a Viking might get such a thing.

"My mother."

"Vikings have mothers? What a surprise. We thought you were hatched in snakes' dens."

"Born like all men. She is a Celt, like you."

From behind her, Arienh heard her sister's haughty sniff, but, drawn by her curiosity, Birgit leaned around Arienh and studied the Viking with narrowed eyes. "Pity the Celtic woman who must give birth to the likes of him."

The Viking's eyes crinkled at the corners, and he cocked his head. "I do not think she minded."

"Ha." Birgit wrinkled her nose to emphasize her snarl.

"The breeches must also come off," said Arienh.

His gaze met hers. A wicked grin twisted at the corners of his lips, forming a blatant implication that sent a ripple of fear through her. He fumbled with the cord at his waist, but the wet knot was swollen tight and eluded his still-trembling fingers.

She gulped and shoved the fear deep inside where he could not see it. He was a little too eager. She decided to amend her statement. "So that you may dry off. It will be easier if you lie down."

The man chuckled almost silently as he eased himself down onto the wool pallet. She dug her fingernails into the knot, freeing it one fiber at a time. Then she eased the breeches down past his hips, and she saw why he laughed.

Not possible. He was surely half frozen. But then he was a Viking, and they were legendary for such things.

"I see it is true, what they say about Northmen," she said.

"What?"

"That their lust is unending."

Wickedness danced in his eyes. "True. Will you dry all of me, little Celt?"

"I will help you with your breeches only. You seem well enough recovered. Dry yourself."

"Nay, I cannot." He gave a pathetically helpless sigh.

Arienh grumbled at his arrogance and picked up the rag, for it had to be done. With gentle strokes that belied her pique, she wiped the damp skin on his legs, her eyes carefully avoiding the obvious sign of the man's unwelcome arousal.

"You've missed something." Laughter danced in his eyes.

"Then perhaps it will freeze and fall off."

"Lie down with me."

"Nay." Arienh sprang back.

The massive hand lashed out and captured her arm, and a smile of beguiling sweetness gleamed on his face. "Lie down with me and keep me warm. You are cold too, little Celt. I will not take your blanket and leave you none."

"Nay." Arienh pushed futilely against his grip.

"Don't let him touch you, Arienh. He'll kill you."

"It's not dying I'm worried about at the moment, Birgit," she said, still straining against his surprising strength. "He seems to be healthier than I thought."

A fraudulent snarl rumbled from the Viking, competing with an oddly cajoling smile. "Tell her I won't kill you. Only her."

Despite herself, Arienh chuckled at Birgit's outraged huff. Birgit's hatred of his kind went much deeper than hers, but her sister was right, and the sweetness she saw in his eyes only masked the evil of his race.

"I did not mean you harm," he said.

"You did not?" she retorted with a sneer. "And for what did you chase me down the mountain and half across the valley?"

"Perhaps I meant to take you home with me." The Viking pulled her toward him.

She jerked against his grip. It was like being pinned in the branches of a huge, gnarled tree. "You did not think I might object?"

His lips crinkled upward. "You would like it there."

Did he deliberately provoke her? He was coming close. She set her jaw, determined not to fall into his trap. "You lie. What are you doing here if you do not come to raid?"

"I came for you."

"Ha. Vikings come only to raid. And they do not come alone. It takes more than one man to sail a longship."

"Aye."

"So you are not alone."

"Not right now." With a sharp yank, he wedged her tightly against him, his arm wrapped about her like an iron band. She could only free herself by hurting him where he was wounded, and she couldn't persuade herself to do that unless she must.

And she didn't want to make him mad.

Vikings were strange that way. They had no fear of death and could summon up inhuman strength when they needed it, in just the way he did now. If he went berserk, as she had seen some do, there would be nothing human about him. She must placate him until he died, for Birgit and Liam would be helpless against him.

"Arienh, get away from him."

Get away from him. Just how was she supposed to do that? What she needed was to keep her head about her, not dissolve into uncontrolled panic. But he couldn't keep this up. Sooner or later he must weaken and sleep, and then she could slip away.

His laughing blue eyes suddenly winced, as the ropy muscles of his body stiffened minutely. Then just as quickly she glimpsed his pain as it ducked back and hid once again behind a winsome mask crinkled with lines of laughter.

Her heart wrenched. She melted inside. He was only a man, no different from any other, more like a small boy seeking his mother's love to soothe his pain, yet unable to say so.

*Lie with me and keep me warm,* he said with words, yet she knew he could not speak of what he really needed. What man could? Not even Trevor, dying in her arms, had been able to ask of her what she had understood he needed most. Why should a Viking be any different?

Aye, he was going to die. She saw it in his eyes, saw the brutal pain he could not quite disguise behind his brash humor and laughing blue eyes. *Comfort me,* his eyes said. *Care about me, care that I will soon be gone. Be my lost love for me, just for a little while. Let me believe I have my love again.*

*He's a Viking.*

*He's a man. Just a man.*

"He will be gone by morning," she finally replied. "Where's the harm? He can do nothing to me without doing worse to himself."

The man laughed, a short, clipped sound. "It would be a good way to die, but I will not hurt you."

He was teasing. How could he be teasing? He was dying.

What did it hurt her to give him comfort? He was not so beloved of her that she would grieve his passing. Perhaps only a little. Because she was at fault.

Nay, the fault was his, whether or not he meant her harm.

And he did not, she could see now. But he had come to her for help, having nothing left to lose. She should hate him. Rage, rage should be engulfing her, rage for the father and brother slain by his kind, fury for the brother stolen away and enslaved, for the torture Birgit had endured. But she saw only agony and the loneliness he struggled so valiantly to hide.

She could no more abandon him than she could a dying child. She would hold him close to her until he died, just as she had done her brother. It no longer mattered if he was a marauder or just an adventurer. He was simply a man in pain, dying.

She ceased her struggling and lay next to him, surprised that he already seemed warmer than she. Beneath the heavy wool blanket, she laid a hand atop his chest, which he wrapped in his own. A broad, strong hand that could easily crush her bones.

"You should sleep," she said at last.

"Nay," he said with his sweet smile. "I do not want to sleep. I do not want to lose any of what is left. Talk to me, my little Celt."

"Talk about what?"

"Tell me of your family."

"I have none. Only Birgit and Liam. All others are dead or stolen, taken as slaves." She did not want to talk about them. Most times, she did her best to forget.

"Birgit is your sister. And the boy? Liam? Her son?"

"Aye."

"Where is his father?"

"No one knows. No one cares. Do not talk of it."

"A Northman, then?"

Arienh shook her head in warning and touched a finger to his lips. "No more," she said.

Despite his struggle, the Viking's eyes soon drooped closed and he slept, his good arm locked around her. Arienh lay still, resolving above all not to wake him. Now and then he stirred and moaned, but he did not wake. It would not be long now, she knew. Regret tugged at her.

Arienh also drowsed, yet she could not sleep, for that wild pounding in her heart would not quite be soothed. She wondered if his grip would still be so firm when the time came that she would have trouble dislodging herself.

And just what would she do in the morning with a dead Viking in her home?

———————————✤———————————

He could not open his eyes. His body felt as if it floated, then as if he rose from it and looked down where it lay beside the girl whose golden hair sprung loose like newly sheared fleece.

He was within himself once again, and still his eyes would not open. Pain pounded like Thor's hammer inside his head. The throbbing agony of his wound would not cease, and his body preserved the memory of the chilling rain, bone deep, almost as if he still lay in it. The warmth of the fire, the scratchy woolen blanket, even the heat from the girl beside him could not chase away the chill. He did not want to sleep, not when so little time was left, but his eyes would not open. *He stood at the prow of his longship. As his ship raced forth out of the churning sea, Hel waited on the promontory before him, one crooked, craggy finger beckoning. Her face, half black, half blue, leered with a toothless grin. Her table beyond, within the cavern that was the Afterworld, boasted bones, split and marrowless, upon its platters, while her minions, no more than skin over bones themselves, scrapped over them.*

*Beyond the headland, his mother. Her voice silenced by the screaming wind, she held forth her bronze Celtic cross for him to take. He reached out to her futilely, but Hel drew him nearer, compelling him into her skeletal arms.*

*Nay.*

*The girl with fleece-like golden hair called to him, her green eyes beckoning. As his ship plunged out of the sea, he reached for her. From nowhere came the silver flash of the blade, and searing pain. Pain. She turned away.*

*And Hel's clawlike hands grasped his arms, tugging him downward, down.*

*Nay.*

His heart raced. His body jerked. His eyes popped open.

Startled, the Celtic girl, her golden hair dried into coiling ropes, raised her head and frowned with an odd interest. Perhaps she thought him ready to depart the world at last.

With a shudder, he drew the girl tightly against him, for his skin was warm but the chill still ached deep within his bones. He shook away the dream that mixed with pain and cold and his confused medley of wants and hopes and fears.

She had grown so beautiful. The moment he saw her, he knew he'd found her again, and in the sudden shock had forgotten they were mortal enemies. To have dreamed so long, to end like this.

He did not want to die. He wanted to live. He wanted to hold her in his arms forever. Never mind that she did not remember him. If only the gods would favor him with more than these few moments of pity and comfort she gave him.

"You are in pain?" she asked, her hand seeking his forehead.

She did not fool him with her tenderness, for he knew the hatred her kind had for his. She only sought to shield her family from danger. Yet he would take what she gave.

"It is not so bad," he said. "I did not want to sleep."

"Your dreams trouble you."

"'Tis Hel that calls me."

"Hell is where all heathens go."

"Hel," he said, knowing she misunderstood him. "'Tis Loki's daughter, and she opens the Afterworld to me."

"I thought Vikings went to Valhalla when they died."

He smiled at her, drinking in the night-darkened beauty of her eyes, as if somehow he might take the memory of them with him into death. "If the Valkyries choose them. But they do not choose a man who has been bested by a small Celtic girl. So 'tis Hel who calls me. But I will not go. I will stay with you."

Ignoring the wrenching pain, he rose onto his elbow and leaned over her. Her dark green eyes widened with fear, and her body constricted, but he didn't care. His palm cupped her cheek, and his lips descended to capture hers as he trapped her with his body. At her startled gasp, he parted her lips and invaded, exploring, memorizing, savoring. He drew her snugly against him, touching from chest to thigh. Her squirming ceased. Perhaps she accepted his advances only out of fear, but if he must die, he wanted the taste of her on his lips when he went.

"Stop it," she whispered, pushing against him, and she threw a wild glance at her sister's bed.

He knew what she was thinking. It was not the kiss that disturbed her, as much as that her sister might see it. And he would cherish that as much as the kiss.

"You are mine," he whispered.

"Never."

"You belong to me. Never forget that, my Arienh."

"Then I have only to wait until tomorrow."

"Aye, if it is so. But if not, then you are mine. I will not let you go."

Agony regathered, swamping him, rolling over him in great, dark, twisting swells. He fought, a drowning man against a violent sea of pain and oblivion, feeling his life force slip from him as surely as if he slid beneath the waves. He fell flat against the wool pallet, still gripping her tightly, lest she escape him before Hel's clutch pulled him down to the Afterworld. With the easing of the tearing pain, his eyes closed and an unexpected contentment engulfed him.

# CHAPTER THREE

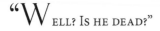

"Well? Is he dead?"

"Nay. Unless dead men smile."

"What would he have to smile about, Arienh?"

Arienh caught the sharp edge of Birgit's taunt like a lash across the face. She doubted Birgit had slept any more of the night than she had, and her sister's keen ears had surely heard all that had occurred between her and the Viking. "Perhaps he is merely happy to know he is alive."

She disengaged from the Viking's arm and rose off the narrow pallet, stiff from remaining so still for so long. Although he had kept his fierce hold on her throughout the night, he now lacked the strength to stop her.

He followed her with his eyes as if she had deserted him, with a gaze that rippled a shiver on her arms. Turning away and grumbling to herself, she tackled the dried tangles of her hair with her bone comb. Never before had she lain down at night with her hair in such disarray, and now she paid the penalty.

Her gaze landed guiltily on the wooden tablet she used to keep track of passing time. In all the time since she had been appointed keeper of the stones, she had never failed to record a day, and now the Viking had so distracted her from her obligation that she had forgotten it. But if she did not make a mark for every day, she could easily lose count, for she could not go to the stone circle very often. From the time the circle had been built by men now long forgotten, no keeper had ever failed his duty, and she did not mean to be the first. She picked up the slab and scraped a mark on it with the point of her knife.

The Viking still stared, as if his eyes held her in an eternal grip. Her heart tripped twice as his gaze roamed over her like a dangerous caress. She turned away, looked back, glanced down again at her tablet, until she could no longer bear his silence.

"I wonder where your friends are, Viking. Will they come looking for you?"

Despite his weakness, a sort of triumph gleamed in his eyes, as if by his very will he had forced her to speak. "They would not know where to look. And when the tide is high in the estuary, they will sail back to the Green Isle."

"Without you? Why?"

"That is what I told them to do. We did not come to raid."

"Why, then?"

"I told you, I came to see you, Arienh."

"You lie."

The Viking smiled.

Arienh tied her knife to her waist cord, then tossed her shawl over her shoulders, grumbling to herself that it was still damp. "I shall see for myself where the others are, and this time, soon enough to raise the alarm."

"Tell them to come for me, then."

As if he thought she might. "You said they would be gone."

"When the tide is high."

"I will not go near them. You will have to do without them, unless you plan to join them on your own."

"No one need fear that," he replied ruefully.

She felt a featherlike tug at her skirt. Liam pressed close to her side. She smiled at the boy.

"Will you come with me this morning, Liam?" she asked, but looked to Birgit for the answer.

"Aye. Please? Can I go?" The boy already bounced in his eagerness.

Birgit's pale green eyes held an odd, uninterpretable message as they often did, but her sharp nod was decisive. Liam could go.

Arienh opened the door and breathed relief when she saw no horde of marauders descending the slopes beyond the field. The sky was clear and bright, patched with bulbous clouds that spelled another coming storm. New rivulets cut through the fields and filled the swollen stream with muddy brown energy, surging toward the equally distended river.

As she had expected, the river had cut a new course through the valley. Debris littered the sodden earth, interspersed with shallow standing water that glistened in the bright sun. They had survived this time, but a flood was easily as dangerous as a Viking raid and could mean the end of Celts in this valley.

With Liam to risk, she resisted the impulse to get closer to the Vikings for a look, so she walked down the valley where the river poured between two low mounts to join the estuary. From there, she could see the great sandy banks and salt marshes that flanked the bigger river as it met the sea.

Liam bounced about like an energetic puppy, alternately speeding away from her and returning to hold her hand. Winter had cramped the boy immeasurably. Sometimes she forgot the extent of his frenetic vigor, for inside the cottage he was always quiet and kept himself useful. It was good for him to get out.

"Who is that man, Aunt?" the boy asked during one of those quieter moments when he walked beside her.

"I don't know. I did not ask his name."

"He is a Viking, isn't he?"

"Aye."

"Vikings are bad."

Arienh said nothing, feeling her throat tighten once again with the muddled mix of rage and tenderness, wishing the Viking both dead and living. How could she explain the welling up of hatred from the very core of her being or the way it inexplicably tangled with compassion? It was like being hot and cold, all at once.

"Is he bad, Aunt?"

"I don't know, Liam. Right now, he is hurt too badly to be any trouble."

"But will he kill us when he gets better?"

"I don't think so. He may be kinder than most of his sort."

"Is he going to die?"

"Perhaps not. It is hard to tell."

The early spring air was cold, brisk, and fresh, almost stinging as she breathed it in. Already water birds were settling into the marsh. For a while, she stood with Liam on a small hummock where they could be concealed while watching the birds search for nesting places.

Beyond the marsh, still soaked from the storm, the ash trees stood like black skeletons against the crisp sky. Between flat, silty shores ran the turbulent river and on it sailed a Viking longship with its blood-red sail and swan's-head prow.

"Is that his ship, Aunt?" The boy's eyes shone with the brightness that revealed his Viking kinship.

"Shh. Aye, I think it must be. Sit down behind the rushes so they will not see you."

Tension stiffened the boy's body, betraying his urge to run out onto the sand, to wave and shout to the strangers who passed in the graceful ship. Arienh watched him struggle to contain himself and sit behind the brush as she demanded. The night before, she had noticed his fascination with the Viking and had thought it born of fear. Now she saw it was also something else.

His own kind. Liam knew he was different.

When the ship had sailed farther downstream, Arienh took Liam's hand and climbed the low hill that looked out over the Irish Sea. They watched as the ship put out to sea, going west.

"Where are they going?"

"To the Green Isle," she said, pointing. "If you look closely, you can see it, far away over the water."

"It doesn't look green to me. Why do they call it the Green Isle?"

"Because most times it looks green, from the sea. But it is winter still. Perhaps nothing is green there in winter."

"It should be the Grey Isle. Why are they leaving him, Aunt?"

"He told them not to look for him if he didn't come back."

"They shouldn't leave him. Will they come back for him?"

"Perhaps."

"Is he like my father, Aunt?"

She studied the boy's bright blue eyes, so full of hungry curiosity. Viking eyes. "Nay."

"That's good. I like him."

Arienh wished she had better answers for the boy. She wished he did not know the horrible truth of his origins. But their village was tiny, too small to keep from him what everyone else knew. Liam was her delight, and Birgit's life itself, but they could not give him what he most needed. And what he needed most was a good father, not a wretch of a raping, marauding Viking.

As they returned along the path by the churning brown waters, Arienh saw Mildread bending over in the field beyond Arienh's stone cottage, her brown braids nearly touching the ground. Mildread straightened, holding the Viking's sword, retrieved from the spot where the man had dropped it the night before. With a hand gripped on the hilt, she awaited them.

"The Viking," said Mildread, almost impatiently. The furrow in the middle of her brow echoed the concern in her voice. "Where is he? Did you not say you killed him?"

"He is not dead, but I think he soon will be," Arienh replied. Mildread was not going to like this. "He found his way to the cottage last night."

"You let him in?"

"Nay. He did that himself. I had naught to say about it. But he is very weak now."

"Not so weak as he ought to be." Mildread's brown eyes darkened with accusation. "And you have left him with Birgit."

"Aye. I do not think he can harm her."

"Why did you not finish him?"

"He is weak. But he could still be dangerous when he holds a knife in his hand. He is best appeased for now. It was not right to let a man die in the cold rain, Mildread."

"They are animals, not men."

"But we are not animals. Give me the sword. We must hide it in case he should recover and try to take it back."

"We should throw it in the river."

"Then we would not have it for our own protection later. Nay, let us hide it in the thatch at the eave by the sheepfold."

Mildread's skeptical brown eyes narrowed, but she handed the weapon to Arienh with a glower as they walked to the cottage.

"You will regret it when he kills you," Mildread grumbled.

"The ladder, Liam," Arienh said, ignoring the impossibility of Mildread's warning, and she watched the boy fetch and raise the wooden ladder to the stone wall. Arienh climbed the ladder and wove the sword into the thatch near the eave. She leaned back to survey the thatch and, satisfied, climbed down.

"I do not think he meant to kill anyone, Mildread." She stepped off the ladder. "He did chase me, but he never did unsheathe his sword. He only meant to stop me from raising the alarm, I think."

Liam tugged on Mildread's skirt. "I saw the ship, Aunt Mildread. It sailed away and left him."

Dark anger lurked in Mildread's eyes, the hatred all Celts harbored toward Vikings. "I do not like this, Arienh. Father Hewil would tell you to kill him. I have heard he is coming. If he tells you to kill the Viking, you must."

With a clipped nod of her head to drive her point home, Mildread walked away from the sheepfold to the muddy path that led down toward the river. Arienh noted Mildread had made no mention of doing the task herself. Mildread had always been good at knowing what others should do.

Arienh turned back to the cottage. Ahead of her, Liam's bright hair gleamed like polished brass in the sunshine as he bounded through the door and ran to his mother.

"Mama, I saw it—the Viking ship! It had a big red sail, and it was going down the river to the sea."

Arienh, directly behind the boy, nodded. "You were right," she told the Viking grimly, for she knew what it must mean to him to be left behind. "They have gone. We watched them sail away."

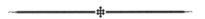

For two days, the Viking lay on her raised bed where she had moved him, with a fever raging through his body. He mumbled strange things in his foreign tongue, threw off the blankets, tossed like waves pounding the sea cliffs in a storm. He called her name, begged her not to let him go.

Then he slept, so quietly, so motionless that she returned again and again to his side to reassure herself he still breathed.

Now and then, she got a few spoonfuls of water or broth past his lips. Sometimes he took enough of the willow bark tea that the fever seemed to subside. Then it would rise again.

For nearly a day now, the fever had seemed not quite so fiery hot. Yet it had continued, and he was running out of strength to fight. She could do nothing.

"Perhaps I should not have stitched it."

"Why?" Birgit asked her. "How could it have harmed him? You can see the wound heals, despite the fever. How can you care, Arienh? If he dies, he dies. You have one less burden."

Arienh shrugged and mopped beads of sweat from the Viking's brow with a dampened rag. "But he did so much better before. I should have left it alone, as I first meant to do."

"You blame yourself too much. That he has lived at all is beyond belief. He improves even now, despite my prayers."

She understood Birgit's hatred, but her own rage mingled with a memory from long ago, of a scrawny, ragged boy who had come with the Vikings yet had hidden her away from his own kind.

It had happened too fast for her to remember much. When the horde had poured into their village, she had been too far away to escape to the cavern, so she ran up into the hills. While her attention was on the hulking Viking chasing her, the boy surprised her. She glimpsed only his light hair and a flash of blue eyes as he pushed her into a small hole hidden by boulders. With a quick, hard hiss to hush her, surely a sound understood in any language, he ran off, luring the marauder away. Her pursuer never found her.

Though this man's hair was far darker, his Viking eyes reminded her of the scrawny lad. She could not give him up until he breathed his last. She could never care for his sort, but she owed him that much.

"I will watch him," said Birgit. A strange flatness tinged her voice. Yet her pale eyes reflected the concern she felt for her exhausted sister. "Take Liam with you to the paddock."

"It is not your duty."

"You must tend the new lambs. I will watch the Viking."

"And give him the willow bark?"

"Perhaps I will do it better than you. Go. You have been inside too long, and so has Liam."

Arienh bit her lip, but it was best. She needed to walk in the sunshine. "Come, Liam, let us see to the lambs."

The bright sunlight stung her eyes as Arienh stepped outside the door, Liam's hand in hers. Clean air swept into her lungs, as delicious as fresh red meat.

Birgit was right, Arienh did need a distraction for a while from her obsession with the Viking's wound and her own guilt, for though her fear might excuse her, it was still her doing that he was wounded. And she couldn't get over the feeling that his wound would not have festered if she hadn't stitched it. The wound was healing and the fever was not as intense, but he was so weak that soon he would not have the strength to continue his struggle.

Mildread and Elli stood by the path, waiting. Arienh shooed Liam off to the paddock.

"Well, is he gone yet?" asked Mildread, with balled fists planted firmly on her hips. Elli placed hers exactly the same way.

"Nay, he lingers."

"You must kill him, Arienh," said Elli. Grim hatred gleamed like ice in her eyes, as cold as Mildread's brown eyes were furiously hot. "His kind are vermin."

Irritation flared in her. Every day they had said this, and she was weary of it. "Well, he is lying in there on the bed, helpless as a new kitten, Elli. If you want him dead, you may go do it yourself. Here, I will loan you my knife."

Elli's eyebrows shot upward.

"Not you? Mildread, then? Here, it is not so hard. Just hold it thus and stab downwards. He may find the strength to fight back and kill you, but I doubt it."

"You should never have let him live, Arienh," said Mildread. "It is your fault, and you should end it."

Arienh smiled with narrowed eyes. "But I chose not to do that. If you want it otherwise, you must change it yourselves."

Mildread spun away angrily and strode down the path. Elli followed, glancing back with a frown.

She could not blame them. Elli could not forget her father's death. Mildread's husband had been crippled in a raid and eventually died of the melancholy, leaving her to raise two daughters alone. And none of them would forgive what had been done to Birgit. But like herself, neither Mildread nor Elli could raise a blade to the Viking.

Arienh forced her thoughts away from them, back to her task, for she had too much to do as it was. Since the flood, the pasture beyond the untilled fields had begun to green, sprouts popping up faster than the flock could nibble them away. She counted the lambs, grateful that none had been lost. Some of them had better survive, for after this hard winter, there was not a single ram left in the valley.

Liam trotted beside her, prattling eager questions about the lambs, about how much they had grown since their winter births. Arienh picked up a lamb to show him how to inspect hooves and bodies for sores or disease.

The sudden blare of Mildread's horn sliced through the air. Her heart lurched and she nearly dropped the tiny lamb she held as she scanned the valley's lower end.

Running women screamed and fled up the valley toward the cavern in the hill beyond. Others, too far from the cavern, scattered up the nearest slopes that lined the valley's outlet.

Vikings. Vikings afoot, a score or more of them.

Yet no hideous howls for blood, no racing hordes in pursuit, not even weapons raised for the slaughter. The marauders strode up the valley as if they owned it, their metal clanging, leather squealing, feet tromping—the sounds of a moving army.

From the day the Viking had appeared, she had feared this. His people had come for him.

# CHAPTER FOUR

"Go to the house, Liam. Do what your mother says."

"Without you? Not to the cavern?"

"Go without me. Now."

Liam's bright curls shimmered in the quick turn before he ran. Her heart lurched. She would do anything to protect him.

They did not come as Vikings usually came, a screaming rush of berserkers. They merely walked, a brisk, purposeful pace, as if they knew exactly what they planned to do. And there were enough of them that, whatever they planned, they would do it.

How much did they know? Had they been watching from the high hills that surrounded the valley, as she suspected her Viking had been doing the day she encountered him?

Only she stood between them and her family. Gulping down her fear, Arienh strode to the sheepfold, climbed the ladder, and removed the sword from its hiding place in the thatch. She threw the long belt over her shoulder, but still the immense scabbard almost dragged on the ground.

The Vikings stopped on the far bank of the stream when one man signaled to the others. He bounded effortlessly over the stepping stones and stood, stance set wide, barely a man's length away from her. Arienh squared her shoulders and glared directly up into the man's bright blue eyes.

Eyes like her Viking's.

This Viking was the tallest man she had ever seen and stocky as a great oak, even larger than the man inside her cottage. His flowing, straw-colored beard, his hair decorated with braids, and the evil sparkle in his eyes gave him a look of maturity, yet she guessed he was quite young, perhaps only a short time into his manhood.

The man pointed to the weapon that dangled from her waist. "That is my brother's sword."

"Is it? It seems to be mine now."

"Where did you get it?"

"Perhaps I took it from your brother."

Blue eyes scrutinized her. "We do not come to harm you, girl. We have come for him. Is he dead? If he is dead, show me where his body is, so we may take it away, for his mother mourns him. I will pay you."

"We have no use for your geld, Viking."

"What will you have, then? I will give you whatever you ask."

Did he mean what he said? Did he think she would trust him? A Viking? What would he think, or do, once he learned she was the cause of his brother's injury? If he should change his mind, she could only hope he would limit his vengeance to her.

"Leave us in peace, Viking."

"Aye, we will do that. I seek only my brother's body, and I will give you a reward for that, be there only a little of him left. What will you ask, girl?"

"A plow," she said. She stifled a gasp. Why had she asked anything at all?

The Viking's bright eyes glowed with shrewdness as he quickly assessed both her and the unplowed fields behind her. She felt stripped bare, all the way to her thoughts.

"A plow? You have none?"

"It is broken."

"And oxen, too? I see none."

She chewed at her lip. The man who lay inside the cottage had been too weak to come out and discover how near to extinction her people were. But this one was accumulating the evidence rapidly.

"They are sickly. It would not hurt." Sickly unto death, but she dared not say.

"A team then, too. Where is he? Have you buried him?"

"You mourn too soon. He is not dead yet. You may come with me, but leave the others where they are."

Arienh turned her back to the marauder and his band of villains across the stream. With deliberate, manlike strides, she walked up the narrow path, keeping her ears attuned to the heavy footfalls and creaking leather behind her. She pressed downward on the sword's hilt to lever the tip of the scabbard over the stones in the path.

The man maintained a discreet distance behind her of about the length of two men, his pace almost exactly matching hers. Although she knew he could capture her in the space of three big strides if he chose, she held her shoulders square and her head high, pretending that fact was beneath her notice. Boldly, she strode up to her cottage.

"Birgit, unbar the door," she called.

But when the door swung open, it was her Viking who stood, gasping and feverish, clasping the doorframe for support. Anxiously she sought out Birgit and Liam, and saw them unharmed.

"Ronan," shouted the huge blond man as he rushed past her and wrapped his big arms around her Viking.

"Aye, Egil, I knew you'd come."

"'Tis a fever you've got."

"And a wound."

"He must lie down," said Arienh.

Ronan. A Celtic name. She had never asked him his name, for she had assumed he would die.

Ronan's legs buckled as the bigger man shifted his arm to support him. "Aye, she's right, Ronan. You must get back to the bed."

The tenderness between them was like an odd parody of a mother and child. Before, she had never even thought of Vikings even as speaking creatures. Then, to find two who seemed possessed of intelligence, kindness, and tenderness toward each other? But they would love their own kind, wouldn't they? Or perhaps there was enough Celtic blood in them to make them human. Her Viking had said his mother was a Celt.

Wrapped in their own concerns, speaking their heathen tongue, the two men seemed to have forgotten the Celts around them. But there were more of their kind down by the stream, and who knew what they might do, once they had accomplished their ends? Arienh flashed a wary look at Birgit and nodded her head toward the door. They left the two men alone in the cottage.

"While they are occupied," she said to her sister, "and while the other marauders wait so patiently across the stream, you should join the others in the cavern."

"I'll not leave you."

"This is different, Birgit. I cannot tell if they mean to trick us or not. But even if they do, they might leave me in peace if there is only me."

"Nay."

"If I must defend you and Liam, too, I will surely die. Go."

Birgit glared. Setting her jaw, she whirled around, snatched Liam's hand, and set out.

Egil had come. Ronan had known he would, for his brother was the most dependable man in the world.

"What have you done, brother?" Egil asked, carefully easing Ronan into the bed as he spoke. "I have never seen you so weak."

"A gut wound."

"I told you not to come alone."

Egil lifted the Celtic tunic to study the wound, then lowered it as if he saw nothing to fear. But Ronan knew his younger brother well and was not fooled. He was still fevered and far from recovered. Perhaps would not at all, and Egil would know it.

"Nay, it was the best way," Ronan said. "This is it, Egil. This is the valley."

Egil's eyes lit, mirroring his own excitement. "And the girl?"

"Aye, the same. I told you she would be a beauty."

"Aye, she is, and the flame-haired one, too. Save that one for me."

"You're the fool, then, Egil," Ronan said with a puny laugh. "She hates us."

"They all do at first, brother."

"She, more than most."

Egil gave a low, assessing hum. "The boy is hers. A Northman's child, you think?"

"Aye. They will not talk of it."

"A boy needs a father."

Ronan could see the speculation in his brother's eyes. He would be hard to discourage. But to his mind, the strange-eyed Birgit was unworthy of his brother. "She has an evil tongue. She is not worth it."

"We shall see. This place—there are no men here, Ronan. Perhaps it is even better than you hoped."

"None? I saw none, either, but I thought they must be away."

"None. The women are struggling with men's work. Most of the fields are unplowed. The girl said their plow is broken, and I suspect her cattle are dead, but she would not say it."

"Aye. It must be so."

Egil's eyes slanted suspiciously at him. "But if there are no men, then who stabbed you?"

He groaned. He had known it would come to this. But he had never been able to hide anything from Egil.

"The girl."

"The girl. You let a girl stab you?"

"I did not know she had a knife. I did not think of her as an enemy."

Egil laughed. "You thought she'd welcome you with open arms? A Celt?"

If he lived to have great-grandchildren, he'd never live this down. "Don't blame her, Egil. I startled her, and myself. It was sort of accidental."

"Accidental. Well, whatever the cause, she has kept you alive. Now we must be sure you stay that way."

"Have you brought everyone?"

"In the estuary. I have only to give the signal."

"Do it, then. But say nothing to these women."

Egil nodded solemnly. His hand went once again to Ronan's forehead. "Your fever cools, I think. It must be that I have come."

"It is the willow bark. Your beloved Birgit just forced it on me. Go, now."

"Aye. And may Freyr watch over you."

"Don't let Mother hear you say that."

Egil flipped his eyebrows wickedly. But Ronan knew his brother would be cautious. He would not tease their Christian mother with their pagan gods. Not too much.

Arienh stood in the sunshine, feeling as if she could absorb from it the strength and courage she needed. It flowed into her, penetrating deeply, as if it reached all the way to her bones. She had not felt such warmth since the leaves had left the trees the previous fall. The tip of the heavy Viking sword rested on a flat stone, and she leaned her weight against it.

From where she stood vigil, she could see in all directions, from the door of the cottage where the big Viking remained with his brother to the group of restless raiders by the river. She scanned the low hills about the valley and the cavern where the other villagers waited. If the big Viking betrayed his promise, at least the others would be safe.

The door creaked open on its leather hinges, and the big Viking called Egil ducked his head to pass. His arms swung easily at his side, almost a contradiction to his purposeful stride toward her. Arienh folded her arms, waiting.

The Viking fixed narrow, assessing eyes on her. "He says you stabbed him."

"Aye."

The Viking's bushy yellow eyebrows raised in pointed arches. "He is a skilled warrior. How did you do it?"

"I stabbed. He fell." She met his gaze like swords clashing.

"Then why do you tend him?"

"It was his idea, I think."

"You lie. He would have died without your help."

"Perhaps. It was a very cold storm, and I do not wish anyone ill. We only wish to be left alone, so please go."

"He cannot go yet. I will stay with him and send the others for the plow I promised you."

"Nay. We do not want you."

"Doubtless, but he is my brother and I cannot leave him. You would not leave your sister."

"My sister would never invade another's land."

A hint of glee flickered on his solemn eyes. "That empty cottage," he said, pointing down the hill. "Is it usable? I could take him there."

"Nay, the thatch leaks badly. It would take too much time to patch it."

The Viking's blue eyes gleamed, and the corners of his mouth danced. He raised an arm and beckoned the restless men near the stream. The Vikings raised a whoop, then dashed across the water and up the hill.

"You treacherous heathen!" shouted Arienh, and her hand shot toward the sword's hilt.

The Viking's hand caught her rising wrist in a tight grip as his eyes narrowed dangerously. "Nay, girl, we do you no harm. I merely mean to patch a roof."

He did not wait for her answer before he lifted the sword from her hand as easily as if she had merely handed it to him, then passed it to a red-bearded Viking behind him.

"Patch a roof? You have no such need. You lie." Her eyes darted about, surveying the horde of huge men who surrounded her. In seconds, she could be dead on the ground and her village overrun. She swallowed, determined to hide her terror.

Egil turned to answer the gaggle of foreign words from men who looked more anxious than murderous, then returned his attention to Arienh. "I mean to make a place to keep my brother until he is well enough to leave. Until then, he will stay beneath your roof under your care while we work."

"I should slit his throat, Viking."

She did not even see him move. The huge raider seized both of her wrists. His eyes turned stormy.

"You will do him no harm. Do not forget, girl, what we could do if we chose."

She knew, yet she sneered. "It would not surprise me if you left not even one babe to breathe."

"Never a babe alone to starve. I would not be so cruel. Make no mistake, girl, my brother is the dearest man alive to me. If you harm him, I will have my revenge."

The big man released his grip, and his eyes warned her he meant what he said. Arienh resisted the urge to rub her wrists, for she would not let him know his threat had been felt.

"So you lied to me," she said.

"Nay, that was a different thing."

"I see no difference. You will kill me if he dies, anyway. You would have, all along."

He fingered the hilt of his own sword as if considering what he would do with her head after he lopped it off. "Think what you will, but do not forget. You've taken good enough care of him thus far. See that he lives, girl."

With a wave of his hand and a flurry of incomprehensible words, the blond Viking led his men along the gentle slope and followed the swollen stream to the cottage that had belonged to her cousin Weylin.

Arienh unbuckled the useless scabbard and pitched it to the ground. Now what could she do? She had never meant that she might take the dark Viking's life, for she had already learned such a thing was beyond her. Yet she dared not let them think her weak.

Never had there been an invasion like this one. What did these men want? Did they mean only to wait until dark and overpower everyone? Perhaps they feared the men of the village would come upon them suddenly and overrun them. Or perhaps they already knew there were no men except Old Ferris.

Aye. They knew. It also explained what the dark one, Ronan, had been doing up on the hill the day she had come upon him.

These men, too, had first spied out the village. No wonder they were in no hurry. No one feared a village of only women.

All he asked now was that she take care of his brother. She had no choice. She might risk herself, but not Liam and Birgit.

Would they ever be free of these Northmen?

# CHAPTER FIVE

———————✤———————

THE VIKINGS INVADED THE MARSHES, SLICING BUNDLES OF last year's osiers and hauling them back upslope to make huge piles by the tumble-down stone cottage they had confiscated. Offended water birds fled their new nesting sites, shrieking as they took to the air.

Arienh was no less offended. The cottage had once been the home of her cousin Weylin, who had vanished years before in a Viking raid, leaving behind a family who had died out one by one.

And the heathens simply walked in and took it over.

The giant blond called Egil twice hiked back up the hill to see the brother he called Ronan, meeting Arienh's murderous glare with only his smug smile.

Ronan. She supposed she should take comfort in the obvious recovery of that darker fellow who still lay on her bed. The fever had diminished with striking speed as the day wore on, and he was already stronger. So perhaps his brother would soon cart him away and they would be troubled by the invaders no more.

Certainly. And new spring lambs would dance in the stone circle.

One by one, the women of the village emerged from the cavern, all eyes warily watching the men who swarmed like yellow bees over the rafters of her cousin's derelict home.

"What is this about, Arienh?" Mildread asked, her voice low and cautious. In her eyes was a look suspiciously like censure.

"I think the big one means to have a place to shelter his brother until he is well."

"His brother? Oh, that is what we need. I told you they would come for him. They will surely kill us for your folly."

"They could have killed us already if they chose to. And why not take a cottage that needs no patching, if all they might do is evict and kill the dwellers? Would it not be easier?"

"They mean to trick us."

"They already have. If you don't like it, stay in the cavern where you will feel safe."

Mildread gave a coarse grunt and stalked off. She was no coward. Arienh knew it and should have never implied so. But Mildread irritated her with her overbearing ways. It probably was a good thing that not many people listened to her.

This time, though, people were listening. No one agreed with Arienh's decision to help the Viking, even if she hadn't really had a choice.

Close to night, as new storm clouds emerged over the hills, Arienh wearied of watching the big men scurrying over the new thatch. She marched to her cottage and gave the door a shove.

Ronan sat at the edge of the raised bed, struggling with his leather jerkin. Birgit stood at her loom, her eyes focused fiercely on the Viking, her shuttle swishing, swishing. Hanging on his mother's skirts, Liam watched the Viking as intensely as his mother did.

"You should not rise yet." Arienh's voice sounded like a scold.

"I should not stay abed when I am well enough to rise."

He gave up on the jerkin, but Arienh was relieved to see that he had managed the leather breeches and embroidered tunic by himself. He swayed a little as he stood.

"You fool yourself," she said.

His wide grin told her she would not win the argument, and in truth, she would be glad to see him gone. But then he sat again. He laughed at her smirk. Perhaps it meant nothing to him that he was a sort of hostage under her roof. Yet if the brother came for him, she could not stop him from leaving, so it made little difference. The giant blond would make good his threat.

That was what she hated most. She was just as helpless as she would have been, had the attack been outright. Silently she picked up a wooden bowl and dipped out broth from the mutton that simmered in the pot on the hearth. She held it out to him.

He shook his head. "No more. I will have food now."

"This is good enough for us. It is good enough for your kind."

"Nay. I mean no disrespect, for you have been generous. But Egil is here, and he will bring us something."

He had no more refused her when the door burst open. The huge blond entered, ducking his head to avoid scraping the lentil. Behind him glowered clouds of the newest arriving storm. Across his shoulders swung a mixed brace of wildfowl. In one hand he carried a bow that he unstrung and set beside the door as casually as if he lived there, and in the other hand, a ham hock, shrunken and dark with smoke, its tantalizing salty sweetness drifting to her nostrils.

"Barbarian," said Birgit, almost spitting. "Can you not even knock before you beset us with your presence?"

"Knock on the door, Egil," said Ronan. "Please the harpy."

Egil shrugged his shoulders and rapped his fist against the door, then slapped the ham and ducks on the table.

Arienh jumped. She had promised herself she would not do that. Egil's lips stretched thin across his teeth.

"I suppose you expect us to cook that for you," Birgit said, her voice like a snake's hiss.

"Do what you want with them. But you are women. I thought it fair to assume you would cook them first."

Egil's big hand pushed down against the table's corner and frowned at its wobble. "You did not fix this, Ronan?"

"I was going to get around to it."

Of course. From his sickbed. What sort of banter was this?

"Aye. Well, I'll look at it after the meal. And the roof has holes big enough to see the clouds. You are remiss, brother."

"Perhaps tomorrow. I've been occupied."

"You're not staying," Arienh said, hoping it sounded like a command.

"Cannot finish the thatch tonight," said Egil, almost as if he were apologizing. "The storm will break any moment. I'll sleep with my brother."

Arienh's gaze caught Birgit's, wide with indignant horror, then turned on Ronan who sat at the bed's edge, his mouth quirking, eyes sparkling.

"Come outside," she said, taking Birgit's arm by the elbow.

"Outside? I vow they'll have taken over our home before we come back in the door."

"Outside," Arienh insisted.

"Nay, I'll not let—"

"Out." For emphasis, Arienh grasped Liam's hand and tugged him out, away from the Vikings the boy found so intriguing, nearly shoving both him and his mother through the door.

As soon as the door shut behind them, Birgit whirled on her. "Arienh, you have toadied to that Viking long enough, and now this irksome brother of his. Do not think I will bow and scrape to the likes of them."

"Hush. Use your head, Birgit. They are teasing us."

"Teasing. If you have not noticed, they have moved in."

"And there isn't a lot we can do about it, short of growing huge muscles on great, hairy arms. Ignore their goading, Birgit, or it will get worse. The dark one has gotten much better since this morning, and he is likely to live. That is good. I would not

49

want the other one taking out his anger on us if his brother dies. I have never seen a man so big."

"I am not afraid of him."

She wasn't. Birgit feared nothing unless it threatened someone else. That was part of the problem.

"What about Liam, then? I do not want to take chances. Perhaps if we just let them have their little jokes, they will go away when the dark one is well. Whatever you do, don't make them mad."

"Don't make them mad. 'Tis you who are mad, Arienh."

Arienh felt her blood growing hot. Sometimes she grew weary of everyone's constant expectation that she solve all their problems. "Very well, then, Birgit, tell me what you would have me do."

"Get rid of them."

"That's not good enough, as I am trying. Tell me how to get rid of them. Would you like for me to challenge them to a sword fight? Perhaps I could persuade them to let me take them one at a time, all twenty of them."

Birgit bit her lips together. Her gaze dropped to the ground.

Arienh felt the sudden sting of guilt for her temper. "I am sorry. I know how hard it is for you, Birgit. But we only have the two of them in our house. At least we can manage them, as they are trying to be agreeable."

"Agreeable." Birgit sneered.

"Aye. For their kind, anyway. Do you see them ordering us about or throwing us down on our beds?"

Both women glanced suddenly at Liam, and the boy flinched. Sometimes they forgot just how aware he was of his origins. How could he not be, in these harsh times? Even at his young age, he had seen women raped and murdered. Arienh was instantly sorry for her bluntness. She put her arm around his shoulder.

"Aye. It is a simple matter," she said to Birgit. "The big one would already have taken his brother away if he could have. If we help them get out of here, they will leave sooner. And he has brought food, Birgit. Think of the ham. We have not even seen a live pig in two years. And ducks. Come, we can set water to boiling and have them plucked for tomorrow's meal."

"I just cannot stand the sight of them, Arienh. But I am sorry. Come, I can at least pluck ducks. Liam can help."

Arienh smiled, relieved. Now if she could just get the brothers to behave themselves. But from what she'd already seen of them, she had about as much chance of that as she did of setting those dead ducks back to flying.

She watched the two men raise eyebrows at each other as the women passed through the cottage door. Birgit, for once not glaring at the strangers, busied herself with slicing up the last of the roots for cooking. Arienh lifted two wooden buckets and opened the door. A sudden flash of lightning startled her.

"I'll go," said Egil, and she was more than glad to let him.

Liam pulled at his mother's skirts. "Mama, can I go?"

"Nay."

"He can help me," Egil offered. But then, faced down by the icy green fury in Birgit's eyes, the big man grimaced and went out the door alone. Arienh laughed to herself. Perhaps not even a fierce Viking was a match for a mother's protective ire.

Liam's face screwed up into a pout. It had been a long time since he had been around men. She hoped his curiosity would not grow too great, yet how could it not? Liam could not be separated from his insatiable lust for knowledge. One more reason she hoped the Vikings would be gone soon.

Egil returned along with the storm, with rumbling thunder behind him, and rivulets running down his hair and into his soaked jerkin. He yanked off the garment, then the smock beneath it, whooshing it over the wet tangles of his hair.

The dark Viking spoke to his brother in the nonsense sounds of their heathen tongue. The big man chuckled, glanced at Birgit, then strutted to his brother's side, where they continued their alien conversation.

He was an attractive man, though not so much as his brother. She doubted even Birgit would deny that. Across a powerful muscular chest, a fleece of golden, springy curls spread. His damp leather breeches clung tightly to his thighs, tightly enough that when he turned she understood immediately the nature of the men's joke. The man was visibly aroused, and it was Birgit who had his attention. Arienh's grip tightened on the knife.

She flashed a glare at Ronan, and the grin vanished from his face. He tossed to his brother her father's old woolen tunic that he had been wearing, along with more of the gibberish they spoke between them. Egil nodded and pulled the shirt over his damp torso, concealing his offending member.

Liam, his bright eyes shining wide with fear, stepped in front of the yellow-haired man, his fists in tight little balls as he tried to stand tall and look the man in the eyes. Arienh edged closer, prepared to snatch him away.

"Are you a Viking?" the boy demanded in a squeaky voice.

Bemused, Egil put his hands to his hips. "I'm a Northman, Liam, not a Viking."

"'Tis the same," said Birgit. "Come back here, Liam."

The boy stood his ground, eyes flashing.

"Nay, 'tis not," said Egil. "I am no marauder, nor have I ever been. But my folk come from the North."

"Blood will tell," said Birgit. "He is a Viking."

"I won't let you hurt my mama."

Solemnly, the man squatted down to Liam's level, placing his large hand on the boy's shoulder. "I am glad you will not, Liam. You are a brave lad, and you will make a fine man someday. And you must always protect your mother. But I give you my word, I will never harm her, nor you, nor your aunt."

"You promise?"

"I do."

"Oh. What do you do in your longship, then?"

"Sometimes we fish."

Arienh noticed the table no longer wobbled. She carved thin slices off the ham hock and laid them out on the board as if she had ham to cut every day.

A gentleness lit the blond one's eyes, as if he had a liking for the boy. "The ship belongs to my brother, Ronan," Egil added. "He built it himself and has taken it to many places in the world to trade. Some of the fine things he has brought with us. He has a fur from a great white bear of the Far North."

"Really?" Liam asked, suddenly eager.

"Aye. They are giants, those great white bears. Ronan has real glass, too, made into fine jugs. Have you ever seen glass?"

Liam shook his head.

"Then he must show it to you, for you have helped to take such good care of him."

"Mama, can I please?"

Birgit glared. "They are not staying, Liam. Come away from them. Now."

Liam's eyes flashed to his mother and back to the blond Viking, assessing his chance for defiance. He didn't move.

"Did you go, too?" he asked.

"Nay. I have always lived on the Green Isle, until now. Some of us have roamed and traded with Ronan, but most of us have lived on the Green Isle, among Celts. Do as your mother says."

A long pout settled on Liam's face as he returned to his mother's side. Arienh knew what the boy was thinking, for he was at an age to test his mother. These men had openly ignored the demands of the two women, and perhaps he hoped they might support him in doing the same.

With the fever gone, the darker Viking regained his appetite. His skin took on a healthier color as the day advanced, and his eyes lost their feverish look. He no longer shook from weakness as he sat propped against the wall, bantering quietly with his brother in their harsh tongue.

Arienh hid her irritation at their foreign words and tried to ignore them altogether, yet her eyes homed back to the man who had been her obsession as he hovered so close to death. Again and again her gaze tangled with his, as if he never looked away. She did, often, quickly.

Soon, she slid into the bed beside Birgit and prayed the men would take the hint. She prayed for more than that.

Egil banked the fire and joined his brother in the bed where Arienh usually slept.

For hours, Arienh pretended to sleep, rigid, still, beside her sister.

The storm no longer roared. Its rage had torn at the thatch for most of the night and whipped back that thin rawhide that draped over the cottage's only window. Arienh had twice risen to check the dark Viking for fever and found none. But a simmering darkness in his eyes replaced his usual affable smile. As she touched his brow, he raised his hand to caress across her cheek. She jerked back out of his reach and hurried back to lie down beside Birgit.

The blond one avoided her gaze, but several times she caught him watching Birgit. And Birgit did nothing but watch the Vikings. Twice had Egil risen to stir and bank the fire, then lay down beside his brother. Each time, he had not taken his eyes off Birgit.

Once more he stood, and this time he jerked off the Celtic woolen tunic Ronan had tossed to him hours before, baring his broad chest. Birgit stiffened. Then with a smoldering flash in his eyes, he pulled on his own tunic and the leather jerkin. He knelt and bound his boots about his thick calves.

"There is a pot beneath the bed," said Birgit, in a calm voice that belied her tension.

"Nay," said the blond Viking with a tightness in his voice. "Come and bolt the door behind me."

Arienh watched her sister rise and edge toward the door. The Viking's eyes seemed to bore into the woman's flesh, as if he meant to grab Birgit and make off with her into the night.

Birgit set her jaw and faced the man boldly. "I suppose you will want me to get up again and let you in."

"Nay. Bolt it." He jerked it shut behind him. The latch clicked.

Birgit slammed the bolt into its slots and dashed back to the bed. Even without touching her, Arienh could feel the tension in her sister, taut as a bowstring.

Birgit would be reliving her horror. For that was what Egil was doing to her, whether he meant it or not. With Ronan, it had not been so bad, for he had been dying and was not much of a threat. And Ronan had paid little attention to Birgit. But Egil was a different story. He was huge and blond, yellow-blond, with great waves of hair and braids, and piercing blue eyes, just like the man who had come in the raid six years ago, the one who had caught Birgit by the hair and thrown her to the ground. The one who had clubbed her against the rock, leaving her for dead, leaving her to go blind.

Be they as innocent as the Virgin, the Vikings had to go.

# CHAPTER SIX

---·❖·---

SHE HEARD GEESE.

They had no geese.

Arienh sat up abruptly in her bed, shaking her head to dispel the sleep. Birgit stood in the open door, jaw tight, glaring, as Ronan yanked on his jerkin and rushed out past her into the bright sunlight.

Shouting. Squeals and squawks, the whinny of horses. Not a battle, nor an invasion. Well, maybe an invasion. It was much like the sound made earlier by the arrival of Egil's warriors, but with the addition of animals. Arienh leaped from the bed and grabbed her shawl.

"Damn them," said Birgit softly.

The dark-haired Viking hobbled down the path toward the narrow mouth of the valley where three great Viking ships, one magnificently graceful longship and two broad *knarrs*, were pulled ashore. Just as Ronan's gait began to falter, several more of his kind rushed up to surround him, shouting, to support him and slap him on the back. The last time she had seen so many Viking ships, her father had been killed, and she and the others had barely escaped into the cavern.

"A raid?" Birgit asked with characteristic cynicism.

"Hardly. Unless they've trained their sheep to do their raiding for them." The second of the *knarrs* was heeled over onto its side to let a flock of sheep with black faces and oddly scraggly long wool descend upon the valley's new grass. Enough sheep that the valley would quickly become brown mud again.

There really were geese. Geese honked and strutted, and challenged little black-and-white dogs. A small herd of horses, shorter and shaggier than the sort Arienh knew, were herded and staked. Cattle. Enough for food, enough for the plow. Not that she expected the Viking to remember his promise.

Arienh released a disgusted huff. "I believe you were right, Birgit. They have come to take our valley. No wonder the Viking sped out the door as fast as he could. I would have stabbed him again if he'd stayed."

"If I hadn't done it first," grumbled Birgit. "What do you see, Arienh?"

Arienh always wondered just how much Birgit could recognize of a distant drama such as this. Sometimes Birgit was simply good at fooling people, often could piece together movement and sound and other clues enough to know what went on.

"They are all men," Arienh said. "Nay, I see one woman."

The woman with arms around her Viking, with hair even darker than Ronan's, small, barely half his size, and almost hidden by the man's embrace.

"I suppose it is too late to head for the cavern. Do you think the others have gone?"

"Aye. Did you not hear their screams?"

Arienh shook her head. Had she slept so soundly that she had not noticed? "They seem to be ignoring us. We could still go."

Hardly a muscle moved in Birgit's rigid face. "Why? They are not like the others, Arienh. If they have come to stay, then we cannot hide long enough to save ourselves. And if they bring their sheep, they do not mean to go away. If they want to kill us, it matters little if they do it now or later."

Arienh's strategy had always been not to give up, even when she could see no solution. Many times in the past, that determination to live just a little longer, even one more moment, had sustained her when she might have been killed. Even that one time when a Viking had chased her up the hill and she had no hope of escape. Yet she had been saved by one of their own kind. You never knew what the next moment might bring.

But Birgit was right; this was different. The Celts probably weren't going to die, but there were worse things, especially for Birgit. Yet Birgit stood tall and calm, so Arienh would stand with her.

"Send Liam to the cave," Arienh suggested.

"Nay. He will be all right with us. Let's go closer so I can at least tell what my fate will be."

"Mama, you're hurting my hand."

The boy was wincing. Fear and excitement mingled in his eyes. Arienh watched Birgit loosen her tense grip on Liam's hand.

They walked down the path and stood by the oak tree by the stream, watching the Vikings swarming around the valley's lower end. Even though Birgit could probably see only movement from here, this was her way of challenging the intruders.

Of the four empty cottages in the lower valley, the Vikings had already taken over three, including Weylin's. Several men with axes worked on the hill trimming out small saplings to mend the enclosures that had fallen into disrepair. Three men and several dogs herded those odd-looking, black-faced sheep along the stream bank to graze.

Toward midday, the two brothers walked side by side up the rise from the lower valley to where Arienh stood with Birgit and

Liam beside the oak tree. Ronan still leaned on the other occasionally, still struggling with his weakness.

There was barely a finger's width difference in their height, and their eyes were the same clear, pure blue. But beyond that, for the life of her, she could see no resemblance between them. Egil was built like a huge tree trunk, straight up and down, where Ronan's broader shoulders and chest tapered to meet slightly slenderer waist and hips. A week's growth of dark beard softened the sculptured features of Ronan's rugged face, but Egil's longer yellow beard and great flowing mustache sharpened already menacing eyes. The pair of them was truly intimidating.

Not until now, as Ronan stood before her, no longer so weak and ill, did she realize how truly massive her Viking was. He could have snapped her in half that day, had she not managed the lucky blow. She had never fooled herself that it had been anything but luck.

Somehow in her struggle for his life, she had forgotten he was such a threat, for he had needed her just to cling to life, and she had freely given what he needed. She had forgotten how big he was and how strong. Forgotten who he was or that he had chased her down the mountain. Nay, no matter how he might frame it, that had been no benign act. Nor was this invasion. She should have killed him, as Mildread said.

Yet she knew she never would, nor could.

She folded her arms, glaring, growing braver with her growing anger. "So this was planned from the beginning. You are like all the others, save that you have come to take everything, Viking."

Ronan shook his head, giving her a beguiling smile that threatened to topple her resolve. "We meant to come here, and I did not tell you that. But we take nothing from you."

"You will graze your sheep on air? I think not. This valley is ours. There is no room for you."

"Nay," said Egil, his sweet smile belied by wicked eyes. "There is more than enough room. We will take your flocks with ours to the upper valley."

"So you will take our flocks from us as well."

"Nay," Ronan protested. "But who else will tend them? You have no men."

"We will do without men, as Vikings will not do to replace them," Arienh replied. "We do not need your kind."

"Aye," said Birgit. "We will tend our own flocks."

"Your fields need plowing and sowing," Egil offered. "You cannot wait any longer for what already should have been done."

Arienh had tried, but the rusty plowshare had crumbled. She had even tried to make one of wood, but it could not cut the stony soil.

"Aye," she said, "and I can do that as well, save there is no plow. But you did not keep that promise, either. You have shown us you cannot be trusted."

"But I have," said Egil. "And the team as well. They have but to be harnessed and led to the fields. When the soil is dry enough, I will plow for you."

"You will not. We do not need you."

"You need us," said Ronan. "We can help you, Arienh."

"And at what cost? Nay, you will not make slaves of us, Viking. Do not think we will cook for you and warm your beds, no matter what you take from us."

Birgit snorted. "This is how they repay your kindness. I am glad I did not waste my time with them. I am going back to my loom." Taking wide-eyed Liam's hand, she stalked back up the hill.

Arienh also turned.

"Arienh!"

She stopped, turned, and lifted her chin high. "I have nothing more to say. And I have work to do."

"We will not go away, Arienh."

A bitter quirk took over the corner of her mouth. "Do not be surprised if you change your mind, Viking."

Once again she whirled away, but the dark-haired Viking rushed around her to block her path. "We will not go away. We will stay and take wives. You are mine, Arienh."

She raked a murderous glare over him. "I thought you addled in the pate before, but I blamed it on the blow to your head. Now I see you come by it naturally. Celts do not marry Vikings."

"You will marry me. I've come for you, Arienh, and I will have you."

He was. He was truly addled.

"You owe me your life, Arienh. Have you forgotten me so easily?"

Arienh stared. "Forgotten you? I know no Vikings."

"But you know me. I came here with my uncle as a boy, and if I had not pushed you into a hole, you would be a Moor's slave today."

Her Viking boy? But how could it be? Surely not this magnificent giant of a man with hair as dark as richest earth. The boy had been little more than a starving waif, his wheat-colored hair thin, filthy strands. Yet, the eyes, blue like summer...

She had prayed for him every day of her life, for his salvation from the vicious man who had beaten him all the way down the hill. The only one of his kind she might have trusted.

Now he returned to take everything, even her valley, from her? Enslave her family and friends, force her to marriage? He didn't know Celts very well.

Fury rose in her like a whirlwind. "When the mountains crumble into the sea, I will still look at you and see only the faces of my murdered kin. Never will I marry one of your kind."

But he met her anger with an arrogant chuckle. "Do not be surprised if you change your mind, little Celt."

She shoved him away, forgetting momentarily his weakness, and he staggered back. The blond brother rushed to protect him, and she flashed a fiery glare at him, daring him to punish her.

She stalked away, never looking back.

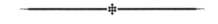

Within the cavern, in the yellow light from smoky reed torches, Arienh studied the anxious faces of her villagers. Seated on rocky ledges, or standing about on the cavern's uneven floor, their eyes reflected back her own grave concern.

"So what are we going to do?" Arienh asked.

"It is entirely your fault," grumbled Mildread. "You think of something."

Elli rose from her stone seat and stood beside her grandfather, a gaunt, bent man whose face glared his hatred for the intruders.

"Nay, Mildread," Elli said. "Arienh is not to be blamed for what they have done. They are the ones who have come to invade our valley and take our land."

"If she had not let that one live."

"And then they would have killed us all," Elli replied.

Old Ferris interrupted. His eyes gleamed as if he sensed approaching triumph. "You have no sense of these things, Mildread. They are animals. They live for blood and revenge. If we are to kill them, we must be sly. Slyer than the fox."

Arienh stiffened, sensing trouble. The man would destroy all of them for his own vengeance if he must. She stepped forward to head him off. "We aren't going to kill anybody. We just need to get rid of them."

Small Selma, her golden curls glowing in the torchlight, winced at the harsh talk. "But we do need help, Arienh. What if they are telling the truth? If they only come to settle, can that be so bad?"

"Settle?" Birgit snorted. "You would live among Vikings? Their sheep will take all the pasturage. And we will die because our animals starve."

"Aye," said Elli, "even if they do not also claim our animals for their own."

"They will make slaves of us, I tell you," Mildread insisted. "They are merciless devils."

Elli nodded. "They are naught but marauding rapists and murderers, Selma, no matter how they disguise themselves. I am surprised you could think of them otherwise."

"I only meant—"

Old Ferris's black eyes gleamed from the narrow confines of his wrinkled lids. "Do you not know they kill and eat the children they capture?"

"They do not!" Liam shouted. The women turned surprised stares at the boy, whose blue eyes shone brightly with tears. "He promised he wouldn't hurt us."

"Who?" asked several surprised women.

"Egil, the big one," Arienh said. "He did make a promise to the boy. We heard it." She put a comforting hand to Liam's shoulder.

"They lie, too," said Old Ferris. "You are foolish to believe him, Liam, for he will beguile you into the woods, and then—"

"Stop it." Birgit threw protective arms around her son. "You do not know any such thing, and you say it only to scare the boy."

"Do you defend them now, too, Birgit?" Elli asked.

"Nay. Only that things are bad enough as it is. You do not need to be making up things to scare children."

Elli snorted and folded her arms. "What do you think they will do to you when they find out about your eyes?"

Birgit flinched at Elli's words.

"Aye," Mildread replied, nodding. "'Tis said they drive the old and feeble out into the winter storms to die, when they don't want them anymore. We must protect our own."

"And expose babies they don't want, too," said a woman from far in the rear.

Elli nodded, certain of herself. "And their sexual appetites. They cannot be satisfied. And I have heard, their organs are so huge that they cannot help but hurt a woman."

"Is it so, Birgit?" Old Ferris's malicious grin punctuated his words.

Birgit's mouth closed tightly.

The old man went too far. If the Vikings got rid of any, surely Old Ferris would be the first, for he had become as useless a human as Arienh had ever known. She stepped between him and Birgit. "And how shall we defend against them if we have no more sense than to attack our own?"

Mildread pushed herself up beside Arienh, buttressing the barrier between the old man and Birgit. She had a soft spot for her dim-sighted cousin and could always be counted on to help protect Birgit. And she didn't like Old Ferris any better than the rest of them. "Arienh is right. We must stick together. We must get rid of them, but Arienh, there isn't any other way except to kill them."

Arienh shook her head. "That is impossible. They are big and strong, and they have all the weapons. They almost outnumber us."

"Not impossible," said Old Ferris. "We have something they want."

"What?"

"It's very simple. You are women. You lure them into your beds. Then all on the same night, we kill them as they sleep."

A collective gasp echoed in the rocky chamber.

Arienh shuddered. "Ferris, how can you even think of such a thing? Are you no better than their kind?"

"They killed my son," Old Ferris retorted with sharp, glistening eyes. "Aye, that's what you must do. Avenge your families.

Kill them for the sons and daughters they have murdered, raped, and stolen into slavery. You, Birgit, do you not want revenge for what they did to you? Your body ravaged, your sweetheart butchered? Do you think we would be so hungry if your father and my son had not been killed? Will you have your revenge?"

But Birgit stood tall and proud against Old Ferris's maliciousness. "Nay, I will kill no one, not in so evil a way."

"Nor I," agreed Mildread. "Besides, it would not work. At the very best, some would escape and kill all of us."

"And I will not kill anyone at all," said Selma. "Do not even think I will help you."

"Nor I." Arienh's words were echoed by others, and she breathed out her relief. "We must outsmart them, for we have not the strength or weapons to combat them. And for all that they are barbarians, they are clever men. But they could be pushed to their limit, I think. We do not need to make life easy for them. Perhaps, in fact, we could make life hard for them."

Selma brightened and tossed her curls. "Perhaps miserable," she added. Her round blue eyes sparkled.

Other women caught the idea as a murmur of interest swept through the crowd. Everyone seemed to speak at once.

"Such as what?"

"Nothing truly harmful," Arienh cautioned. "We must beware the Northmen's fury."

"Ruin their food supply," suggested Selma.

Mildread shook her head. "We are all too hungry ourselves. I could easier slit their throats than ruin perfectly good food."

Everyone laughed.

"Of course," Mildread continued, "we could steal it and eat it. That would be fun."

Other voices babbled in the cavern's dimness, overlapping each other, so fast that Arienh was not entirely sure who spoke.

"Pranks. Like boys do to old men."

"Steal their tools and bury them."

"Scatter their flocks."

"Forget the sheep. The dogs would just herd them back. Scatter the horses."

Giggles.

Silence.

"Can no one think of anything else?" Arienh asked.

"We might not lure them into our beds, but how about into the woods?" Selma said sweetly. "They are strangers here."

Arienh nodded. "Get them lost. I like it. But we need more. We must convince them we're too much trouble. Enough to make them leave, but not enough to harm any of us. It will be hard."

A rumbling chorus of assent echoed in the cavern.

"But what if it doesn't work, Arienh?" Selma asked. "What if they just decide to kill us all?"

That was what Arienh feared. "We have no other weapon. We have no power at all, except ourselves. But we are not cowards. We must either take the chance, or give in to them."

"Aye," Mildread agreed. "'Tis better than more bloodshed. You are right, Arienh. Though I think you should have killed the dark one, perhaps it would have brought us more harm. Who can say? This might be a better plan."

"Now," said Arienh, "I have something. And it will cost us nothing but a little time."

"What?"

For an answer, she merely grinned and motioned for the villagers to follow her out into the clear, dark night.

From Weylin's cottage in the lower valley came the sounds of deep and rollicking voices singing.

"They're drinking," she said. "Mead. Celebrating their triumph. Let them. It will keep them busy."

"For what?"

"Come and see. Selma and Mildread, bring three others. And buckets. Lots of buckets."

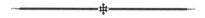

Hidden among scrubby oaks, Arienh watched a silent figure, silhouetted by the bright half moon, glide across the shining sand to the distant surf's edge. Skirts billowed in the stiff wind as the figure bent down, filled a pail, then walked back the long trek to low dunes. Not a bird pipped as the bucket passed to another hushed figure, who turned and trudged just as quietly up the slope, following the tiny stream that flowed between two hills. Arienh reached out in silence for the bucket Mildread handed her, exchanging it for an empty one, then turned and climbed toward the ridge, and handed the bucket to Selma. The bucket passed over the crest, down the far slope. Another joined it, and another, until several full buckets rested in the shadows at the foot of the hill, within the valley. Silent women collected around them.

Pairs of vigilant eyes watched. At the edge of the forest, Arienh waved a hand. A shadowy chain of women emerged and followed, creeping upon the provisions stacked beside Weylin's cottage.

Small kegs came off the stack. Lids pried open. Half of their contents poured into empty buckets, full buckets poured into half-empty kegs, lids replaced. Shadowy women crept into the silent forest, their footsteps muffled by the soggy earth.

Inside the cottage, Ronan reclined against a stack of woolen blankets, furs, and pillows, watching his companions at the tables and benches and letting the sweet warmth of the mead curl downward all the way to his toes. The fever was gone, and his strength was returning rapidly. It was good to be back with his family and friends, good to see his mother relaxed into Gunnar's arms, good to see Gunnar active after his last bout of illness.

"I know which one I want!" Tanni shouted, too loudly, and tossed back his head to drain the last drop of mead from his horn. "That little one with the golden curls."

"I care not, so long as you stay away from the redhead," Egil retorted, chuckling.

"Well, you can have her. Strangest eyes I've ever seen."

"But big enough to be a woman, at least."

"You'll both be lucky if they even look at you," said Olav solemnly. "The problem here is they're all Christians."

"So?"

"So Christians can't stand it until you become one of them. You know how it is when you try to trade with them. They've got to say their words over you first."

"So let them say their words," Tanni answered with a shrug and laugh. "They say it really doesn't make a difference as long as they don't sprinkle their water on you. But if they sprinkle on you, you're doomed. You'll never see Valhalla."

Ronan's mother sat up to interrupt, but Gunnar eased her gently back to his side. She'd explained things often enough.

Ronan had heard stories of the Christian faith all his life, and had considered it, so at least he understood it. But the new religion of the Christians made little sense to most Northmen, so they interpreted it the way that pleased them most.

"Aye," said Ronan, and he stopped to gulp the remainder of his mead. "But that's just for trading. We're talking about taking wives. A few words won't appease them."

Bjorn snorted. "Why bother to appease them? They're just women."

"In Frisia," said Olav, "my uncle must have converted six or seven times so he could trade. Got white robes each time. He swore it was the way to do it. Always got the best deals that way. But he died fighting the Danes and found his way to Valhalla anyway, I'd swear by Thor's hammer."

Ronan smiled and watched silently. Wynne just shook her head at the hopelessness of it all.

Olav took another gulp of mead, draining his horn. "That's what we've got to do, take their white robes and everything. Then once we've got them, we can do whatever we want."

Ronan suspected that was a little too simple. "Some of them might not fall for that."

"Then pick another," said Bjorn. "There's plenty of them. One woman's pretty much like another."

"You're forgetting, the women have something to say about it, too," Ronan objected.

"Don't see why," Bjorn replied, lifting his horn to his lips. The pale scar that slashed into his reddish beard flexed with the movement. "Pick the one you want and take her, I say. It's all the same to me. I'll let you have them all."

"Nay, there will be no taking of unwilling women here. We'll court them properly."

"Let me speak, son," interrupted Wynne. It was not her usual way, but Ronan had watched his mother's edginess for most of the evening. She had once been a Celtic woman taken against her will. He nodded to her.

"These Celtic women are proud women," she said. "In times past, they fought alongside their men, and they have not forgotten. You will not subdue them easily, and if you do, they will make sure you regret it. Best to pretend they all have fathers ready to lop off your heads if you dishonor them."

"Meaning, to court them, not just take them," Ronan said.

Olav contemplated the bottom of his horn, tipping it to see if it was truly empty. "Aye, Wynne. I see what you mean. They could all be had, if we do it right, if we get past their rage. Until we persuade them we're worth having, there's not a one of them worth the chance."

Olav's careful speculation of the future shone in his eyes. He was an intelligent, serious man, and Ronan prized that in him. Ronan nodded. "And once we have their trust, it will be easy enough to take over. All women need men to take care of them."

"Did you see the redhead's sister?" said Tanni, as loud as if he shouted over the roar of the sea. "That's a beauty."

"She's mine," Ronan replied quietly. Tanni had had so much to drink, he'd lost the point of the whole debate.

"Aye, you and Egil, you'll get the feistiest ones. There's a tongue on both of them."

Ronan laughed. More than they knew. "Aye, that one's not like any other, for whatever you say, Olav. Tanni, fetch us a few more casks."

He laughed some more as he watched Tanni stagger through the sagging door. Good thing the bad weather had finally ceased, for Tanni didn't have enough sense left to get the door back in its jamb and properly shut. Ronan sighed and followed. He was not so weak he couldn't heft a couple of small kegs.

Outside, in the dark shadow of the cottage, Tanni stumbled about, grumbling as his toes stubbed on unseen objects. Ronan reached out to steady his friend, but Tanni yelped, grabbed his arm, and fell, toppling Ronan with him.

"What?" Ronan fell against the stack of kegs, which collapsed, sending little barrels tumbling and rolling over the soggy field. "Thor's beard, who stacked these things? We're lucky we haven't lost the whole batch."

Disgusted, Ronan gathered up the casks and stood them upright by the cottage. No point in restacking them until they had some light. He gave Tanni a boost to his feet and tromped back inside with his mead.

Wynne rose from her place beside Gunnar to decant the mead. She had ceased fussing over his wound, and Ronan was glad, for with Gunnar's failing health, she had enough worries. Soon Gunnar would be gone, and they all knew it. Wynne would lose her second husband, and Ronan would miss him even more than his first father, whom he hardly remembered. It was Gunnar who had rescued him as a boy and fostered him to manhood.

Now, at last, Ronan had the chance to repay him, and Gunnar would have his dream fulfilled, a green land with valley and fields stretching out as far as a man could wish.

Pensive, Ronan lifted his drinking horn to his lips in a toast to their new home. He tossed back his head to swallow a big gulp of the delicious mead.

He choked as a foul brew snorted back into his nostrils.

"Aaagh!" Egil stood suddenly, his hand flung to his mouth.

Ronan darted for the doorway, jostled his way past his fellows, and dashed for the rain barrel to scoop water into his mouth.

"Salt!"

The rain barrel was also salted.

He dashed for the stream, gulping water down his gagging throat, slapping water upward to rinse flaming nostrils.

As he sat gasping on the stream bank with his men, Ronan slowly realized the other men suffered the same fate as he did.

"How did that happen?" he asked.

"On the crossing?" asked Egil, still hacking.

"But you said it was not stormy. It would take some mighty waves to break over and flood the casks. Even that I could understand, but the water barrel, too?"

It must have dawned on the rest of them at the same time it did Ronan, because nobody said a thing.

It looked like a declaration of war to him.

# CHAPTER SEVEN

As the morning sun threw brilliant shafts of light on the village, Arienh and Birgit stuck their heads out the door and looked around. The village sounded perfectly ordinary, with the usual noises of men and animals. It looked perfectly ordinary, too, except that not a woman was in sight.

Unlike the other women who had fled and spent the night in the cavern, Arienh and Birgit had gone home, for they had intended from the beginning to put themselves on the front line of the confrontation. Someone had to do it.

Arienh and Birgit set off down the path.

"What do you suppose they'll do to us?" Birgit asked as they sauntered along.

"Us? You didn't do anything, Birgit."

"I am no more innocent than you, for I am just as guilty in my heart."

"But you can truly say you did nothing."

"You will say you did nothing, too, so what difference does it make?"

"Perhaps they will not make the connection."

Birgit tossed her a look of disgust.

And here they came. Ronan and Egil, with the one woman she had seen. All smiling, as if nothing had happened.

"Arienh, Birgit," called Ronan, halting directly in front of them. "We bring you our mother, Wynne." He nodded, his face lit with affection. "Mother, the child is Liam, Birgit's son."

His mother. The woman who had embraced him was his mother, although she hardly looked old enough. Her long, very dark hair, lightly streaked with grey, was looped into a large knot of the Nordic style. She was not tall, even for a Celt, and had the slimness of a very young woman.

Arienh nodded coolly to the woman, carefully keeping Ronan in view as she debated what to say to a woman who had spent her life with heathens. "Ah. You are a Celt, as he said."

The woman smiled, and in her smile Arienh suddenly saw the resemblance to her son. Yet she saw nothing to connect her to the yellow-haired Viking who stood at her other side. Perhaps his profuse beard obscured the resemblance.

"I am of the Cymry, though I have not been among them since I was a young girl." The woman proudly held out a goose egg. "My favorite goose has already laid her first egg here. I have brought it for you, to thank you for saving my son."

Arienh quickly scanned Ronan's blue eyes, which crinkled at their corners in a secret laugh. Had he already forgotten last night? Why didn't he say something? Do something? What kind of man was he that he let such a challenge as they had given go unanswered, and laugh instead?

But even in the beginning he had tried to tease her, before he had sunk into the depths of his fever. Then, she had not minded, even knowing who and what he was. Now, he sought to beguile her even as he betrayed her kindness to him with his invasion. Well, he was a Viking. And he meant to possess her. He had even said as much.

Never. The fight had just begun.

"I did nothing," she said. "I did not expect him to live, and he brought himself in from the cold. I could not have done that."

Again she flung a glare at Ronan, whose eyes still held laughter. What was he thinking? Did he mean to say nothing about the night before?

"But I am still grateful, for he is my son. So please, take the egg. It will make a good meal for you."

Arienh resisted the urge to reach out for the egg. She had not eaten a goose egg in a long time. Birgit gaped speculatively at the egg, and in Liam's eyes she saw what could only be defined as pure lust. She hoped the boy would learn to be less obvious when he reached the age to lust after women instead of food.

"Perhaps you should keep the egg, in case there are no more."

"Oh, she is a good layer, have no fear. There will be many a new gosling soon. We will soon have a new flock for you. Come, perhaps we can talk while the men repair your roof."

"The roof? I did not ask—"

"But nay, we did promise," Ronan replied.

His eyes sparkled with hidden merriment. She hated that about him, hated the incredible blueness of his eyes that was brighter than the warmest day of summer.

And he did what he pleased, took what he wanted, ignoring her objections. Arienh could only watch as Egil led men to swarm up ladders over the aging thatch. Bundles of osiers were passed up to yellow-haired men who wove them in place. Inside the cottage, Ronan poked upward with a pole to indicate holes.

Arienh seethed. She didn't want him to be nice to her. It was all a ploy to gain their goodwill while taking the last of what was theirs.

And not a word had been said about the mead, as if it had had no effect whatsoever. Well, let them pretend. She knew what she had seen last night. From the cover of underbrush, she had watched the Vikings rush for the stream and cleanse their assaulted mouths.

That was just the beginning. She would make him regret coming to her valley. And this Wynne, this Celtic woman who was no Celt. All right, she would talk with her, even accept her egg. But she would tell her nothing of any importance.

Wynne helped her lay cloths over the furnishings to protect them from the debris that dropped from the thatch as the men worked, while Birgit and Liam covered the loom and the spun wool that awaited weaving. Arienh worked in silence, determined not to converse unless she must. Yet she nearly burst with questions. This woman would be one who knew about these men, and she was a Celt. Why not ask her?

She glanced at Birgit, who responded with a questioning look. Birgit would follow her lead. Arienh decided to probe cautiously. "Is your husband not with you, Wynne?"

"Aye. Gunnar." The woman studied the thatch, looking wistful. "He is not well. Although he does much better, these days I cannot leave him for long."

"Do you not fear the change in climate for him?"

"It is not so different from the Green Isle. But he will not get well. And he longs for land of his own before he dies."

"This is our land," Arienh objected.

"But you are few and there is enough to share. They thought at first they would go up into the hills where the Celts do not go, for that is land like many of them from the North know. But there is room here."

Perhaps, then, if they could not persuade the Vikings to leave, they might be able to talk them into taking over the mountains instead. But Arienh decided to save that argument for another time. "Father Hewil tells us that the Vikings take the old and weak out into the wilderness to die."

A dark cloud of memory seemed to pass over Wynne's face, and for a moment, the woman was silent. "It is done, sometimes. It is part of what they believe, that sometimes a life should end.

Life and death are much the same to them. But I do not think Gunnar will go."

Shudders ripped through Arienh as Birgit shifted her gaze down to the basket of wool at her feet. It must be true.

It had been little more than a sennight since the Viking had offered her his dagger to kill him. But he had lived, when he had expected to die in freezing agony. Would that cause him to see things differently? Or would he still see Birgit as useless?

And how could she know without risking Birgit's life? She couldn't take that chance.

✦

"Ready? He's coming."

"Which one?" Selma asked.

"How should I know?" retorted Elli. "It makes no difference, anyway. Go on, swing. Yell."

Yell? Selma screeched as she swung out over the cavern's dark pit. Never mind that it really wasn't all that deep, and she had already been down in it earlier that same afternoon. It was just hanging out over the pit that made her heart leap into her throat.

Elli gave her a shove.

"Stop it, Elli," she cried out, and hooked her foot outward, perfectly serious in her intent to get back to safe footing.

Elli just grinned and gave her another shove.

"What's going on?"

Oh, good. Tanni, the handsome one. Selma thought if she had to be rescued, she'd rather it be by him. He was more like a normal man, not so huge and frightening like the other ones.

Then she recalled just what they meant to do to her rescuer.

"Oh, help me!" Elli cried to the man, and Selma thought she was not at all convincing. "Selma is trying to rescue our lamb

76

that has fallen into the pit. And now I am trying to rescue her, for she can't go down or up on the rope."

From the darkness of the pit, the little lamb bleated as if he knew the plot.

Tanni reached out his hand and grabbed Selma's wrist to pull her and the dangling rope closer. With a swift scoop, he had both rope and Selma in his arms and pulled her to safety. Selma sighed genuine relief as she rested her head against the rugged chest. A gentle hand rubbed affectionately across her back. She didn't mind his rumbling chuckle. Perhaps he did think her silly. He wouldn't for long.

"Thank you," she whispered, as if a whisper was all she could manage. "I don't know how we will get the little fellow out."

Tanni held the reed torch over the rim of the pit. "It is a long way down. He must be injured."

The lamb bleated pitifully.

"Perhaps," Selma told him. "But we cannot afford to lose him, as we have no rams now. We must rescue him."

Tanni's warm grin almost strutted across his face. "Well, I will get him for you."

Selma felt her own flirtatious smile fade from her face. Suddenly she didn't want to do this. But she had promised. They were depending on her.

With cocky pride, the man swung out on the rope and descended into the darkness. She held her breath as she shone the torch over the edge and watched the leather rope play between his muscular legs until he reached the rock beneath.

"The torch," he called, and Selma tossed it down to him.

His hands skimmed over the lamb, which bleated and rubbed against him. "He is not hurt. How could he have fallen so far?"

Elli shrugged. "If you will tie him onto the rope, we will haul him up."

With the extra length of the hide rope, Tanni fashioned a sling around the lamb. The two women pulled upward, bringing the lamb out of the pit, and shooed the little creature out the cavern's entrance.

"Maybe we shouldn't—" said Selma.

"Don't be silly." Elli signaled to Mildread above, who suddenly unfastened the rope and let it drop into the pit.

"Hey!"

"Oh, dear," said Elli. "The rope has fallen."

"How am I going to get out of here?" shouted the Viking.

"I don't know. We don't have another rope."

"Then go get another one." Even the man's desperation seemed to echo in the hollow chamber below.

"Aye," said Selma, glancing hopefully at Elli. "We could do that, couldn't we?"

Elli glared back, then smiled sweetly to the Viking. "There are no other ropes."

"Then ask my friends," the man shouted back. "Send one of them for me."

"There's another way out, Viking," Elli said. "If we can't find help, I'm sure you can find the way."

Mildread slid down from her hiding spot, into the passage beside Elli and Selma. "Come on," she whispered, "let's get out of here."

The three women skittered for the cavern's entrance, but not before Selma turned back to give a rueful glance at the man they abandoned in the pit.

Ronan walked along the edge of the valley where steep, forested hillsides abutted gently sloping grassland, carefully surveying his valley. The battle for the land had been the easy part, but the women themselves would not be won in a day.

Perhaps he had been a bit naive. Ronan had really expected these women to be a bit more grateful. They were being saved, after all, even if they did see it as a conquest.

Four of the smaller abandoned cottages in the lower valley had been made over to house his men. New pens enclosed horses and sheep awaiting the greening of pasture land in the high valley. Over Arienh's objections, he and his men had patched thatch, repaired enclosures, and begun the plowing and sowing that had been dangerously neglected. But the women went about their business as if the intruders were not even there. He could not get even one of them to look him in the eye.

"Somebody? Help!"

Ronan stopped, puzzled, his ears straining at the sound.

"Help. Anybody out there?"

A man's voice, faint, echoing, indistinct. With a frown, Ronan studied the hillside and saw a cavern scooped into the steep grey cliff, about a man's height above him. The echoing sound seemed to come from there. He scrambled up the rock to the cave. A dim glow came from the dark, damp air, but he could not see his footing.

"Help!"

"Who is it?" he called back, feeling his way along rough rock.

"Tanni. Is it you, Ronan?"

"Aye. Tanni, where are you?"

"In a pit. Be careful."

As Ronan groped his way into the cavern, the light grew brighter, reflecting off water-slick cavern walls. As it brightened more, he spotted the pit before him, and looking down, young Tanni below with a torch in his hand.

"Tanni? How did you get down there? Are you hurt?"

"No, I'm not hurt. Get me out of here."

"How did you get there?"

"With a rope. But the rope has, uh, fallen in. The sides are too slick to climb."

"But why?"

"Never mind why. Just get me out of here!"

Never mind why? That didn't bode well. He shrugged. He'd get it out of him later.

"I'll go for help," he suggested.

"No. No, just—just catch the rope and pull me out."

With a thud, the coiled rope landed at Ronan's feet, and he snagged it before it could slide back down into the hole. Ronan looped one end around a column of rock the size of a man and tested it for safety. The other end he threw back to Tanni.

"Climb."

Tanni shinnied up the rope, and as soon as Tanni had solid rock beneath his feet again, Ronan grabbed the man's jerkin and pulled. As they emerged from the cavern, Ronan checked him to confirm Tanni was unhurt.

"All right, Tanni, how did this happen?"

A flush crept onto the man's cheeks as he studied the ground. "I uh, went after a lamb."

"Where's the lamb?"

"It's already out," Tanni mumbled.

"Out? How did you get it out and leave yourself behind?"

"I—never mind."

"Ah. The women. Well, they said they'd make us regret coming here."

The smaller man's light blue eyes pleaded for protection. "Don't tell anybody, Ronan."

Ronan agreed it was a secret worth keeping, although it was probably hopeless to try, just as it had been futile to expect Egil to keep quiet about how he'd got his wound. His men loved nothing more than a thorough teasing of their fellows. He had been right:

he'd never live that down. But it would behoove them to be more vigilant in this little war.

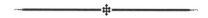

Tanni was in a rare fit, and drunk, to boot. Hardly surprising, Ronan thought, considering the humiliation he'd suffered this afternoon. Then again, Tanni was usually the first to tease, so it was his turn.

"So why can't we just pick the ones we want and take them?" Tanni demanded.

"Nay."

"Why not? Stop their pranks." Tanni guzzled ale from his horn. Much more, and someone would have to carry him home to his bunk.

"Nay," Ronan said again. "You wouldn't do that to women back home. You'd give a girl a proper courting, and that's what you'll do here."

Olav swirled the mead around in his horn, frowning, instead of drinking. "A girl back home wouldn't be pulling pranks like this. Maybe they really just need a strong hand, Ronan."

"And a hard rod. That's what a woman really needs." Bjorn, too, had been drinking hard all evening. He tilted back his horn so far that the liquid dribbled down his red mustache.

"Not this time," said Egil. "They've had too much of that."

"Aye, your Birgit, has, it's obvious. Beyond me why you want another man's leavings."

Egil got up from his bench, and the room went silent. In three deliberate strides, he faced Bjorn, the smaller man by far. Egil folded his arms. "Never say that again, Bjorn, or you will not live to face the morn."

Bjorn shifted his startled glance about him and found no supporters, not even Tanni.

Ronan stiffened. This was dangerous. For a young man, Egil had an even, mindful temperament, but he had a line he would not allow to be crossed. Bjorn, no longer young, had never learned moderation. Bjorn was the one who worried Ronan the most because he didn't know much about the man, beyond that he was an adventurer, battle-scarred and hard, but a good black-smith.

But Ronan did not intend to let him cross Egil's line, and stepped between the two men.

"Nay. We propose to stay here and live with these Celts," Ronan said. "But all that they have suffered teaches them not to trust us. So we will earn their respect and trust. You agreed to this, Bjorn. If you have changed your mind, we will see you back to the Green Isle or the Manx Isle in less than a day."

The man grunted and turned away. He raised his drinking horn and downed the contents in one long gulp. Still grumbling, he pushed his way past his companions and stalked out the door.

"We came expecting to have to fight for a place," said Olav. "Bjorn is a good man in a fight."

"But it's all he knows, Ronan," said Egil. "And smithing. He's never been a farmer or trader like the rest of us."

"Nay, we'll give him a chance."

The door burst open again, and Bjorn dashed back inside. "Damn women!" he shouted. "The horses!"

From the darkness came the roar of hooves pounding the earth, raucous neighs, dogs barking. Men raced for the door, out into the chilly night as the last of the horses sped through the breach in the paddock and across the open meadow.

# CHAPTER EIGHT

D AMN WOMEN, INDEED.

Grabbing the flowing tail of a galloping horse, Ronan hurled himself into the flow. As he groped for the mane and leapt onto the animal's back, a flash of sympathy for Bjorn's attitude surged through him. It was the women's doing. He'd checked the paddock himself.

As another horse galloped past, Ronan snagged its mane and yanked, reining it in as it slowed with a harsh whinny. Tanni caught up with him and alit onto the horse's back.

Ronan dug his heels into the flanks and raced after the stampeding herd to cut off and slow down any beasts he came upon. In the light of the waxing moon, he saw other riders who had also captured horses. Bjorn rode up, then Egil. The roar of hooves drowned out their voices, so he waved to signal directions. The two tore off toward the river after part of the herd.

A good thing about horses. They didn't run headlong very far. The creatures slowed as their stamina faded and fear abated. And the valley was narrow, so there weren't many places for the animals to go. Soon, the Northmen had gentled most of the horses and coaxed them back toward the fold.

"Still three missing," Egil said at last as Ronan and Bjorn closed up the gap in the enclosure.

"They'll probably wander back by themselves when they discover there's more grain in the paddock than grass on the ground."

"Aye. They know what's good for them."

Unlike women.

"Damn women," Bjorn snarled, "must've used this place for a sheepfold. Never saw such a mess."

Ronan repressed a smile as he watched the blacksmith fuss about the abandoned smithy, sweeping debris with a broom that was in such bad shape it needed to be discarded. The forge had gone unused for a while, that was obvious, but it was hardly a mess.

"The mill's worse," Ronan replied.

"Well, then, the mill's no use at all, is it?"

"Only because the millstone's cracked. Not anything the women could help. I've sent a ship for a new one from Caen. You know that."

"And you're all a bunch of fools," Bjorn insisted. "They'll put rings in your noses and lead you about like pigs to market. A man's got to take a firm hand with a woman."

"Don't lay a hand on any of them, Bjorn."

Bjorn's gaze flicked at him dismissively. "Didn't say I'd hit them. There's ways to control a woman without hitting her."

"And it works better to persuade her she wants to do things your way."

"Bah. Bunch of women yourselves. I should've stayed on the Green Isle."

Ronan snickered as he watched Bjorn turn back to his task of refurbishing the old forge. The man puzzled him. He didn't know if he was dangerous or just a grouch. What he did know was Bjorn was a good blacksmith, and their community could not survive without a smith. Maybe he'd watch the man more closely.

Despite Bjorn's grumpiness, Ronan left the forge feeling invigorated. His strength seemed to surge back into him.

The day was bright, although still chilly. A knot of women gathered near the stream, which continued to run muddy and strong. As he approached, their chatter silenced and all eyes turned to him. Then, as if he were of no significance, they all looked away. The women parted then dispersed as if they had intended to leave anyway.

Only Arienh remained, along with the village sheep, swinging her crook and encouraging the flock away from the riverbank.

A dog. She needed a dog. Better yet, someone to help her with the flock. But she had already turned that offer down.

"Good morning," he said.

She looked at him silently, muted anger still seething in her eyes. But something else. Was it a flicker of scheming satisfaction at the success of her mischief? There was plenty of that in her.

His entire body hummed in anticipation of a challenge. Should he ignore it as he had before? Or was this the time for confrontation? His men were getting impatient.

"You look tired this morning," he said impishly. "Did you not get enough rest last night?"

"I am rested. You look like you could use more sleep."

"Horses got out last night. You wouldn't know anything about that, would you?"

"I don't know much about horses." She concentrated her attention on her flock.

He stepped up beside her. "I see. And you wouldn't know how the salt water got into the mead, either, I suppose."

"Salt water in mead? As I have never been to sea, I cannot imagine what you might have done to cause that."

"Mm. Nor would you know why three young women forgot they had left one of my men stranded in the bottom of a pit after he rescued their lamb."

An evasive glint passed her eyes before she quickly turned away. Ah, as he thought, she was the mastermind. As if he had said nothing at all, she riveted her attention on her unruly flock, swinging her crook to urge them up the trail.

Ronan pounced into her path. "I can think of other things I would rather do with my nights than chase ponies, Arienh. Making love, perhaps."

"Vikings make love?" she retorted with a sneer, pushing him aside. "I would not call it that. I doubt you know what love is."

"I could keep you happy."

"Nay, only a man could do that. Vikings do not qualify."

He had not forgotten kissing her. The memory of her body flexing against his sent a shiver of energy through him. It had been more than mere sympathy for an injured man. He reached for her arm.

"Do not touch me. I want no part of you."

"Yes, you do," he replied, laughing. "You want a very specific part of me." He drew her close. She squirmed free.

"You are but a beast. Stay away from me. And keep your brother away from Birgit. If he hurts her, I will kill him myself."

Again, she shoved at him with her free hand, and he reluctantly released her. She shooed at her flock to hurry them away from the water toward the upper valley. The sheep continued to move at their same ambling pace.

She had no great skill at herding, and too many sheep for one small woman to control. Ronan picked up a fallen branch and hacked it clean with his knife. With a few bounds, he caught up with her and swung the makeshift crook at the animals to move them in the direction she had chosen. He scooped up a young lamb that couldn't keep up and draped it around his neck.

"Go away. I don't want your help."

"But without it, you will not make the upper valley until midday tomorrow."

"That is my affair." Even in profile, he could see angry frustration flashing in her eyes.

"Then I make it mine. How will you manage the sheep and still do what you must do at home? Tanni is a good shepherd, with good men and good dogs. He can tend the flock for you."

"Birgit will tend to things at home. I take care of the animals."

He said nothing but kept swinging his improvised crook, redirecting strays. She could hardly deny it took both of them to move the flock along.

Earlier this day, he had sent his men up the valley with their flock of black-faces for the first time, and Ronan suspected that was likely the reason she sought to move her animals now. Sheep were notorious for cropping grass too close. She must fear that the Northmen would find and use up all the good pasture before she got there. Ronan wished he could find a way to persuade her he meant to help.

"It is a good thing Tanni's bitch will whelp soon. You are going to need some good dogs."

"We can do without."

"But why do you want to, Arienh? You need not suffer any longer, nor the other women. We have more than enough for all."

"We would rather die than to take from your kind. You do not fool us with your gifts."

He sighed. "There are those of us who wonder if we should not simply take brides and be done with it."

"Slaves, you mean. You have already taken our land. Do not think we will come so easily. Celtic women will never submit."

"Perhaps we could make an agreement. We will tend your flock for you, and in exchange, take some of Birgit's fine cloth."

"We do not want to deal with you. We only want you to go away."

"But we will not go away, Arienh. Ask Birgit if she will trade."

"She cannot. The cloth she makes now is already promised. It is Mildread's wool she weaves now."

"Oh? She weaves for everyone?"

"Aye, as she cannot…" She paused. "She is the best weaver. So everyone spins for her loom. They bring her other things in return."

"Oh. Well, it is a good thing. She does not seem to be of much use at anything else."

Arienh's jaw dropped open. "She is not useless. She can do anything anyone else can do. She just chooses to weave."

An odd response. "I did not mean she was useless. Not when she can weave the way she does."

"Well, she isn't."

"Of course not. I suppose you are right. She spends so much time weaving that she does not have time to do other things. And it matters not, when her weaving is so fine. Not even Flanders wool is so well done."

Arienh glared and swung her crook at a stray.

In the upper valley, short grass was already growing tall enough to graze, although snow still clung to the high slopes. Arienh chose her spot to graze on the far side of the valley from the flock of black-faces, perhaps purposely. Ronan lowered the small lamb from his shoulders to the ground and gave a swat to its hindquarters. The little creature bawled as loud as a calf, and its ewe trotted up. He had always been amazed at how a mother could identify its own.

The sheep quickly settled in to their task of devouring everything in sight and no longer needed close watching. Arienh left the flock to its grazing and climbed a deeply worn path uphill along rocky slopes. He followed.

"Where are you going?"

"To the stone circle."

"Stone circle?"

"I must move the stones."

Ronan hadn't the slightest idea what she meant, and she obviously didn't intend to explain. He climbed after her. She reached a lightly sloped plateau, backed by a tall mount, overlooking the sea. The stiff breeze ruffled the golden curls that escaped her tight braid.

In the new green grass, tall, upright stones, mostly about the height of a man, marked a broad circle on the ground. Just within the perimeter circled another ring made up of low, weathered posts. Arienh walked up to one rotting post and picked up a red stone at its base, then paced around, counting off the posts.

"Yan, tan, tether…"

"An odd way to count," he said. He leaned back against one of the larger stones and folded his arms to watch.

"What is odd about it? That is the way we always count."

"It is not the way other Celts count."

"Well, I care not. It is how we count."

Arienh continued her count as she carried the marker stone from point to point. "I thought so," she said, and placed the stone at the base of one of the upright ones.

"Thought what?"

"With all the rain and other things, I was losing track. The Alban Eilir, the end of the long nights, comes in a sennight."

"How can you tell?"

"It is the way the ancients told, before they had priests to keep the days of the year. But the priests do not often come to us, so we have kept up the old ways. I count the posts around the circle, one for each day of the year. But I have not come up here for fifteen days. Sometimes in the winter I cannot come for a long time."

The wind whipped her skirts, teased her heavy golden braid, and she seemed to meld with the ancients and the connecting force with their descendants, a vital, living link between past and present. It was important to her, this place. She was different here, softer. Yearning, perhaps. Did she not want what all women wanted—a man, a home, children? Yet she was wild and fierce, a Celt of bygone days, part healer, part warrior.

"Then what do you do when you cannot come?"

She flashed an impatient glance at him as she again paused. Then with a shrug, she continued.

"I make a mark on a wooden slab every night, so that I don't lose count. This year, I could not even come at midwinter, because there was too much snow. But in seven days, the sun will rise over the horizon exactly where the large stone pillar touches the sky. And that is spring's first day."

"Will you come to see it?"

"Aye."

"Does everyone come?"

"Nay, I am the only one. The others only come when there is something important, like Beltane. Sometimes they do not even come for Imbolc, if the weather is as bad as it was this year. They leave it to me."

"But why to you?"

"Because I am the appointed counter of days, the keeper of the stones. It is a very old custom, and I will not let it die."

She rarely looked at him as directly as she did now, and her clear green eyes dared him to scoff.

"I will come with you," he said.

"It belongs to us, not you."

"Well, I think I will come anyway. Perhaps it will belong just to us, since no one else will come."

Arienh flipped him a disgusted look and walked away, descending the slope of the hill by a path worn deep as if people had been climbing up this route since the creation of the world.

Ronan followed her, no matter that she made it clear she didn't want his company. In the valley, a small lamb bawled, and its ewe bleated pitifully, even though they had been gone only a short while. Arienh scanned around with a worried frown and scurried to a muddy hollow where the little lamb had wandered into muck and couldn't get out. Gently, she lifted the little one from the mire and wiped the worst of the mud from its hooves before setting it down.

But behind her, the remainder of the flock scattered widely. Arienh tried to direct the flock toward more concentrated grazing, but there were just too many of the beasts.

"Tanni would willingly loan you some of his dogs," Ronan suggested.

"Leave me alone. I'll do it myself."

"There is no longer need for you to work so hard, Arienh. Leave men's work to men."

Her eyes bored into him like icy knives. But even she had to know she could not manage the flock. She was just so stubborn that she would not give up until the situation was beyond hopeless.

He sighed. He hated to make her angrier than she already was, but he saw no choice, knowing she could not afford to lose any of her animals for her stubbornness. Tanni and his men and dogs had moved closer. He blew a shrill whistle that carried across the glen.

Her head jerked in his direction. "What are you doing?"

"Calling for help."

"I told you—"

"Someone's got to rescue you from yourself."

Across the valley bounded Tanni and one of his shepherds, slowing when they saw there was no danger.

"Aye, Ronan, what is it?" asked Tanni as they sauntered up.

"Take the white-faces and graze them with our flock," he replied.

"They are ours. You have no right!"

Tanni studied Ronan quizzically, then with a shrug directed the little black-and-white dogs that had accompanied him to round up the flock.

"We will have no trouble telling yours from ours, Arienh, as yours are all white-faces. Tanni will bring them down at night until the weather is warmer."

For a very long moment, she just glared at him, her green eyes blazing with the ferocity of a woman slapped. She pitched her crook off into the wild shrubbery. With furious strides, she left the valley and climbed back up into the hills to the grassy plateau that held the stone circle.

It would not be easy now to convince her he meant well for her. But he'd had little choice.

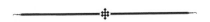

Heavy clouds approached, and the stiff wind wrested strands of hair free from her braid to lash her eyes as Arienh climbed the mount above the stone circle. She scowled out over the dark, sparkling Irish Sea, taking the wind full in her face, waiting for the worst of her rage to pass.

The rage was for the helplessness. If there was anything more frightening to her than being helpless, she couldn't imagine what it was. She feared it even more than the Vikings themselves. She had always thought she could depend upon herself, even when all else was lost. The entire village had learned to rely upon her that way. Always, from the day her father had died, they had depended upon her, and she was failing them.

Now he had taken her sheep, and that meant everything. The flock was the lifeblood of her people, their food, their clothing, their very survival. Perhaps it had been true from the moment the Vikings landed their great longships, but not until he had taken possession of their flock had the point been driven home to her that the Vikings now owned the valley and everything, everyone, in it. The Celts lived and breathed at the whim of these heathen giants.

Especially Ronan. For they all followed him.

What would happen to Birgit? To Liam? To Old Ferris? What would the Vikings do to them when they discovered Birgit couldn't see well enough to perform common, everyday chores? When they learned she memorized the patterns she wove and counted the rows in order to produce the cloth they considered so perfect?

Her rage slowly subsided, replaced by a great, empty aching, akin to an enormous loneliness. An ache for what was lost, a fear for what was still to disappear. She couldn't define it, for it seemed to be both everything and nothing, all at the same time.

It was a longing for past and future, and, yes, a yearning for a man who both beguiled and betrayed her. For some traitorous thing inside her kept letting him into her heart, no matter how hard she tried to slam the door.

Nay, she must not let him in. This last, this taking of her sheep, was just one more thing that showed his true character, no different than his thieving, marauding ancestors.

But she would not win this battle against these heathens by displaying her own temperament so openly. Arienh took a deep breath. It was not in her nature to quit.

Nay. The battle had just begun.

---

Egil reached the door of Birgit's cottage and remembered to knock. He hoped she noticed. But Birgit could see him through the open door and barked out resentful permission for him to enter. Her pale green eyes glowered as he entered and plopped his brace of mergansers down on the table.

"What do you want?" she demanded, never stopping her weaving.

"It is a gift. I have not come for anything."

"We do not want your gifts."

"Too bad. I will not take them back. You may waste them if you choose."

Egil met her glower without flinching. Liam, with his round blue eyes, hid behind his mother's skirts and peered out at him.

"Perhaps if Liam learns to hunt, he may provide you with birds, and you will have no need to accept any from me. Would you like to come hunting with me, Liam?"

"Nay." With a squeak like a hare running from the hawk, Liam ducked back behind Birgit, two fists tightly clutching the fabric of her kirtle.

Egil watched, confused. The boy seemed terrified of him, yet he had not been afraid before. Had he done something? "You don't want to go hunting? I thought all boys wanted to hunt."

"You aren't going to eat me!"

Egil stared in horror. "Eat you? Where did you get such an idea? Birgit, you did not tell him this."

"Nay. Liam, I told you not to believe that. Old Ferris is just trying to frighten you."

"Old Ferris? The old man?"

Birgit gasped and her pale eyes widened. Horror spread on her face. "I did not mean—he is just an old man—it is not his fault. It is a common belief. Old Ferris merely gave it voice, and Liam heard."

"Perhaps I should go talk to the old man."

"Nay, please, he is a harmless old man."

Did she think he meant to hurt the old man? "But it is a terrible thing to tell a child. Surely you do not believe such a thing."

"Who knows what atrocities Vikings will commit? Nay, I do not. But some do, and a child is easily frightened."

"Then I must teach him this is not so."

Her old rancor returned as she stepped deliberately between him and the boy. "It is my job. You are not his parent, and I do not want him around you. Perhaps you are not as evil as those who have been here before. But you are still Vikings."

"Northmen."

"It is all the same to us."

"But it is not the same, Birgit. And I will teach you that it is not."

"I care not for that. But he is my son, and I will raise him."

Nor would it help her cause as a parent to argue in front of the child, Egil knew. The boy needed a father, anyone could see that, but he was young yet, and needed his mother, too, and it was not good for someone such as he to question her decisions.

"As you wish," he said, and with a nod that was almost a bow, he went out the door.

If there was a way to her heart, though, it would be through the boy.

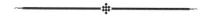

"Ducks?" asked Arienh. She wrinkled her nose at the acrid smell that feather plucking made.

Birgit looked up, smiling sheepishly. With a pail of still-steaming water before her, she sat in the sunshine plucking feathers from the mergansers. "You're home early. I didn't hear the sheep."

"That's because the Vikings took them away from me."

Birgit's eyes widened as her mouth dropped open.

"They say they mean to tend them for us," Arienh added.

"Do you believe them?"

"Does it make any difference? If I did, I still wouldn't have the sheep."

"Do you think it is punishment for our pranks?"

"We'll find out soon enough. I'm not through with them yet. Where did you get the ducks?"

"The Viking, Egil, brought them. It grows cool," she said of the water. "I will have to reheat it soon."

"I'll heat it, Mama."

Arienh frowned, glad in a way for the distraction of ordinary cares, but suspicious of Liam's intentions. The boy required a lot of watching and liked fire too much. Arienh recalled the time he had lit rags to watch them burn.

"Nay," said Birgit. "It will do for now. Put the feathers in the sack."

"Perhaps he could come along with me and watch," Arienh suggested. They had always tried to contain Liam's fascination this way. He was just too curious.

"Aye."

"I thought you weren't going to take presents from them."

"They would have gone to waste. I have had enough of hunger, Arienh. Liam, take a bucket to the creek and bring more water."

"But we have enough now, Mama."

"Do as I ask."

Liam pouted and picked up the bucket, with his lanky legs swinging and his arms feigning the heaviness of the bucket as he departed.

"What are you thinking?" Arienh asked as soon as the boy was out of earshot.

"I don't know. He wanted to take Liam hunting."

"The Viking? You didn't let him."

Birgit shook her head. "Liam is afraid of him. He remembers Old Ferris's words. I don't want that old devil to influence Liam."

"Better him than the Viking."

"I'm not so sure. I cannot see them from here, Arienh. But that is the big Viking who stands near the stream, I think."

"Aye. It is Egil."

"What is Liam doing?"

"He can't take his eyes off him. But he is trying not to get close to him."

"And what does the Viking do?"

"He is fishing, I think. He pretends not to see Liam."

"Because he knows Liam is afraid. It is the way a man coaxes a stray dog to him."

"I don't understand."

"He has a liking for Liam, Arienh. Do I have the right to keep Liam away from him?"

"Of course you do."

"But is it right? For Liam?"

"We cannot let these Vikings take over, Birgit. We will all suffer if we do."

Birgit was silent as she plucked feathers. Arienh knew she was remembering again. And she did not want Birgit to suffer anymore. But what if she would suffer more if they drove the Vikings away? And what would this Egil do if he learned Birgit could not see? Birgit was not useless as his kind might think, but she was helpless alone.

She could not tell if Egil was cruel or kind. Like Ronan, he had a way about him that made one want to trust him. But Ronan had turned on her and stolen her flock. And even if he meant well, he now controlled their food supply, their entire livelihood, and them.

Visions of an ominous future fluttered before her. She pictured Birgit shivering in the cold alone, slowly dying high up on some lonely, windswept mountain, where no one could rescue her. Or Liam walking off with the huge blond Egil, never coming back. Or of her village, fallen entirely under the control of heathens, and women bending to their pagan demands, little more than slaves.

Nay, she was not through with them yet.

Yet, could she be wrong about these men? If she could only find a way to ask without revealing her reason for concern. But any word at all could trigger their suspicions. She would not run that risk. They must be driven out before they learned the truth.

She looked back to the stream bank. Egil casually tossed in his fishing line and trolled through the water. Liam, his bucket forgotten at his side, hid behind the big oak tree, his eyes fixed in intense concentration on the giant Viking.

# CHAPTER NINE

---❖---

"Ronan, have you seen my ax?"

From where he sat planing an oak timber, Ronan turned to see Olav coming up behind him. "No, I did not have it."

"But you asked to borrow it."

"Aye, and I could not find it. But Bjorn has finished forging a new head for mine, so I do not need it anymore."

"You are sure? It was hanging on the peg on the shed post."

"But it was not there when I looked. Use mine. I am through with it."

Olav shrugged, his brow wrinkled tightly as he picked up Ronan's new ax, hefted it to test its balance, and joined the men who went to cut timbers for a new cottage.

Ronan frowned. Hoes were missing from the fields. Tongs had disappeared from the forge. And then the anvil. How in Hel's pit had those women managed to carry off Bjorn's largest anvil? Since Bjorn rarely left the forge except to eat and drink of an evening, they must have done it then. Or when the man was too deep in his cup to know anything was going on. That happened often enough.

What would the women think of next? And what was he going to do about it? He'd better think of something, because he'd seen the women quietly gathering in one of the cottages last night. And that meant more mischief coming.

Ronan returned to shaping the lintel, running his plane over its surface for the last smoothing finish. He straightened his back and stepped back to admire it. There was much old, rotten wood to be replaced here, enough to test his skills at carpentry for some time.

Close to dusk, Wynne's brass supper bell rang.

Long past the supper hour, Olav and his men had still not returned. Ronan finished off his mead and set the horn down on the slab table.

"So where are they?" he asked.

"Don't know," said Egil. "They went off to fell timbers in the far hills, and a few trees are down. We found their axes. But they seem to have wandered off. No signs of violence."

Another one of the women's pranks, or so he hoped.

"This could be serious, Ronan," said Egil.

"Could be. But I doubt it. Their tricks have been getting worse, it's true. But I don't think they'll do anything truly harmful, or Tanni would have been pushed into the pit, not tricked there. No real damage has been done. And they could have, if they'd wanted to."

Egil chuckled, and an amused twinkle shone in his eyes. "In an odd sort of way, there's a kind of trust in all this, Ronan. As if the women believe they'll be safe, no matter what they do."

Ronan raised his eyebrows. It was a thought worth considering. "Or maybe they mean for us to prove we can be trusted. Surely they would not pull such stunts if they expected to be slaughtered for them. I wonder if they recognize that."

"There's another possibility. They are Celts, after all."

"Hmm. You mean, they'll fight back, even without weapons, even if it means their death. Aye, I thought of that. But these pranks, they're a nuisance, but they're also funny, in a way."

Egil snickered. "Tanni didn't think so."

Ronan grinned. "Aye, but everyone else did. What about all of your hoes standing upright in the mud of the stream? Meant to make you feel foolish, I'll wager."

"True." Egil chuckled again. "Nothing broken or harmed."

The anvil had been found by an ash tree in the forest. The tongs were close by, half buried by leaves. Of Olav's ax, nothing more had been seen.

But now the men themselves had disappeared.

Misgivings were beginning to flourish.

Then the old wooden door to Ronan's cottage burst open. Olav straggled in, followed by his men, clothing snagged and bare skin scratched, their faces fixed with tight-set jaws and frowns.

"What happened to you?" Ronan asked.

"Got lost," grumbled Olav. He seized the horn of ale handed to him and downed it as if he had had none in a sennight.

"Lost?" Oh, this was ripe for merriment. The other men gathered around Ronan, their eyebrows rising with increasing interest. "But you were not so far away that you could get lost. Did you forget which way the sun sets?"

"We uh, decided to explore a bit."

"Ask them what they were exploring," Tanni suggested with a sly grin.

"Or maybe who," said Bjorn. "Which little witch has got your eye, Olav?"

Olav's face reddened, and he tried to object, over the roar of laughter. It would do him no good. Tanni's mishap had been easily unearthed by Olav, so he was not about to let Olav go unscathed.

"Told you," Bjorn said. "You don't take control, the women will run you."

"I suppose you'll do better."

"Aye. I'll have no women in my life. Nothing but trouble."

Bjorn emptied another horn of mead. His cheeks were flushing from indulgence. But there was none of the laughter of camaraderie in his voice, only an odd bitterness.

Ronan decided to probe. "Why did you come with us then, Bjorn?"

"Just wanted some peace. You said nothing about women, just a chance to make new lives. That's all I want, to work my forge and be left alone. You can keep the women, for all I care. Do what you want, but I won't let a woman make a fool of me."

Bjorn raised even more jeers than Olav had. Bjorn ignored them and ladled himself more mead.

"But he's right, Ronan," said Egil, settling down from a hearty laugh. "The imps. We've got to get a handle on this, or they'll just get worse."

"Aye, I know. They're as mischievous as Loki himself, as if Loki gave birth to the whole lot of them. But they're not like Hel. This time Loki made his daughters beautiful instead of ugly, to add to the torment. We'll have to outwit them."

"How?"

Ronan almost laughed aloud as inspiration struck. "Gather all the sacks you can find, big, sturdy ones. And cord."

"Why? What do you have in mind?"

"You'll see."

After the last torch was damped, Ronan's men hid in their cottages. When darkness was almost total, they gathered their materials and set the watch.

Ronan hardly slept for the waiting. Long after he'd taken his turn at the watch, then crawled into bed fully dressed, he was still awake when Olav tapped his shoulder. He sprung to his feet. With the waxing moon hidden behind the clouds, the Northmen filed out of the cottage and lurked at its corners.

Ronan spotted his own special quarry among the shadowy figures prowling cautiously up to the cottages, at the head of the furtive gang. Whatever her scheme, this time he had her.

At his signal, the men dashed forth, whooping great war cries like berserkers, and leaped upon the creeping women. Loud shrieks and squeals erupted as men stuffed flailing women into heavy woven bags and tied the bags shut.

Tightly securing his squirming victim in his sack, he hoisted her over his shoulder and strode up the slope. Fists pounded through the cloth on his back, accompanied by shrieks as Ronan swatted her rump.

"Ouch! Don't you dare! Put me down!"

*All in good time, my sweet.* As Egil caught up to him along the path, Ronan slowed and they walked silently apace to the door.

Egil banged his fist on the door. "Open the door, Liam."

"My mama said no," the boy called from inside.

Egil laughed. "Open it."

"I can't. Mama said!"

"Open the door, Liam," grumbled out Birgit's voice from inside Egil's sack.

"Come on, Liam, let me do it," said a young girl's voice.

Ronan roared out his laugh as the door gaped open, with Liam and an astonished young girl standing aside. Bursting in, he tossed the wriggling sack down onto Arienh's bed and gave a parting swat to her rear. Egil plopped Birgit down just as unceremoniously. Leaving both women still incarcerated in their sacks, the brothers headed for the door.

"Try to keep your mother out of trouble, Liam," Egil said.

"And your aunt," Ronan added. "Since you seem to be the only one with any sense around here."

Down the path, several other men joined them, laughing, clapping each other's shoulders.

"Ah, you were right, Ronan," said Tanni. "That was fun."

But it had been too easy. Ronan frowned. "Don't get cocky. We haven't won the war yet."

Wild shouts echoed up the valley. Ronan strained his eyes against the darkness. More women?

Clouds parted and the waxing moon shed its puny light on the longship as it slid from its berth into the stream.

"The *Black Swan!*"

Ronan broke into a run. Egil sped beside him.

Ahead of them, shouting men leapt into the stream, splashing after the ship as it caught the current and turned toward the estuary, gliding smoothly away.

His ship. All the years of effort. Perfectly fitted clinkered planks, the lovely, graceful swan's head bow he had painstakingly carved, all disappearing before his eyes.

*Not his ship!*

Ronan ran faster down the narrow trail than he'd ever run before, faster than either the *Black Swan* or the swimmers in the widening stream.

"Come on," he yelled to Egil, who sped along with him, racing apace with the boat and swimmers.

Bjorn cut in behind them. "Damn women!"

"The women?" Ronan asked between hurried breaths.

"Thor's beard, aye, it was the women. What do you think, Loki himself cut the damn thing loose?"

They had to make the estuary before the ship, or they'd never catch it. Dashing past the *Black Swan*, they rushed on. Bjorn turned and made for the riverbank.

"Not here," Ronan shouted. "Get ahead of it, and let it catch up with us."

"You mean swim after it?" Bjorn asked, slowing.

"Got a better idea? Come on."

"Can't swim," Bjorn said, slowing more.

"Hel's tits," sputtered Egil. "Go for a rowboat. You're no use here."

At the stream's mouth, where it joined the estuary, Ronan dove into the river, Egil after him. With choppy strokes, they cut through the rippling water. The ship drifted toward them.

"Go to larboard and catch her as she drifts past," he shouted to Egil. They split apart, one for each side, treading in the water, waiting for the ship to glide up to them.

Ronan felt the ship rocking as Egil grasped the larboard side, and he lunged and grabbed the starboard side to maintain the balance. He threw his body aboard, landing roughly on the planked deck. With a huge sigh of relief, he lay for a moment on his back, feeling the change of the water as the *Black Swan* caught the river's current in the estuary and slowly pivoted toward the sea.

"A small problem," said Egil, who sat up on the deck, still breathing hard.

"What? All we've got to do is row back."

"No oars."

Perhaps he should resign himself to his fate. The gods had joined forces with a small band of Celtic women and were determined to thwart his dreams.

Nay. Not as long as he drew breath would he let a bunch of women defeat him. He leaped to his feet.

"The deck. Rip a plank off the deck."

"Aye." Egil leapt to the task as the graceful ship glided in the current. Iron nails and wooden pegs squealed like mice as the brothers pried and ripped up two long boards.

Ronan grabbed one and dashed to larboard, while Egil took starboard. They dipped their planks into the water, paddling the way an Irish Celt paddled a round coracle. The *Black Swan* slowed in her wayward journey toward the sea, but they made almost no progress against the current. And if both of them had to paddle against the current, who would steer? Despite its keel, the *Black Swan* was unbelievably awkward when used as a giant canoe.

"Try to head for shore. Any shore."

"Good idea. If we can move at all." Egil cocked his head toward the stream mouth. "Look. Help's coming."

Ahead of them, two small boats entered the estuary from the stream, Bjorn and Olav, and other men, rowing hard. The small boats bristled like hedgehogs.

The oars.

The little vessels pulled alongside. Men jumped aboard. Egil sighed as hard as Ronan.

"Thought you could use these," Olav said as blandly as if he were loaning a knife, and passed the oars aboard. "At least the imps didn't get a chance to hide them, too."

Ronan glared. There wasn't a lot left of his sense of humor. He barely spoke as he directed the replacement of the oars and joined the men in rowing back upstream to the *Black Swan's* berth.

"Loki's daughters," he grumbled. Ronan jumped down into the water and used the last of his strength to help shoulder the longship onto the bank. It could not have been an easy task for a few women to have shoved her out into the flowing water. Particularly when most of them were being carted back to their homes in sacks. They had to have planned it carefully, and worse, figured out what the men were going to do.

"What's that?" Egil asked, looking about as exhausted as Ronan felt.

"Loki's birthed a whole tribe of women, solely for the purpose of driving us crazy."

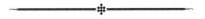

The women gathered around Arienh's cottage hearth gabbed excitedly as she stirred the coals and added an extra faggot to ward off the early evening chill. She joined their laughter. But it worried her. They were having entirely too much fun.

"It was funny," Mildread said. "I wish you could have seen it."

"Took too long to get out of the sack," Arienh replied. For some reason, everyone thought that was funny.

Selma sighed, perhaps wistful, perhaps satisfied. "But how did you know they'd come looking for us? How could they have known we'd be there?"

"They probably didn't," said Arienh. "But we became very predictable. We've done something every night, after all. Wouldn't you think they'd figure that out?"

Birgit sniffed. "First time I go with you, and look what happens. Why do you have all the fun?"

Arienh laughed. "I thought you did rather well," she said. "Of course, I didn't think they would sack us."

"As long as I had your skirt to hang on to, I did all right. But then, when that sack came down over my head, I thought I'd lost my sight entirely."

Selma joined Elli in a fit of giggles.

"Never mind, Birgit," replied Elli, when she finished laughing. "I'm sure we can find something more to amuse you."

Birgit's eyes sparkled with pale green devilment. "Actually, I did overhear something yesterday."

All heads turned in Birgit's direction, surprised. Mischief was not a usual part of Birgit's solemn disposition.

"They're looking for a place to bathe. Where the water is clear. Away from us."

"Oh?" sang the chorus.

"The Bride's Well," Birgit announced triumphantly.

"Good choice," Arienh agreed. "Meets all their requirements. Of course, the water's cold, coming off the falls, but they probably don't care."

"They're Northmen," Elli said with scorn. "They're used to the cold. Imagine how much could disappear while they're gone."

Birgit shook her head. "Nay, they'd be onto that. They'll have a guard. The picking would be better right under their noses."

"Hmm." Mildread stood, rubbing her hands together. "I wonder if it's true, what they say about the Northmen's organs."

"I'll wager they're no bigger than any other man's," Elli said.

Arienh didn't like the way the conversation was shifting. She'd have to proceed cautiously if she didn't want to lose control.

"Oh, I don't know, Mildread," Elli countered. "From what I've seen so far, they're of a fair size."

Mildread laughed. "And I think their breeches are stuffed."

Arienh knew better. She'd already had a good look. But this was taking a dangerous turn. And it wasn't a good time to try to issue orders. Every day, it seemed, the women listened to her less. She tried a less direct approach. "That's not what you said before."

Mildread sneered. "A week's washing says they're stuffed."

"Can it really be worth that much to you?" Arienh asked.

Birgit's green eyes took on an evil gleam. Her smile had faded away. "Can it matter? They say cold shrinks things. And they'll be cold enough when we're finished with them."

Selma stood, clasping hands together and grinning. "It would be worth that much just to watch them walking back without their clothes."

Arienh was aghast. "You cannot mean it."

"Done, then," said Mildread, matching Selma for wicked glee.

"And this time," said Birgit with a cunning smile, "you will watch the children, Mildread. I am going."

"You think so? I wouldn't miss this for a year's baked bread."

Arienh folded her arms. "Have none of you any sense? These are Vikings we're dealing with."

As if she had said nothing, Mildread turned back to Elli, Selma, and Birgit. "All right then, when we take their clothes, what'll we do with them?"

"Hang them up," said Birgit with a very sweet smile.

Arienh groaned. Even Birgit? What was the matter with them?

One by one, the women left the cottage, each peering around the doorframe to check for Vikings. Arienh huffed to herself. If the men hadn't suspected their adversaries were up to something before, they certainly would know now. They were blockheads, all of them. But she might as well join them. How else could she avert disaster?

The bleating of the lambs drew Arienh to the door. Stepping out into the twilight, she saw the mixed flock of Celtic sheep and the ones the Vikings called black-faces coming down from the upper valley.

Furtively, she scanned about, seeking out the Viking who was her bane. She found him quickly, near the ash grove, bare-backed even in the chilly air, with a sheen of sweat over lightly golden skin. He gave one more healthy swing of his adze at the beam he was shaping, and straightened, looking straight at her as if he had known she was watching him. She snapped her head around to concentrate on the incoming flock, but she knew he wasn't fooled.

She watched in fascination as the little black-and-white dogs culled out the white-faced Celtic sheep from the flock and, following the sharp whistles of their herder, sent the ewes and their lambs scurrying for her paddock.

Without a word, she threw a glare at the shepherd, whose name was Tanni. Well, at least they had returned the sheep as he had said. But that didn't mean much. She closed the gate and began examining hooves and checking lambs for cuts and wounds.

Arienh didn't like Birgit's plot. In fact, she didn't like the way anything was going. The women were having entirely too much fun, and that was not the aim, not at all.

She herself had stolen the hoes from the shed and hidden them in the forest, only to find them standing heads up in the stream the next day. And every time she looked at Selma, the girl quickly looked away.

She had the sinking feeling she was losing control.

It would be funny, she had to admit, to see those grown men having to run about without their clothes. She had thought it a much better idea to get rid of the clothes entirely, or at least dump them into the pit where they had hidden the food they had stolen, but everyone else liked Birgit's plan better.

The truth was, she was as cowardly as the rest of them, unwilling to provoke the Vikings' outrage completely. But if they did nothing, they would be stuck with these men forever. And that one in particular, who had vowed to make her his wife.

"I told you the sheep would come back," he said.

The very air sizzled with his words, like the wild sea spray from heavy waves against the sea cliffs.

She made no answer. She hated him. Hated the way he commanded her attention. It was as if she couldn't help searching him out, the moment she stepped outside her cottage. And he always seemed to be there. Even now, she could not stop her eyes from seeking him.

Of its own volition, her gaze skimmed over him in a way that brought heat to her face, studying the sheen of perspiration that collected in rivulets and gathered the sprinkling of dark hairs into a waving trek down the center of his chest. She knew where the trail led as it narrowed to a line that broke, then picked up again, to gather around the organ of which he was clearly so proud. It seemed to be in its usual state, she noticed. Some unruly thought in her kept wishing she had touched it when she had had the chance, just to see if it felt anything like what it looked. She gritted her teeth, willing the errant thought away, the way she chased away all thoughts of wanting to touch him. Then her gaze flitted to the scar, ugly and still dark. The stitches were gone. She winced, recalling his pain.

Nay, she should not care.

"It does not hurt," he replied as if she had spoken her guilt aloud, and a wide grin crossed his face.

"You seem almost to have forgotten it," she grumbled back.

He laughed. "It is not something I will ever forget," he said. "They will not let me."

"They will not?"

"Nay. Nor will they let Olav forget that he lost his way in the woods, trying to catch up to a laughing Celtic imp."

"They laugh at you?"

"Of course. I was stunned by a pair of beautiful green eyes and let down my guard. They think it's funny."

A Viking would let others laugh at him? She could not imagine it. Yet the first time she had seen him, she had noticed the laughing lines around his eyes. Even then he had tried to tease her into laughing with him.

She recalled what she had thought then, not of making jokes with him, but the tugging of regret at her heart that wished somehow this impossible man might live.

"They seem to have fared well enough," he said, examining one of the lambs, then setting it down.

Again, she did not reply. Even though the lambs were fattening already from their first tastes of pasture.

"As you see, the dogs have no trouble telling your sheep from ours."

"You merely tease us with your empty promises," she retorted. "Why don't you just get it over with, Viking?"

His dark eyebrows flitted up and down in speculation. "Would you like that, Arienh? It would be easy enough. But nay, I think we will take our time. When you are through with your pranks, perhaps."

Pranks, he called them. He did not even take their efforts seriously. "I want nothing from you, save that you go away and quit taking what is ours away from us."

"Ah. But let me see. I give you back your sheep every night. And you may have the plow back now, for Egil has finished plowing the fields for you."

"You bring back the sheep now. But what about later?"

"We'll shear them and give you the wool."

Arienh snorted. "For nothing?"

"For your love, Arienh." Laughter crinkled around his eyes in just the way that irritated her most.

"Aaah!" She threw up her hands and whirled away from him. The man was insufferable. "You think us fools, as well. Do you think we do not know treacherous heathens when we see them?"

He laughed. "We know what you think you see. We are only farmers. But we do not expect you to understand that yet."

"Hah. Egil said you are a trader, not a farmer." Arienh passed through the paddock gate and closed it, lifting the ragged leather loop over the post. The frayed leather broke in her hands. Frustrated, she whipped off the cord about her waist and tied the gate closed.

"I was, once. I built my ship and sailed her both north and south for years. That is the wealth I bring now, to settle."

"What did you trade in? The slaves you captured?"

"Nay, I have never trafficked in slaves. The far north has an abundance of furs and goods, and the south has many things the north hungers for."

"But slaves are more profitable," she guessed. Against her best efforts, she slowly turned back to face him, seeking out his wonderful blue eyes in spite of herself.

"Aye."

"Then why should I believe you?"

"Well, I cannot make you believe me. But it is still true."

Some strange part of her wanted to believe him. Yet would he admit otherwise? She knew better. It was for slaves that the Vikings raided this coast, since there was so little other wealth.

He had been here before, and on that raid, two of her cousins had disappeared. Her brother, not long after.

But the questions burned holes in her soul. Could it hurt, if she asked? She drew a dark, dangerous breath, wanting to know, afraid of the answer. But she had to know, that very thing she had shoved so deeply inside her she had almost forgotten. "What happens to them?"

"To slaves?"

"Aye, to slaves," she said impatiently. "What happens to them?"

"Some are taken north to Hedeby. The Danes mostly do that, but the Northmen, too. Some go south to the Moors. Pretty young women especially bring a better price with the Moors."

"But what happens to them?"

He paused, reluctant. Sad eyes searched hers. "It is not a good life."

"I never thought it was. But could a person return?"

"Probably not."

She set her jaw bitterly, glaring at him. Well, what had she expected anyway? That they were wined and dined by princes? "So they are as lost to us as if they had been murdered."

"It is likely. Who have you lost, Arienh?"

"Everyone."

"Who?"

"There are many—my brother." So Niall would never be back. Angry tears stung at her eyes, but she fought them.

"I wish I could bring him back to you. But I would not even know where to look."

"You know too much about slaves, Viking. I do not believe anything you say." Arienh hurried inside her cottage and shut the door. Deny it he might, but he was part of it. And it was unforgivable.

In the morning, Birgit answered the rap on the door to find Egil holding a fishing pole. She stepped outside to keep him from entering. Liam slowly emerged from behind his mother's kirtle, with his eyes trained on the coveted object.

"You may have it," Egil said as he held out the pole. "But there are rules about catching fish that must be followed. You must agree to them."

Liam warily nodded and reached out for the pole.

Birgit clenched her jaw but did not intervene with the transaction. "Set it in the corner and go to the stream for water, Liam."

"Water? But we have plenty."

"I said go."

"Aw. Why do I always have to go for water?"

The blond giant raised thick eyebrows into high pointed arches. "Boys who don't do what their mothers ask don't get fishing poles."

Without another word, Liam fetched the pail and scurried for the stream. As the boy ran down the hill, Birgit turned her icy glare on the Viking.

"I told you I did not want you around him."

Egil let a silly smile creep onto his face. "I only gave him a fishing pole."

"You know better. He is only a little boy and easy to beguile with gifts. I will not have my son grow up to be a Viking."

"Northman."

"Viking."

"He knows what he is, Birgit. If he thinks badly of us, he thinks badly of himself. Can you not see it?"

"I can see it. I cannot change it."

His blue eyes turned stormy grey beneath frowning yellow brows. "He is our kind. If you hate us so much, do you hate him too?"

"Of course not. He is my son."

"He has to feel your hatred, Birgit. Let me take the boy with me. I will raise him to be a man."

"Never."

"He needs a man, Birgit. You say you love him, but you cannot teach him what he needs to know to become a man. Here, he does not even have other boys for companions. What could be more cruel than to deny a boy the path to manhood?"

"I will do the best I can. But he will not become a Viking. Stay away from my son."

Birgit turned on her heel and stalked toward the stream after Liam.

Egil still stood with his brows wrapped in a frustrated frown as Ronan walked up the hill to his brother. "Did not go so well, then?"

"Nay. I am only trying to help. Can't she see that?"

"She is very angry. All of them are. I think there have been far more terrible things in their lives than we have ever considered. It is more than a matter of winning their trust. They are just so very angry."

"Aye. I cannot see how we will get around it."

"You aren't thinking of quitting, are you?"

"Nay. I decided I want her, and I'll have her."

Ronan clapped a hand to his brother's shoulder. "Well, you have always been a very patient man. Have patience a bit longer. Olav has gone upstream with the others to that pool he found. Let's join them."

The diversion pleased Egil. "Aye. It will feel good to get really clean. I am tired of muddy water."

The path wound along the small stream that cut through the village and between two low hills. Away from the village, the canyon narrowed, faced with tall, dark cliffs. Ronan and Egil followed the path as it grew narrow and steep until they reached a sheltered cove surrounded by cliffs and split by a small waterfall about the height of two men. On either side, nearly vertical cliffs towered even higher. In the rock-bottomed pool below it, several men swam and splashed in water that was pure and clear.

Ronan didn't relish the thought of the cold water, did not like the idea of being cold again at all. But baths were always hard to come by in the winter, and once in the water, it would not be so bad. He looked forward to the sleek feel of real soap on his bare skin, instead of sand. He had even brought a sharp knife and metal mirror to shave.

He stripped off his clothes, although not quite as eagerly as Egil, who quickly undid his braids and threw off his clothes before splashing into the pool. Ronan paused at the water's edge, then plunged in. Shock waves of icy cold rushed through him. Invigorated, he surfaced, slung his hair to shake the water away, and lunged into a swim across the pool to the waterfall where the others cavorted.

Ronan loved the first swim of the year as much as the first bath. This place would be a joy. Throwing himself into the frolic, splashing, jumping, diving, Ronan let the great pleasure flow through him, of being wet and cold below and warm with the bright sun above. Of being alive, free, with all his dreams at the tips of his fingers. This green valley with its verdant fields. The beautiful woman for whom he had yearned for so long.

Standing in the shallows, he dipped into the little vat of soft soap and worked a lather into his hair, then spread the soap over his skin, scooping up handfuls of sand to aid his scrubbing. Then he threw himself into the water, diving under, then breaking the surface with a rush like a seal.

Above him, Egil leapt from the high cliff, drawing into a ball, and smacked the water like a great rock. Instinctively, Ronan ducked just as the splash slapped him. He grabbed Egil by his long, yellow hair as he surfaced and shoved him back beneath the water. But Egil's great, hammy arm lashed about Ronan's neck and dragged him down under the water with his brother.

Shouting voices above them called out wagers on which brother would come out the winner of the impulse match. Egil had the edge this time, having launched the attack. Ronan knew his cause was lost as his feet slipped from under him, leaving him with nothing to grasp but his opponent. Under he went. Egil came out on top.

Ronan dove for Egil's legs, normally a fruitless ploy. But Egil stood on the same slippery rock where Ronan had been, his footing equally vulnerable. With a whoop, Egil slipped under, and Ronan stood victorious.

A great cheer rose from half the men. The other half who lost the wager would all be poorer by at least one silver coin.

"Enough for me," said Egil, slinging his dripping yellow hair out of his eyes.

A disgruntled Tanni showered Egil with a huge wave of water from his hand. Egil dove for Tanni and a second match was on. Tanni was smaller, but wiry and wily. Ronan chuckled quietly and crawled upon a level ledge to watch while he absorbed the warmth of the sun. He had not yet regained all his strength, but it was coming back. As sure as summer was coming, he could feel it.

He leaned back and allowed his gaze to roam across the water, taking in the beauty of the sparkling pool enclosed by forbidding dark cliffs. New green leaves dappled the shrubs where the men had draped their garments.

A small hand on a slender arm groped through the greenery, snagged a jerkin. The jerkin disappeared into the bush.

So had everything else.

"Hey," he shouted. "They're stealing our clothes!"

All heads came up. Men rose up, shedding water in rushes. Ronan dove into the pond, stroking furiously toward the far side. Others sloshed with wild strokes alongside him. When his feet struck bottom, he waded, forcing the bulk of his body through the water to the rocky shore with frustrating slowness.

"Thor's hammer. Gone. They got everything." Voices around him echoed his thoughts.

"Every damn boot and tunic."

"They can't have gotten far. Come on." Egil hobbled over the pebbly shore, and Ronan followed, quickly realizing how tender his feet had grown through an entire winter of wearing boots.

"Ow! Damn!" Tanni stumbled, lifted his foot, hopping.

"Ow!" Shouts, grumbles, oaths colored the air.

"Ouch! Hel's tits! Thorns!"

Stinging pain stabbed Ronan's foot. He bent to examine it. "Burrs!" He yanked the barb out of his skin.

Ahead of them, the trail was littered with burrs, scattered like grain sown in the fields. And there they stood, naked as the gods had made them, in the chilly, bright day, and nothing for it but to set out walking, very carefully.

The rocky trail soon smoothed into fine dirt, and the scattered burrs grew scarcer as they came closer to the village. The path widened as the valley spread out and trees thinned.

"Let's hurry," said Egil.

Ronan spread out his hands as sudden inspiration seized him. "Nay, let's not. Odd, that they should pick such a ploy. Maybe there's something they're curious about."

"What?"

"The obvious. Or at least, it's going to get obvious. Take a look." He pointed down the path. "They're hiding in the bushes to watch what happens."

Egil slowed, checking out the shrubbery ahead. "Aye, there's something they've come to see."

"Damn women," snorted Bjorn. "Got no respect, that's what."

"No fear, I'd say," Olav retorted. "We've been too easy on them. They need something to worry about. A good scare."

"Aye," Tanni agreed, suddenly hopping on one foot again, picking at his sole. "Let's shake them up a bit."

Aye, it was about time. Time they really got even. "Then let's show it to them. Think, men. Think about those tits."

"What do you want to do, Ronan?" asked Egil with a laugh. "Start an orgy?"

"Just show off. Use your imagination. Tell me you haven't thought about what's under those kirtles. Just think about it. Imagine yourself with one of them in your arms, what you'd be kissing. Show them what they're missing."

Hearty chortles spread through the group as they marched, Ronan at the lead. There wasn't a one of them that didn't have plenty to display.

# CHAPTER TEN

———————❖———————

"They're coming. Hide." Selma dashed up the path and ducked into the bushes at the edge of the ash grove, gasping for breath.

Arienh winced at a bad idea that was getting worse. The men had discovered the plot far too soon. They weren't ready, but she seemed to be the only one worried about it. Not even Birgit. But then, Birgit had always been ridiculously daring.

Raucous male shouts came from the forest path.

"Maybe we should go, Birgit," she urged, tugging on her sister's arm.

Birgit shrugged her off. "Not yet. I've got to see who wins."

"I'll concede. I'll do Mildread's laundry. I'll do it for a month. Come on, they'll see us here."

No one seemed to hear her. Birgit shook her head and peered through the bushes, squinting hard as if that somehow might improve her sight.

The very ground pulsed with heavy footfalls. Naked men tromped around the bend in the path, Ronan in the lead. Arienh gulped.

"Well, what do you think?" asked Birgit, straining her eyes.

"That they're all nude," Elli whispered, her eyes big as daisies.

"Well, I know that. How big are they?"

Selma craned her neck around Elli to see through the dense shrubbery. "Don't look so big to me. Maybe the cold does shrink them."

Elli shoved Selma aside so she could peek through the opening. "Well, they've got cold enough in that water to shrink them right off. How can they stand it?"

"It's probably nothing to them," said Mildread with a quiver in her voice. "Maybe Arienh is right."

Arienh tugged at Birgit again. "They're Northmen, remember." By Arienh's experience, it would make no difference at all. Ronan was no bean sprout, even in the freezing rain.

"I heard Vikings never bathed. That's what Father Hewil said." Elli scowled, yet couldn't take her eyes off the men.

Mildread grumbled something under her breath. "I'd say he was wrong," she said. "Maybe we should—"

"The question is, who wins the bet?" Selma asked, still peeking around Elli. "They look pretty large to me."

"Come to think of it—oh, dear." Mildread grabbed Elli's arm.

"Oh, dear, what?" asked Birgit. She stood up, trying to see.

"They're...erect."

"Erect?" Birgit strained to see.

"Aye. As in—erect," Arienh replied. "Get down, Birgit. They'll see us." She tugged her down by her arm. "I think Mildread and Elli will be doing lots of laundry."

"A month's worth," agreed Selma, her eyes wide with fright. "Let's get out of here."

Mildread bolted.

With a bevy of squeals, Selma and Elli spun around and scurried down the path.

The strutting men broke into a trot.

Arienh's anxious gaze quickly scanned the lot of them. The closer they got, the bigger their organs became. Her eyes caught

Ronan's attention fixed directly on her. She gulped. "Come on, Birgit, let's go."

"Wait, Arienh. I want to see, too."

"You don't understand. They're—they're coming, Birgit. And they're not just nude, they're—erect. And really big. Can't you see it?"

"Of course not. Are you sure?"

"Birgit!" Arienh tugged at Birgit's arm, but Birgit just stood there.

The pack of naked men marched closer, coming within Birgit's range of sight. Birgit's pale green eyes rounded as her jaw dropped open. She froze where she stood.

A battle cry roared out, like berserkers on the attack, as the Vikings dashed forward. Arienh's courage failed. She dropped her sister's arm and fled. She screamed as Ronan's huge arm snagged her waist and swung her up into his arms, then over his shoulder. Her fists pummeled futilely against his back.

"Run, Birgit!" she screamed.

Birgit spun around to escape. Her foot caught a rock in the uneven trail, and she fell, arms flying. Egil leapt and caught her, taking both of them rolling onto the dirt path.

"Let me go!" Arienh screamed, suddenly more fearful for the sister she had deserted than herself. "Let me go! She's hurt!"

Ronan laughed as he knelt beneath the trees, among a sprinkle of old leaves and new violets. He swung her to the ground, pinning her with his massive thighs. "Nay, she's not. Egil has her."

"Has her?" Arienh pushed against his chest as he leaned over her. "He's on top of her. Let me go."

Ronan glanced back. "Looks now more like she's on top of him."

Egil's great rumble of laughter burst forth. His voice boomed. "Not the usual way for a tumble, girl."

"Stop him! He's—he's—"

"Naked?" Still Ronan grinned as he imprisoned her among the violets with their conspiratorially heady aroma. "As he has no clothes to put on, you should not be surprised."

"But he'll hurt her. He'll—"

"Easy, love. Egil will not hurt her. I have no clothes either. Don't you worry about that?" Ronan leaned his magnificent body over her, his eyes grew dusky, his voice gravelly. "Did you get to see what you wanted, sweet? Is it enough to satisfy you, do you think? I'll show you more if you like."

As if there were anything she hadn't seen.

With her face captured between his hands, Ronan teased at her lips with his tongue, and nipped with his teeth. "Like that, love? I think you do. You're touching me, Arienh. I like it when you touch me. It feels like a caress. Is it a caress, love?"

She jerked her hand away from the enticing ridge of his spine just at the very moment she realized she had been fingering it. The hand floated downward past the blocky bone of his hip and the hard curve of buttocks.

"Even better," he said, sounding like he had gravel in his throat. "I think you like to touch me, don't you?"

Arienh flung her hands into the air and balled her fists, determined not to let her fingers touch his flesh again. "You are so arrogant," she said with a snarl. "Let me go."

"Let you go? A prank for a prank, my darling."

"But—"

His voice became a husky purr. "Don't you think a man can contain himself when he should?"

"It isn't very funny." She lay still, her fists balled, unable to move without touching him again. And she would not.

"Neither are burrs in the foot, if it's your foot. But 'tis a dangerous game you're playing this time, girl. 'Tis a good thing it's with men who won't do you harm."

"Let me go."

"Soon. I'm not finished yet." Ronan drew her tightly against his body, molded to him from thigh to breast. His hard erection pressed against her thigh so that she could discern its entire length and shape. His lips descended to hers. Softly, gently, he ferreted out the urgent passion she had been burying, exposing it for what it was.

She should make him let her go. She should break this bond. But it was so sweet, tingly. The tip of his tongue caressed like a feather, as if it tickled her whole body, all the way down to her toes.

She moaned. Sweet saints, why had she done that?

That wasn't all she was doing. Her hands escaped her control again, eager to touch every part of him. She traced the elegantly masculine curves of his spine and back. Hungry, hungry for all of him.

A tremor shuddered through him, and his body flexed and tensed, grinding into hers while his knee forced her thighs apart. His eyes deepened, dark, like a storm over the sea. Anchoring her head between his hands, he drove a deep kiss into her, voracious, as if he meant to consume her. Deep in her core, something wild stirred and sprang to life. Something wild, meant to devour him in turn.

"Touch me again, love." His words were a ragged whisper.

What was he doing to her? He had the power to reach inside her and control her.

Then, his hands let go as he raised up and hovered above her, touching only where their lips joined. His tongue still probed. Excited tremors still rippled through her. He held her prisoner only with his kiss.

She could do it, break the kiss. Just stop. She could. Just stop. It was not so wonderful that she could not, just…quit…just…She could not let go.

His eyes squeezed closed as another shudder rippled through him. With a reluctant sigh, he sat away from her, drawing deep, ragged breaths.

Arienh sat up, staring, too stunned to move.

"It was meant to be a joke," he said between gulps of air. "I'm sorry."

Sorry? A joke? It was more like—she didn't know what it was like.

"Go on, leave," he said.

She wanted to flee. She wanted to stay.

"Go on," he yelled. "Get out of here."

She saw in his face that same look she had seen once before, of a love long lost, tangled with something darker, more frightening. Lust. Arienh scrambled to her feet and ran, shaking away her fuzzy thoughts.

She ran to her sister, who sat on the ground beside the naked blond giant, leaning over him. Egil, sprawled on his back on the path with Birgit's flaming red curls spilling down over his chest, reached up to trace his broad fingers over Birgit's cheek.

"Birgit?" Arienh called. Her voice seemed like a distant echo in a canyon, lost in the raging blood that still pounded in her ears.

"Aye" came the quiet response, another echoing sound.

"Are you all right?"

"Aye, 'twas only a little fall."

"Let's go home."

"Not so fast, my pretty girl," said Egil as he grasped Birgit's arm. "I won't let you go until you tell me where our clothes are."

Once more, mischief decorated Birgit's face as she pointed upward at the huge oak that grew near the stream. Garments of all sorts, from tunics to boots, stretched and sagged all about its upper branches.

Egil gave a great hoot of laughter. "I begin to appreciate your wicked mind, girl."

Had Birgit already admitted her part in the plot to the Viking?

For a moment after he released his prize, Birgit merely sat, staring senselessly at him. Then, freed of the spell, she jumped up, away from him, and scurried off with Arienh down the dirt path till they reached their cottage. Safely there, Arienh looked back. Nude men climbed the oak tree, scrambling along its branches for their garments. Chagrined women wandered toward their cottages.

Everything was unraveling.

Ronan watched her skitter away. Sitting in the soft bed of old leaves, he dragged great gulps of air into his lungs to clear his head of the cloud of passion. He could have done it, so easily.

Could have? Nay, he almost could not stop it. She had inflamed him so suddenly that he had nearly let passion take control. But even though she had responded to him, she hadn't really understood. It still would have been wrong.

He had never been out of control before. He shuddered at the force of that primal drive that had so nearly overtaken him. Perhaps he was, after all, that very dangerous predator she so feared. He'd never had any sympathy with men who took women against their will, yet now he had an inkling of the power that was involved.

And now she knew, too. He wouldn't be surprised if she wouldn't let him near her again.

Ronan stood, feeling a sudden, almost painful stiffness in his body from neck to toes, but the heat of his passion was slowly cooling. He walked out into the path, hearing the chuckling laughter of victorious men. He hoped none of them laughed because they had carried it too far. None of them seemed quite as shaken as he felt, and he hoped that wasn't why.

They laughed and slapped each other on the back, while women hurried away toward their cottages. Already, Tanni and Olav had climbed up into the big oak tree and unsnagged breeches and jerkins. Boots and belts tumbled all the way to the ground, but lighter smocks merely caught again on lower branches.

"You didn't—" Egil asked him tentatively.

"Of course not," he snapped back. "I hope no one else did."

"I doubt it. But you were the only one who headed for the bushes. I don't think I'd have enough control to do that."

"That'll teach them," said Bjorn. It was the first time Ronan had seen that man grin.

Ronan didn't share Bjorn's mirth at all. But he promised himself he would bridle his passion carefully. However much he might desire her, his first duty was to protect her, even if that meant protecting her from himself. He would never force her against her will, or even trick her.

But now she understood exactly what it was and where it all would lead. And whatever she gave willingly, he intended to take.

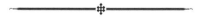

Arienh lay on her bed in the darkness, unable to sleep. Ronan's kisses still burned her flesh. An aching hung in her throat, and bottomless longing, deep inside her, that she recognized as the very root of passion.

She had seen couples making love before and had thought she understood it all quite well. But natural as it was, as interesting as it was, she had always wondered what was so compelling. Now she was beginning to understand. Now she realized she had ached with desire for him, from the first day he had come to her valley.

Once again, she flopped her restless body over on her side, and saw that Birgit sat at the edge of her own bed, staring at the banked hearth fire.

"Are you sure you're all right, Birgit?"

"Nay, I am all right."

"You don't look so."

"But I am. It is just—"

"Does Liam sleep?"

"Aye."

Arienh threw back her blankets and rose, crossing the hard-packed dirt floor to sit beside her sister.

"What is it?"

Birgit sighed. "I think they tell us the truth, Arienh, that they will not hurt us. They could have, any number of times, so far. They could just take us if they wanted, couldn't they?"

"Aye. Then what disturbs you?"

Birgit's eyes held a wistful longing. "He is amorous enough now. But when he learns the truth about me, he will change his mind. He will not want me."

"But isn't that what you want? Why not just tell him, then?"

"He wants Liam."

"Liam?"

"He said so. The men of his kind take the boys and raise them, even if they are not kin, so that they learn how to be men. I told him to stay away from Liam, but if he learns how helpless I am, he will take him from me. Arienh, he is right. I cannot give Liam what he needs. Without you, I could not do it at all. And he will know it."

Through all the terrible things that happened to her, Birgit had never cried. Now the tears flooded her eyes and poured down her cheeks.

Arienh held Birgit's head to her chest and stroked the red curls. "We won't let him, dear. He will not know."

Birgit was right. The Vikings would not harm them, not in the ways that others had harmed them. Despite that heady desire she had seen in Ronan's eyes, she had known he wouldn't harm her. Its intensity had frightened her, yet he had let her go when he saw her fear. She could only guess what it had cost him.

It was not at all what she had expected from a Viking.

She was caught in a terrible tangle, fearing, yet drawn to him, yearning, desiring, yet raging. Worse, the Vikings were going to win, and she was helpless to stop it.

Yet she could not give up. She remembered once again the boy who had come from nowhere and yanked her away from certain capture, perhaps death. The boy who had taught her by his deed never to give up. Ronan.

How often she had fantasized that he would grow up and come back, yet somehow in her dreams he was no longer a Viking. The man in her imagination had had light, straight hair, but still those wondrous blue eyes. He would not have been as big as these men, for the boy she remembered had been slight. But she had never been able to quite picture the face. Now, it was as if Ronan's face had been there all along.

It had been a false dream.

Aye, everything was definitely unraveling.

Arienh rose before dawn to move the stones and wait for spring's first day, setting out in the brittle, cold night before the first twilight streaks crossed the horizon.

It was the day when the sun would rise over the pointer stone, to mark the day midway between midwinter and midsummer, the day when day and night were equal. Those markers of the seasons were like affirmations to her that life could go on, even when things seemed darkest, when her people seemed destined for extinction.

Today, the marker of the first of spring, represented the waxing of new life, of hope. She had to be there.

A nearly full moon, close to setting, traced a silver path leading up the valley. Arienh followed the path to the little plateau where the ring of stones had awaited daybreak since long before any living man remembered. Nothing had ever been written down of those distant folk who had left the stones on the plateau overlooking the sea. They were not even Celts, her great-grandfather had said, but she felt the kinship with them all the same. They were her people, who had longed then as she did now to understand and predict the world in which they lived.

Climbing up onto the plateau, she recalled the last time she had been here, the day Ronan had taken her sheep from her. As he had taken everything else.

He waited for her. She was not surprised, although she had hoped he might forget to come. Ronan rose from the pallet of furs and blankets spread within the circle on the damp new grass. A corona of fading moonlight outlined his magnificent form against the black night sky.

Arienh forced herself to look away, wishing she could avoid acknowledging his presence. She drew her woolen cloak closer about her neck to ward off the chill and stood directly across from the pointer stone. Every year since she had become the counter of days, she had come and stood in this spot. Yet now it was so different, for the Viking came to stand beside her, silently placing his blanket around her shoulders. She was cold enough that she did not resist his invasion of her sacred place. He could not belong here, yet somehow, he did.

Heart pounding, she waited, the Viking beside her, as the first grey streaks appeared in the east. A dim line grew below the clouds, growing, paling, charging the air with the sort of energy it held before a storm. The deep midnight gloom faded to eerie, expectant twilight as long ribbons of red fused into the darker purple.

Yellow light breached the horizon.

"There," she said, her voice barely a whisper that shattered the silence.

His hand gripped her shoulder as if he, too, felt the magnificence of the moment. The glowing golden line brightened to a bulge of light and merged into a globe as it rose over the pointer stone and broke free of the earth to join the sky. A new dawn, new life, as surely as the birth of a child.

His arm came around her waist beneath the blanket, drawing her against his side. Her own arm found its way about him, taking in his pure, solid strength, a strength they shared beneath the heavy blanket as dawn took on life, light, sound.

Somewhere, far down the valley, a young lamb bleated and its mother bawled back. The chitter of a tit, and honks from the faraway estuary as ducks and geese awakened. Slowly, the grey of twilight brightened into a brilliant, pale morning. His eyes were brighter blue than the sky, deeper than the vast majesty of the passing night. The tip of his smallest finger caressed over her lips and back, pleading.

Perhaps she had come here to see him, rather than to move the stones and wait for the arrival of spring. Perhaps...

She didn't know. She knew only the warmth of his body as he held her, the tender ecstasy of their lips where they joined. Knew only the wanting, desiring, aching need that kept her in his arms. She had not slept the night for thinking of him, remembering his brazen, blazing touch, wanting, needing it again.

It was a need he had awakened in her from the night of their first meeting, one that had grown and stretched its bounds to the point of bursting. A need born of knowing, seeing, learning.

A touch caused it to grow; a kiss, to expand dangerously. Every thought that slipped past the barriers she had erected pushed her closer to the brink of explosion.

Enveloping them in the blanket against the biting cold, he took them to their knees, and with a hand to her back, eased her gently onto his pallet of furs. Her cheeks burned with the rasp of his beard, and she rubbed against it, memorizing the feel.

"Arienh, my Arienh. I've yearned for you so long." The words snuggled against her ear. His hot kisses trailed with his raspy words down her neck, nestling near the hand that cradled one breast. Teeth and tongue teased at her nipple, sending fire surging through her. She abandoned thought, letting sensation overwhelm her.

The skirt of her kirtle rose with the other hand that skimmed and caressed the untried flesh of her inner thighs and, she gasped with the newness of it. At first tentatively, then with boldness, she foraged beneath his smock to find warm flesh taut over muscle and bone in the age-old pattern of all men, yet uniquely his. Ridge and valley, hard and firm, silken and smooth. A crinkle of curls ran in a narrow line down the center of his chest, tickling the tips of her fingers.

Before she understood the movement, he lifted her kirtle up, over her head, baring her beneath the blanket and momentarily letting in a shaft of icy air. Just as rapidly, he closed the blanket about their shoulders, again capturing her lips in his kisses. She shivered. With a knee between her legs, he slid atop her, his warmth like a second, welcome blanket.

She took his probing tongue into her mouth and felt him stiffen and bend into her with a heavy moan. Whispered nonsense words, begging words, sounds of pleasure and pain flowed from him. She wanted everything from him, wanted the heat of flesh against flesh, the wrap of his hand around her breast, the sucking of his mouth on her nipple, the feeling that stars grew bright within her.

He lowered his body in position between her thighs, swept her legs upward over his shoulders, then slid back up to kiss her lips quickly. Poised over her, his organ at the juncture of her thighs, he waited, as if to wait was agony, as if expecting her to suddenly jump up and flee. She could not find words nor desire to deny him.

Then she felt him enter her, and she stiffened, expecting some awful pain to engulf her. Instead, a sharp twinge, and the oddly pleasant sensation of being filled where she had not known emptiness existed. He lunged, suddenly fully within her, filling so that she could feel him all the way to his tip. She tightened her legs about him, wanting to make time stop and keep him there forever.

Passion looked like torment on his face. His love words came in wispy gasps. He began to withdraw. Perhaps it was pain she saw. Could it hurt him, if it felt so wonderful to her?

Then, as he began slowly stroking in, out, gradually deeper, harder, longer, faster, she began to understand the nature of his passion as it became like her own, growing stronger, compelling. Something wonderful. And his hand found an unexpected center of pleasure that rippled through her again and again, doubled to passion, to something beyond words.

She breathed his name, a sweet sound, melding with the flow of passion within her until she thought she couldn't breathe. And still it built, this nameless everything, with the stroke of his hand, the stroke of his body, ever deeper, stronger, harder, faster, and she could bear it no more.

Wave after wave of light and pleasure rippled through her, the sensation that seemed to lift them to the heavens together. He stiffened, cried out, and plunged deeply inside her, his strong body coursing with a rigid force that dissolved into trembling.

They floated together, like a feather caught in a light breeze. They were the universe, the stars, all of life from the beginning of time. Arienh closed her eyes, floated, letting the being of it fill her. The tickle of his breath against her cheek, the silken rasp of his finger pads cuddling the blanket snugly against her neck.

Sliding aside, his arms remaining about her, he whispered in her ear. "Told you."

She opened her eyes. Sharp, cold air stung one cheek while the warmth of his breath caressed the other. "What?"

"Told you. You're mine, love. It's done."

"Done?"

A contented smile draped across his face. Almost as if it took great effort, he raised his head to capture a nipping kiss from her lips. "I'll build you your own house. We're much too noisy, you and I, to share with anyone else. Wood, though. Stone would take too long."

The cold air slapped her. "House? To live in? With you?"

"It is usually done that way." He gazed triumphantly at her, and he nipped her nose again. "I will always give you the best that I can."

With the suddenness of a plunge into icy water, reality returned. Flinging his arm away, she jerked to sitting. Blankets shed off her like water, leaving nothing between her bare skin and the dawn's early light.

Blessed saints, what had she done? She had lost her head, her body, her senses. Everything recklessly abandoned. Against all common sense and decency, against the safety of herself, her people, and most of all her sister, she had given herself to the Viking.

"But I can't live with you."

Ronan sat up abruptly, his brows knitted with confusion. "How else do you propose to conduct a marriage?"

"Marriage?" She scrambled to her feet. "You're a heathen, a Viking, a—a—I can't marry you!"

"You just did."

"I did nothing of the kind. This is not marriage."

He looked at her as if she had just slapped his face. Arienh snatched her discarded kirtle and tangled herself as she tried to pull it over her head.

"Nay!" she screeched as he reached to help. The armhole that had maliciously hid itself finally submitted. She wiggled the garment into place.

Already he was on his feet, his garments fastened. He stepped toward her. She retreated.

"Arienh, you know it is enough, among your people or mine."

"Yours, maybe, but I have given you no promises."

"I have given you mine."

"Nay, there must be vows," she lied. "They must be said before others. At the church steps."

"Nay, there is no need, but if that is what you want, I will do it."

"Then you do it alone. I do not consent."

She turned to flee, but he caught her arm. His mouth quirked bitterly. "Then what was this?"

Oh, what was it? She'd known perfectly well what she was doing. She just had not cared. She had wanted time to stand still and keep that moment forever. Something separate and apart from the life she must lead, which had no room for Viking lovers.

"Arienh?" Confused pain etched his face.

"Foolishness. That's all. Foolishness." She snatched up the cloak that had been discarded unnoticed in that time before, before everything inside her had been turned upside down. And she ran, throwing the cloak over her shoulders as she went.

And perhaps she was a little disappointed that he did not follow.

Oh, what had she done? She needed to think. Her head was too muddled to make any sense. He could force the issue. He had only to tell. Then Birgit would be stripped of the protection she needed, and she would be helpless and alone. Egil might think her pretty enough now, but no man wanted a wife who could not see. And if he took Liam? Birgit would die inside. How could she have been so careless with Birgit's life? Nay, she could not betray her sister this way. She had to do something.

But she had no idea what that was.

# CHAPTER ELEVEN

————— ✠ —————

ALL RIGHT, SO THEY DIDN'T EAT CHILDREN. OF COURSE, Arienh had never believed that one. It was too bad that Liam had.

And no matter how big their organs were, they weren't too big. She certainly was glad of that. Trouble was, she couldn't tell anybody.

As she fluttered about the small cottage doing useless tasks, Arienh was aware of Birgit's eyes following her almost in rhythm with the quiet swishing of her shuttle. She dared not even look up to meet Birgit's gaze. She needed to leave, yet Ronan could be out there, anywhere, and she couldn't face him.

What if he told? And why wouldn't he? Surely he did not really believe her lie about saying vows at the church door. And not even the Celts would support her if they knew, for marriages had been made in just this way for as long as there had been Celts. They would see her as the traitor who gave in to the Vikings. Once he had her, all the others would simply fall into place. And where would that leave Birgit?

It was hard to tell what to believe about these Vikings. They were not filthy, but in fact very clean. At least, these Vikings were. Perhaps some of the other rumors had begun with frightened villagers or passing tinkers with always a dramatic tale to tell. But which ones?

But one had come from Father Hewil himself, in a sermon about Christian duty. He had told a story about heathen Northmen who sent their invalids and elderly out into the freezing north storms to perish so that they didn't have to take care of them. She remembered it well.

On the other hand, there was Wynne's husband, Gunnar, father to Ronan and Egil, who was thin and bent and had an unhealthy pallor. Did it apply only to certain people, perhaps those who were poor or who had no relatives? Wynne seemed to feel Gunnar was exempt. Maybe they only did it to slaves. Or Celts, perhaps.

But she couldn't run a risk like that, not with Birgit's life. Poor Birgit had been through so much. Arienh must not fail Birgit again.

Really. And what had she just done?

Arienh dropped a wooden bowl on the table, and porridge slopped onto the earthen floor. Birgit winced.

Nay. She had to find out. It was the only way to protect Birgit. But how? If only there were someone to ask.

His mother, Wynne.

Aye, she was a Celt, and she knew the Northmen. She would be the perfect one to talk about how the Northmen were different from other folk.

But how to go about it without giving away the secret?

When Ronan stomped into the cottage and threw his pile of blankets down on the low platform bed, Egil's eyebrows rose to pointed arches. Ronan hurried out of the cottage without saying a word. Nobody knew him the way Egil did, and at the moment, that was not a good thing.

He snatched up his adze and hacked at the new beam he was making for one of the cottages. That should take him all day.

Good, hard work was what he needed now—sweat pouring over his body, draining every ounce of strength from him.

By Thor's beard, what was the matter with the girl? He hadn't done anything she hadn't welcomed and enjoyed. Why would she go that far if she didn't mean to marry him? That business about vows. That was nonsense. Wasn't it? Oh, he knew it was a common enough thing to say the words on the church steps, in front of the village. And the priest blessed the marriage bed, when there was a priest. But when there wasn't—ah, he knew better.

Ronan swung the adze with a fury, sending shavings flying. Maybe he'd better ask his mother. They might do things differently here.

"Enjoy the sunrise?"

Damn. Egil.

"You didn't go out there with all those blankets for nothing."

"It was fine." Ronan turned away, renewing his effort on the beam.

Egil let out a hearty laugh. "By Thor's hammer, you got some, didn't you?"

How did he do it? Sometimes he thought Egil could read his mind.

"You did, didn't you. Then why by Hel's frozen tits are you so mad?"

Ronan gritted his teeth and concentrated on his adze.

"Went sour, did it?"

"Damn, Egil, back off."

"Ah." The blue eyes twinkled halfway between merriment and concern. "Scared her off."

"How should I know what's in her head? Damn the stars, Egil, keep it quiet, will you?"

"If you want. Why? Most men would be bragging."

Ronan gave up and set the adze down, leaning against a tree. "I'm not most men. I don't know. I pushed too hard, I suppose. Everything seemed just fine until I mentioned marriage."

"Marriage to a Viking." Egil carefully examined a wood shaving he had wrapped around his finger. "Pretty hard for these Celts to swallow."

"I know, but then why would she…? She's skittish, like a pony in a lightning storm, running from something."

"Well, it's better than most of us are doing. Not a one of us doesn't get hard at night dreaming of tits, but that's all we've got. Dreams."

Ronan mopped the sweat from his brow. "Looks to me like I'm right back there with the rest of you."

"But if she'll do it once, she'll do it again. Plant a babe in her. That'll settle her down."

Ronan glared fire. "That sounds pretty strange, coming from you."

"Aye." Egil nodded. "It's not my way. And 'twould be the wrong thing entirely for my Birgit. But maybe it's the right thing for her. But keep your own advice, at least, Ronan. They don't know us. They only know the worst of our kind. That's a lot to overcome."

"I'm not as patient as you."

"Yes, you are. You've waited half your life for this girl. Don't ruin it now. Maybe you should talk to her."

"Tried it."

"Try again." With a sweep of his hand, Egil gestured down the valley toward the estuary. "She went out with Liam toward the beach about an hour ago. Several of the women are out there."

"Trust you to know. No, I don't want anyone else to know about this. Not till she's ready. I know that's part of what's upsetting her."

"Then be careful what you say. But if the others are around, she couldn't run away. She might have to listen."

Ronan shook his head and picked up his adze again. It looked pretty hopeless to him. "She just needs some time. I think I'll just finish this beam. We can replace the thatch on another cottage when it's done."

"Suit yourself," Egil said, clamping his hand on Ronan's shoulder. He started to walk away. "By Thor's beard, would you look at that?"

"What?" asked Ronan, his head already turning in the direction Egil was staring. But he saw it immediately.

"By the forge, with Bjorn. Who is that?"

"Elli, I think, by the long blonde braids."

"No women in his life, huh?"

"Maybe, maybe not. Her father was the blacksmith. Maybe she has some business there."

"You think? Let's go see."

Ronan was not really of a mood to do such a thing, but he was greatly in need of a distraction. The brothers sauntered down the path toward the old forge that Bjorn was renovating, keeping a careful eye on the man and the girl to whom he talked.

Their footfalls got Bjorn's attention. He glowered at the girl. "Go on, girl, go on. I've got work to do. Don't need a woman around to bother me."

The girl looked slapped. She turned swiftly and left. Why was Bjorn so brusque, if he had been so willing to talk with her before?

"No women, is it, Bjorn?" Egil asked.

Bjorn shot an evil glare at Egil. "Woman just hangs around," he said. "Said her father was the blacksmith."

"So he was," Ronan agreed. "Does she have a liking for the forge? Or do you have a hankering for her?"

"Don't want nothing to do with women," Bjorn insisted, bristling. "But she knows things. There's things here that are confusing, and she knows about them. Girl knows more than most folks."

"Oh? Like what?"

"Guess her father had some idea about getting iron so hot, it'd flow like water, and using molds, like a goldsmith does."

"Not possible, is it?"

With the return to a safer topic, tension eased in the blacksmith's face. "Not that I know of. But I've thought of it myself. Thing is, can't get a fire that hot. I've tried, but there's nothing hotter than a charcoal fire. Bellows make it as hot as it can get, but not hot enough. And molds, anything that hot would crack any mold. But he must've been trying. Found a bunch of them."

Ronan's eyebrows raised. "Interesting discussion for a girl."

Bjorn set his square body, feet spread, bulky arms folded. "Aye, but she's still a woman. Got no use for women."

---

The rains came again. Arienh was relieved, for it kept the Viking away. When the sun shone, she stayed away from him only by judiciously watching where he was and making sure she was somewhere else. Every day he helped Tanni bring in the sheep, and she left Liam to tell him she was off on other errands. Knowing he would then watch to see where she went before the sheep were brought in, she took off even earlier. For over a sennight, she had avoided him. But she could not keep it up forever. He was only humoring her, and she knew it.

At least there was never a loss of things to keep her busy. She needed more time, time to think. Especially since she couldn't find the courage for more tricks.

She took Liam to gather clams. The boy ran ahead, then dashed back, taking her hand and tugging, then he ran off again.

"Come on, Aunt," he said, pulling her along. "The tide'll be back up before we get there."

She laughed. Never could she look at the child without reveling in the incredible gift he was to them. "The tide's still going out, Liam."

"Well, you're so slow."

She quickened her pace along the narrow trail that wound between the curve of the hill and the estuary. Brilliant sunshine lit up pale sand and gleamed on Liam's brass-colored hair. The boy was beautiful, special. For all his horrible origins, she could not be anything but glad he had come into their lives. She wondered if they were right in shutting the huge blond Viking out of Liam's life.

Nay, they had to do it. Egil would want a healthy, whole wife. All men did. And the more time he spent with Liam, the greater would be the risk of discovery. He was a greater threat to Birgit than the man who had raped her and fathered her child.

A child. She hadn't thought of that either, when she had so easily given herself to the Viking. She hadn't thought of anything except her own desires. He hadn't just stirred her body. He stirred her soul. And addled her brain.

She had been so angry with him for moving in and taking over, and all the while denying he did what he did. So angry, she had been determined to resist him. And so sure that anger was all she needed to protect herself from him. Yet, all he'd had to do was touch her and her resistance had crumbled like fine-grained sand.

She should be angry with herself. He had only done what any man would do.

"Look, Aunt. See? It's low enough to dig already. Hurry!"

The boy was right. In her dallying, she was going to miss the best of the low tide. Out by the far sand spit, Selma with her two cousins, and Elli with their kirtles knotted up high, walked the edge of the surf, dodging the occasional high wave.

"All right," she said, handing Liam his little shovel and one of the knotted mesh bags she had made to hold shellfish. "But stay close to me."

"Aw." He shuffled in that ungainly way he had, meant to make his reluctance known. He would spend more time running in and out of the surf than digging, but she didn't mind. He would be eager enough when he found something.

Spotting the telltale clam squirt, Arienh dropped to her knees, rapidly shoveling sand with her trowel until the trowel struck the shell. She latched fingers around the shell before the creature had a chance to dig away and escape. She plopped the clam into her bag, then walked on along the strandline, glancing up now and then to be sure Liam hadn't gone far.

"Liam," she would call when he wandered.

"Aw." But he would hurry back.

When he lingered around a clutch of boulders that lay in the warm sunshine, she called out again. "Liam, come away. There could be adders."

"Aw. I don't see any."

"Just because you don't see them doesn't mean they aren't there. Come away."

Liam flailed his lanky arms in disgust as he stomped away and returned to the wetter part of the beach.

"You would not want to be hungry tonight because you did not dig, Liam."

Liam dug, but his heart was not in it. A world of fascinating things awaited him, and he did not often get so far away from his mother. But he was too curious and had no natural caution. This time of year, as the sun began to warm the rocks, the adders came out to sun themselves, and their mottled markings hid them well. Engrossed as he often became in minute things, Liam would not see a snake before it struck.

She bent to her knees again and again, digging, most of the time achieving her quarry. She soon became engrossed in her task.

A shadow fell across her.

Ronan, leading his favorite pied horse. Her heart beat faster. Nay, not here, not now.

"Go away," she said, trying not to look at him, but it was not possible. He was too compelling, too huge, and by far too handsome. Her eyes swept a path upward over hard-muscled thighs and flickered away at the bulge beneath his breeches. Was that all it took for him, just to be face-to-face with a woman? Truth to tell, she did not want him any less.

Bright sun glinted off the silver trimmings on his sword scabbard and illuminated golden strands in his richly dark hair. She recalled how that same scabbard strap had looped twice about her own waist, and the scabbard itself had nearly skimmed the ground.

"We need to talk," he replied. His eyes were dark with a hidden kind of hunger.

"I do not need to." She cast an anxious glance over her shoulder, hoping Liam was out of earshot. He had found a small tidal pool among the rocks.

"Aye, we do, Wife."

"I am not your wife."

"I say you are." His jaw set hard. "Arienh, what is wrong?"

She looked down, studying the debris of the strandline. "Nothing is wrong. I have nothing to say to you."

"If I have done something wrong, I would like to know."

"You know what you did."

"Aye." His brows rose high. His tongue licked across his lips. "And I know what you did, too."

"Hush. Someone will hear."

"That's a thought. Shall I tell them? I could force this if I wanted to, Arienh."

"It wouldn't surprise me. You do whatever you want, with no regard for others. We don't want you here, Viking. Can't you get that through your head?"

"We're not leaving."

"That is my point." Arienh spun away, striding across the wet sand toward the tidal pool where Liam dangled his fingers, but it did not discourage the Viking. Very little did. Leading his piebald horse by its reins, Ronan loped up beside her and took up her pace.

She could walk faster, of course, but so could he, so what would be the point in it?

"You cannot say you didn't enjoy it."

Her jaw tightened as she fixed her gaze on a scraggle of dead seaweed at the strandline.

"Can you, Wife?"

"I'm not your wife."

"Can you?"

"No, I cannot."

"Then what is wrong?"

She whirled on him, her fury blazing. "That is not marriage, Viking. Marriage is a lifetime of living. And I do not want to live it with a heathen Viking."

"Heathen, aye. Viking, nay."

"You say you are different, but you have come and taken from us, just like the others."

"We have taken nothing."

"Land. Sheep. Houses."

He was silent. The horse's hooves squished the wet sand as they walked. Then Ronan leaped in front of her, walking backward when she refused to slow her pace.

"Arienh, your people are dying out. No matter how hard you try, you cannot save them by yourself. Can you not see it, for their sake?"

Aye, she knew it. But how was she to choose? She could not sacrifice Birgit. Surely if she held out long enough, an answer would come to her, but now she could only defend her position. "That is like opening the door to the wolf."

As they reached the line of shingle above the sandy beach, a shout rang down from the high cliff above them, faint against the wind. Curious, they both strained their eyes against the glare of the sky to look up to the top of the cliff. Egil stood, shouting at Ronan, pointing out to sea.

Ronan turned, frowning as he scanned the wide horizon. She followed his line of sight, squinting out at the bright sea.

"Blood sails!" Ronan shouted. "Go, Arienh, run!"

A striped red sail crowned the horizon. A speck. A square, growing as she watched. The chill ran deep into her bones.

*Run! The children!*

"Elli! Selma! Vikings! Run!"

The gusting wind stifled her voice as surely as it brought the invaders toward shore.

"Liam, run!" she screamed.

But Liam only stood beside the tidal pool, his face a mask of blank fear. She screamed again at him and at Selma.

Suddenly hearing, Selma jumped up from her knees, grabbed her two cousins by the hand, and sped across the sand toward Elli, her mouth open in a yell they could not hear.

Ronan dashed to Liam and hauled him onto the piebald's back. "Liam, we need you. Ride for help. Find the first man you can and tell him the raiders are coming."

The boy came alive, eyes shining. "Aye."

Ronan slapped the horse's rump and sent it trotting back along the path. Arienh prayed Liam would not fall, but Liam leaned into the horse's dark mane, his bony knees gripping the horse's flanks.

Selma shoved one of the girls to Elli as the larger woman caught up to her. Hitting the dunes, they sloshed across the loose sand, headed for the far slope of the hill. They would be all right if they could make it inland to shelter. Too far for Ronan and Arienh.

Ronan grabbed Arienh's arm just as she turned to look back at the approaching ship.

She gasped. "Ronan, look. Blessed saints!"

Two little girls played alone in the surf near the mouth of the estuary, where the Viking ship would enter the river.

Mildread's girls!

Arienh slogged over the sandy dunes, fighting the loose sand with agonizing slowness, to the firmer, wet beach, screaming the alarm. Ronan dashed past her, yelling for her to follow her friends, but she sped on.

The longship drew closer, its striped sails billowing like storm clouds. With his heavy sword banging at his side, Ronan sped across the sand into the water, swung one child under each of his strong arms, turned, and raced for the beach. As Arienh rushed up, he passed the smaller girl to her.

"Run!" he yelled. They ran together along the narrow trail between the steep cliff and the river, slipping in the mud where the high tide brought the water onto the path.

Alien shouts rang out behind them. Long oars slapped the water.

"Take them both, Arienh. Run. Don't stop, don't look back!" He shoved the second girl toward her and pivoted around.

He meant to make a stand. Alone against a ship full of marauders, to protect her and the children. Arienh set the child to her feet with a quick swat to her rear.

"Run!" she shouted, as the sister caught up. "Don't wait for us."

Yanking out her knife, Arienh planted herself alongside him.

"Get out of here." Ronan shoved her behind him.

"Nay."

Too late for a contest of wills. The raiders sprang down from their shallow ship into muddy water at the river's bank. Ronan raised his big sword, ready for the onslaught.

The man at the lead stopped. His mouth widened into a malicious grin of recognition.

"Hrolgar," said Ronan, as if fate had just struck a crushing blow.

# CHAPTER TWELVE

———————— ⁂ ————————

"Aye," said the toothy marauder, glaring from malicious eyes as he waved his crew to a halt. "'Tis my little nephew, grown to be a brawny man," the man said, speaking in harshly accented Celtic words. "'Tis a man you are, isn't it?"

Arienh saw the resemblance in his eyes and strong jaw. The man was easily as broad as Ronan, but squat and potbellied, with short, beefy arms.

"Try me out, Hrolgar." Ronan raised his sword, poised for the first blow.

"Settling down, are you, boy? Gunnar make a farmer out of you? How long's it been since you swung that sword?"

"Too long. It's hungry for your blood." Without a backward glance, Ronan stepped in front of her to block the grizzled Viking. "Arienh, get out of here."

"Nay."

"Women fight your battles now, nephew? Maybe old Gunnar's too feeble to do it for you now."

"I fight my own, Hrolgar. And this place is mine. You'll harm no one." Ronan stepped forward, set his stance.

"Who's to stop me?" The marauder grinned, baring darkened teeth, and raised his sword. With a lunge, the blade crashed down toward Ronan's bare shield arm.

Ronan leaped away and swung. His blade slashed down as the raider's wooden shield rose to block it. Hrolgar roared, dodged and swung, his blow parried by Ronan's sword, and countered Ronan's reply with an upward swing. Hrolgar staggered back from the force. His foot slipped into the muddy riverbank.

Ronan slashed downward, his blade gouging into the upraised shield. Fiercely, he yanked it free.

The older Viking lunged at him and swiped at empty air as Ronan leaped aside, again set his stance.

He glanced over his shoulder at Arienh. "Get out of here!" he yelled.

Angry shouts poured from the band of raiders, but the older man bellowed back at them. Wiping at his mouth with the back of his hand, Hrolgar crouched, then with a raging yell, he hurled himself at Ronan, sword swinging wildly. Ronan leaped back and slashed, first down, then up. The upswing cut through flesh.

Startled, Hrolgar yelled and staggered back, clasping his shield arm. Blood poured like a torrent between his fingers. The wooden shield dropped to the mud, revealing a deep gash on the arm's underside. He glanced over his shoulder toward his long-ship as he backed up, slipped, and tumbled into the mud.

Angry curses, roars of rage came from the marauders behind as they hurtled toward Ronan and their leader.

"Run, Arienh!"

She could not leave him. Her heart thumped wildly.

Behind them roared thunderous hoofbeats, and the shrieks of berserkers turned loose. She leaped aside, only to be snatched about the waist and swooped onto one of the galloping horses.

"Nay!" She screamed. "See to Ronan!"

"Egil will see to him." It was the smaller one, the one called Tanni, who held her. He turned his horse.

"Do not leave him. There are too many of them. Let me down!"

Tanni's grasp around her waist tightened, threatening to cut off her breath as he reined in his horse.

Spotting the defenders, Hrolgar's men spun in their tracks and raced for the longship as Egil and his Vikings descended upon them.

With one foot, Ronan pinned Hrolgar's sword arm to the ground while he jerked the weapon from his hand. Enraged, the older Viking rolled and kicked Ronan in the gut.

Where the knife wound was.

Arienh screamed.

Ronan staggered back, barely holding onto both swords as Hrolgar scrambled to his feet and splashed into the water after his departing ship, just ahead of Egil's horse. The ship, sail furled, raiders rowing hard, slid into the estuary, Hrolgar dangling at its side, and his men hauled him aboard while ribbons of red blood ran down his body and brightened the dark water. Egil reined in where the water deepened and rode back to his brother. He jumped down from the horse's bare back.

Seeing the situation safe, Tanni released Arienh to slide down, and she ran back to where Ronan had fought.

"I'm all right," Ronan said to Egil, his chest heaving as he held his gut.

"You lie," Egil replied. "You take the horse." Egil lifted Hrolgar's sword from Ronan's hand.

"Nay." Ronan straightened, the movement almost taking away his breath. He sheathed his sword and whirled on Arienh. Bloody rage darkened his eyes. "Next time I tell you to run, you run."

The fury caught her off guard, and she staggered back before she recalled her intent not to be intimidated by the Vikings.

"I meant to help," she said, setting her jaw to bolster her determination as she squared her stance.

"Meant to help? I had to limit my stroke for fear of slicing you. Never stand so close to me in a fight."

"I didn't mean—"

Ronan expelled a disgusted breath and flexed his hands as if trying to make them relax. "Arienh, get it straight. Defy me in any other thing if you must, but in a battle, there must be only one leader. It will be me. You will do as I say."

"Nay, it is not only in a battle that you want to have your way. You do mean to rule the entire valley."

"Aye, I do." Power and fury jerked the muscles of his jaw. "We will not go away, Arienh, and you'd best get used to it."

"Nay."

"You will. I have had enough of your pranks and defiance. Tomorrow, Arienh. On the green. Bring your women. We are going to have this out."

Never had he frightened her so much as now. Arienh folded her arms to bolster her sagging composure. "We will not negotiate with you."

Ronan's eyes narrowed and he closed in, to stand so close she could feel his heated breath. He leaned over her and whispered, his voice like the rustle of dry autumn leaves in the breeze. "Aye, you will, Wife."

She had never realized a whisper could be so forceful. As he stomped away, struggling to disguise his pain, he abandoned her and Egil on the path.

"He will be all right," said Egil as he led the horse to walk beside her.

"I suppose he is right," she said. "I was in the way."

"Aye, you were," the man replied pleasantly, as if the battle for their lives had not just taken place. "And he would take it to heart greatly if you were harmed. He should have killed Hrolgar when he had the chance. I would have. But then, he is not my uncle."

"Not yours? But you're brothers. I do not understand."

"Hrolgar is brother to Ronan's first father, who is dead."

"Gunnar is not his father?" She wanted to stop but forced herself to keep walking.

"He is now. His father was Gunnar's cousin. When Ronan's father died, Hrolgar took Ronan away from Wynne. Gunnar did not learn for a few years, for we were on the Green Isle, but when he did, he went looking for them and forced Hrolgar to give him up. Hrolgar has never forgiven either of them for that. After that, Gunnar married Wynne and took Ronan as his son. So we are brothers." He smiled. "I think that is what you wanted to know, isn't it?"

"Then it is true that your people take boy children from their mothers and raise them?"

"Hrolgar did. It was his right." The blond Viking winced lightly, as if he himself had felt the pain. "But it could hardly be called raising. Hrolgar is a plague. Everyone hates him. He forced Ronan to raid with his band, and he was ill treated, beaten, ill fed. I am glad my father went for him."

Egil paused to face her, his eyes entreating. "He is a good man, Arienh. Will you not give him a chance?"

Her fleeting glance caught the Viking's eye, but guilt forced it away. Like Ronan, he had a kindness about him that entrapped her. She wanted to believe in it, but it was Egil's kindness that worried her most, for he would do what he thought was right. And that would mean he would take Liam, for Liam's good, because he needed a father, not a blind mother. That would destroy Birgit as surely as if they took her life. And if Arienh accepted Ronan, she would also be letting Egil in the door.

"Nay," she said. Yet to say it was like a stab to her heart.

"Aunt! Aunt!" shouted Liam as he ran down the path, far ahead of his mother. "I did it! I didn't fall off, and I rode all the way to the village, and I told them."

Catching the boy as he sped into her arms and hugging him tightly, she said, "Ah, Liam, you are my little hero today. You brought help in time to save us all."

"Only I didn't, Aunt. 'Cause Egil got there first. Did Ronan save you, Aunt?"

"Aye, he did. He was very brave. I did not think either of us would live. But we did because he was brave and you were brave, and Egil brought everyone to save us."

Egil slanted a glance at her, then swung Liam up onto the horse for the ride back into the village. Far up the path, Mildread stood with an arm around each of her girls, watching solemnly. Elli and Selma hovered close by with Birgit.

Unraveling.

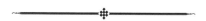

Birgit stood near the slit window looking out at stars she could not see. "I can hear them singing."

Arienh leaned back on her pillow, propped against the stone wall. "They like to sing at night. They sing more when they're drinking, I think."

"But it is beautiful. Listen."

Arienh was listening. She wasn't sure beautiful was the right word. The voices were deep, sometimes raucous, haunting, strangely lilting. A sound that told of their close bond with each other. A masculine sound unlike any she had heard before.

"You're worried about him," Birgit guessed.

"He must be in pain."

"They wouldn't be carrying on like this if he were truly hurt. But maybe you should go see."

She shook her head. Probably Birgit couldn't see the movement. "Nay."

"You were right not to let him die, Arienh. We were wrong."

"But if I had, perhaps we would not face this now."

"You could never have done it, anyway. And the others still would have come. They already meant to." Birgit turned from the window to fix her pale eyes on Arienh. "I know how you feel about him, Arienh."

Arienh returned her focus to the embers of the banked fire. "I don't feel anything, Birgit."

"Aye, you do. He saved Liam today. And you, too."

"Mildread's girls, too. He meant to die for us."

"And you say you feel nothing?"

She chewed her lip. Of course she did. But she didn't want to admit it. "I'm grateful."

"More than that. What will you do tomorrow?"

Arienh pulled her brown blanket around her and sat on the bed's edge. "I don't know. He is right. We cannot survive without them. But somehow we must not let them get too close."

With a sigh, Birgit left the window. She stirred the fire in the stone hearth with an absent sort of movement. "I think you fight a losing battle. They are going to find out about my eyes no matter what we do. They have earned much respect today."

"Aye."

"Arienh?" A curious knot of anxiety tinged Birgit's voice.

Arienh sat up, away from the pillow. "Aye?"

"Perhaps you should bow to the inevitable. Perhaps it would not be so bad. At least for Liam."

"It would not be good for him to lose you. I will not allow it."

"You must think about it. Think of everyone's needs."

"You don't know what they will do to Liam, or to you, if they learn you cannot see. I will not sacrifice you. There must be another way."

Whatever that might be, she had no idea. Mildread, Selma, all of them, were beginning to look at the Vikings differently.

If only she could talk with Wynne.

Arienh watched as Birgit walked back to the window, alternately clasping and dropping her hands to her side. "What if he is badly hurt, Arienh? He saved my Liam and you. I cannot stand not knowing."

"You could do nothing about it."

"Aye. But I did not say—someone must tell him I am grateful, Arienh. You must go."

Birgit was not saying what was on her mind, and Arienh could not divine it.

"Is there not some betony or lettuce you could take him?"

So that was it. Birgit felt guilty, in the same way Arienh had on that day that now seemed so long ago when she had first wounded him.

"Aye, I still have some lettuce syrup made up. I will take it to him." She quickly tossed her cloak over her shoulders, took up the little jug of syrup, and left the cottage.

A full moon spread its silver over the path and danced on the ripples in the river. The night was bright and clear enough that even Birgit could have made her way with little help. Arienh passed the lone oak and crossed the stepping stones in the little stream that divided the upper village from the lower. The deep voices grew louder as she drew closer to the big cottage that had once belonged to Cousin Weylin, now claimed by the Viking. She hesitated, then pushed against the door.

The raucous voices suddenly grew louder. The smoky, warm air assaulted her eyes and nostrils. Words spoken in their guttural tongue brought a course of back-slapping guffaws that rippled through the crowd. Something else was said, and sudden silence reigned. Men turned and stared at her with horrified expressions.

Had she broken some law? Only men allowed, perhaps? But Wynne rose from the platform bed where she reclined with her husband and, speaking calmly to the men, walked to the door.

She took Arienh's arm and led her away from the cottage.

"Did I do something wrong?"

Wynne laughed. "Only caught them at their jokes. Now they are wondering if you understand enough of their language to know what they said."

"Really? What would make them feel so guilty?"

"They are making up stories about Loki's daughters."

Arienh recalled the one Ronan had mentioned, Hel. "Who are Loki's daughters?"

The small woman who was more Viking than Celt smiled, her every feature clear in the bright moonlight. "That's the secret they hope to keep. According to their legends, their god Loki has but one daughter, Hel, and she is a Northman's nightmare. But Loki is the god of mischief, so they have decided he must have had more daughters, and made them beautiful Celts, to bring them nothing but trouble."

"Perhaps they should have thought of that before coming here to take over Celtic land." Then Arienh regretted her words, for Wynne was a kind woman and loved her sons.

Wynne laughed, a warm and happy sound, reminding her of her own mother, who had died with the babe born after Niall. Arienh had been little more than a young child herself, then.

"They would not be happy if they knew I told you," said Wynne. "But it is very funny."

The twinkle in the woman's eyes was compelling. "What?"

"Ronan's story. It's about men coming to the Island of Loki's Daughters. The men are enchanted, and the women lure them into their beds."

"In their dreams."

"Aye, that, too. But then the men discover to their dismay that they are the ones who become pregnant."

Caught off guard, Arienh spewed out her laughter, and Wynne laughed with her.

"Surely a man did not make up that tale," she sputtered out, still laughing.

"But he did. You see why they don't want you to know it."

She answered with a smile and a nod. The woman was more Celt than Arienh had thought, and had clearly been deprived of women too long. "I have not seen you often," Arienh said.

"I do not get about much, for my husband is not well. But I am glad to see you."

"I have brought something for your son, if he is in pain."

"I think Ronan is all right. He does not complain. But then, they are drinking."

"They drink often."

"Aye. They do not have women to keep them busy, so they sit around of an evening telling wild stories and singing and drinking their mead. Sometimes it is too loud for me. It is quieter out here." She set a hand to Arienh's elbow, gently guiding her toward the path. "The night is fine. Will you walk with me, Arienh? I do not often have the company of a woman."

Arienh nodded as they stepped into the shadow of the trees, knowing the darkness obscured her gesture. "You have been long among their kind?"

"Many years. I was probably younger than you when I was taken from my home by Ronan's father."

"You must have been glad when he died."

"Glad?" She smiled. "Nay, I had come to care for him. It must seem strange to you."

"It does. How could one care for such a man?"

"He was good to me. I was fortunate that he did not sell me but kept me for himself. My life could have been far worse. Yet he did not understand for a long time why I did not appreciate his efforts. After a while we struck a bargain. I agreed to stay with him and try to get along with him for a year. And then if I still wished to leave, he would honor the Celtic custom and would take me back home."

"But you did not go?"

Wynne paused. Arienh wondered if perhaps she had not been heard. Then with a wistful sigh, the older woman began again. "By then, I was with child. But I lost that child. He won my heart when I watched that great, crude warrior cradling that tiny infant in his hands and crying, before taking her out to bury." Wynne chewed on her lower lip. Her eyes seemed too bright in the moonlight. "So I stayed another year. And then I had Ronan."

"But he died. Ronan's father."

"You know how Gunnar took Ronan away from Hrolgar?"

"Egil told me."

"Tonight, my sons celebrate their triumph over Hrolgar. He is an evil man. I hoped we would never have to see him again."

"Did you never wish to have a man of your own kind?"

"Perhaps. But a woman could not do better than Gunnar. Or one of his sons."

Another voice interrupted. "You brag too much, Mother."

Startled, Arienh turned. Egil's yellow hair shone almost silver in the moonlight as he walked noiselessly up to them.

"Go away, Son, this is woman's talk."

"I came only to see if everything is all right. Do you seek my brother, Arienh?"

"I only meant to bring him something in case the pain bothered him."

"He is feeling no pain. Or if he is, he doesn't know it."

Wynne laughed. "Egil means he is drunk. It is also a way to treat pain."

"I was afraid…"

Egil smiled as if he knew the rest of her thought. "The wound has not opened. Hrolgar's kick would not have mattered at all if there had been no wound. I will tell him you have come."

"Take this to him." She held out the jug. "If he does not need it, it must be saved, for it is the last until summer."

A pleasant chuckle rumbled through the man, and he pushed it back to her. "He will not take it, not from one of Loki's daughters, lest he spend the rest of the night running to the pot. Take it back. He will be all right."

Wynne suppressed a snicker.

"Birgit sends a message. She is grateful for Liam's life."

Egil smiled. It was odd, how his wicked-looking eyes could sometimes seem so warm and affectionate.

"We have all made our decision, Arienh," he said. "We are here to stay. And we will protect all of you with our lives."

She knew that, and knowing it made things even harder. If there were only some way that Egil would still look upon Birgit with loving eyes after he learned how little she could see. But when that happened, he would not recognize how much Birgit could do, but how little. Not enough to be considered a satisfactory helpmate. Nor, when Ronan understood that Arienh was sworn to take care of Birgit, would he be willing to take on the added burden. Nor would they leave. She knew that now. The Vikings would rule the valley, not the Celts.

"I must go now," she said. Arienh turned away and plodded back up the path. Her feet felt weighted with lead.

# CHAPTER THIRTEEN

---

CLOUDS HAD FORMED IN THE NIGHT, THEN VANISHED WITH the dawn, leaving a sparkling coat of dew on the new blades of grass. Arienh stood on the green, arms folded, observing the gathering.

Women stood in a half circle around her, men around the Viking. Everyone was there, even Old Ferris, his black eyes as full of hatred as ever. She doubted Old Ferris would ever give it up, so intent was he on his vengeance.

Like her, Ronan folded his arms. But unlike her, he strode about, confidently studying her and her women from all angles. She refused to show her relief, but it pleased her to see Ronan stride about with no signs of pain, with fresh garments, cleanly shaven, even with his rich brown hair neatly trimmed. No trace remained of his fierce battle the day before, except the man himself and the natural power that radiated from him. His great size made her feel insignificant as she faced him, standing in front of the cluster of Celts.

It took all of them together, including the children, to outnumber the Vikings. How could she win?

She controlled what the Vikings wanted. Yet giving it to them would mean losing.

"Well, Viking, you have called us here. Get on with it."

His laugh had a hollow sound as he turned to face her. "Get on with it? Aye, we will end this feud, Arienh. You have nothing to gain by it."

"You think we will gain by giving all to you?"

"It is simple enough. We give all we have to you as well. You have what we need. We have what you need. Together, we can all prosper."

"We do not want what you have."

His hands went to his hips, and his fascinating blue eyes fixed on her. "Have you asked the others, Arienh? Are you sure they would rather go hungry, watch crops fail, see their cottages fall to ruin?"

She met his gaze, equally determined. "If we give you what you want, we will no longer be Celts. We will be no more than possessions of Vikings."

"Northmen."

"Blood will tell, Viking. You have not shown us you are anything less. Like all those raiders before you, you have come to take from us. Only this time, you have come to take it all."

"We do not take without giving back, and you know that."

"It is because you would have us believe we can trust you. But we learned our lesson about your kind a very long time ago."

His eyes flinched, as if the barb had stung them. "Very well," he said, "have it your way. If that is how you insist on seeing it, then I claim this valley as mine. But all your bitter words will not chase us away, nor will your tricks and traps. You live in my valley now, and you would be wise to learn to live with us."

"It is not your valley and never will be." Arienh felt uneasiness stirring behind her. The Celtic women were losing their zest for a fight, and Arienh herself wished for a better way. Perhaps she was being too strident. "But we will listen to what you propose."

He knew he was winning. She could see it in the narrow gleam in his eyes. His hands propped on his hips. The man could strut, just standing there.

"You do not have men to do what men must do, and so you try to do it yourselves. You are much to be admired that you have not simply given up. But no one can lead two lives, Arienh. You may try to plow your fields yourselves, with nothing but a stick to do it, but you take time away from the things that women must do to survive."

His eyes scanned over the Celts, then glanced back at his horde of Vikings. He continued. "We need what you have to give, too, just as you need our skills. We can provide venison and barley, but we cannot make it taste very good."

A chuckle rumbled through the Vikings. She wondered just how terrible their cooking was.

"Wynne cannot continue to cook for all of us, and we waste too much good food with our clumsy attempts," he continued. "We can tend the flocks, shear the fleece, but then, who is to card the wool, spin it, weave it?"

She snorted. "I cannot tell if you want wives or slaves. Or if you know the difference."

"You cannot? Is that not the difference between sharing and taking? We know it, Arienh. We are not the animals you make us to be."

"We will not be your wives, either."

"Aye, so you have said." And he grinned knowingly at her. She prayed he would not suddenly decide to divulge her secret. Yet why had he been willing to keep it when he could so easily use it to gain control of her? Then she realized his game. He needed only the threat of exposure to control her.

And it was working. But if she watched for her opening, maybe she could beat him at his own game.

"And we have something you need even more," he said, his eyes narrowing slyly.

"Do you, Viking?"

"You wish to defend yourselves, yet you have no weapons. We can help you with that."

A low murmur coursed through the women.

Arienh sneered. "Swords? Then we would be dependent upon you for the making of them."

"Nay, a sword would be a bad choice. You are all too small, and your sword arms too short. A balanced sword for you would be little better than a dagger."

"Looks to me like she did all right with a dagger," said Egil. A hearty chuckle rumbled through the men. The women smirked quietly.

"And they can't always count on luck, Egil," Ronan snapped back, yet a silly grin tugged at his lips. "They need something that doesn't put their size to disadvantage, something easy to make of ordinary materials."

"What then?"

"Bows."

"Archery?" snorted Olav. "You'll make archers of women?"

"Why not?"

Egil laughed back. "Aye, why not? Bows, arrows, bowstrings, quivers, all of it they could make themselves, and the materials are common. Only the arrowheads need to be forged. Perhaps the bows would not be as powerful, but they still would serve."

It was too good to be true. "And what if we turn what you teach us against you, Viking?"

He grinned, that irritatingly disarming grin that made her want to kiss him and slap him at the same time. "We will not give you the opportunity, my beautiful little Celt. If you want what we have to give, you will have to cease your pranks. We will teach you to make and use the weapons, and we will benefit as well, knowing that you can defend yourselves if we are not around. Think of it, Arienh. Imagine a sudden onslaught of those such as Hrolgar, met with a hail of arrows from women they thought defenseless. Tell me, all of you, does it not thrill your hearts?"

A speculative giggle came from a woman behind her. Arienh suspected it was Selma.

"And you, men, you all know Hrolgar and hold him in great disgust. Perhaps not as much as I, but would you not like to see his vicious career cut short by the very women he would enslave?"

"I for one," said Egil, "would personally go back to the Green Isle to spread the news. Aye, Ronan, I support this wild scheme of yours."

"Aye" rose the chorus from the men.

Despite herself, Arienh blinked at the sudden response. What was he up to, and why did his men support such a proposal? Did they really despise the Viking Hrolgar that much? "But you would not like it if we should shoot some friend of yours."

"Our friends do not raid, Arienh, so there is no concern."

She eyed him suspiciously. What purpose could his strange plot have? It surely could not be merely revenge against his uncle, no matter how much he hated the man. "What could you possibly gain from this, Viking?"

"'Tis simple. To teach you we are not Vikings."

He was quick to exploit an advantage, mischievous and sneaky. He meant to gain far more than that, but she could not tell what. Arienh folded her arms again and turned her back to him, facing the collection of women.

"What could it hurt, Arienh?" Mildread asked.

What? It would give them an opening. Closer to Birgit and danger.

"Even if they leave, we would still be able to defend ourselves," said Birgit. "We would not have to go all the way to the cavern to be safe."

"Aye," said Elli. "Anyone can carry a bow and a few arrows around. We could have it with us all the time."

"Silence, girl." Old Ferris shoved himself between Elli and Arienh. "You'll have no truck with their kind and stay in my house."

"No, Grandfather, you are not thinking. Such a skill could be used in many ways." Elli's brown eyes focused intently on her grandfather.

The old man frowned, confused. He stepped aside to mull over what Elli had said. By itself, that puzzled Arienh, for Ferris had never been one so easily silenced.

But she sized up where everyone stood, and realized what they wanted. Yet they expected her to find some way to preserve Birgit's safety too. How?

"We will do your cooking then, Viking, if you are so bad at it. You will provide what must be cooked."

His blue eyes widened suddenly. Perhaps he had not thought he would win a point so quickly. Looking about her, she saw the women were as equally taken aback.

"And we will spin and dye and weave. We will do the chores that have always been for women to do, and you will provide in the way men do. But we will not share our houses with you or clean up after you. You will live south of the stream only, and we will stay to the north. You will not come to our houses."

"But if something needs repair?"

"We will negotiate it. And if a man has a need for a service that is not usual, that will be negotiated."

"It would best be done if a man chooses a household and provides for it." One dark eyebrow arched expectantly.

She saw the guile behind the seemingly innocent suggestion. "Nay, for we do not wish your companionship. You asked only how we may get along together in the same valley. You will bring your provisions here, to this place. We will divide them up and

return them properly prepared here, to this place. You will bring
your laundry or mending here, and it will be returned here. The
wool, when it is sheared, will be dealt with here. And we will
decide among us who will do which task."

"It need not be so complicated, Arienh."

She knew it. She didn't want what she asked for, either, but
it was necessary. "I find it easier. Then we need not worry about
what game you may be playing. You are sly, Viking, but we will
not be fooled. We will not become wives to heathens."

He shrugged and his bright blue eyes took on a merry twinkle. "If that is all, we will convert. Send for your priest."

"We do not send for Father Hewil. He comes when he comes."

"Then we will wait. I heard he always comes in the spring."

Any day now, but she would not say it. "He will not be
seduced thus."

"Nay, he will accept us. We will become Christians for you."

And how could she oppose him then? Simply wearing the
cross would not change him or his heathen customs. "For the
wrong reason, clearly, for your heart is not in it. But that is far
from all. You cannot so blithely wipe out all that has been done
to us."

"'Tis so, you have lost much, and nothing can change that.
But we did not do any of it, for all that you blame us. We offer you
help, not more pain."

And she wanted what he offered. Oh, how she wanted it.
Arienh raked her eyes over the gathering of men. "You carry battle axes and swords even now. Can you tell me none of you have
ever raided? Have you never killed a man, Viking? You swing
your sword like a man who has done so many times."

"And who better to defend you from Vikings than one who
knows the sword? We will carry our swords, Arienh, for the danger of a man like Hrolgar lurks at all times. And we shall post a
man from dawn to twilight every day atop the cliff that overlooks

the sea so that none may catch us unawares. We will do what men must do. We ask only that you do as well for us."

"Aye. We agree. But we will not be your wives. And we will keep to ourselves."

"And no more pranks."

"If you leave us alone, we will leave you alone."

"We will accept."

At that, Arienh turned away. Temptation clawed at her, but she resisted and strode on through the gathering of women who parted for her passing, then followed her.

"Pardon me, Brother, but will you tell me what we have won?"

Ronan allowed his gaze to follow after the departing women before replying to Egil's snide remark. "It is a crack. And everywhere there is a crack, we will fill it."

"Huh," sniffed Bjorn. "These women will make slaves of all of you. Bunch of fools. Didn't anyone ever tell you men are supposed to run things?"

"Bjorn has a point," said Olav, a heavy frown furrowing his brow. "I don't know what you hope to gain."

"The point is to win their trust. When they begin to do things for us and accept things from us, they will begin to trust us."

"If they don't put an arrow through someone's heart first."

Ronan chuckled. He doubted the women had the courage to take it that far. "You are not Northmen if you cannot see the opportunities here. How close will you have to get to teach them to shoot?"

A murmuring hum spread through the men.

"Do you really think they can do it, Ronan?" Olav asked.

"They're Loki's daughters, aren't they? They will give up the idea of defending themselves eventually, once they learn how hard it is. And when they begin to let us defend them, we will have won the battle. Tomorrow we'll begin with choosing the wood. Olav, keep an eye out for a beehive, for the wax. And Bjorn can get busy forging arrowheads."

"Bunch of fools. Give a woman a foot and she'll take a whole damn furlong," snarled Bjorn. With a great, gruff noise, he stalked away.

But Tanni's boyish face erupted in a wide grin. "Nay, Ronan, I think as you do. 'Tis willing women who give the best pleasure. And the price is not so awful."

"Aye," said Egil, "I'll have mine willing or not at all. But it seems to me we have lost ground, not gained it. We have just agreed to stay away from them."

"Find the cracks and fill them," Ronan repeated.

"When we cannot go near them?"

"Oh, ignore that."

"Ignore it?"

He grinned. "For good enough reason, of course. But you can think of something. Just make the opportunities."

Egil stared at him as if he were suddenly speaking a language none of them understood. Then slowly a broad, wicked grin spread beneath the long, yellow mustache that draped across his face. "Aye. And I think I just found mine."

Mildread stood with her girls by the huge old oak on the green and watched the crowd fade away. She had listened, but her heart had not been in what was said. She had tried hard to watch the dark-haired Viking and Arienh, but her gaze kept slipping to Olav, standing among his comrades with his arms folded. Only once had his slate-blue eyes looked at her, then slid away with a mild disdain. Although tall like the others, he was slimmer, and handsome in a rather normal way. Once, when he had first come here, he had looked upon her with interest. But he never would again.

Although dark-haired Ronan had plucked her girls from beneath the very noses of the raiders, it had been Olav who had carried them up the trail when they were too exhausted and terrified to keep going. He had run with them all the way to the cavern, not even pausing to allow her to help. She had not understood at the time, but now she did. If his friends had not succeeded in holding back the intruders, her girls would never have made it to the cavern safely.

"Go to your Aunt Elli," she told the girls now. "I have something I must do."

Mildread walked alone along the trail that led down toward the Bride's Well, and when she reached the cutoff that led through the south forest to the sea, she climbed the gentle rise. At an outcropping of grey rock within an ash grove, she stopped, then bent and dug beneath the old leaves, rooting around with her hands where she could not see.

She felt first the wooden handle, then the spreading width of the iron blade. She lifted up the ax into the dappled sunlight.

"I thought you knew where it was."

Olav. And she held his missing ax in her hands. She was too ashamed even to blush. "I meant to return it to you."

"Did you? Or merely to see if it was still there?" He took the ax from her hand, his fingers running over the blade.

"I stole it and hid it. But I meant to give it back. I was wrong, and I was wrong to lead you off into the woods and get you lost."

Nothing in his solemn face changed. "The first, I blame on you. The second was my own stupidity. You could at least say thank you."

"For my girls. I—yes, thank you."

"It is rusting."

"I'm sorry. I don't suppose you will ever trust me again."

The slate-blue eyes regarded her slowly as he tucked the ax handle into his belt. "Perhaps. When you begin to trust us."

Olav turned and walked down the hill as silently as he had come, leaving Mildread standing alone.

Smoky heat from the fat-soaked torches warmed the cavern's damp air. A nervous excitement infused the women who stood there with the lone man, Old Ferris, with his brooding rage. Arienh was glad she had asked Selma's older cousin to keep the children while they talked, for Old Ferris loved nothing more than stirring up the children.

"You have betrayed us all, Arienh," shouted Ferris, his finger shaking in her face. "Your father, your mother, all of them, all of us. There is no bargaining with their kind."

"Oh, be quiet, old man," said Mildread, folding her arms as she faced him. "You are letting your hatred think for you."

Ferris whirled on Mildread, rage blooming like roses in his cheeks. "It seems I am the only one who thinks. They killed your husband."

"My husband died of his own malingering."

"And who would not, with his manhood destroyed?"

"His manhood worked just fine. It was the rest of him that would not."

A muffled giggle spread through the crowd of women, and Old Ferris's black eyes widened. "And you think a Viking will serve you better?"

"I said nothing of that, Old Ferris, but none can deny they are hard workers. These are not bad men. We all would have died today if it were not for them. You, as well."

"I care not if I live or die. I just want them dead. I want all Vikings dead."

"Then kill them yourself. I will not help you."

"Nor I," said Birgit.

Ferris sneered, and his eyes seemed to sizzle as he turned on Birgit. "As if you could. The big blond one turns your head, does he, Birgit? Well, he is about the best that you could do, but even he will turn on you, for they have no use for invalids. Not even a Viking wants a blind wife. When they discover how helpless you are, they will not even let you live, and it will be your sister's fault, for she has sold us all to the heathens."

Birgit stiffened her back, seeming to grow taller. Perhaps her outrageous courage came from years of facing down Ferris's taunts. "Nay, the fault will be my own. But I will not hide, and I do not fear they will kill me."

"Huh. You are cowards, all of you. You dishonor the Celtic women of old, who fought beside their men. You are afraid to do what must be done."

Birgit shrugged, and a bitter smile wobbled on her face. "Oh, well, we are just ordinary women."

Ferris faced the crowd of women, glaring, studying each face separately, finding no support among them. Arienh doubted if anyone regretted Old Ferris stomping out of the cavern, only that he dragged his reluctant granddaughter after him. Perhaps some of the women even speculated on just how much of a shove it might take to topple him into the pit, but more probable, like her, they remembered a time when the old man had not been so consumed with rage. All that had changed when his son died.

Arienh regretted more for Elli than for Ferris. Poor Elli, for no matter how she tried, she could never please the old man, never replace his lost son. Yet Elli could never stop trying.

The moment Ferris passed out of their sight, silence gave way to urgent chatter.

"I know they won't kill you, Birgit," said Mildread. "They have proven much too gentle for that. But I do not like the way that big one plays up to Liam."

"They don't eat children, either," Birgit retorted.

"Of course not, but he shows him too much interest. What if he does take him away?"

Selma nestled up close to Birgit as if, despite her diminutive size, she might protect her larger but more helpless cousin. "He wouldn't. Liam is just a little boy. He needs his mother."

Birgit shook her head, and a flash of pain crossed her eyes. "I don't know. He already asked for him. He thought I must not love my son because I hated Vikings, but he knows better now. I think."

"And I am not so sure, either," said Arienh. "They have a tradition of taking over fatherless boys. Egil himself told me that Ronan was taken first by that raider, Hrolgar, who is his uncle, and then Gunnar, when he was a boy. Egil said it was Hrolgar's right."

The silence was broken only by the quiet sound of women breathing.

"They admire your weaving," Selma said. "They won't think you helpless."

Birgit sighed. "But you forget, they want wives. I cannot do the things that are expected of wives, and I must depend upon you. They will not want you to spend time taking care of me."

Selma pursed her pretty lips as she frowned. "Aye. We must not let them know." She frowned, then brightened suddenly. "I know. Let's offer to trade Birgit's cloth. Then we will say she is too busy weaving to come outside."

"That won't stop Egil," Birgit said.

"We could all flirt with him."

"Nay." Suddenly blushing, Birgit amended her outburst. "I mean, that would make the other men mad."

Mildread raised an eyebrow at Birgit's objection. "Yes, I suppose it would. It could make them mad at him, but more likely they would be mad at us. Besides, we agreed to no more pranks. We need a better plan. The trouble is, we don't really know them, and we don't know what they'll do. We think they won't hurt her, but we don't know."

Birgit gave a despairing smile. "I think it is hopeless. It would be better if you make your peace with them, for you cannot hide me forever."

"Nay," said Arienh. Sometimes Birgit's fatalistic attitude frustrated her beyond words. How could she even think about defeat? "I will not hear you talk like that. I will never give you up, Birgit."

"Aye, Birgit, you should listen to your sister." Mildread slipped a comforting arm around Birgit. "And she is not the only stubborn one, for you are very precious to all of us, and so is Liam."

A chorus of assent echoed in the cavern.

"Then we must find out," said Mildread. "There is much we do not know of them, and much we have assumed has proven false. I propose to ask them. Carefully, of course."

Last year's old leaves on the forest bed rustled with the footfalls of men cutting slender logs of yew and trimming out saplings of ash. Olav found a hive and robbed it of its wax. Arienh watched the men assembling their collected leather, beeswax, linen thread, and sinew, and at Egil's request, she grumblingly produced the wing feathers she had saved from the ducks he had given them.

The forge billowed smoke while the blacksmith Bjorn turned out iron arrowheads.

Her gathering of women observed, fascinated, as Ronan showed how a bow was carved from a sliver of yew, how to shave it down to weaken it if it was too strong. Egil rolled the little ash saplings on a flat stone to show them how to choose the straightest limbs for arrows, how to attach iron arrowheads, split feathers to fletch the arrows, and twist and wax the linen to make bowstrings. With each step, the men insisted the women participate in the making, no matter how clumsy their efforts.

Arienh grumbled beneath her breath to cover up her fascination.

"You cannot expect the best for yourselves without practice," Ronan responded. "You will learn with time, but these will do for now. Eventually, we will see that all of you have the best we can make for you, but you still must know how to make your own."

Standing beneath the old lone oak beside the village green, Arienh watched Ronan and his men scurrying about, setting up targets on the green, humming about like yellow bees harvesting pollen. She gazed up at the oak's greening branches and laughed, remembering the men's clothing hanging from its higher boughs. It reminded her of the rags tied to the trees at the Bride's Well at Beltane to represent prayers and wishes, except that the wishes were so different.

Well, perhaps not so different. At Beltane, they wished for prosperity, fertility, long and happy lives. And lovers. Arienh was no longer sure what her people wished for now. She wasn't even sure what she wanted.

No, that too wasn't true. She knew exactly what she wanted. Ronan. She just knew she couldn't have him. He was a Viking after all.

A Viking who had saved her life, twice, who had saved them all. Yet he was a threat to Birgit, and it was not as if Birgit could defend herself. Birgit was Arienh's responsibility, conferred upon her with their brother Trevor's dying words.

Guilt swamped her. She was failing. Yet she could not see a way to win. If only she had not been left with all the responsibility, for she was not up to it. If any of the men were still alive, they would know what to do, but Arienh was alone—surrounded, yet alone. No one knew she was afraid, and she could never let them know, not Viking nor Celt.

Perhaps she should have turned the Viking down. Yet they needed what he offered: more than food or shelter, they needed to learn to defend themselves. And for all its simply obtained equipment, archery was not a simple skill.

Ronan towered before her, seeming even larger, mightier than when he had first come. He had a laugh in his bright blue eyes as he held out the bow to her.

"You first, my love," he said.

She flinched at his endearment, more than she would have had he struck her. She did not want to be held dear by a Viking. She wanted to refuse, to run, but she stuffed her fear back inside her as she raised her chin and accepted the bow.

As if he read her thoughts, he laughed, but a darkness like roiling clouds hid behind his merriment, as if a hundred turbulent thoughts tumbled in his mind. With his giant, gentle hands to her hips, he positioned her properly, standing sideways to the target, her arm outstretched with the bow.

His plot became clearer as he nestled his body behind hers. She stiffened at his warm breath stirring her hair. Every inch, every familiar inch of him, molded against her. Her body tingled everywhere they touched, screaming its awareness of his maleness. Heat crept into her face at her irrelevant thoughts. She was supposed to be thinking about shooting.

Nay, he did not mean for her to be thinking about arrows and targets, unless it was his particular arrow, which she could feel quite well where it pressed against the small of her back.

"Slant the bow," he said, "not straight up and down." His left hand wrapped around hers to cock the bow a little to the right. His other hand came around and, grasping hers, led it to the bowstring.

Arienh tried to pluck the string between thumb and forefinger, as she had seen her brother do.

"Nay, love, use your two fingers to hook the string and draw it." He manipulated her fingers into the position he wanted.

She struggled to comply, but she seemed to move in the wrong direction with each move. He carefully repositioned her stance, his hands lingering at her hips, smoothing around her waist, snuggling around her hands. A quiet, humming sort of growl edged his voice.

After three practice pulls, he let her nock the arrow into the bowstring, correcting her only in its placement to the left of the handle.

"Slant the bow," he said again, and Arienh realized in her agitation she had changed her position. She resolved to get it right, for every mistake on her part gave him another excuse to touch her and prolong her agony.

As she pulled the string, the arrow dropped away from the bow. Ronan moved her left forefinger over the top of the arrow to steady it.

"If you don't want the arrow to fall, you must slant the bow. And you must move the top finger away before you release, or the feather will cut your finger as it passes. Don't shoot yet. Just pull back the string, then ease it back."

Arienh hadn't thought there could be so much to shooting. She cocked the bow to the side. Yes, it did help to keep the arrow in place. She drew back the bowstring. Ronan's massive hands turned her posture sideways again.

She couldn't do it. She couldn't stand this close to him for as long as it took to get this right. She'd be in his arms till sundown, and long before that, she'd be shaking like a quaking leaf in autumn, begging him to release his own arrow to its target. But she must. Surely she could manage just a little bit longer. She'd just have to learn faster, pay more attention.

Once more she felt his fingers turn her hips. "Just lean into me, love. That's all you have to do."

And that was the last thing she wanted to do.

Wrong. It was what she wanted most to do.

Arienh gave in, yielding to her body's need to feel him nestled, hard and excited, into the curve of her backside, exactly where he wanted her to be. He rewarded her. As she drew the arrow, sighted down its length, he let her release it.

The arrow flew and plopped to the ground a few feet in front of the target. A high-pitched giggle floated through the air.

Ronan didn't laugh. She turned to see his eyes, darkening like storm clouds, but not from anger. "Don't feel bad, love. It is a good first shot. They will be lucky if they do as well. But an arrow does not fly straight. It falls as it flies, so you must aim above the target, about as much as it fell short."

Arienh sighed again and ignored the female and male snickers as Ronan settled once again into her backside and positioned her. She nocked the arrow hurriedly and raised the bow, angling it just so. Anxious to finish, she drew the string, aimed above the target, released.

The shot flew wild, skimmed the grass, and landed near where Olav's feet would have been, had he not had the sense to jump away quicker than a hare avoiding an eagle's dive.

Ronan's chuckle rumbled in her ears as raucous laughter echoed around her. "Never rush yourself. You make mistakes that way. Always do everything exactly the same. Of course, that only applies to shooting."

The men roared with laughter. Arienh recognized the allusion. Everyone knew how much men liked variety in their love play. Well, she'd give him "exactly the same." She'd give him perfection. She'd get every little part of this absurdity exactly right, and end it. This time she'd concentrate.

Determined, Arienh nocked another arrow, checked her posture, checked again. Angled the bow just so. Drew the string back so that her thumb touched her ear, exactly as he had shown her. Sighted, and raised the elevation.

"Take your time. Hold very still. Be sure. Move nothing but your fingers when you shoot. Now."

Arienh checked everything once more. She released the two fingers that hooked the bowstring. The arrow flew, arcing across the green, catching the lower edge of the painted sheepskin.

The men cheered. The women laughed.

"That's enough," Arienh said. "Let someone else try."

Relief flooded her when Ronan didn't protest.

Egil stepped up. "Birgit," he said.

From where she sat on the grass, Birgit jerked around. Her pale green eyes widened in horror.

# CHAPTER FOURTEEN

⚜

"N AY." BIRGIT'S VOICE SOUNDED AS FRAIL AS HER EYES WERE weak. Even Liam's brilliant blue eyes gleamed with fear.

Egil shook his head, holding out his hand to Birgit. "It is your turn. Everyone must learn."

Frantic thoughts raced through Arienh's mind. She had to think of something quickly.

But what?

"This is foolish," Birgit said as she rose and turned, trying to mask her fear. But it cavorted in her eyes.

Egil took Birgit's arm and led her toward the green before she could walk away.

"I must get back to my weaving."

"Aye, in good time." Egil handed her the bow he had made.

Birgit stared at the thing as if she held a snake. Hesitantly, she yanked on the bowstring a few times. "I cannot pull this thing," she said. "It is too strong."

"Only because you do not hold it right, Birgit. You are no weaker than the other women. Come, we will do it just like your sister. You will see, it is not so hard."

Arienh's heart lurched as Egil took Birgit into his arms. She must not panic. Egil did not press himself against Birgit in the way Ronan had done to her, but Birgit's eyes bugged with fear, begging Arienh to think of something. She would not even be able to choose the direction to shoot.

Unless…

Arienh picked up the bow she had left on the ground. "Well, while you figure that out, I think I will practice," Arienh said, forcing composure into her voice.

Standing as close to Birgit as she could without being obvious, Arienh positioned herself as perfectly as Ronan had taught her. But her back faced Birgit, so she glanced back over her shoulder, hoping Birgit comprehended.

Unsmiling, Birgit returned a tiny nod.

Arienh squared herself to the target, and elevated the arrow exactly. Birgit was an excellent imitator, for the symmetry of her weaving had taught her exact proportions. Arienh glanced back again and saw that Birgit imitated her sister's position precisely. Then the arrow slipped and dropped to the grass.

"I cannot do this," Birgit said. "I am too clumsy." She tried to hand back the bow, but Egil refused. Reluctantly she nocked the arrow again and carefully tilted the bow exactly as Arienh did.

But Arienh had stalled too long. Her shoulders ached from holding back the string. If she held too long, the men might suspect her ploy. She let the arrow fly. It struck low on the target. She bent and chose another arrow from the arsenal beside her, covertly checking Birgit's position, perfect in all respects except that she squeezed her eyes shut. With a silent prayer, Arienh turned back.

"How can you aim with your eyes shut?" Egil asked.

"I already aimed."

Two arrows flew together. Two arrows thudded into the target. Arienh stared, astounded. Hers was still low. Birgit's had split the center.

In the unearthly silence, Birgit stood still, eyes pinched tightly shut as if she waited for a blow to descend on her.

Elli shrieked. Mildread rushed up to Birgit, laughing, and shoved Egil aside to hug her cousin.

"You did it, Mama!" Liam tugged excitedly on Birgit's skirt.

Birgit had the good sense not to reply.

"Of course she did," Arienh said calmly, and she raised her chin haughtily as if she had expected nothing else of her sister. "She has always been good at such things. It is a shame she forgets that."

"Well, it was a good shot," Egil agreed. "Do it again."

Again?

Birgit frowned. "Don't be silly. I told you this was stupid. I'm going back to my weaving."

Before Egil could stop her, she spun away and raced up the hill to the little stone cottage. "Well, I have had enough, too," Arienh added. "The rest of you may carry on, but I must get back to work." She set aside the bow and hurried after Birgit, Liam in tow.

As soon as Arienh shut the door behind them, Birgit threw her arms around her, trembling almost to sobbing.

"It's all right, Birgit." Arienh rocked Birgit gently in her arms. "It was a shock, though. A perfect shot, Birgit."

Liam squeezed his way in between them. "Aye, Mama, it was perfect."

"Was it really? If I lived to see the millennium, I could never do that again."

"And I will never let it happen again," Arienh promised.

Somehow, she wouldn't. She didn't know how, but for today, she simply wasn't going to let Birgit out of the house again.

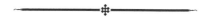

"A bit strange, those two," commented Olav.

Bjorn snorted. "All women are strange. And you're all fools."

Ronan had begun to wonder, himself. Arienh's consternation had been easy to understand, given how determined she was to fight off her attraction to her Viking enemy. But after that, nothing had made sense. He laughed at Egil's confusion but slapped his brother's back.

"Come on, Egil, let's get back to the lessons. You can chase your sweetheart later."

Egil's wicked blue eyes sparkled beneath his thickly fringed blond lashes. "You do it, Ronan. I have other things to do."

Ronan watched Egil saunter up the slope to the little stone cottage where the sisters lived.

Arienh answered the knock on her door, glaring at Egil. His wheat-colored beard was gone, freshly shaven away, and his splendid yellow hair was flowing entirely free, without the tiny plaits he usually wore beside his ears. He looked like an eager suitor. Fresh resentment bloomed in her.

"What are you doing here? You are not supposed to come here."

Egil gave Arienh a coolly triumphant smile as he wriggled past her. "This is a different matter. It is my duty."

"Duty? Your duty is to abide by the agreement and stay away from our houses."

"Nay, I must speak to Birgit. It is about Liam."

"And Liam is my responsibility," Birgit replied. "You may not concern yourself with him."

An eager grin laced across his face. "But I must. We have all agreed to do the things men must do. It is a man's duty to train boys in men's ways, and he has no father, so I must do it."

Arienh shared glances with her sister. Had he somehow detected the truth in spite of Birgit's accurate shot?

184

"Nay, you will not take him from me," Birgit replied, and she gently shoved Liam behind her.

"Take him from you? I only mean to teach him. Do you not share your skill at weaving with the village girls, Birgit?"

Arienh had not expected that argument. As she focused her anxious gaze on Birgit, she saw something else, something different, something turned upside down. She had expected her sister's pale eyes to radiate fury at the Northman's audacity. Instead, Birgit thoughtfully folded her arms and turned her gaze on her son.

"What do you mean to teach him, Viking?"

He had the gaze of an ardent suitor, soft, sweet, intense. Definitely, that was what it was. Arienh might not have seen such since childhood, but she knew it when she saw it.

"I do not know everything a man may know. But I am a hunter and a fisherman, and I have some carpentry skills. I can show him the ways of farmers, and I know some of smithing. But more than that, I would have to turn to my friends."

Birgit rested her hand within the nest of Liam's bright curls. "And of raiding?"

"I have no experience with those things."

"But you have admitted you are a warrior."

The man folded his hands before him. "As all men must be if they are to defend their own. On the Green Isle, I often fought in battles with the Celts against the Danes."

"I do not want my son to be a marauder."

"He will not learn it from me. But I will teach him to defend himself and those he loves."

Birgit's eyes roved longingly over her son, whose bright blue eyes beseeched, echoing both fear and excitement.

"Nay, Mama," he said, pulling on her kirtle.

Arienh and Birgit exchanged glances. There was nothing Liam wanted more than to go with the giant blond Northman, but Old Ferris's words still terrified the boy. They both knew Egil was far too kind and gentle to bring the boy any harm, but that was not their real fear.

"How do I know you will not hurt him?" Birgit asked, fixing her pale stare on the Viking.

"I will give you my oath, and a Northman may not break his oath. If he should come to harm by me or by my error, I must give to you my firstborn son."

"You have such a son?"

"Nay. So I pledge you my very future."

An odd, undecipherable light flickered in Birgit's eyes, then quickly tucked itself back down beneath her solemnity. "Let it be so, then."

Liam gasped. "Mama, I'm afraid."

"There is no need, Liam. A Northman may not break an oath made on his firstborn son. You will be safe with him."

Arienh's jaw dropped open, along with Liam's. Had they made a pact? Or had Birgit merely picked up the thread of Egil's plan, just as she had done with the archery earlier?

Egil gave Liam a very solemn nod. "Then I will come for you in the morning, Liam, so that we may join the other men in choosing wood for more bows. Now, if you wish, we will go to the river to fish."

"With my pole?"

To his credit, Egil did not laugh. "It is the best way."

Liam glanced back and forth between his mother and the fascinating Northman, then even briefly looked at his aunt. His natural exuberance could no longer be constrained by fear. "May I, Mama? Please?"

With great solemnity, Birgit nodded. "That is the agreement, Liam. You may go."

The boy dashed for his fishing pole, and his brassy golden locks bobbed as he hurried off behind Egil. Egil flashed a magnificent smile for Birgit, and a sly wink, as he left.

Fury boiled up in Arienh as if it began in her toes and rose all the way to her ears. "Birgit, how could you? After all my work?"

Birgit gave a shrug. "I was going to give in to him anyway. There was no point in wasting time with a fight."

"Birgit, don't you see the danger in letting the man get too close?"

"Aye, I do, Arienh. But it is clear Liam needs him. I will just have to be careful."

"It is not your loose tongue I am worried about. But Liam is just a little boy. You cannot expect him to guard his words."

Birgit turned away her head, looking off out the door as if she stared into some far distant time. "I know, but I must risk it, for Liam. It does not matter about me, Arienh. I do not think you can stop it."

"Then why don't you just run right out and tell them, if you are so intent on giving up?"

"You do not understand, do you?"

"Nay, I do not." Arienh stalked out of the cottage, and as she swung the door to bang it shut, the leather hinge broke. In her fury, she left it sagging in its frame.

Unraveling. Everything. Birgit was unraveling!

# CHAPTER FIFTEEN

———✦———

"IT IS NOT A VERY GOOD TIME OF YEAR FOR TROUT," SAID EGIL to the small boy who bounced along beside him. "The water is still too murky, and trout do not like it."

"Then where do they go if they do not like the water?"

Egil laughed. He had never thought of that. "Hmm. Well, they cannot leave the water. Maybe they look for a place where the water is not so muddy."

"But isn't all the water muddy?"

"Aye, but some of it is clearer. Maybe I am wrong. Maybe they are there all the time, but they just don't take bait when the water is muddy."

"Don't you know? I thought you knew all about fishing. How can you teach me if you don't know?"

Egil studied the child's suspicious gaze and suppressed a laugh. "Well, I can teach you what I know, but no one knows everything. And I do not. I'll show you the best ways to catch trout, but even the best ways don't always work. You will have to make lots of mistakes before you learn everything I know."

"I don't want to make mistakes." The boy frowned.

"But mistakes are important, Liam. It is true with hunting, too. You must first learn what makes noise before you can learn to be silent. With the trout, they have very good eyes, for they must see their food before they strike, so you must learn how not to be seen. But first you must learn what they see."

Liam studied the murky water from all angles, squinting beneath his frown. "Can they see when the water is muddy?"

"I don't know, but they do not feed when the water is too muddy, maybe because they cannot see their prey. You are a very smart boy, Liam. Maybe I will learn some things from you."

"Truly?"

Truly, Egil thought. He figured he would learn something very special from this boy.

Arienh stomped down the path toward the river, determined to do something, but with no idea what that would be. Anything besides remaining in the cottage where Birgit continued with her incessant weaving. Swish, swish. She couldn't stand it any longer.

Well, what? She couldn't tend the animals. That Viking, Tanni, had already herded them from the pens into the upper valley. He did that every day, leaving her no other task but to check them for murrain when they came down of a night. Soon, he would be keeping them in the high mountain valleys, and she would not have even that to do.

Everywhere, she saw signs of the Vikings' labor. The Vikings had plowed the fields and sown them, and green sprigs already broke the ground. Smoke billowed from the forge. Cottages all wore new thatch, even some that had been topless for years. She had refused Wynne's offer of geese, so she had no geese to tend. And there was no point in gathering clams, for the Vikings brought fresh game or meat every day. Her people had not eaten so well in years.

She certainly couldn't go back to the green where the Vikings exercised their tender ploys along with their archery.

There had to be something to do. It hadn't been so very long since she had complained to herself that there was too much to do. Now, the Vikings were taking over everything, and Arienh wasn't sure where she belonged anymore.

But what?

Ah, the stones. In all the tumult over the Vikings, she had not been into the hills for a long time. In fact, last night she had counted twenty-three scratches on her board. The moon had passed through three phases. She had not been up there since...

The Viking. The man had taken over her life.

That left only a little less than three more moon phases before Beltane. She had grown careless, all because she hadn't wanted to be reminded of what had happened within the stone circle.

With a flip of her skirts, Arienh spun in her tracks and headed toward the trail that led to the upper end of the valley and the stone circle. But she was making her pique obvious, and she hardly wanted the men to notice she had quarreled with her sister. She slowed to a more natural stride.

Ronan stopped to watch her pass, but she pretended not to notice. Perhaps he would tend to his other students.

Perhaps bats would fly in the bright of day.

The trail, widened by the passing of sheep to the high pasture, and recently well muddied from the necessity of bringing in the flock every night, wound familiarly along the river where Liam fished with big, blond Egil. Seeing them together only reminded her more painfully of Liam's terrible heritage. Liam looked enough like the man to be his own son.

"Aunt, look! I'm fishing!" Liam's excited voice carried from the riverbank to the trail.

"Aye, I see, Liam." She continued her trek.

"Come and watch me, Aunt. I'm going to catch a fish."

She gritted her teeth. She didn't want to watch. Did she not want the boy to be successful? Or perhaps she wanted the Viking to fail with the boy? Nay, her anger was senseless. Birgit was right, Liam needed the man.

"Not now, Liam. Catch a fish for me."

But what about Birgit? No matter that Birgit intentionally risked herself for Liam's sake, Birgit would fade away to nothing if the Viking took Liam away from her. Birgit had so little to live for. Only Liam.

What was she to do? There had to be something.

Nothing came to her. Arienh stalked up the valley, turning west into the hills and taking the back trail that led up into the circle, where she felt safe, embraced by all that was past, that stretched back beyond the time that men recalled.

In the dim recesses of her mind, she could still hear her great-grandfather telling her the stories of the stones, how once men governed their lives by the circles. There was so much more to it than she knew, for most of the lore of the stones was lost. All she knew how to do was move the small marker stones around the circle to keep time, so that everyone knew when crops were to be planted, or harvested, and when the feasts were to be held.

Sighing, Arienh picked up the marker stone and counted off the markers in the ancient way, "*Yan, tan, tether, ted...*," until she reached the twenty-fourth marker, and set the stone down.

Beltane was coming. The moon would pass through two phases and four nights. They would build great fires and drive the flocks between them. It was a time for men to dance in great circles.

Except that they had no men. Only Vikings.

Sudden tears formed in her eyes. Beyond their blurring, she pictured within the circle the great, crackling fires of Beltane, sending tongues of fire to the heavens. Past her skipped the dancers, grandfather with arms entwined with cousin, father, uncle, as they circled. Almost, she could hear the shouts and laughter, deep and mellow voices singing words no longer understood by living man. The tingling of smoke in her nostrils was only a memory. They were gone. Brother, father, cousin, uncle, all gone, because of Vikings.

Because of the kind of men who had invaded her village and taken over their lives. And they thought she would just forget?

She wiped at her eyes. She must not cry. If she ever started, she might never stop.

With a fierceness welling inside her, she spun around to fix her eyes and her fury on the circle's center, the place where she had lain with the Viking.

As if thinking made it so: there he stood, hands resting on stocky hips, above those massive, tree-trunk legs with their muscular calves and bulky thighs. Broad shoulders above broad, tapering chest, with the thick plates of muscles she knew so well. Beautiful, bright, anxious blue eyes in a face so handsome, she wanted to die for him.

How could she? He was going to destroy everyone, and worse, do it kindly. And traitor that she was, she wanted to tell him everything.

Anger and grief thickened in her throat. "Leave this place, Viking. It is mine."

"It is ours, Arienh. We shared it. Together."

"That was an accident. It will never happen again."

"It will. We belong together. I have known it from the beginning, and you know it, too."

Two quick strides, and he swept her into his arms. She shoved against him, her efforts puny against his strength.

"Nay, do not fight me so, Arienh."

She could see the aching, yearning, in his eyes, and it only made her angrier. "We had an agreement. Already you break it. You said you would leave us alone, yet even before the sun reaches noon, your brother violates it by coming to my house for Liam."

"That was different."

"It was but an excuse. And you have not even that. Leave me alone, Viking."

"I come because you are so unhappy. Tell me, love. Let me help you." His arms folded around her gently, yet gripped her as tightly as if he had lashed his body to hers.

Fury fought with anguish. Then despite her resolve, a flood of shaming tears poured forth. Her fists tightened, gripping the leather of the back of his jerkin, pulling him close while she desperately wished she was pushing him away.

"Tell me, love. Tell me what it is that hurts you so."

"You. It is you. You will destroy all of us."

"Nay, I swear to you, I will hurt no one. What is it you think I will do?"

She could not tell him, for telling him would only bring it about sooner. Arienh could only tuck her tear-stained eyes into his chest, ashamed that she cried when she should have been strong, that she was too weak even to push him away. This would be how he would destroy her, with his tenderness.

"Go away," she said, choking back a sob.

"Not just yet." She could feel his lips against her hair, feel him nosing back the strands of hair at her temples, making way for gentle, nibbling kisses. Soon he would have her down on the bare rock, making love to her as easily as he had the first time. Nay, even more easily, weakling and coward that she was. Selfish, weakling coward. It was Birgit who would pay the price for her selfish desires.

"I am so hungry for you. Do not say you are not as hungry for me. Give yourself to me. You are my wife, love."

Wife? That did it.

"I am not. Not." Her weakness springing into strength, she shoved hard, catching him by surprise.

He released her. A puzzled pain mingled in his eyes. "Arienh?"

"That's all you do. Take. And you think after all you've taken from us, we'll blithely encourage you to take more. Enough. Enough, I tell you."

"Arienh, you only fight yourself." Again he reached for her, but she lunged away, lifting her kirtle to run. He snagged her arm.

A curdled scream laced with rage rolled down the hill toward them. "Heathen! Barbarian! Let her go!"

Father Hewil.

Arienh spun around, astonished. Like a whirlwind, fierce as any Viking, the wiry priest rushed at them, swinging his staff.

Ronan whirled, drawing his sword.

"Nay!" Arienh screamed, and grabbed Ronan from behind at his waist. "He's a priest. You heathen, haven't you had enough of killing priests? Leave him alone!"

Ronan lowered the sword and pitched it aside. But the priest came on like a berserker, ranting, swinging with both hands, his staff slamming down on Ronan's shoulder.

"Ow!"

"Seize our women, will you, Viking? Take that!" The staff swung again.

Ronan blocked it with his arms, then twisted it from the priest's hands and threw Father Hewil to the ground.

"Stop it. He's a priest!"

"I know that, Arienh. That is the only reason he isn't dead. Kindly realize it was he who attacked me."

Arienh knelt beside the priest, who groaned as he rose, rubbing his elbow.

"My poor Arienh, has he hurt you?" asked Father Hewil.

"Hurt her? The only one with bruises here is me." Ronan glared at both of them.

Well, that was true, but it must have looked very odd to Father Hewil, who had surely thought her as good as dead.

"Nay, Father Hewil, I am unharmed. He has been here for a while, as they have taken over our village, but they have not hurt anyone."

Surprise lit the priest's face as he trained his suspicious gaze on Ronan.

With a snort of frustration, Ronan retrieved his sword and shoved it into its scabbard. Well, at least there was one thing Arienh didn't need to worry about. Today she wouldn't end up in the grass making love.

"Ah," said Father Hewil as he rose to his feet and dusted off his cassock. "It is the same everywhere. Northmen are everywhere these days, spreading their heathen ways. I suppose we should be grateful they are mostly of the kind to settle."

"I am not so sure." Arienh replied. "At least the others went away."

"Ahh." Ronan almost yelled his disgust. He pitched the priest's wooden staff to the ground. "It would be nice, Arienh, to be given a little credit for what we have done. You could at least admit you are no longer living on boiled bones."

"Well, that is true, Father Hewil. They have fed us. And we have made an agreement with them."

"You make agreements with heathens, now?" The priest's eyebrows rose high.

This would not look good to the priest. She shrugged. "Since we have no men, save Old Ferris, of course, but he cannot do anything. They will do all the things that men do in exchange for our cooking and mending and such."

"Hmm. An unusual solution."

"A reasonable one," said the Viking, glaring. "Save they could be friendlier."

The priest straightened his cassock and bent to retrieve his staff, then turned a superior scrutiny on Ronan. "I suppose you think they should be grateful that you have not enslaved them.

But you do not know these Celts, Viking. They do not give up their dignity so easily."

"So I have noticed." A sly look formed in the Viking's eyes. "But now that you are here, you might as well get busy."

The priest cocked his head to the side and frowned. "Busy?"

"We have all agreed to convert. It is the influence of these fine women."

"They think it will help them convert us into wives," Arienh replied with a sneer. She took hold of the good father's arm, although it was clear he had no need of assistance.

Father Hewil's eyebrows raised in interest as he looked back at the Viking. "Perhaps it would, as such good Christian women do not marry heathens."

"And rebuild the church," Ronan added. "Bigger, of course, with a tall bell tower."

"A bell, of course?"

"Of course."

Arienh watched with alarm as the priest's warm brown eyes took on a gleam of newborn enthusiasm for his potential convert. He was a greedy man at heart, greedy for converts and the glory of God. And the Viking had taken little more than the space of a moment to discern that and turn it to his advantage.

"And," Ronan added, "of course we must have a true Bible. I know of one that could be had on the Isle of Man, where it sadly languishes in the hands of unbelievers."

Arienh shifted her gaze back and forth between priest and Viking, watching in disgust as Father Hewil's excitement grew. Soon he would be bouncing about like Liam.

"A wonderfully illuminated work, embellished with gold fittings," Ronan continued. He was fishing, just as surely as his brother was, but he had an even better chance of landing his fish. "Perhaps it could be had before it is destroyed for its gold."

"You could obtain it? Restore it to the Church?"

"It would take much geld. But then, I have that."

The priest fairly danced with the news. "Then let us get down to the village. Come along, Arienh. I have had a long journey over the pass, and I am weary to my bones."

Arienh glared her fury at Ronan, but the Viking just let his beautiful, twinkling blue eyes laugh for him. Father Hewil picked up the hem of his garment and trod along between them, chatting amiably about his journeys, more as if he had just begun the journey than was ending it. Weary to the bones, indeed.

Even Father Hewil. Everyone was betraying her.

Arienh stood with Birgit and the other women, along with the wiry priest in his plain brown robes, beside the bank of the small stream at the Bride's Well, just below the falls.

She had never thought she'd see this day. Father Hewil, who had cursed and railed against Vikings as long as she could remember, had accepted a mass of converts who had no more sincerity than frogs. She had argued mightily with Father Hewil, hoping he would see the great risk the Vikings posed to Birgit, and tried to make him see how the Northmen manipulated him. But all the good father could see was the glory of God. Sacrifices must sometimes be made, he had said.

The Vikings had indeed pleased the priest, for they had poured their great enthusiasm into the building of the church, a large wattle and daub building with thatched roof, with a tower that might someday hold the bell Ronan had promised. Even Arienh had to be excited about that. She had never heard a real bell.

Their energetic efforts for the glory of God might well cease the moment the priest left and they had his blessing to take wives. If so, it wouldn't be long, for Father Hewil always left before the Beltane began.

Yet she believed Ronan would keep his word to the priest, for the sake of his mother. Arienh had not forgotten the awe in Wynne's face when he had announced he was sending the broad *knarr* to the Isle of Man to rescue the illuminated Bible. Today's event was as much for the sake of his mother as to please the priest.

Arienh decided to make one last assault on Father Hewil's rational mind. "Surely you do not accept them, Father. They are not sincere."

He folded his arms as he watched the string of men that marched up the trail to the pool. A slightly wicked smile traced across his pious face. The priest enjoyed this day far too much to please her. "Be they devious as foxes, I must accept them, Arienh."

"They do it merely for their own gain."

"Perhaps, but that is for God to judge. I would not have it on my conscience that a man turned to Christ and I refused him. And if they merely fool us, well, it is only the way of pagans, who petition their gods the way a child does his father, for their own gain. We are not so different, hmm?"

"Except that they do not believe. They will go on worshiping their pagan idols."

"Well, that is not so different, either, for you have your Beltane. But God is patient with their kind. They have not been raised the right way as we have, and as their children will be."

The priest's mention of children sent a chill up her spine. Perhaps Father Hewil didn't realize it, but the Vikings intended to have their children of the women of this village. On the other hand, she suspected he not only realized it but considered it one of those necessary little sacrifices.

Priest or no, she intended to prevent it. Somehow.

"He is right, Arienh," Birgit said quietly. "They do not know any better, and we have known the Christian way all our lives. Perhaps we criticize too soon."

Father Hewil nodded. "There are those who believe God is not patient with ignorance, but I think He must be, else no man would ever enter Heaven."

A long train of men, their fair hair gleaming in the sunshine, walked up the trail, singing their newly learned Christian hymn. At the end of the approaching procession, Egil and Ronan supported their frail father as he struggled up the long path and joined the congregation around the shallow pool of the Bride's Well. The old man chose a large grey boulder by the water's edge for his seat. Gunnar would be the last, so that he would not suffer the cold water so long. Only Gunnar wore the traditional white robe of the convert, for the entire village could not come up with enough white cloth for more. The lightest tan and grey had to substitute for all the others.

Father Hewil stepped into the water, taking up the back hem of his robe between his legs, bringing it forward to tuck into his waist cord as he went, even though he had no hope of keeping it dry. The collected women watched silently as each of the Vikings, beginning with Ronan and Egil, lined up for their turn to be dunked by the Christian priest. Their deep, warm voices resonated the hymn against the canyon walls.

Wynne wiped at her eyes. Father Hewil said his words over the only dark-haired Viking, then grasping Ronan by his hair and back, tossed him backward under the water. Somehow, it reminded Arienh less of a baptism and more of the rough water games she had watched the Vikings play.

Ronan floundered and emerged, blinking back water that streamed into his eyes. He slogged to the bank. Wynne rushed forth and hugged him, then hung a leather thong with a beaten bronze cross about his neck.

The love for his mother shone in Ronan's face as he bent to kiss Wynne. Then he turned to see what Arienh thought, and his smile faded. She realized she was frowning, but she could not encourage what she felt was no more than a maneuver for his own gain.

Egil took his turn, dunked heartily by the priest, who breathed a deep, satisfied breath of triumph as if he had just slain the Viking in battle. Next Olaf, then Tanni. Each Viking in turn, even the grumpy blacksmith with his wild, pale blue eyes, who stomped away alone, out of the water, all the way down the path. Arienh suspected the man had not voluntarily converted. Perhaps the priest was right and God would be patient with him. She certainly hoped so, for she didn't feel particularly merciful.

At last, Gunnar, helped into the water by his sons. Wynne grasped Arienh's hand, her tension pouring into the grip. The chill from the water could easily kill a man so weakened by illness. Gunnar trembled with the cold as he went under, then rose, aided by the priest, and groped his way along the slippery stream bottom to the shore. Only this one time did Arienh see a glimmer of compassion in the priest's brown eyes.

They wrapped Gunnar in blankets as soon as he stood on dry land. Wynne rushed up to place the cross around his neck, just as she had for each of her sons.

Arienh saw then the love, the concern, the fear in the sons who would willingly die for the crippled old man. And in the gaze between Gunnar and Wynne, she saw something more. Now she understood. This was a gift, a gift Gunnar gave to his beloved wife, perhaps his last.

"Now we will be together," the ailing man said, trembling despite the blankets, and his lips blue with cold. Arienh shared Wynne's fear for Gunnar's life.

Wynne's face streamed with tears as the procession returned, alongside the stream that fed into the larger river, through the wooded valley to the village, with Gunnar carried, sling-fashion, on the arms of his sons.

# CHAPTER SIXTEEN

"So, they are all Christians. Now what will you do, Arienh?" Birgit slipped the shuttle back and forth through her loom as calmly as if this day were like any other. Her green eyes followed Arienh's movements around the cottage.

"I don't suppose anyone else could consider doing anything," Arienh grumbled.

"Not likely. Certainly not Father Hewil. He salivates whenever he thinks of that beautiful book Ronan has sent for. No one else has the courage, and I can do nothing anyway."

"You might try making it a little harder for them to learn the truth. I do this for you, anyway, Birgit."

The shuttle swished back and forth, and Birgit betrayed no feeling in her face. That was what irritated Arienh the most. Birgit didn't even seem to care.

"And it is probably useless. I have decided to just make myself unlikable. Then Egil will not want me anyway, and he won't come around as much."

"How will that help?"

"He won't notice anything if he stops looking. And Liam has promised not to tell him."

"Liam is a little boy. Little boys let things slip."

"He will do his best. It is all I can ask. So far they haven't noticed, Arienh. I must be doing pretty well."

"Aye, you do, and the way you weave, they all admire it. They would not think you could do it without seeing. They all want to trade for your cloth."

A faraway wistfulness traced across Birgit's face. "Just think, I could stay home and weave to satisfy their demand, and they would never see me. It could work."

Arienh shook her head. She wished she, too, could stay inside and avoid the Vikings, but she couldn't control anything by staying inside.

"Who fixed the door?" she asked as she noticed the repaired leather hinge.

"Egil."

"Egil," Arienh grumbled as she passed through the doorframe.

"Leave it open. The warm air is good."

Arienh let her eyes adjust to the bright, crisp day. From the upper end of the valley, a troop of Viking men lugged timbers on a sledge pulled by oxen as they tromped along, their deep voices singing an unintelligible chant with a vibrant beat to match their steps. Little Liam trotted beside Egil, looking up at his idol and swinging his arms in exactly the same way.

The oxen dragged the sledge down the trail and halted in front of her cottage. Still belting out their work song, the men unloaded the timbers into a pile. Then all but three of the men turned the cumbersome sledge and oxen back up the trail.

"What is this?" Arienh asked.

"We're going to build Mama a weaving place, Aunt," shouted Liam. The boy hopped about, with his springy curls bouncing in the sunlight.

"A what?"

"A weaving gallery," Ronan said. "It is a shame for her to have to stay inside on these fine days, so we will build her a shelter against the house. If we make it big enough, then others can come and spin there, too."

It would be like a dream come true for Birgit. A chance to be with others while she worked, instead of cooped up in the cottage alone. But how could they do it? "But the loom. You cannot move it, and it would not do to leave it out in the night air."

"We'll build her a new loom, too, and move it from the outside frame to the inside one."

"But that is so much work. You'd better ask Birgit."

"We already did," Egil responded with a chuckle. Arienh was always amazed at how wicked his eyes looked when he laughed.

Arienh turned her frown on Birgit, who now stood in the doorway. "Stay inside, you say."

Birgit shrugged. "The light is better on the south side," Birgit told the men.

Indeed, Birgit had her own way of doing things. Arienh quietly spun her wool while she watched Ronan and Egil splitting timbers and trimming narrow boards with their adzes. Other men brought a second load of logs. And Birgit directed loudly, shrilly. Before Arienh's astonished eyes and ears, Birgit became a shrew.

Birgit knew everything about what they were doing, and none of what they were doing was right. Their cuts not straight enough, the adze marks too rough, the frame not square, none of it good enough.

Finally weary of the sniping, Ronan straightened his back, laid down his adze, and glared with narrowed eyes.

"Do something," he told his brother, "or I will."

"Mama, you aren't very nice," Liam said.

She saw Birgit wince. It was one thing to make the Vikings hate her, but quite another to look bad in Liam's eyes.

Egil laid aside his mallet. "Liam, take your mother for a walk."

Take her? Did he know? Nay, he was just giving Liam something to do and hoped Birgit would go along.

"Aye. Come along, Birgit, let's walk," Arienh said.

"Walk? And let them make a mess of things? They will get it all wrong."

"Take a walk, Birgit," Egil said firmly.

"Do not think you can tell me what to do."

Egil sighed and began gathering up his tools. "Very well, let us go, Brother. She can tell us when she wants us to come back and finish."

Ronan gave a grim nod and gathered up his tools.

"Wait. I—we'll take a walk," Birgit said.

They could not know how much it cost her to be cruel to them, but they certainly did know what it would mean to give up the gallery. Arienh hurried Birgit away from the cottage, close to the river.

"I didn't think you could keep it up," Arienh told her. "It is utterly contrary to your nature."

A wan smile crept onto Birgit's face. "It seemed like a good opportunity. I guess I ruined it."

"You almost ruined your weaving gallery."

"It has worked for you. You have persuaded Ronan you are a barb-tongued harpy, when I know you are not. But I am too selfish. I wanted it too badly. But at least he won't stop seeing Liam if I'm snippy. He'll just stay away from me."

"You hope."

Back up the slope, blond Egil shouldered a heavy beam, and dark-haired Ronan lifted its far end to fit it into the mortise he had carved for it. Even from here, their light skin glistened with dewy sweat on magnificently muscled torsos. How very beautiful they were.

"Go on back, Liam," Arienh told the boy, for he could hardly contain his eagerness to rejoin the men. He needed only those few words to speed back up the hill.

Arienh watched the Viking with the long yellow braids patiently teaching Liam to shave a peg.

She stayed with Birgit by the side of the clear-flowing river, and together they harvested early buds of horsetails. Soon the men grew tired, or perhaps they merely reached a point when they must quit. Egil and Liam wandered back to the river, fishing poles in hand.

How could something be so good for the boy, yet be so devastating for his mother?

Liam threw in his line and jerked it back.

"Not so fast, Liam," Egil said. "It needs to look like a bug, so it has to move like a bug."

"Aw. I'll never get it right."

"Yes, you will. Remember you have to do it wrong before you can do it right."

"Well, at least I'm doing it wrong, right?"

Egil chuckled. "Let's try it again, and just wait. Don't do anything until I tell you to."

Liam grunted and rolled the pole around in his hands.

"Throw in the line."

The line hit the water only a little way from the shore. Egil ignored the poor throw. The fly hung on the surface of the clear, slowly moving water. Just as it began to sink, Egil told Liam to pull. "Slowly," he said.

Liam jerked the line. But it was only a small jerk.

"Slowly. Just raise the tip of your pole, and it will come toward you."

The boy raised the pole, and the fly came out of the water.

"Aw." Liam turned away from the stream and flung the pole on the ground. "I'm tired of fishing, anyway."

"Well, it is not good to quit when you are just tired. Let's try again."

"I don't want to." The boy's mouth screwed up into a pout.

"This time I will help you hold the pole, and we will practice getting it just right."

"I don't want to. Can't we do something else?"

"Aye, but we must finish here, first. Bring the pole."

"Aw." But Liam picked up the pole, and carried it back to where Egil waited.

Egil stood behind Liam with his big hands wrapped around the small ones, gently guiding the movements of the pole as the bait fly swung into the water, then casually trailed away, to flick back again to the surface. In, out, up, down, carefully repeating the motions over and over.

"Look, do you see it?" Egil pointed to a pale flash that rippled beneath the flowing water.

"Is that a fish?"

"Trout. Just watch him. He thinks your fly is interesting. Let's just tease him awhile."

"I want to catch him."

"We will. Just tease him until he can't stand it anymore."

Egil flicked the line out of the water. The trout flew into the air after it and missed. It splashed back beneath the surface.

"Did you see that?" Liam jumped about with excitement.

"Shh. Yes. He's getting mad. Now he'll have to try harder. Watch."

Again Egil plied the line up, down, and the fly danced about the water. With a great rush, the trout leapt from the stream and nabbed the fly. Liam screeched. Egil calmly kept the pole in Liam's hands and set the hook. With a great flip, he swung the trout through the air and landed it beside the bank.

"We did it! We did it!" the child screeched.

The fish flopped on the bank. Egil dispatched it quickly. "It isn't fair to let them suffer," he said. "Now, are you ready to go do something else?"

"No, let's catch another."

Egil smiled. He could get to liking this.

He spent the remainder of the afternoon working Liam through the motions with the pole until he no longer felt resistance in the boy's arms. Then he let Liam try it alone.

"You are doing very well," he said finally, "but I think we've caught all the fish that are here today. Let's rest awhile."

Egil sat down on a snarled root at the base of the oak tree that overhung the stream, and Liam snuggled up to his side.

"I thought you wouldn't like me anymore," said the boy.

"You did? Why?"

"'Cause my Mama was mean to you. She isn't mean, really."

"I don't think she's mean, Liam. Maybe she was worried."

"She's just scared."

"Scared? Of what?"

Liam's eyes twinkled mysteriously. "I'm not supposed to tell."

"Ah." Egil leaned back against the great tree trunk and put his arm about the boy, who giggled about as he nestled in beneath Egil's arm. "Well, I hope she is not afraid of me. I would never hurt her or you. Remember, I promised. And I will always like you, Liam."

"Really? Even if I'm bad?"

"You will never be bad, Liam, even if you do bad things. But you must try not to."

"Sometimes I'm bad."

"Little boys misbehave sometimes, but that doesn't make them bad. I have known some very bad men, and so I know what bad really is."

"Like Vikings? My father was a Viking and he was bad."

"Who told you that?"

"Nobody. I just figured it out. He was very bad, and he hurt my mother and made me be born, and I shouldn't've."

Sometimes the boy tore his heart. He wished he could just will away the evil from the boy's life. He reached his arm around Liam and drew him to his side.

"My mother told me that all babies were meant to be born because God decided He wanted them here. I don't know much about God, but I'm glad He decided to give you to us. And your mother is, too."

"What if I'm like my father?"

"I think you are more like me. You can be like whom you want, Liam."

Liam looked as if he didn't know whether to believe him or not.

"Let's take the fish to your mother. She will be happy to have them."

"She won't. She'll be grumpy 'cause she wants you to think she doesn't like you."

"That's all right. We know better, don't we?"

He laughed at Liam's wicked little grin and shouldered the string of fish as they hiked up the stream bank toward the stone cottage. Ronan would be waiting for him, to help finish the weaving gallery.

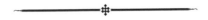

They returned to the weaving gallery the following day as soon as the morning chores were completed. Only Egil worked with Ronan, but now and then others brought materials Ronan had requested. He had watched Arienh leave the cottage early, and for the remainder of the day, she was gone.

Ronan paused in the middle of hammering in a peg that joined a cross brace to its post. "There goes another one."

Egil raised his head. "Who?"

"Olav. Off into the woods."

"So? You sent him after timber."

"That's an ash grove. I asked for oak. Besides, he's alone. Doesn't even have the sledge with him."

Egil gave out a chuckle. "Jealous, Brother?"

"Hel's frozen tits, of course I am. First Tanni, now Olav. And that little one with the blonde braids has been hanging around the forge all day."

"Elli?"

"Don't know what she finds so interesting in Bjorn."

"'Don't want nothing to do with women.'" Egil's voice took on clipped and sullen tones in a perfect imitation of the blacksmith, but merriment danced in his eyes.

Ronan responded with a weak smile. "The man's ugly as a boar. How does he manage to attract women?"

"Maybe he's the only one saying no. Could be a good sign. One woman won't hold out if the others defect."

"Or they could be up to something again."

"Maybe. Come on, Ronan, hit the peg. Let's get this done."

Ronan grumbled at Egil's lack of sympathy, but pounded in the peg. At the other angle, he fitted in another to hold the rafter firmly. "Arienh might. I've never met a woman as stubborn as she is. If I could just do something really special just for her, like this weaving gallery for Birgit. There must be something."

"Give her something."

"Like what? Gold, silk? Those things don't mean anything here."

"Herbs? Wine? She might like some good Frankish wine."

He shook his head. He had a better idea, but the problem would be persuading Egil to help him. "Something really wonderful."

"What, then?"

Ronan grinned broadly. "Down."

Egil's face sagged abruptly. "Oh, no. The last time you nearly got us killed."

"Why not? I was up on the cliff yesterday. The fledglings are nearly all gone."

"You've lost your wits. It would be safer to kill all Mother's geese."

"Ha. Now your wits have gone begging. Anything would be safer than that. Come on, let's finish this."

"So you can drag me off to dangle over some cliff?"

"This time, you can hold the rope, and I'll go over the edge." He didn't intend to give Egil the chance to argue further. Ronan stepped back away from the gallery and studied his work. "Birgit, come and see what you think."

Birgit's bright red hair flashed in the sunlight when she appeared at the door, her strange green eyes tracing the shape of the gallery's frame. She skimmed delicate fingers over the wood. He could almost see the imaginings in her mind of a bright, hot day and her loom in the shade, where she could see the green and the river, watch her child frolicking while she kept to her beloved task. Egil had guessed right when he had chosen this gift for her.

"Why are you doing this?" she asked.

Egil, sly devil that he was, recovered from his previous consternation. "So that when I am working, all I have to do is look up the hill to see you," he said.

The girl was impressed. Ronan could tell by the way she sheepishly lowered her gaze to the ground. Now if he could only get that much out of her sister.

# CHAPTER SEVENTEEN

"R ONAN, YOU'VE ADDLED YOUR BRAIN."

Ronan laughed as Egil stretched his neck out to peer over the edge of the high sea cliff as if getting even a finger's breadth closer would topple him over the edge. Fortunately, Ronan didn't have the same fears.

"It's very simple, Egil," he said. "The best nests are in groups, so we won't have to move the rope but a few times."

"What if it slips? Or breaks? Ronan, you can't be sure."

"That's why the second rope, just to appease your fears, brother. And you've tied it to a tree, and you have the ox team. Don't worry so much." Egil had insisted on so many precautions, Ronan was surprised he would be able to get over the edge at all.

Egil's wild eyes gave him no reassurance, but that was good, for that meant Egil would take no chances whatsoever. Ronan grinned as he lowered himself over the edge of the cliff on the tough walrus-hide rope, walking his feet down the vertical rock face as the roaring waves crashed against the rocks far below. He also would take no chances, for even though the tide was at its highest, a fall would mean almost certain death.

He had no intention of dying. He had more to gain by living now than he had ever had. He needed only to win Arienh's heart, and he had great hopes this gift would do it for him. What woman could resist a sack of down? It was more precious than gold.

The fledglings had flown from most of the nests, but he made a point of not disturbing those that had not yet tried their wings. There was plenty more down in the empty nests, where the chicks had left behind the remains of their first molt, the most highly prized feathers of all.

Reaching the first clump of nests, Ronan dodged irate parent birds as he swung out to empty crags and scooped handfuls of the soft feathers into his bag. Down was such an odd substance, one that seemed to compress into nothing and weighed nothing as it drifted into the sack. The sack would fill rapidly, yet he would lift it to his shoulder like a sack filled only with air. Convenient for hauling it back to the cliff top.

He picked there until the nests were clean.

Egil peered over the cliff, looking like he was going to be sick. Ronan laughed and sent the small sack aloft and waited until Egil lowered an empty one. Giving a light kick against the vertical cliff face, he swung away to another group of nests.

He imagined the delighted expression on Arienh's face when he presented her with his gift, something that few kings could afford. She would surely be persuaded of his love then.

Again, he filled a sack and tied its top tightly, marveling at its lightness. Nay, there was truly no gift like down. When winter came, they would snuggle beneath the blanket she would make of it, warm together. And over the years ahead, they would cuddle beneath it, and she would remember again and again how much he loved her.

Ronan went as far as his rope would reach by rappeling to each side and called for Egil to hoist him up.

"Isn't that enough?" Egil asked, studying the sacks he had tied onto one of the ponies they had brought.

"It would not make half a blanket," Ronan replied.

Egil groaned and lowered him over the cliff in another place with great reluctance, trying to swallow away his horror.

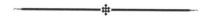

In the dark cottage, Arienh sorted and cleaned the horsetails she had gathered, preparing them for drying. It was one task the Vikings hadn't taken from her.

She had never been one to sit around and spin like other women. From the time her last brother had died, when she had been barely thirteen, Arienh had been shoved into the place of a boy, to help her father, and she had never resented it. The way things had evolved, Arienh had more and more assumed the role of a man, and strangely, the village had come to expect it of her.

Now the Vikings were here and had taken all that from her, and the only thing she had left was her herbs. Restlessness overwhelmed her. But outside, there were Vikings, and as soon as she set foot beyond the door, she knew she could count on Ronan's amorous assault.

"They're coming again," said Birgit in a resigned voice.

Arienh heard the sounds that Birgit's more attuned ears had picked up first.

Liam ran to the door, which stood ajar to let in the late-afternoon warmth. "Mama, they're carrying sacks. Lots of them."

Birgit stuck her shuttle through the warp threads. "Well, I suppose we should go find out what has him so excited."

Arienh set aside her bundles of horsetails, and they went to stand with Liam at the door. It was a strange sight. The two men each carried two large sacks over their shoulders, yet they moved as lightly as if they carried nothing at all. They were strong men, true, but almost any man would have lumbered up the hill under such a large load. They not only walked sprightly but grinned widely while doing it.

Without asking permission, Ronan swaggered in, followed by Egil, and the two men deposited their sacks on the packed earth floor. They stood aside.

"For you, Arienh," Ronan said, proudly presenting the sacks.

Puzzled, Arienh frowned. She did not mean to accept their gifts, but her curiosity demanded satisfaction. "What is it?"

"Look and see."

For a moment, Arienh eyed him with anticipation but saw he did not intend to tell her. Irritated, she reached for the closest bulging sack and with a flourish, roughly whipped off the binding cord of a sack, suddenly noticing it felt oddly like it contained nothing.

"Don't!" Ronan cried as the sack slipped from her hand and fell.

The bag toppled over with a whoosh and hit the floor. Little white puffs billowed out, flying into the air like giant snowflakes of a spring snowstorm.

Feathers. Feathers everywhere, floating, flying, landing in hair, on eyelids, clinging to nostrils. On the floor, in the soup. Drifting to singe and stink in the fire. On clothes and benches. And covering Ronan's dark hair.

Egil groaned. Birgit squealed.

"Mama, look. Feathers! It looks like it's snowing! Why did they bring feathers, Mama?" Liam danced about, snatching at feathers that whooshed away faster than he could move.

"I'm sure I don't know, Liam." Birgit pursed her lips tightly.

"Feathers?" Arienh asked. Was this a joke? They did like to joke. But what was funny about feathers all over the house?

"Not just feathers," said Ronan. Horror sagged from his face into disappointment. "Down."

"Down? All right, it's down. But why? Whatever am I going to do with this mess?"

"It's down," Ronan said again. "You're supposed to—never mind. I'll help you clean it up."

"Nay, I'll do it." Arienh reached for a likely looking handful of the stuff, only to have it scatter away as she touched it. She grabbed again but caught only a few feathers.

"Not that way. You have to move slowly," said Ronan. Frustration oozed in his voice.

She had really hurt him this time. But why? Why had he given her feathers? Why were they so important?

Birgit's face puckered up like a dried apple in her determination not to laugh. Arienh wished she'd leave.

"Ah, maybe we should go for a walk," Birgit suggested.

With a grumble, Arienh nodded and spit a feather from her lips as she watched Liam and Egil rush after Birgit out the door.

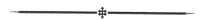

Egil almost had to jump out of the way before Birgit slammed the door shut and burst out laughing.

"That isn't nice, Birgit," he said, but he couldn't help grinning. He'd never seen solemn Birgit laugh before.

At that, her giggles rose to shrieks. "Tell me you didn't want to laugh. Tell me it isn't funny."

Egil chuckled, enchanted by mirth he had not seen before. "All right, it's funny."

"Why did he give her feathers, Egil?" asked Liam, looking up at him in confusion.

"It is down, Liam, not just feathers," the man answered. "And it is more precious than gold."

"It is?" Liam's eyes bulged. Greedy little rascal.

"Aye. It is very dangerous to collect it. It comes from the abandoned nests of seabirds on the high sea cliffs. A man must dangle on a rope over the edge to take it."

"But why?" Birgit asked. "What can she do with it?"

"Make a blanket."

"A blanket?" Birgit giggled wildly. "Oh, I do not believe it. How could anybody weave those little things? No one could spin them."

Egil laughed again. It was such fun to see her so merry. Even more fun to see her confusion. "Nay, they are not woven. But you have feather pillows. I have seen them."

Birgit frowned as her puzzlement deepened. "Aye, but—"

"Ah, I see you really do not know what to do with it. Then I suppose your sister does not, either. It is much used in the north and makes the warmest blankets, so I think Ronan did not realize you would not know. It is done much the same way as the pillows, with the down in between two pieces of cloth."

That didn't seem to help much, and he suddenly realized she was imagining a giant pillow. "But it is tied together in many places so that it lies flat instead of round, but puffy. It is said the king of the Franks has his bed filled with down, and it is softer than floating on water."

"And how would you know about the Frankish king's bed?"

"When we were younger, Ronan decided we were going to get rich by collecting down and selling it to kings."

"But you didn't?"

"Nay, the one time hanging over a cliff was enough to keep me from ever going back."

"Were you scared?" Liam asked.

*Never so terrified in my life.* "Aye. Just looking down at the waves crashing on the rocks makes me sick. It is not a way I would choose to die."

"But you went with him this time, didn't you?" Birgit said, and a warm smile lit her face. "If it is so dangerous, why did he do it?"

"Well, he loves her. And a man sometimes does foolish things to win a girl's love."

Birgit's beautiful pale eyes studied his with a curious wonder. "And I suppose a man sometimes does foolish things for his brother."

"Sometimes. Look, Liam, do you see my mother and father down by their cottage? Will you run and tell my mother we need her help?"

"Why?" asked the boy.

"Because she knows what to do with the down."

With a gleeful shriek, the boy sped down the path, his brassy curls bobbing. His hair was much like his mother's with its tight, springy curls but was much lighter than her fiery red hair. He loved her hair. Never had it looked so wonderful as it did now, with a brilliant sun shining through it and hundreds of colors dancing in the strands. He thought of lacing his fingers through it and drawing her into a kiss.

But he only thought of it. He did not even reach out to touch her hand, lest he frighten her. Though he had his brother's aggressive impulses, Birgit was not like her sister and could not be taken in such a way.

Now, she laughed so naturally, trustingly, beside him as they walked, as if suddenly something inside her had broken loose and begun to sparkle. Time. She still needed time. He would give her all she needed.

"What kind of cloth?" she asked.

"What kind? I don't know. Just cloth."

"Nay, just cloth will not do. The wool is too springy. It gives too much. The feathers could poke right through it."

"They could?"

"It would have to be a tight, firm weave. Very tight. Linen, maybe, or nettle."

"Mm. I had not thought of that."

Her pale eyes held an odd, scheming look. He had seen it once before when he had watched her decide to let Liam go with him to fish.

"Nay," Birgit said, her eyes still focused intently on him. "Men do not often think of such things. But we do not have anything that will do."

"There is silk. And the Moors have something they call cotton."

"Cotton? What is that?"

He shrugged. "I've never seen it. But it is not heavy, and they say it is nice when the weather is very warm. It is even more costly than silk."

"Well, we don't have that either. And we have no flax crop. That leaves nettle. It usually must be retted, but if we could find last year's stands, it may have been retted naturally by the weather. My mother used to gather it this time of year."

"Then, could you weave it?"

"I don't think so. My loom is too coarse for the fine weave we would need. Mother had a very fine loom, once."

He stopped her, taking her arm in his hand. "But Ronan wants to build you a new loom for the weaving gallery. He could build it if you tell him what you want. He is a very good carpenter. He built his longship."

Her pale green eyes danced with excitement. "He could? Oh, but I don't know where to find the nettles. I do not get out much because I am always weaving, so I do not know those things."

"But someone must. I will tell everyone, and we can look for the nettles as we do other things. I was going to take Liam very early tomorrow to show him how to hunt water birds. We could look then."

Birgit bounced about and grabbed his arms. "Oh, would you? It would be wonderful. Then for once I could do something for her instead of—she is always doing things for me, I mean. Oh, please, would you?"

Egil felt his heart wrench in his chest. He had never seen her like this, jumping excitedly about, just like Liam did. He had never seen her excited about anything. And maybe this would be the gift he could give her that melted the ice away from her soul. "Of course."

"You promise?"

"I promise." And he laughed and gave her a quick hug.

A pink flush colored her face, and Birgit regained her composure. He was sorry to see it end. But it was a start.

Egil quickly explained to Wynne as she arrived with Gunnar and Liam, and they hurried back to the cottage.

In silence, they picked feathers from the dirt floor, the oak table, even from the porridge that simmered over the hearth fire. It seemed they had been picking up feathers for hours.

The scrambling sound at the door caused Arienh to look up from her misery. Wynne stepped into the cottage, her mouth agape at the remaining mess. The older woman wrinkled her nose, and Arienh realized she had become accustomed to the acrid smell of burnt feathers that still permeated the cottage air.

Behind Wynne trooped Egil, Liam, Birgit, and Gunnar. Without a word, they joined in plucking feathers from incongruous places and depositing them in the sack.

"I see you have been cliff-hanging, Ronan," said his mother as she plucked a feather out of her son's hair. "And rather successfully. But it appears you did not think to clear the way before you."

"It was my fault," he admitted sadly. "I thought everyone knew about down."

"Everyone in the north. But then, the winter nights are so bitterly cold there that it is a necessity. Here, it is only for the very wealthy. No one else knows much about it."

"I'm sure it is a wonderful gift," Arienh said remorsefully, yet not even knowing for what it was she felt regret. "But truthfully, I do not know quite what to do with it."

"I would say you do not know what to do with it at all," replied Ronan.

She nodded, feeling very sheepish.

Wynne scowled at him. "That is not her fault. It is yours because you did not tell her. I have told all of you, you cannot assume that everyone here thinks the same or knows the same things that you do. This is a different place, and if you would live in it, you must take the time to learn about it."

"It is not his fault," Arienh insisted. "It was a nice thing to do. I'm sure."

"Of course. Now, let us talk about making a down blanket."

Arienh eagerly listened as Wynne tied back her hair in a Norse knot and began her explanation. Only lone bits of fluff still lodged in odd places, but Arienh was determined to retrieve every one. She tried to avoid Ronan's glances and the terrible disappointment on his face. And her cheeks burned with humiliation when she learned from Egil the extent to which Ronan had gone to provide her with his gift.

"Well, now I understand how it's done." Arienh said. "I had some very strange ideas at first."

Birgit laughed. "So did I. I tried to picture weaving those little tiny feathers. I am going to weave the cloth," she announced proudly. "It will be nettle. And Ronan will build me my loom, for he has already promised."

"Of course I will," said Ronan. "You have only to tell me what you want."

"Nettle?" Arienh asked. "But we have none."

"Egil is going to find what has rotted over the winter. Mother used to do that, and I remember how."

"But it will take so much."

Egil smiled. "Everyone will look. We will find it, do not worry."

"It will be fun, Arienh. And just think of the fine cloth I will be able to make."

Arienh saw something different in the dancing light-green eyes where nothing but sadness had been for so long. Birgit was laughing again. If only it could be that way forever. But if only for now, it was a gift more precious than any he could have ever given her. And he did not even know he had given it.

"It is truly a wonderful gift, Ronan," she said. "I am sorry I ruined it for you."

Slowly a smile spread from the small crinkling at the corners of his mouth. She did not resist him when he wrapped his arms around her, giving her an affectionate hug.

"Nay, you did not ruin it. I'm glad you like it." Then he snuggled his lips in close to her ear. "Wife," he whispered, and took a nibble at her earlobe.

She didn't resist that either. But she felt a crimson blush rise in her cheeks when she saw the raised eyebrows on everyone but Liam.

And Liam just grinned.

"Smells like burnt feathers," said Mildread, her nostrils flaring.

Birgit giggled. Arienh narrowed her eyes at her sister, hoping her frown would be enough to earn her silence. But Elli and Selma giggled too. So then, the story was out.

Arienh stirred the fire in her hearth, seeking a bit more warmth for the gathered women on this chilly night. And it was better than giving credence to their jokes.

The Vikings would be drinking their mead and telling their wild tales. The children were all safely out of earshot and bedded down in Selma's cottage, with her older cousin watching them. Old Ferris was no problem since he probably wouldn't be coming back, and Arienh had seen that Father Hewil was kept busy by sending him off to try to cajole Ferris out of his pout. This was women's business, after all.

Anticipation hung in the air as heavy as smoke. Arienh rose to her feet. "Well, what did you learn, Mildread?"

"That they are not so big after all."

"You didn't."

Mildread laughed. "Nay, I tease you, Arienh. I have not tried Olav out, even though I think he would fit just fine. But that could be more because he doesn't trust me. I am having to work on that."

"But did you ask him about the other things?"

"Aye. It is true, they do foster fatherless boys, if they have good possibilities. He says sometimes a man feels he has more claim on a nephew than the mother does. He told me that story you already know about Ronan."

Silence hung thickly in the small cottage.

"And he thinks Egil plans to take Liam, eventually."

"But they don't always do it," Birgit said hopefully.

"Well, I suppose not. Apparently a man must be willing. They take it very seriously. Like Selma took her cousins."

"But what about Grandfather and Birgit?" Elli asked, her brow furrowed like the newly plowed fields. "Are they safe?"

"Well, I could not tell, exactly. He said he knows it is done—this sending of people off into the wilderness to die. I didn't understand exactly, but it sounded like it was something an old man might choose to do when he felt his time had come. But I have been thinking, Elli. We have hidden the truth about Birgit, but we cannot hide Old Ferris's age. Yet they have not done anything to him."

"But maybe it is only something they do when times are hard," Arienh countered, though that was not enough surety for her.

"Aye," said Elli. "Maybe they will not do anything until they are sure they have us where they want us. Then it will be too late for us to object. I do not think they will be patient with us much longer, anyway."

"We have to know," Selma said in a very quiet voice.

Arienh nodded. Selma also loved Old Ferris, for all his bilious nature, for he was her father's uncle and had taken her in when she was very young and had lost her parents, then her two little cousins as well, until Selma had grown old enough to provide for them herself. And Selma was cousin to Arienh and Birgit on her mother's side. Young as she was, Selma had suffered as much as any of them from the raiders. Yet she had the softest heart.

"Your Olav is much too serious, Mildread," Selma proclaimed. "I do not trust him."

"Nay, it is because he is so serious that I think he may be trusted," Mildread countered. "He may not believe as we do, but he is very strong in what he does believe. I think he is an honest man. And a hard worker."

"Swings an ax well," Selma agreed with a grin, batting her thick lashes. "With his jerkin off, too, Mildread?"

"That has nothing to do with it. Even if he does have a fine back."

A chuckle rippled through the clutch of women.

"Mildread would like a hard worker," said one.

"She deserves one, for a change," said another.

Mildread shook her head. "But that is not the point. It is his honesty that counts here."

"Nay, what we need is more information to compare," Selma said, flouncing her long curls. "I will see what I can learn from

Tanni. He is very friendly, not so suspicious or serious. And not quite so big."

Arienh didn't like the way the discussion was going. She had never thought Mildread would show interest in the Vikings. Certainly not Selma. Yet she could see why. These big men were purely masculine and as attractive as any Celt she had ever seen. And no man could work harder than they. But surely they all remembered the pain the Vikings had brought to them and would not look at their kind with anything but disdain.

Of course. The way she looked at Ronan. Lascivious disdain, that was it.

"Selma, be careful," Arienh said, frowning. "You are not as old as the rest of us, and you could be easily misled. That Tanni is a charming one."

"Aye, he is, isn't he?" Selma's eyes sparkled.

An excited cooing sound spread through the women.

"You wouldn't be thinking of trying him out?"

"Well, someone is going to have to do it. That's the other thing we have to know: if they're too big for us. And we have already seen they are pretty big."

To Arienh's consternation, no one seemed to be disagreeing.

"Tanni is a smaller man than most of the others," Elli said.

"So, what kind of test would that be?" Mildread asked.

"He isn't small in that way," Selma protested. "I looked."

Mildread folded her arms, then stroked a finger across her chin, the way a man would do. "Well, it should not be a virgin who tries them. A virgin might not know the difference between that and the usual pain of the first time. It would not be a good test."

Arienh struggled to keep her calm and her silence. She could tell them. And then she could end up married.

Of course. That was it.

"You don't realize the risk," she said. "If you lie with them, they could claim you as wives. You would be stuck. And that would only encourage the others. And the closer you let them get, the more likely Birgit will be exposed."

"Well, that is true," said Mildread. "We will have to be very careful. After all, we don't want to marry them."

So Mildread had already made up her mind. And probably Selma had, too. Arienh doubted she could change that. But she could use them to bolster the claim she had made to Ronan. Ah, good idea. "You could tell them it isn't a marriage without a public vow at the church steps. It isn't that different from the way we did things before the church burned."

"True," Mildread agreed. "But not everybody did that."

"Well, we don't have to tell them that." Now, that would take the sting out of Ronan's threat.

But Mildread shook her head again. "No, Arienh, it simply isn't true. It would be a marriage, and we all know it. Unless one of the two was already married or if it was a rape. And it would not be rape. Or, if we made it clear before the act that we were not consenting to marriage."

"Aye, that's true, Arienh," Birgit agreed. "The act itself has always been considered consummation of marriage. Even Father Hewil would agree to that, Vikings or not."

"I think the entire thing is too risky. But if you are so determined, you'd best make it clear or be prepared to be married to one of them." She felt her jaw tighten. It was a good thing she hadn't told them.

But what was going to prevent Ronan from telling? Why hadn't he already?

# CHAPTER EIGHTEEN

———————❖———————

THE LAST OF THE THATCH WAS BEING TIED ONTO THE SLANTING
roof of the weaving gallery. Arienh glanced sideways at Ronan as
he surveyed his accomplishment. It was sturdy and square. He
truly was the fine carpenter Egil had claimed.

Birgit's new loom stood waiting for its stringers and heddles,
a marvel of fine, delicately drilled holes and smoothly polished
wood. The pile of retted nettles grew daily, waiting to be stripped,
spun, and woven. Birgit's impatience was barely controlled and
growing difficult for others to bear. Yet for Arienh it was as wonderful as Liam's ill-contained energy. Birgit was suddenly young,
like she had been so long ago.

And the way she secretly looked at Egil, thinking Arienh did
not see. Arienh smiled and said nothing, wishing Birgit could
have a love that could grow and become wonderful.

Was there some way Egil could be persuaded to accept Birgit
as his bride, even knowing how helpless she would become?
Arienh tried to imagine Birgit with a new babe. She knew the
love the child would receive. But would she be able to care for
an infant? Possibly now, but not if things got any worse. When
Liam was born, they had not realized that Birgit's sight was
already fading. But by the time the boy was toddling, his mother
had to keep him very close, lest she not be able to see him.

Even as a very young child, Liam had to learn to accommodate his mother. Sometimes he rebelled. He was far too curious for his own good, so the risk of trouble always lurked. That was why Arienh took him with her whenever she could and why Egil was so good for the boy.

Would Birgit's sight continue to fade, or had it gotten as bad as it would get? Who could tell? How could a blind woman be a wife? Life was too hard as it was.

This morning, Arienh had watched Liam go off with Egil, with his eyes focused in adoration on the big Viking. And there was no doubt of Egil's delight in the boy. How old did a Viking child have to be before he was taken from his mother to be fostered?

Arienh felt a prickling sensation on her neck and knew its reason even as she turned. Ronan. While she had not been looking, he had come up behind her, standing close enough to touch. She felt the heat of his body close, too close. His smoldering gaze roamed over her, seemed to speak in silence of the ways he wanted to touch her. Or perhaps that was only what she wished him to be thinking, the way she wished to be touched.

Did it matter, since she could not let it happen? If he called her wife in anything more than a whisper in her ear, he would gain the power to decide what happened to Birgit.

She could not have him.

"Come and see." His sensual voice and breath tingled against her cheek.

She nodded, afraid to speak aloud, lest any word she uttered betray her. With Birgit, she stepped out from beneath the gallery into the sunshine, back far enough to survey it thoroughly.

A scream lashed through the air, from the stream.

Liam!

"Liam!" screeched Birgit. She dropped her spindle and ran.

Arienh's heart lurched as she bolted after Birgit, Ronan beside her. She was almost as afraid for Birgit as she was for the screaming child, but at least Birgit had memorized every bit of the valley.

From the clutch of birches along the bank, Egil burst forth at a run, carrying the writhing child.

"Mama!"

"Give him to me," Birgit screamed, her arms begging for her child.

Egil stopped suddenly, his blue eyes wild with fear.

"A snake, Mama!" Liam cried. "A snake bit me!" Amidst his sobs, the boy's arms reached out.

Birgit lifted the boy's leg. The lump was already growing, reddening. Horror spread over her face.

"Adder bite," said Arienh. She swallowed down the bitter gorge of terror, forcing herself to keep her head. "Take him to the sunlight so I can see it."

"Give him to me," Birgit demanded.

But Egil sped up the slope to the open green. Birgit ran behind him, screaming and grabbing at him.

"Nay, Birgit, let him," Ronan insisted. "He is faster."

Birgit, infused with the strength of a frenzied mother, shoved Ronan away and dashed desperately after Egil. Arienh grabbed Birgit's arm as she stumbled against a rock, steadied her as they ran.

"Hurry." As if her sister somehow needed urging.

Liam's screams grew louder, higher. His legs and body thrashed. Reaching the knoll where the sun was bright, Egil sat down with the boy, his arms wrapped snugly around him.

"You've got to hold him still," Arienh said, trying to get a good look at the wound. "Liam, you must hold still for me."

"It hurts, Aunt!"

"Aye, I know. And it will hurt for a while. But you must try to bear it so that I can help it. Will you try for me?"

Through his sobs and gasps, Liam struggled to nod. He clung first to his mother, then to Egil, then again his mother, his little body trembling.

Arienh ripped off her cord sash, wrapped it tightly several times around Liam's leg just below his knee, then tied it.

Birgit shoved at Egil, clawing her way to her child. "Get out of my way."

"Birgit, let me—"

"Get out of my way. Get away from my son."

Egil shook his head in confusion. "He needs—"

Terror and fury filled Birgit's eyes. "He needs his mother. He needs someone who can watch over him, not a careless Viking who lets a snake bite him. Get away from my son. I don't want you ever near him again."

Stunned, Arienh watched Egil's mouth drop open. His blue eyes grew wide as he swallowed a lump of horror. He sagged away, letting Birgit snatch the boy from his arms. Egil rose, turned, and walked slowly away, as if he had lost his world.

Liam screamed. "Egil! I want Egil!"

"Hush, Liam, you must be still," Arienh begged. The boy's leg swung wildly, slipping from her grasp. She lunged and caught his leg in a downward swing. His foot broke free and kicked her jaw, knocking her backward.

The wiry child bucked out of Birgit's grip, but she threw her arms back around him, struggling to contain the child.

"Mama, it hurts. I want Egil. He hates me, Mama."

"No, Liam, no. You must hold still." Birgit clamped a tighter grip around the boy.

Liam's hysteria rose like a whirlwind, a melee between his fear and pain. "He hates me, Mama. I was bad. I saw the snake, and I didn't tell him. Mama!"

He could die from his own frantic exertions. The more the boy fought the pain, the more the poison would spread.

Somehow, Arienh knew, she had to stop his writhing. She threw her weight over Liam's legs, pinning him to the ground, at once wrapping her arms tightly around his legs in the strongest grip she could manage.

The screams escalated as the child wriggled beneath her.

"Nay, Liam, stop it," she shouted. "I will not let you go until you stop thrashing."

"It hurts!"

"And so it will." Fiercely, she fought against him. "I will not lose you, Liam. I will not. And you will do as I say so I can save you. Do you hear me?"

"I can't, Aunt!"

"You can. Hold still."

"Let me hold him," Ronan begged, reaching for Liam.

Fiercely, Birgit swung Liam away from the Viking. "Nay. I want none of your kind to touch him."

She was losing control. Liam's foot pulled out of her arms. She grabbed his ankle, pinning it down, and the other leg swung free. He could die.

*Please, God. Oh, please. Not Liam. I could not bear to lose him.* Her heart pounding wildly, Arienh lunged for Birgit's arm and jerked, hard, as she again rolled her body over the child. "And you'll have him die for it, Birgit?" Arienh yelled back. "For what? Pride?"

"He promised me," Birgit cried in terror. "He said he'd keep him safe, and he didn't even look out for adders. They lie to us, Arienh."

"Nay, Birgit," said Ronan. "Egil has never seen a snake." His strong hands gripped Liam's thin arms, despite Birgit's demand.

"That's stupid. Everyone knows about snakes."

"There are no snakes on the Green Isle, and Egil has never been anywhere else. He would not know to look out for them."

Had not Vikings been everywhere? But no. Egil had said the first day they met he had not been trading with his brother. Arienh glanced at Birgit.

Stunned horror spread over Birgit's tear-stained face. Her hand went to her mouth. "None?" She squinted off in the direction Egil had gone. Giant Egil leaned in despair against the huge lone oak. Arienh could see his chest heaving in sobs.

"I want Egil, Mama." Full of terror, the stricken child gasped and jerked beneath Arienh's weight.

Tears flooded down Birgit's cheeks as she gulped, struggling for composure and clinging to her sobbing child.

"It hurts, Mama. I want Egil."

"I'll get him, Son. You must hold still. Promise me."

Ronan jumped up. "You stay. I'll go. I promise you, Liam. I'll bring him."

"Mama, I want Egil."

"He's coming, love." The nod she gave was for Ronan. "But you must hold still."

Liam nodded jerkily, amid moans and whimpers. And Birgit rocked her son mournfully. Arienh took a deep breath as the boy's hysterical cries lessened and flailing eased. He was exhausting his strength. But so was she.

Ronan sped off, shouting. With a quick glance, she saw him grab Egil's arm and nearly tug his huge brother toward the green. Egil took up the pace, both men tearing down the hill.

Egil knelt beside Birgit. "Birgit, I didn't mean him harm, truly not." Tears streamed from his eyes. His stark terror mirrored Birgit's.

Birgit choked on her sobs. "Nay, forgive me. I was wrong, I did not think. I know you would not hurt him. Please, Egil, he needs you. We cannot calm him."

Silently, Egil sat cross-legged on the grass. Arienh released her grip as Egil cradled the boy in his arms.

"I'm sorry I was bad," cried Liam, and he snuggled into the big man's chest.

"You weren't bad, Liam." Huge hands smoothed over the little boy's golden curls and wiped at his tears.

"I didn't tell you about the snake, and it bit me. Please don't be mad at me."

"You should have told me, and you should have stayed away from the snake. But you aren't bad, and I don't hate you. You are as precious to me as my own son." Egil's cheek rested like a caress against Liam's bright curls.

"It hurts," cried the boy.

"I have to cut his leg, Egil," said Arienh. "It will help."

"Do you want me to do it?"

"Just hold him still. Then I have to try to squeeze out the poison."

Egil nodded and with gentle words soothed the boy. Ronan held Liam's legs in his firm grip, while Birgit stroked a wet rag over Liam's brow. The boy screamed at the sight of the knife, yet did not seem to feel the strokes of the knife as she cut small slits over each fang mark.

Kneeling, Arienh tied cords above and below the dark lump, then pushed and squeezed against it, forcing out blood and venom, until she could get no more. The swelling did not seem much smaller. She needed something else to draw out the poison.

"The snake, Egil. Did you kill it?"

"Aye. Why?"

"I need the head. Mother told me the head tied to the wound will draw the poison back to itself."

Liam screamed, his blue eyes wide with terror. "Nay, Aunt!"

"It is dead, Liam. It cannot hurt you anymore. We must get the poison out."

"Nay. Please, Aunt!"

One of the men was already running toward the stream after the dead adder. But if Liam was so terrified of it, would it not do more harm than good? Her mother had always said a snakebite victim must be kept calm, for their fear helped spread the poison.

There must be another way.

"We will use mud," she decided. "It's good for drawing out poison, too. And there are some herbs. Most of them I do not have. Bugloss, maybe. The leaves of the ash tree may help, and I have the lettuce, and that will help to calm him. Cleavers in wine would help to protect his heart."

"Cleavers," Mildread repeated as she knelt beside Arienh. "I found some stuck on my kirtle yesterday. I think they are by the woods."

Behind Mildread, Olav jumped up. "Aye, get them, Mildread, and I'll fetch the wine."

"I will go for the ash leaves," Selma offered. Tanni hurried off with her.

As Egil carried Liam to the cottage, some went to the stream for mud, others to fetch the herbs Arienh specified. Egil stretched Liam out on Birgit's bed, but Liam cried as Egil tried to stand back. So Egil sat on the bed, his back propped against the wall, and held Liam against his chest, his deep voice crooning an alien lullaby.

Birgit walked toward the door after the wine brought by Olav, and Liam screamed for her return. Arienh took the wine to mix, letting Birgit crawl onto the narrow bed and wrap her arms around her son.

Twice, Arienh tried to bind the snake's head to the wound, for it was said to be the best relief for bites, but Liam screamed and kicked violently. So she had no choice. Instead, she treated his wound with compresses of mud and herbs, and he drank the wine laced with the cleavers and young ash leaves.

Liam's cries slowly diminished to whimpers, and Arienh gave him the syrup of lettuce to make him doze. He slept fretfully, crying in his sleep and waking himself up. As the mud dried, Arienh scraped it off and applied a fresh coat, covering his leg all the way up his thigh.

Each time the door opened, Arienh looked up. Wynne brought a broth made from her chickens, and Mildread brought a porridge for those who tended him, and bread fresh from the village oven the Vikings had rebuilt. Father Hewil slipped in and spoke a prayer over the child, then quietly slipped out again. Ronan hovered close, bringing to her what she demanded. He pressed against her, giving her a place to rest her back, and massaged her aching shoulders.

Outside, villagers and Vikings kept watch, going to their duties when they must, returning whenever they could. Egil and Birgit together held the child, who cried when either left.

Day merged with twilight, then into night. Arienh changed the mud compresses again and again. The swelling grew so large that she reluctantly untied the cord sash and moved it higher up his leg, lest the leg itself die.

The swelling stopped. Beneath the packs of mud, a huge knot of darkest purple bulged from Liam's leg. Skin sloughed off, and Arienh rubbed with a cloth to clear it away. She thought of maggots, to eat away the dead skin, but she hated the idea. Only if she must would she run the risk of the pus they sometimes caused.

The child slept, wrapped in Egil's arms as the big man leaned against the wall. His deep voice sang on and on, so soft it caressed like a feather.

Exhaustion enveloped Arienh and threatened to swallow her. When at last she and Ronan stepped outside the cottage for the first time in two days, she drew the clean, chilly air into her lungs as if she had never tasted its freshness before. She answered everyone's questions and sent them home.

Then she and Ronan walked, drinking in the freshness of the night, the clean aroma of a recent rain. Even the darkness seemed to have a smell of its own. Silence hung between them as she racked her tired brain for anything else that could be done.

"Will he live?" Ronan asked for the first time.

"I think so." She could think of nothing else to say. "I cannot tell. I have never known an adult to die of such a bite, but some children live, some die. Or he could lose his leg. Only God knows if we have done enough or done it in time."

"You are so weary. Could you not rest awhile?" His voice was soothing, and his face mirrored his concern.

"Nay."

"I could do what you are doing and wake you if you are needed."

A frisson of terror ripped through her heart, but she shoved it aside. He meant well, but he did not understand. She could not let go, even for a moment, until she was certain Liam was safe. It was like giving up, and giving up was unthinkable. "Nay, there would be no point. I could not sleep anyway."

Silence returned as they walked on. The air from a wet day had chilled with the clear night, but a stiffening breeze foretold another storm blowing in. She needed the freshness of the wind to invigorate her and the quietness of his company to calm her.

When they returned to the cottage, the mud had dried again and needed once more to be replaced. Arienh gave Liam another dose of the lettuce following the broth, adding bugloss, cleavers, and ash leaves. And they waited.

Waited.

Night became morning, day faded to evening. Liam worsened, improved, worsened again.

And everyone waited.

The worst of the poison stayed in Liam's leg, and the swelling began to shrink. Beneath the mud, the skin that had turned hideously dark, almost black, finally began to fade to brown. Dead skin crumbled away, leaving an ugly, gaping hole with bright red flesh beneath it.

By the middle of the third night, Liam slept quietly. Egil slipped out for a little while for the first time, then Birgit. Each returned to take their vigil on the bed with the boy. After a while, they took turns eating, then curled back on the bed, with the boy between them, and slept. Egil's long arm stretched over Liam, to rest atop Birgit's hand.

"Now you will sleep, too," Ronan announced to Arienh.

Aye, now she could sleep. She could not tell if Liam would be crippled from the bite, but he would not die. Silently, with a hand to her waist, Ronan guided her back to her own bed.

She could no longer even find the strength to remove the old cloth she had tied to her skirt to protect it from the mud and blood. As she sat on the bed, Ronan untied it for her and removed her soft leather boots. His deft hands smoothed the woolen hose down her legs, evoking a fleeting memory of the night she had so gently done the same for him.

She was beyond thinking, anyway. Willingly, she succumbed to his tenderness, not caring where it led. Ronan pulled back the heavy woolen blanket and eased her down. Linen sheets, soft and cool, caressed her skin.

She closed her eyes. The mattress dipped, and Ronan crawled in beside her.

"Hush," he said as she started to object.

Aye, surely he must be as weary as she was.

Beneath the covers, his arm slipped around her waist, drawing her body against his, not so much an amorous thing as one of comforting affection. And the bed was small, hard for two to sleep in without touching.

He leaned over her, lips descending, touching, caressing, a soothing touch she needed, more than she ever had any other.

Tomorrow, she didn't know what she would do, but tonight she would accept his warmth as he once had hers.

In the other bed, Birgit sat up abruptly. A garbled gasp escaped her as her pale eyes widened in horror.

# CHAPTER NINETEEN

————— ✠ —————

SMALL NOISES FLOATED THROUGH THE HUSHED ROOM FROM Arienh's bed. Birgit sat up, shaking off her exhausted sleep.

He was kissing her. And she was allowing it. Arienh, who had made such a fuss about the Vikings. A sudden terror arose in Birgit's throat, tightening it as if she were being choked.

Egil, too, sat up. His big arm wrapped around her as it reached over the sleeping child. "Nay, love, let them be."

Let them be? Her fists tightened, fingernails biting into her palms. Birgit had tried to keep her fears to herself. She knew they weren't logical, even though they welled up from deep inside her, but every time she saw the dark Viking touch her sister, she cringed. She knew what was in the man's mind, even when she could not clearly see his face. Lust. Horrible, terrifying, dredging up all her painful memories of the past.

Nay, she knew better. She truly did. Such things were part of the normal way of life, that very same normalcy she hoped Arienh would have someday. Yet all she could think of was her own nightmare that had never really left her.

"He will not hurt her, Birgit. Don't you know that? What is it you fear?"

She opened her mouth, but words would not come out. She knew. It was not that. How could she tell him? How could she say aloud her fears when his very knowing would cause them to come true? How could she say she feared for Liam, for Arienh, mostly for herself? In the daylight, she could joke with Mildread about the size of the men's organs, but how could she tell anyone how much she feared the joke might really be the truth? Her only experience with a Viking had been one of terror and pain. She had nearly died from the man's brutality. And she had seen enough, both of Vikings and normal men, to know these Northmen were indeed of prodigious size.

Her tongue seemed firmly wedged in her mouth, her throat too tight to let out words.

"Birgit," he said, his blue eyes the color of smoke in the dim firelight, "what happened to you was not a normal thing. It is not the way of things between a man and a woman. You must know that."

She did. Yet she could not dislodge the memories that told her otherwise. How was it she could look at this man and desire him so much, hunger for his simplest touch, yet fear him so much? Why did she long to finger the yellow mane of his hair, crumpled from having been so long without a comb because he had given his full measure of patient attention to her stricken child? Or to run her hand across the newly grown prickle of yellow beard he had so recently shaven off?

She knew what lay beneath his jerkin and breeches, for she had seen all of it. Yet she wanted to see it all again, the square-set, bulky muscles of his heavy-boned body. Even the huge organ she so feared, she wanted to touch.

She wanted to know what it felt like to be loved by a man such as he. But she had no courage.

"A kiss cannot hurt. Have you never been kissed, Birgit?"

How had he known? Once there had been a boy, but he had been only a boy, before he had been killed, and it had not been a real kiss. No one had ever wanted to kiss her after that. Men had always thought her too strange. Even when there were still men around, they had thought of being father to a Viking's child and the burden of a wife going blind. No one had wanted her.

Nor would he, when he knew.

But he didn't know. And he wanted her.

The rough pads of his fingers skimmed lightly over her cheeks. His thumb caressed across her lower lip. "Your first kiss, Birgit? Will you give it to me?"

She thought she would drown in the smoky depths of his eyes. She drank in his scent, salty from the long ordeal, yet so sweet to her, for he had given everything he could, even his penchant for cleanliness, for the sake of her son. His rumpled clothing, scratchy beard, uncombed hair, were all precious to her, for they were the badges of his caring.

"I promise you, it will be the sweetest you will ever have."

Birgit licked her lips in anticipation of the touch. Yet she could not find words to say what she wanted. Fear still held sway, fear of pain, fear of...

The brown fringe of lashes shaded his eyes as Egil's sensual lips gently touched hers. Birgit nearly jumped from the sudden tingling, then slowly melted, yielding to the tender pressure and sinuous flexing, as if they formed whispered words of love.

Fear of love. Even more, fear of losing it.

She had no courage. None to say aye, none to say nay.

The tip of his tongue teased against the tender flesh of her lips, seeking entrance between her teeth. Callused thumbs paraded boldly along the curve of her cheekbones. She opened to him and found herself suddenly lost in the whirlwind of sensation in the play of his mouth and hers. A timid moan escaped her, startling her. She pushed against him, a tentatively silly push that said more of wanting him than of resistance. He was right. It was good. Sweet.

Egil understood far too much of her. With a gentle caress across her cheek, he released her, quietly smiling.

"Stop that. Leave her alone!"

Lurching out from the dreamlike state of the kiss, Birgit whirled her head toward Arienh, who was trying to rise from the bed.

Ronan held her back. "Leave them be, Arienh, it is only a kiss."

"Will you never cease, either of you? Leave her alone."

"Arienh..." said Birgit, not at all certain what her objection would be.

"Do not think just because we are so weary that we do not know what you do. You take advantage of our troubles. You, Egil, you pretend to care about Liam, but you only use him. You think you will win Birgit by your false caring. You do not even care about her, only how you may use her."

"Arienh!"

"It is true, Birgit. 'Tis nothing but seduction. Both of them. That one is no different from his brother."

"How is that, Arienh?" laughed Ronan. "Does he mean to make her his wife? Perhaps if we left, he would finish the task."

"Stop it. You see, Birgit?"

"See what?"

"He is trying to do the same thing to you that—"

"Do what, love?" teased Ronan.

Birgit felt the silliness of a half smile creep onto her face. So that was it. Now, she understood. Arienh really was harboring a secret. She could not exactly see Arienh's face, but she could tell by the sudden silence and the stillness of her form that Arienh had let something slip. Exhausted as she was, Arienh couldn't be thinking clearly. So they had made love. And that was why Arienh had been so jumpy.

Now that she thought of it, Birgit even knew when it had happened, on the morn of spring's first day, when Arienh had gone to await the sunrise at the stone circle. For just afterward, Ronan had been confused and furious, and shortly after that, brazenly cocky.

It was love, if ever she had seen it.

Egil slipped a nibble of a kiss at Birgit's earlobe, and a quiet chuckle rumbled through him. Birgit bit back the smirk that teased at her lips. So Egil knew, too.

"Come on, Egil," Ronan said. "It's time for us to go, lest this one do you harm for molesting her sister."

"Aye," Egil replied. "'Tis more than time. The boy will be all right, and none of us will get any sleep until we leave."

Liam sat up, wakened as surely as if he had been swatted. "Nay, Egil, don't go."

But the huge blond man shook his head. "'Tis time, lad. We've been here three nights, and we should be going home. You are well enough. Listen to your uncle, and go back to sleep."

"Uncle?"

"He's not—" Arienh stammered.

Birgit smiled. Arienh was far too tired to engage her usual wit. The battle was lost, anyway. Didn't she know it?

"Mama."

"Sleep, Liam," she said as she watched the two men, dark and light shades of each other, unbar the door and exit into the chilly night.

"Mama, I want Egil for my father."

She knew. The Vikings were right. All boys desperately needed fathers. It was something God had put in their hearts, from the beginning of time. It was what Liam needed most.

She didn't know how she could survive it. She couldn't, really. She had lived only for Liam for so long, she knew no other way. If only Egil would love her, too, as she knew he would love the boy. But no man had wanted her once he learned her sight was fading, and no man would. There was too much a wife must do that she could not.

Ronan. Arienh. They belonged together. Arienh needed a love, needed her own children. For years, Arienh had been taking care of everybody. It was almost a joke, the way people had begun to turn to her when she was little more than a girl and expected her to have all the answers, solve all the problems. Arienh had taken care of everything for so long, she had lost track of who she was meant to be.

Birgit was in the way, between Arienh and Ronan, between Liam and Egil. She stood in the way of happiness for everyone in the village.

Perhaps there was something in that strange Viking custom that made sense after all, and it did not seem so different than the martyrdom of the saints. If it came down to a matter between her life and Liam's, she knew what she would choose. But she was neither saint nor martyr. Only a useless woman in everyone's way.

Besides, she would not be able to make the cloth for Arienh's down blanket, and she wanted so badly to do that, for the sister who had done everything for her.

*The cliffs, above the Bride's Well.*

Egil was afraid of the high cliffs. Birgit was not. But then, she could not see what was at the bottom. She would not see the danger until it was too late.

But it was a sin. An unforgivable one. And she was no saint.

*I'll do the best I can for you, Son,* she said, but only to herself.

It was a strange thing, to wake with the sudden knowledge of having slept, when Arienh could barely remember having touched the bed. Perhaps the turmoil she had expected to keep her awake had lulled her instead.

Arienh studied the motes floating in the narrow shaft of warm sunlight from the little slit of a window.

Liam. She could hear his small voice, pale like the dimmest of light. And Birgit sat on the bed beside him.

Arienh rose. She rubbed her back, convinced it ached all the way down to her toes. Before seeing to her morning needs, she went to Liam's bedside.

"Morning, Aunt," the boy said. "I didn't mean to wake you."

"You didn't, Liam, it is time to wake. I see the sun has been up for a while. How do you feel this morning?"

The boy wrinkled his brow and, along with it, his nose, as if he had to think about it. "It still hurts."

Arienh washed the mud pack and examined the wound. The tissue beneath it was healthy, living. "It will, for a while. I am not convinced the poison is all gone yet, but I think you were lucky. Maybe it was a weak snake and didn't have much poison."

"It didn't look weak, Aunt."

She had seen the head. It was a good-sized snake. But who knew? Perhaps all she had done had worked after all. "Perhaps it is because you are strong, or it is God's will. But you must never take such a chance again, Liam. We would be very unhappy without you."

"I don't think Egil will take me now."

Arienh exchanged a glance with Birgit. "Take you? Did he plan to?"

"Aye. He said we will go hunting and fishing together. And we'll go into the hills and find the nettles for Mama to weave."

"Liam, you belong with your mother."

"Can't I have both, Aunt? I want him to be my father."

What was she to say? She did not want to turn him against the big man he adored. She doubted if she could. And she knew

Liam understood the circumstances, the danger to his mother. It was not his fault, but he was just like all the others. He expected Arienh to solve an impossible problem. Sometimes she felt like she was drowning, fighting against the water, with huge waves washing over her, yet with everyone else calling out to her to save them.

"We will just use herb poultices now, I think, Liam. And I think you must be quiet for a while yet, until we are sure the poison is gone."

She repacked the dark wound with the pounded herbs and grease and wrapped a bandage around them, then went about her morning chores in a sickly sort of silence. Birgit, turning to her loom for the first time in days, avoided Arienh's glances. Usually Birgit's pale green eyes would have followed her, obscuring the fact that Birgit could distinguish little more than the movement.

Liam slept again, for Arienh had given him the last of the lettuce syrup.

Arienh tightened her jaw with the silent rage building in her, bit by tiny bit, making her want to slam things around. Instead, she made conscious effort to place everything very carefully, exactly where it should be.

"Stop banging things around, Arienh."

"I am not banging things around." She meant to whisper, but the words came out like a shout. "What is the matter with you, Birgit?"

"Matter? Nay, I am fine. What is it that ails you?"

"You heard what Liam said."

"Aye. Perhaps Egil merely means to continue as he has been doing."

"You know better."

"Nay, I do not." The shuttle swished quietly.

"How could you be so foolish? Don't you see the danger?"

"I see very little, Arienh."

Arienh's fists balled so tightly, her fingernails cut into her palms. "Oh, do not think you will toy with me. You know very well what I mean. It is you who are in danger, Birgit, yet you all but invited the man to kiss you."

"It is so. And I know the danger. I do not deny it."

"I am trying to protect you from him. The whole village tries to protect you, yet you ignore our efforts and throw yourself into the midst of danger."

The shuttle ceased. Birgit's eyes hardened. "I know what you do for me. I know how useless and helpless I am."

"You are not useless and helpless."

"Yet you treat me that way. Nay, Arienh, I know I survive only by your good graces. But at least the Vikings would recognize it honestly."

"How dare you say such a thing?"

"Because it is true. They would not protect me and pretend it is out of caring. You do not value me, Arienh. You only see me as a useless burden, like a child, yet one with no potential."

"Nay, Birgit, you are only as useless as you see yourself. But if you are so determined to give up, I suppose I should not stand in your way."

Birgit shrugged. "It makes no difference. In any case, you will not give up. You never do."

The knife in Arienh's hand slammed down hard on the table. "You are right, Birgit. I never do. And I never will. Say what you will, you cannot goad me into anything else."

Arienh stomped out of the door.

"Leave it open," Birgit called.

"Do it yourself!" she shouted back as the door banged shut.

If Birgit thought herself so useless, could she imagine Arienh's fumbling hands on a loom? Birgit would sneer at the very best Arienh could do. How could she not see her own worth?

Thick moisture filled her eyes as she stalked down the path toward the river trail. She'd go into the hills to gather her own nettles. She did not need the Vikings to do that. And there were herbs to hunt, which would be showing their first tops about now, and she would know where to retrieve them when they were ready to be plucked from the ground. Besides, the stones needed to be moved. Beltane would soon be upon them. She had to...

There was too much to do. Like a devil wind, Arienh threw herself into her tasks. With fierce steps she hurried up the trail beside the stream, hardly noticing its rushing waters until she remembered she should check the progress of the sprouting horsetails on the marshier slopes of riverbank. Their odd sprouts poked pointed heads up everywhere. Nearby, she found meadowsweet showing. If it were only a little bit further along, it would be good for Liam's pain.

In the upper meadow, she found more nettle and could see bare places where men had gathered last year's plants, which had lain and rotted over the winter. But Arienh's concern was the new plant, already prickly in stem and leaf. As she yanked the plant from the moist earth with a firm grasp, the stickers flattened harmlessly. The root was not much, but when boiled, it would make an excellent elixir for Mildread's girls, who always suffered from the phlegm this time of year.

She next walked up the hill, past where Tanni pastured the sheep, and into the stone circle. For a moment, she only stood at its center, then turned to look back the way she had come. But she was alone this time, with only memories for company.

What had she expected? Had she not thoroughly chased him off once again? How could she want and not want? It made no sense to her. She felt all tangled inside.

That was why she was so angry. But she had taken it out on Birgit.

She moved the stones, counting off the marker posts and noting to herself that some of them were badly decayed. It was her duty to replace them this year, lest they fall to ruin and be forgotten. Then those who came after her would not know how to count the days properly. She had never understood why the ancients had not used stones instead of wooden posts, but they had not. So she would follow the instructions she had received and someday pass on the knowledge to another.

They had but a sennight to Beltane. She wondered if the Vikings celebrated it. They did not know about stone circles. Did they build great bonfires and drive the cattle between them, then stay up through the night, dancing and singing, and watch the sun rise over the stones? And take their sweethearts into secret, sheltered places among the trees and rocks?

That had not occurred to her before. Another secret the Celts had better keep to themselves.

She ambled through a mixed grove of beech and oak along the southern flank of the hill, down toward the narrow little canyon that contained the Bride's Well and its falls, thinking how good a bath would feel. The very thought calmed her jangled nerves. She spotted a patch of violets nestled among moss, and stopped. Of all the plants that flowered, violets were her favorite. Deep purple blossoms suspended above dark green leaves spoke something to her heart. She picked leaves regretfully, relishing the fragrant scent, wishing she did not have to damage the perfect plants. But violets, too, were good for the phlegm.

If she could have, she would have stayed there, among the violets, feeling calm and safe, hiding herself from all her troubles in the village. There were times when she would like to leave them all to their fate, but she couldn't. Perhaps they would have all been better off if she had not always been there to take over whenever one of them faltered. Perhaps they would have learned strength if she had not.

Or perhaps they would have simply died. Perhaps strength was something they simply did not have.

She didn't know.

Arienh chewed at her lower lip. She had too much to do to lounge about among the violets. She picked up her willow basket and tucked the violet leaves into it, then started down the trail. Thinking of the bath, she left the trail and crossed the field, until she reached the rocky ground that formed the back side of the Bride's Well. She climbed the gentle slope that soon grew steeper, then merged into solid, dark rock laced with deep, regular cracks, bare of soil or plants.

The massive stone bluff leveled out at the top and was split by the deep, tiny gorge where a small stream ran, then plunged to the pool below. She heard splashing in the pool.

Ronan. Wearing nothing but his smile. He saw her before she had a chance to duck away. A deep heat spread over her face that she was sure he could see even from the pool. Standing in the knee-deep water, fists planted on his hips above his magnificently muscled legs, his organ grew visibly as she stared. Perhaps the other things said about Vikings were not so true, but she had unquestionably been right about their lust.

She should have stayed on the path. She hurried away. But she had only two choices: to go back the long way through the forest or down the path around the hill and down into the valley beside the Bride's Well, which was much shorter. Perhaps if she hurried, he would not be dressed in time to catch her.

And pigs cooked their own bacon.

But what was the point? Either way, he would catch her before she made it home, if that was what he wanted to do.

She shrugged her shoulders and, resigning herself, took the little path that wound through the valley.

He was predictable this time.

# CHAPTER TWENTY

H E WAS STILL BUCKLING HIS SWORD BELT WHEN HE CAUGHT
up to her. His damp hair had an enticing curl to its ends, and the
shadow of dark beard that had grown on his face over three days'
vigil was cleanly shaven away.

"How is the boy?" he asked, reaching for her basket.

She snatched it away. "I can carry it. He is fine. Was fine
when I left."

"So can I," he responded with his sunny smile, but he left the
basket in her hand. "I thought he might be, or you would not be
abroad so soon. Egil has already gone back to the cottage."

She stifled her startled look, although not before he saw it,
and averted her eyes to the trail.

"Are you still angry?"

"I'm always angry," she replied glumly. "You know that."

And he was not even the true target of her anger. Just the
brunt. She was being so unfair. She didn't want to hurt him. She
wanted to love him. But she didn't know what else to do.

"Aye, I know that for a truth, Wife."

"I'm not your wife."

"So you say. But you are my love, at least, and that you cannot deny."

This time as he reached for her basket, she let him take it.

"Have you been to move the stones?" he asked as they walked.

"Aye. I count but a sennight to Beltane."

"Beltane?"

She sighed. "I suppose you do not know of Beltane."

"I have heard of it. The Celts on the Green Isle celebrate it. It is a festival."

There was no way around it. They would need the Vikings' help this year, or there would be no festival, and she could not imagine a year without Beltane. Then everything really would be dying. "We begin at sundown with two great bonfires, and we drive all the cattle between them. All hoofed animals."

An ugly grimace covered his face as if he had just bitten into a bitter root. "I hope you don't think of that as fun."

"Well, not fun, exactly, but it must be done. After that, they may go up into the mountains."

"Tanni was going to take the sheep up tomorrow."

Sudden foreboding struck her. "Oh. He must not!"

"They must go between the fires first," he guessed.

"It protects them from disease. All hoofed animals."

"Ah." His big hands rested casually on his hips. "Are you sure?"

"Of course. We have always done it that way." Arienh tried to remind herself he didn't understand Celtic ways.

"Even the horses, I suppose."

"They have hooves, too."

"Well, that leaves out the geese, at least. I don't suppose you know what it takes to drive horses near a fire."

She contained her impatience. After all, he did not understand these things. "It must be done, or their hooves will rot."

"All right, but isn't there more?"

"To Beltane? Of course. It is a time of great joy. The nights are still chilly, so the fire warms us, but we dance around it and sing, and whole families sit together and wait for the sun to rise." She left out the part about lovers slipping off into the woods.

"And will you teach me your dances, my Arienh?"

"That is silly. Men don't dance with women."

"Then how will we do the men's dances?"

Arienh stared at the ground. How was she to say she did not want him learning the dances? It was not right. In the memories of her childhood, Celtic men leaped and danced around the flames. Not Vikings. Her mother's arm had rested on her shoulder, and her little sister squeezed her hand excitedly as brothers joined the men for the first time in a great circle around the scorching flames. There were no Viking men in their midst.

Yet were these men so different? They were muscle and bone, like ordinary men. They bent to the plow and adze in the same way. They laughed and sang, and drank their mead, perhaps a bit louder than she remembered, and perhaps the sound of their blended voices had a deeper cast. She was not sure. They grew sad or angry. And they certainly had the same sort of interest in women. They even cried.

"I am not sure anyone knows the steps," she said.

"Old Ferris surely must."

Old Ferris. He would die before dancing with the Vikings.

"I do not think that is a good idea. Do you not have dances of your own?"

"Aye." His reply seemed stuck in his throat. "Why don't we divide the fires, then? You take one and do whatever it is Celts do, and we will take the other and do what Northmen do."

"Well, it might work," she agreed.

Ronan halted and turned on her, his eyes flaring. He grabbed her arm. "And you would do it, wouldn't you?"

She fell back a pace, astonished. What was he so angry about? "Well, it was your idea."

"And you think I meant it? You mean to use us to drive your flocks, just as you use us for everything else, but you will not dance with us or share your fires."

"You made the agreement with us. Of course, you do not even keep that."

He glowered over her, huge, menacing. "You do not seem to mind when it is convenient for you. You are willing enough to have Egil when you need him to calm your nephew."

"I do not want him kissing Birgit."

"Why? Why do you object, Arienh? Egil will make a good husband for her and a fine father for the boy. He understands her fears. No man could be kinder or more patient than he."

She had no answer, none she could tell him. She wanted Birgit to have Egil as much as she wanted Ronan for herself. She ached with the wanting. She loved him. But accepting him was a betrayal of Birgit. She could never do that, nor tell him why.

"Why, Arienh? What have I done? What have I not done?"

*Tell him. Tell him.* Aye, she ached to say it. He was right, he didn't deserve this terrible silence. If only she could find a way, something that wouldn't endanger Birgit. "It is not anything you have done. Or not done."

"We are here. You need us. You accept what we offer you, but you do not accept us. We have done all you ask. We have converted, for you would not have heathens. We take care of you and protect you. We share all we have. We do not harm you, do no rape or murder. We have not made you slaves, but equals. I have never failed you, Arienh. What more do you want?"

*I am afraid for Birgit. And myself.* But she could not say it.

The heavy muscles in his jaw worked fiercely as he glared. "So it comes down to this. I could not please you, no matter what I did. The truth is, you will never accept me, will you?"

If he could only know how badly she wished she could.

"Answer me, Arienh. You could at least give me an answer."

If only she could think of a way. "Ronan, it is not that way."

Bitter pain squirmed in his eyes. "You will not marry the Viking simply because he is a filthy Viking."

"Nay, it is not so."

"Isn't it? Thor's beard, I should have never come back. I should have known better. Your kind will never harbor anything but hatred for mine."

Her Viking boy. How he had changed. So terrible in his magnificent male beauty. Only in the eyes, so beautifully bright and blue, did she see the boy. Somehow, she had always loved him. An aching, hopeless love, still.

"I thought I might somehow win your love. But I see now how hopeless it is. Then worry yourself no more. I will stay on my side of the stream from now on."

Ronan grabbed her wrist and shoved the willow basket back into her hand. He swung around and stalked away. The very ground seemed to shake with each step he made.

Helplessness poured over her. Her throat grew painfully thick, and her eyes burned with tears. He could not know how she felt about that strange boy who had violated his own customs to save a girl he did not know. He did not know how many times in the night his image had come to her, a boy with bright blue eyes full of fear, who ran, leaving her crouching in the hole, praying, afraid she would cry out in her own terror. She could still hear the marauder's angry shouts, unfamiliar words so clearly understood, and the blows. And the boy's cries of pain. Then silence.

Thick tears filled her eyes, obscuring the path at her feet.

Ronan. So many times she had prayed for him. And he had come back, hoping his sacrifice had meant something. Hoping she would find room in her heart for him. But she was too full of hatred and fear.

It *had* meant something: her very survival. It had saved her, her family, even her village, for she wouldn't let them quit, either.

And look what she had given him in return.

Clutching her basket to protect its contents from spilling, Arienh ran down the shaded path. He was already beyond sight, obscured by the curve in the narrow trail. She hesitated, then ran again. What would she say if she caught up to him? There must be a way. There must be something.

But what?

Perhaps if Egil grew to love Birgit, somehow. She had tried to understand these men, know what they believed, so she could guess what they might do. That would be what they believed was right, but she didn't know what that was.

But she had to tell him she had not forgotten him, had to tell him how important that boy, in that one minute, had become to her. That she had dreamed, hoped, but never believed, the boy would grow to be a man who would come back.

She ran, stumbling, frantic to catch him. Ahead of her, now she could see him as he left the shade of the ash grove for the bright, open green around the village. She quickened her pace.

He broke into a run. Did he run from her?

Then she heard the din, loud shouts and screams, like a battle. Or an attack. Terror gripped her.

*Run! Hide!*

Birgit! Liam! Her village was in danger!

She sucked in a sharp breath, shoved panic deep inside her. Dropping her basket, Arienh sped toward the village. She cleared the edge of the forest and stopped cold.

Village women screamed and flailed at Viking men who held them back. In the midst of all, the red-bearded blacksmith, Bjorn, forced Elli to her knees with one hand and by the other gripped her unbound hair.

A line of blood dripped from his neck.

# CHAPTER TWENTY-ONE

RONAN REACHED THE CROWD ONLY PACES AHEAD OF HER. From all directions, other men and women ran into the meadow. Mildread screamed, beating her fists against Egil, who grabbed her wrists, twisted her around, and pinned her against his chest.

Ronan grabbed Bjorn, forced Elli out of the blacksmith's grip, and shoved him away. "What happened?" he demanded.

"Damn woman tried to kill me!" Bjorn yelled, his face as fiery as his short, red beard.

Arienh gasped. She reached for Elli, but Ronan pushed her away. "Nay, Elli wouldn't."

But if anyone, Elli would, for her grandfather. Arienh bit her lip lest she say something dangerous.

"You think so?" shouted Bjorn. "You think I sliced myself? Tripped on my sword, maybe?"

"Easy, Bjorn," said Olav, pinning Bjorn back by his arms.

"Let go of me."

"Not till you calm down," said Ronan.

Bjorn's eyes blazed like fire, but he stopped struggling. Olav loosed his hold, and Bjorn tossed off Olav's grip.

Elli squirmed against Ronan's strong arms, choking on her frightened sobs, as Arienh pried futilely at the Viking's hands.

Ronan spun around, keeping his massive body between Elli and Bjorn, forcing the girl farther from Arienh.

"What happened?" Ronan demanded.

"Damn witch tried to slit my throat as I slept."

"Slept? It's the middle of the day, Bjorn."

"Well, I was—I'd drunk some."

"She was in the forge with him, Ronan," said Olav, who joined the guard holding back the women. "I saw her go in. Bjorn was lively enough then."

"Meaning?"

"I saw them kissing, nothing more."

"The rest of it, then, Bjorn."

"She tricked me, damn her. Acted like she cared about me. Then she waited till I dropped off, then quick as a wink, had a knife to my throat. She was going to slit my throat, damn her!"

Arienh couldn't breathe. That was exactly what Elli would have done if she followed Old Ferris's scheme. And who better than his own granddaughter? She glanced about and spotted Ferris hanging back behind the clutch of women, his eyes fierce with hatred, sparkling with anticipation.

She had to do something. The Vikings could finish Elli off in seconds if they chose. And why would they not, for trying to kill one of their own men?

Arienh threw herself in front of Ronan. "Let her go."

His blue eyes darkened with smoking rage, a command to back away. She could not. She blocked his path.

"Let her go? She attempts murder, and you want me to let her go?"

"Is this the equality you speak of, Viking? Will you execute her when you have not even heard what she has to say?"

"I see blood. Where do you think it came from?"

"Ask her, if you dare, Viking."

His eyes smoldered. He released his grip, and the terrified girl crumpled to the ground, her blonde hair spilling over her face. Arienh dashed in, but Ronan blocked her.

"Nay, you will not touch her. You want her to speak? So be it. Well, girl?"

Ronan glared at Elli, who shrank away.

"Well?"

Elli's lip trembled, but she set her jaw and raised herself to her knees. "He killed my father."

Ronan's dark brows furrowed until they almost met. "Your father is already dead."

"And he killed him. I was there. I saw it."

"That's not possible."

"Why not?" Arienh asked angrily. "You have been here before. Why not him?"

"But Bjorn has not. She has confused him with someone else. Or she lies altogether."

Arienh wedged herself in front of Elli. "Elli does not lie. And I will not let you harm her."

"Is this another one of your pranks, Arienh? If so, this time you have gone too far."

"It is no prank. She testifies it was he who murdered her father. Is that not grounds enough for revenge?"

Ronan hesitated. His eyes shifted toward the blacksmith. "Bjorn? What say you?"

The blacksmith had lost his florid rage, and he stared in confusion. His fingers probed at the thin red line of blood. "Nay, I know nothing of her father."

"So you will believe him," Arienh said, "for he is your kind. And you accuse me of hating your race, Viking? I say it is yours that hates mine, for hatred excuses your violence to us."

"Ronan." Egil carefully placed his hand on his brother's arm. "Shouldn't we think this out?"

She had been lost in the intensity of the struggle between Ronan and herself, forgetting the others until Egil interrupted. Egil couldn't know about their fight in the forest, so his brother's anger must seem out of proportion to him. But it was no surprise to Arienh, especially that he blamed the entire thing on her. But blame or no, she had to protect Elli.

And there was only one way.

"Let her go, Viking, and I will give you what you want."

"Will you?" he sneered.

"Aye. I will be your wife. Let her go."

She'd caught him off guard. Never mind that she had just trapped herself.

Ronan quickly surveyed the crowd of bystanders and frowned. "Nay, that choice is not mine. I have not been wronged. Bjorn must decide what to do."

The blacksmith looked pale enough to faint, yet he had lost very little blood. Beneath his wild coppery brows, his pale blue eyes looked deathly ill. He shook his head. "Nay, Ronan, I should have known better. Damn women can't be trusted. But I don't want her hurt."

"What are you talking about, Bjorn? It's your right."

"I give it to you. Let her go and take your wife. You wanted wives. This is your chance." Without another word, the blacksmith pivoted around, shoved his way through the gathering of men, and stalked off toward his forge.

Arienh watched the retreating blacksmith with mounting confusion, and Ronan seemed equally puzzled. But she knew the blacksmith's departure would not ease her problem. Ronan was not one to miss an opportunity.

"So be it, then." Ronan's fierce glare pierced Arienh to the core as she saw the hurt that lay beneath it. Her throat tightened, aching the way her heart did. She hadn't wanted it to be this way, but she couldn't let them hurt Elli. She reached down to Elli, helping the girl to her feet.

"Come to my cottage," she said, motioning to the others. "We must figure out what to do next."

"There is nothing to figure!" shrieked Ferris. "She has betrayed us!"

Startled, the women turned to face the old man.

"What do you mean?" Arienh demanded.

"She is no granddaughter of mine," he railed, black eyes flashing. "She has failed."

So Ferris had done this. Set up his own granddaughter to be murdered. "Hush, Ferris. How can you say such a thing? Do you truly think she is a match for such a huge man?"

"She did not do it right. She failed because she lacked the courage. Her own father was killed by that fiend, and she will not avenge him."

"She's lucky she isn't dead," said Mildread. "We're lucky we all aren't dead because of your stupid scheme, Ferris."

Ferris wheeled on Mildread, unleashing his rage on her. "And you. I've seen you sneaking off into the woods with that thin one. You have betrayed your own people to consort with heathens."

Mildread raised her chin high and looked down her nose. "They aren't heathens anymore."

"They will never be anything less. Heathens. Barbarians. Thieving murderers. And you make your bed with them."

Mildread drew herself up to her full height, looming over the old man. "Well, now, how do you know I didn't mean to follow your advice and do him in? But I would not, for he is a true man. You would not know about that. If you want them dead, go slit their throats yourself instead of sending women to do it."

"Slut!"

"Stop it!" shouted Elli. Tears stained her reddened cheeks. "Stop it, Grandfather. You are right, I could have killed him if I'd wanted to, but I didn't want to, and I tried. I've always tried to please you, but you cannot be pleased. No matter what I do, you will never be satisfied, not even with this. You will never be satisfied until we are all dead, and we will not die for your warped vengeance."

The old man bounced about in his frenzy. "He killed my son! Your father! You said so yourself."

"Aye, it was him," Elli said, "I'm sure enough. But there has been enough killing, and I will do your bidding no more."

"Then you are no kin of mine. You will never darken my door again."

The women gasped. Old Ferris flitted his cold stare over the group of women, turning his hardest scowl on Arienh. Then he turned around in the path and stalked away despite his hobbled gait toward his cottage.

"I wonder who he thinks will look after him now," asked Selma. "I am not inclined, even if he is my uncle."

Mildread's mouth formed a grim line. "I will see to him. I cannot let him starve. But he cannot bully me, either."

"Elli, you will come home with us," Arienh said. "And we will all protect you; do not fear."

Elli already gathered strength from somewhere inside her, or perhaps she absorbed it from her friends and kin who stood by her. Arienh was proud of her. She had stood up to both the Vikings and her grandfather, and survived both times.

With an arm about Elli's shoulders, she started toward the stone cottage where Birgit awaited. Liam, still perched on Birgit's hip, spoke into his mother's ear, pointing in various directions, and Arienh guessed that he told his mother what he saw. But Birgit's sharp ears had no doubt heard enough to guess for herself.

"Arienh," shouted Ronan, angry and fierce.

Arienh jerked and glanced back.

He stood wide, like a man ready to do battle. One massive hand wrapped around his sword's hilt. His eyes blazed. "Your place is with me, Wife."

Her jaw gaped. Now? She had thought to stall him at least a little bit longer. "Nay, Viking, it is the middle of the day."

"Is your word worthless, then?"

"Nay, but there are things that must be done first."

"Vows at the church door? You have run out of excuses. Now there is a church."

"There is the Beltane—"

"A time for lovers. You neglected to tell me that as well."

"And a time for marriages."

"A marriage may happen when it happens. And you have just given your vow, before your people and mine. The time is now."

Arienh gulped down her fear, and out of the corner of her eye spotted the coarse brown robes of Father Hewil. She would get no help there, for Ronan had thoroughly won over the priest. If she tried to stall, Ronan might regret his decision to free Elli. But if she went with him, his triumph would encourage the other men, and soon one of them would discover Birgit's weakness.

"Don't do it for me, Arienh," Elli pleaded. "You should have let me take my punishment."

But what was marriage compared to death? Nay, she could not risk Elli. And she had given her word.

Mildread's hand alit lightly on Arienh's shoulder. "Nay, you must, for you agreed. Don't worry, it will be all right. We will take care of them."

Arienh wasn't sure exactly what Mildread meant, but her solemn brown eyes held a softness in them that could be understood, all the way to the soul. Arienh nodded. She stepped forward and walked down the path as if to her execution.

Fear was her enemy, far more than the enigmatic Northman who was one moment tender and kind, and the next fierce. They vied for power here, and if she showed her fear, she might just as well hand it all over to him. Give up.

Never had she given up, and she could not now. And she was well practiced in disguising her fear.

Then she would give him what he asked for, but she would give it like a warrior. Strength she might not have, but she had the wit to win. Boldly, she strode toward him, faced him squarely. Silently, eye to eye.

Swift as an adder, his hot grip latched onto her arm. She met it, not with resistance, but with challenge in her eyes, her gaze raking from his hand to his eyes. He meant to possess her. He thought control of her body would give him dominion over her soul, but she was a Celt, descendant of Celtic women warriors, and she would teach him what dominion meant.

Abruptly, he released his hold, as if sensing her compliance. With haughty strides, jutting out her chin, Arienh trod the length of the path to the new timber church.

The path seemed interminable but all too short. The beautiful Viking caught up to her in only two strides and kept pace beside her. Arienh fixed her sight on the freshly limed walls and bright honey-colored thatch. She dared not look at his face, lest her resolve crumble.

As Father Hewil took her hand and laid it atop the Viking's, she focused on the tiny pits in the bronze cross that hung from a cord over the brown cassock. The priest's words of blessing seemed far away, vague and shapeless. Her awareness of the throng of Celts and Vikings surrounding them was nearly smothered by the intensity of the huge man beside her.

She shook off her stunned reverie when Ronan's strong hands turned her by her shoulders to face him, then held her face still as he leaned to touch his sensuous lips to hers. Neither hard nor gentle, a kiss of possession, not passion. But a hundred kinds of passion seethed in his eyes.

Before she could recover, he tossed her over his shoulder and stalked with huge strides down the path by the river to the Vikings' cottage.

At the threshold, he paused and set her down.

"In," he said.

She met his demand, shoulders square, head held high, still focusing on the route ahead of her, and the door banged shut behind her. The latch slammed into its slot. It was an alien place now, this cottage, furnished in strange, Northman-like ways. The beds for his family were built along the walls and covered with furs and plump blankets, which she guessed were filled with the precious down he had collected. The scent of mead mingled with stale smoke from the previous night's hearth fire.

She could not let him win this battle. She would give her body, yes, but would not let him take it, nor her soul. Arienh whirled suddenly to face the Viking, feeling the flare of fierce aggression rise in her.

Like a ravaging wolf, he closed in, eyes gleaming with his voracious thoughts as his garments shed away like water: jerkin, smock, breeches. He kicked away his short boots. Corded muscles rippled with tension in the yellow glow from the banked hearth fire. His huge male form loomed like a dark shadow, darker than the gloom, so that only its outline was clear. She hungered to run the pads of her fingers over his skin, to sense with her fingers the rugged male beauty her eyes saw.

*Think.* Men did not like aggressive women. They sought to conquer, not be conquered. His weakness was his lust for her. Could she use her own lust to conquer him?

She became the wolf. In one motion, she grabbed the hem of her kirtle and jerked it over her head, to stand before him bare.

"Hel's frozen tits," he whispered hoarsely.

"Do not compare me to your heathen goddess, Viking."

"'Twould be like comparing plenty to starvation." He shifted closer.

Swift in her attack, she pounced to him, breast to chest, her hand clenched the prize of his masculinity, hard and solid with silken heat. Once, she had been in awe, wondered if the legends of Viking prowess were true, wondered how it could be possible for a woman to take something so huge into her body without pain. Then she had learned. It had not been pain he had brought her but pleasure so intense it had left her reeling.

A groan ripped from deep in his chest as he clutched her to him, trapping her hand between them, until she pulled it free and left his magnificent organ to press against her belly. He forced his lips against hers and, with her sharp gasp, drove his tongue within. She retaliated, like swung swords, stroke for stroke, dueling, meeting, probing, parrying, eagerly seeking to learn every corner of him. Her freed hand rushed to join with his sleek skin, discovering all the hard male curves and ridges that formed his back, while the other hand combed the darkness of hair that flowed to his shoulders.

Ronan broke away the kiss and swept her into his arms so quickly she almost thought she would fall. Two paces to the bed, and he had her down on her back atop the white bearskin, as he hovered over her, pinning her thighs against his knees. His eyes darkened to wolfish ferocity. "You think to end this quickly, do you?"

Her heart climbed into her throat. Whatever had made her think she could best him at his own game? She rolled to the side, trying to duck beneath his arm, but he caught her hands and pinned them down to the heavy fur.

"The idea was yours, remember?"

She could hardly deny that. It was just that fear had momentarily conquered her. She ceased her struggle. "Then get on with it, Viking."

Anger darkened the lust in his eyes. "I have a name."

"I do not care."

"You will, Arienh, you will." Ronan lowered the full weight of his body onto hers, encompassing her, as if he sought to capture all parts of her at once, his mouth taking hers, hands cupping breasts, thighs surrounding thighs. Callused pads of his thumbs rubbed across the hard tips of her nipples, sending sheets of fire blazing through her.

"Say my name, Arienh," he demanded hoarsely between the rough bite of kisses.

"Nay." It was a gasping cry.

He shifted lower and took one urgently erect nipple into his mouth, suckling, flicking with his tongue. She thought she would scream. She bucked against the constraint of his hands holding hers, but when he released them, they wound into his hair, splayed to savor its silkiness, and sent it spilling over his shoulders.

"Say it." His hand explored that intimate place where he would enter her, and raw, ravenous fire engulfed her at his touch.

"Nay." And any moment, she would say anything, do anything he asked.

One large knee nudged its way between hers, then the other, and the immensity of his body spread her legs apart. Expectation loomed as she awaited his entry, wanting again that heated, sleek pressure that had imbedded itself in her memory.

Shock set in as he shifted again, lower, lifting her legs as he moved, and the tender explorations of his tongue took the place of his fingers. Her body flexed wildly, involuntarily, as she moaned. Passion wound through her like dark red smoke.

She thought she would die if he continued. Would die if he stopped.

"Say it."

"Nay."

"Say my name, damn you."

She moaned, long, hard, plaintive. "Ronan." She moaned. She screamed, as the colored streamers of passion tangled with bursts of light and her whole being turned inside out. "Ronan!"

He was above her once again. Passion looked angry, dark, and painful on his face as he lowered the weight of his body onto hers. She welcomed his entry as an aftermath to her spent desire, the last caresses. It would be easy from here on.

But he was not spent. And she had only thought she was. In her greediness, she had not realized his need continued. She felt his thrust within her still-heated body, still tightly enclosing him as he plunged deeply, and suddenly spent desire regained its loft. His mighty strength gathered, curled, and thrust, again and again to the rhythm of his hips, first slowly, withdrawing almost fully, and planting deeply, then faster, harder, deeper, wilder, wilder. Her mind spun with the frenetic, hungry, demanding sensation.

She thought again she could take no more. He stiffened with a ragged cry, and thrust deep and hard, his body shuddering. Once again, the world folded in on her and she felt him streaming over her, engulfing her, as if they melded into one.

A sated sigh escaped him as the tension eased from his body. He lay atop her, heedless of his weight, and she welcomed it, feeling the rightness of it. One gentle, big hand cradled her head and held it against his cheek. She could feel the touch of his lips on her scalp and turned her face so those sensual lips would catch her forehead instead.

In the quiet, cool darkness of the cottage, Arienh lay in his arms, wishing the afternoon were night and they might lie together just like this. She didn't want to think about Elli or Birgit and Liam, only about stopping time and staying here with him forever.

Slowly he slid to her side, turning her with him as he rolled. No longer entrapped beneath him, she could have risen, but she yearned to prolong the quiet perfection of the moment. In the silence, she slid her arm over him, letting her fingers trail across the plains and valleys of his chest and left her hand to rest there. She nestled herself into the snug cradle of his arm and was not exactly sure how he managed to pull a soft, cloudy down blanket over them.

She closed her eyes. For now, she would not think of the disaster she had made and instead let herself ease into a quiet, mindless serenity.

She was not aware of having slept, yet a stiffness filled her body that could only have come from lying still for a long time. And beside her, Ronan breathed the quiet, easy breaths of sleep.

She had lost. Well and truly lost. For he had not merely conquered her body but her soul as well.

He was so handsome. Beautiful in body, magnificent in soul. She wanted to trace his dark brows and the straight length of his nose, the curve of his strong jaw. But she did not want to wake him. The down blanket had slipped below his chest, but she knew all of what was hidden beneath it. If she could, she would spend forever with him, eagerly touching him, welcoming him into her body.

She remembered the Viking boy, a thin wraith of a child with filthy, scraggly, sandy hair and wonderfully blue eyes. The boy she had prayed for and even dreamed might come back to her someday. He had come back, far different from the memory she had cherished for so long. And though he had come back to take possession of her and all that was hers, somehow she had stopped minding about that. Somehow she could not be angry with him anymore. She had held up her anger as a shield to protect herself from him, but he had battered it down, leaving her weak, vulnerable. Frightened. Worst of all, he had reached within her and stolen her heart. Or had she simply handed it to him?

Aye, she had lost, but she must not let him know.

Quietly, she sat up. They were still wild, these Vikings. This afternoon had shown her their threat. Elli might have been killed. Arienh had been right in offering herself.

Yet what would she do now? The other men would press their demands now, especially Egil. Somehow she still had to keep the Viking at bay.

Carefully, determined not to stir him, she slipped herself from beneath the cozy down blanket into dark, chilly air. She crept silently across the hard earth floor, gathering her garments, and pulled the kirtle over her head. Deciding not to take the time with her boots, she reached for the door.

"Where are you going?"

She didn't turn. "Home."

"Your home is with me."

The slat bed creaked as he rose, and footsteps padded on the earth. Against her will, she glanced over her shoulder. The glance became a longing stare at his massive, muscular body. She forced a hard brittleness into her voice. "I have work to do. Do not worry, Viking. I will not deny you access to my body whenever you require it."

His jaw took a hard set, and anger blazed in his eyes. "Don't waste your time. It isn't worth that much."

His angry words stung like a slap. Arienh turned quickly, so that he could not see the pain in her eyes, and rushed through the door.

Gloom permeated the air of the Viking cottage. No one sang or laughed. Horns of mead were emptied in large gulps surrounded by silence.

Egil passed through the door and quietly pulled it shut.

"Did you find Bjorn?" Ronan asked.

"Dead drunk. He made it back to his bed, and he's out cold."

Ronan wasn't doing much better. He'd had enough to lighten his head, but it hadn't done anything for his dark mood. "Well, better than up to mischief. I was afraid he might seek vengeance against the girl."

Egil folded his arms. "Something strange about that whole thing, Ronan."

"I know, but it couldn't be true."

"Are you sure you know that much about Bjorn?"

That was the bad part. He didn't know. "He was a mercenary, true, but only on the Green Isle. I suppose he does have a lot to forget, though."

"There has always been something strange about him."

"It's not strange for a man to do what he can to survive. That's the way of things. He's a good man with a sword or a forge, and I'll wager he chooses the forge whenever he can."

"Aye," Egil agreed, accepting the horn of mead his mother handed him. "Most men fight only because they must, Valhalla or no."

"The girl must have seen some other red-haired man. There are enough of them, especially those of mixed blood."

"Aye, she could have been mistaken. Seeing her father murdered could have been enough of a shock that she didn't remember things quite right."

"Aye, I've thought that. And the cut was pretty shallow, like she lost her nerve or had no heart for it."

"He is in no danger. But it's a bad way to be rejected."

Ronan nodded. "Odd, isn't it? With all his talk about having nothing to do with women."

"Well, I'd say he's not the only one to lose his heart," Egil replied, and he almost smiled. "You're not going to give up, are you?"

Was he? What was the point?

He wanted to leave. Felt like shoving the *Black Swan* into the river and sailing out into the Irish Sea. Felt angry enough to become that very raider Arienh so heavily condemned and thought he was.

No, that he could never be, no matter what she thought. But he didn't know how he could continue living here, every day seeing her and knowing she would never quite let go of her hatred.

He could not leave. He had committed to this spot, brought his kin and companions and rooted them here. Gunnar needed to stay, for all his life he had roamed, yet had fixed his hopes on a future in which his family had a homeland and not just a berth in an alien port. Wynne needed to stay wherever Gunnar would be buried.

Nor were any of the men inclined to leave. Egil, Olav, Tanni, and most of the others probably couldn't be pried loose. And truth to tell, he really didn't want to go, either.

He just wanted her back. Back? He'd never had her.

He supposed he had always known it would be like this, even though he had not been willing to accept it. Saxons and Celts alike had suffered so much at the hands of raiders, and they knew so little of the world at large, that it was natural for them to assume all men from the north were vicious, violent, conscienceless. But he had just assumed she would only have to come to know him and her fears would be dispelled.

He hadn't realized how deep her hatred ran. Not hatred, exactly, but he didn't know another word to explain it. It was as if she thought he and his kind were something not quite equal to mankind. A higher sort of animal, perhaps, but not human.

"No, we aren't leaving, no matter what. But if there's a way to make all this right, I don't know what it is."

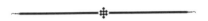

Night had not been so quiet since the Vikings had come. They had grown used to the raucous sounds of an evening as the men gathered together, laughing, drinking their mead, telling stories, sometimes singing. Tonight, the dark air in Arienh's cottage seemed empty, yet curiously heavy.

"He really isn't a bad man," Elli said, almost in a whisper, addressing her statement to the hearth fire.

"If he killed your father, doesn't that make him a bad man, Elli?" Birgit asked.

Elli shook her head sadly. "Perhaps he was then, but I don't think he is now. He is gruff, though. I think it is because he thinks no one will like him anyway. Especially women. He thinks a woman won't like him."

"But you do, don't you?" Arienh guessed.

Elli sighed, still studying the glowing embers. "I suppose I do. Well, I tried not to. He just wanted a chance to start over, Arienh. Could that be so bad?"

"Perhaps he didn't like the life he led if he wanted to change it. I suppose that's not so bad."

"I wish I'd never listened to Grandfather. No matter how much hatred I might have, I could never have killed him."

"I didn't think so."

"And now I've ruined it for everybody."

"Except for Birgit."

Elli looked up from the fire, her eyes almost pleading. "Arienh, they didn't kill me. If they were going to kill someone, wouldn't it have been me? Do you really think they'll hurt her?"

"Nay, I think not. But Liam belongs with us. I can't let them take him away. And who knows if they'll still want to stay here?"

"What are you going to do?"

"I don't know."

Perhaps it meant they had to do the Beltane alone, since it was not something Vikings believed in. Perhaps, for the protection of the sheep and cattle, they would at least drive the stock between the fires, but Arienh could do little more than hope.

The women formed groups. Some stayed to prepare food, and others gathered brush for burning in the bonfires, choosing dead branches broken off in the previous winter and carrying bundles to the ancient ground within the stone circle. It would take all day to assemble enough wood to keep the fires burning through the night, from dusk to the first glimmer of dawn.

Birgit tagged along, bringing Liam on his first day out, prepared to carry him if he tired. Arienh supervised the boy as carefully as Birgit did, but Liam wasn't up to his usual bouncing around yet.

Arienh was determined they would carry on. The traditions would not die. Today the wood; tomorrow they would begin assembling food for the feast.

If only they could have poles for dancing. They had not had poles for years.

Would there be dancing? The women would dance. She could not tell what the Vikings would do.

Maybe she couldn't see what the answers were, but that had never stopped her before. Thanks to the Viking boy who had saved her so long ago. Ronan.

Her breath caught in her lungs. With a silent sweep of her hand, Arienh summoned Elli to follow her. With the large bundles they had slung onto their backs, they trudged up the trail that led onto the little plateau where the stone circle faced out over the restless sea. Elli busied herself in glum silence, plodding through the forest where the trees thinned and out onto the grass-covered hillside. Dappled sun filtering through leafy trees soon gave way to the brilliant light of the open plateau and sparkles flashing off choppy waves of deepest blue.

Her place of healing, where past and present met and joined. Today she needed that sense of wholeness. On Beltane, just a few days hence, all those who had danced and died before would come back, to share their love and lives with those who still struggled. The time would come, someday, when she also would be among those who came from the hazy time past to dance with living folk, part of the living thread of time.

Arienh set down her bundle, stretched her back, and walked to the far side of the stones to gaze out over the dark and sparkling sea.

Elli screamed. Arienh swirled around as the smell of human filth assailed her nostrils.

Vikings.

Hrolgar.

# CHAPTER TWENTY-TWO

"Vikings, Mama!"

Birgit jerked at Liam's urgent whisper.

Screams pierced the quiet forest air. Terror tightened like a band about her chest.

"What do you see, Liam?"

"It's the bad one, Mama, and he's got Aunt," Liam whispered.

Birgit squinted in the direction of the stone circle, in vain. She could not even tell if a tree stood between her and the grassy plateau of the stone circle. It was like a thick, pale fog with occasional darker blotches.

"The one who is Ronan's uncle? How do you know?"

"I can see him and his ship, too, with the striped sail, way up the coast, where the iron pits are. Come on, Mama." Liam jerked at her skirt. "Come on. They've got Aunt Selma, and Aunt Elli, and the girls. Mama, they'll get us. Hurry!"

Fear warred with guilt. Liam couldn't run. She'd have to carry him. She could not save Arienh. She could only go for help, and she was nearly worthless even for that.

But Liam could be her eyes. "Aye. Study it so you can tell our Vikings what you see. Lead me, Liam."

Purpose filled the little boy's face. He grabbed her hand and scurried through the brush. Branches she could barely see flew in her face, scraped her body. At the narrow path, she broke into a run, Liam before her. They sped through clearings, Liam hobbling on his good leg. When he slowed, she knew there were obstacles, even before he called back to her.

Shouts and crashing, rustling brush sounded behind them. Her mind raced back to a time when a Viking seized her, threw her to the ground, tearing, ripping, forcing his hideous body into hers. Liam. She could not let them get him.

"Run, Liam. Run."

"I'm running, Mama. My leg hurts."

His breathless cries tore at her heart. But she couldn't let him stop.

He stumbled.

*Nay, Liam, don't fall. Don't let them get you.* Birgit dashed to him, scooped him up onto her hip, and staggered back to the trail. Rough shouts echoed through the forest. She gasped, her side aching as she sped along.

*Please, God. Please don't let them get us!*

"They're going back, Mama. They've turned around."

Birgit prayed as she ran. Guilt clawed at her. That could only mean the Vikings would take Arienh with them. Did God save her at the cost of her sister's life? He must not. But Liam? She must save him.

"Look out, Mama. There's rocks here."

Birgit studied her footing and the darker smudges where rocks and their shadows lay. Her toe caught and she stumbled, caught herself, tottered to her feet.

"Put me down, Mama, I can run now."

"Nay."

"You can't see it. Just here, Mama."

How safe would he be if she fell with him in her arms?

"They're gone. We can slow down."

"Nay. We must get help. We're almost there."

Birgit's lungs burned, her gasps deep. She could see the blotches of green that told her the village sat in the sunlight just ahead. "Run ahead of me, Liam."

"Nay. Mama!" He tugged at her arm.

"I'm all right. Just run ahead and get someone to come back for me. I'm still coming, but I've got to slow down. Hurry!"

His bright blue eyes were wide and round with fear. His brassy curls bobbed as he spun around, and blurred to a wheat-colored spot while his arms flailed, until even his movement disappeared into the fuzziness.

Birgit ran on. She gasped, again, again, deep and futile gulps, and she clutched her side where a sharp pain threatened to double her up. What would they do to Arienh?

*If she's lucky, no more than they did to me.*

The horror of it spurred Birgit on, suddenly heedless of her pain. She must find Egil. Ronan. He would save his wife, wouldn't he? She focused on the blotch of blurry green ahead, begging her saint for strength. With a renewed burst of speed, she rushed on.

An explosion of light, pain. She hit something...Nay. She must...Her head...Light, dark...She had to...Swirling, throbbing, pounding, her palms hit the dirt.

Screams.

Ronan dropped his adze and lunged for his sword.

"Help!" cried the breathless boy, stumbling with exhaustion as he ran. Behind him, his mother, running and clutching at her side. Birgit suddenly picked up speed, then—

Horror struck him as Birgit ran straight into a low tree limb. The branch caught her in the middle of her forehead, stopped her cold, knocked her to the ground. Clawing at formless air, she crumpled, lay still.

Ronan blew the alarm as he ran to her, caught Liam in his arms, and scooped him up.

"Vikings!" the boy gasped. "They got Aunt!"

Vikings? But how? He had set up a watch. "Where?"

"The stone circle. I saw them. They sneaked up."

Egil sped to Birgit just as Ronan reached her. Both men knelt beside Birgit as she moaned. From all sides, men and women came running, weapons at hand.

"What happened?" Egil demanded, but already a darkening knot formed on Birgit's forehead. Egil folded Birgit into his arms. Mildread plopped down beside them with anxious concern.

"Hurry. You got to hurry!" Liam insisted, pulling on Ronan's arm.

"Aye, Liam," Ronan replied, but he turned to Birgit, who touched the knot gingerly as she struggled to sit up. "Birgit, tell me everything, and hurry. Where are they?"

The pale green eyes he had once found so hellishly eerie stared with fear. Birgit licked her lips. "It's like Liam said."

"Aye, but we have to know where to go to head them off. How far up the coast were they?"

Liam yanked at Ronan's sleeve again. "Mama can't tell you. She can't see."

Ronan stared. It couldn't be. "What?"

"Oh, Liam." Birgit sighed.

"You didn't say I couldn't tell him, Mama. Only Egil."

Egil muttered an ugly curse. With a sickening thud in his heart, Ronan understood his brother's thoughts. Egil clasped Birgit's face between his hands, turning it to him. "What does he mean, Birgit? You ran right into that branch, didn't you?"

Mildread sighed. A secret they all knew, then. "He means she can't see," she said. "Not much, anyway. Liam is the only one who can tell you what you want to know."

278

"Hel's tits," Egil said. He flung his hands to his side and stood abruptly, leaving Birgit sitting on the ground. "All right, Liam, tell us."

The boy still breathed hard. "Up there where the iron pits are, past the stone circle, that's where their boat is. I saw it. It's that bad one that's your uncle, and he's got Aunt, and Elli, and Selma, and the girls. You got to stop them."

"They've got too much of a head start, Ronan," said Tanni.

Terror constricted Ronan's throat as he wracked his brain for an answer. "Nay, that's miles away, with struggling women. We'll take the *Black Swan*."

Wild-eyed, Bjorn shook his head. "But how? Olav's gone to the iron pits, and Solvi's gone after that holy book. Seven of us can't man a longship."

"Take us," Mildread said, suddenly grabbing Ronan's arm. "We can row. We're strong, you know we are."

Women? Women rowing his longship?

He frowned. "It takes training, Mildread. If the oars clash, they could shatter."

"We'll do it right, I swear."

Birgit sat up, tentatively touching the lump on her forehead. Her pale green eyes impaled him with their intensity. "Please, Ronan. They took Arienh. And Elli and Selma, and the children. I know what they will do to them."

They were Loki's daughters. Why not? He had to do something or Arienh would die.

He had already decided. "Aye. We might all end up at the bottom of the sea, but there's no choice. Mildread, get the women and their weapons to the ship. Egil, Tanni, to the ship."

"Take me," Birgit begged. "I can't see, but I could row."

Ronan only glanced at her and the purpling knot on her head. "See to my father. Get everyone that's left to the cavern," he told her. "And try to find someone to run to Olav. We need him if he can be found."

Ronan raced down the path after the others to the *Black Swan* on the riverbank. The men shouldered the big craft into the shallow river as men and women scurried aboard, and poled it downstream to the junction with the estuary. The receding high tide gave them speed.

Ronan's mind raced as he barked orders to the women and paired them with men at the oars. He swallowed down his fear. One rower out of rhythm could wreck the entire ship.

But what would happen to Arienh if they didn't? What was happening to her right now? He dared not think it. But he would kill Hrolgar. That, he knew.

The oars slapped the water, striking the rhythm. Tanni released the rigging. The big sail caught wind. Ronan adjusted the sail, securing its tackle to hold its position steady. The longship plowed across the rolling water, sleek and swift, under both sail and oar power.

Tanni's eyes blazed with horror and rage. It would be for Selma and the two little girls who had won Tanni's heart. And Elli? He glanced at the fiercely rowing blacksmith and wondered.

With the sail set, Ronan dashed to the helm. Counting the women, he had a crew of about twenty. About six men had gone with Olav in the woods. With luck, Olav would get the message or would see Hrolgar's ship, for the iron pits were only a few miles from the cove where Hrolgar had most likely landed.

Could he count on Loki's daughters to fight the way they had been taught? They were not cowards, but would their arrows cause more harm than good? If they even caught up with Hrolgar.

If not, they'd follow him all the way back to the Manx Isle.

The sleek longship broke free of the estuary and slowed as it turned across the tide. Ronan swung the sail to catch the wind, and the ship lurched forward, turning north.

The rowers grunted as they strained over their oars. The oars slapped the water in rapid cadence, matching Egil's booming voice.

"There. I see them," shouted Tanni.

Ronan spotted it. The aging grey longship with its faded, striped red sail. Deep hatred surged inside him. "Close to shore, just putting out. Thought they'd get farther than that. Head them off."

"Damn women must be putting up a fight," Bjorn shouted. He heaved his massive weight into his oar as hard as any other man.

The sail shifted to catch the wind at its best angle once again, and Ronan set course to cut off Hrolgar's ship before it could reach open sea. The *Black Swan* was the sleeker, faster ship. It could go up against Hrolgar's old and battered ship and win, any day.

Ronan stifled a plea to the old gods. They were Christian now. He said his prayer to the Christian God and hoped his mother was right.

Closer, closer, closing. Hrolgar had spotted them. He turned his ship, angled to the shore, nearly paralleling their path. Running.

Closer, closer. He could see Hrolgar on the deck. Hrolgar's longship turned sharply again, cutting back toward shore, against the choppy current and receding tide. The ship bucked, its clinkered planks squealing. Ronan, too, cut against the waves, fighting. The sail swung so far, he thought he'd lose the breeze altogether.

If he did, so would Hrolgar.

The battered grey longship reached the breakers, wallowing in the crosscurrent. Closing in, Ronan's rowers strained as if their lungs would burst.

"Gut their oars," he shouted. "Ship oars."

Women moved as fast as men. The *Black Swan*'s oars rose high into the air and inward. Its prow skimmed starboard of Hrolgar's ship, cracking the oars of every raider who didn't think fast enough. Grappling hooks lashed the sides. Thuds mingled with clashing iron and fierce shouts.

Hrolgar's ship heeled over. One captive sailed overboard, almost poised in the air, before she hit the water facedown.

"Thor's beard!" shouted Bjorn. He leaped to the pirate deck and dashed across to heave himself into the choppy sea after her.

Raiders jumped overboard into the surf, swam for shore as Ronan leaped onto the ship, slashing at whatever marauder was too slow to get out of his way. Lashed together, the two ships ground through choppy breakers, bouncing, rolling. Women clung to ropes and slid across the deck. The ships rushed on, pressed by the wind, and slammed against the shingle beach.

The women remembered their orders. The instant the *Black Swan* grounded, they took careful aim at the marauders slogging through the surf, and shot. Arrows flew. A second volley launched. Raiders staggered and fell beneath the onslaught.

Ronan scanned rapidly around, counting captives. Three aboard, one overboard. Only Arienh still missing. So was Hrolgar. On the pebble beach, raiders dashed to high ground, a low dune studded with sea grass, and formed a shielding circle.

Within the circle, a husky, rough-hewn raider forced Arienh to her knees. Next to them, Hrolgar.

Hrolgar had but one arm.

"So that's it," Ronan said, leaping into the surf.

"What?" Egil asked, trudging beside him, sword held high.

"Vengeance. The slice I gave him at our last meeting must have cost him his arm."

"Thought even Hrolgar would realize he's outclassed."

Ronan shook his head as they advanced. "The women themselves outclass him, but he'd never have the sense to know it. I should've known he'd be back."

Hrolgar had lost several men. Some of the raiders lacked weapons. With a sharp jerk of Ronan's head, his men formed a battle line and marched on the dune, swords and battle axes ready. Ronan's rage leveled into cold resolve as he fixed his concentration on Hrolgar.

Hrolgar's dark teeth showed in a humorless grin. "Now it's women for archers, nephew?"

"They are Loki's daughters, Hrolgar. They are your hell on earth. Let the woman go."

Hrolgar's grin widened. "Thought you'd come for her. This one yours? You want her, do you?"

"Let her go or you're dead, Hrolgar." Ronan tightened his jaw, containing the rage that threatened to boil over.

"Am I, now? Maybe she's dead, instead. You want it that way, nephew?"

"Let her go."

"Oh, aye. For a price."

Ronan shifted his line of men just below the dune. "What do you want?"

Hrolgar's grin vanished suddenly. Deadly evil spread over his face.

"Give me your hand."

# CHAPTER TWENTY-THREE

---

ARIENH WINCED AT THE WRENCHING PAIN OF HER ARM twisted behind her back, sharpening the scents of salt and sweat. Waves of oddly colored light blurred her vision.

Like an alien god rising from the sea, Ronan marched through the surf, the last thing she saw as the raider forced her to her knees.

The Viking's knife cut the skin at her nape. Blood trickled like sweat around her neck and down her chest. The slightest movement could kill her.

"Give me your hand," Hrolgar demanded maliciously.

*Think. There has to be something.*

Hrolgar had no shield, no arm to hold one. But her side vision spotted his sword flashing menacingly. He meant to cut off Ronan's hand. In trade for her. Ronan surely would not.

"No, Ronan, don't." It was Egil's calm voice. She couldn't see him.

"Let her go first," Ronan replied.

"No!" she squealed. The knife bit in deeper. Its prick quickly stilled her.

"Take me for a fool, nephew?"

"The worst fool. You've made a bad mistake this time. Nor is there any honesty in you. If I give you what you want, you'll kill her, anyway."

"It's a chance you'll have to take." She could almost hear laughter in the evil growl.

All she could see of Ronan was his soggy boots in broad stance, the tip of his gleaming sword beside him, ready to swing.

"Nay," he said, his voice calm and cold. "There's no chance to it. But you know me as well as I know you. And you know I'll keep my word. Let her go and I'll give you what you want."

*Nay. Never. He must not. She could not let it happen!*

She dared not move backward or to either side. The dagger would penetrate her skull instantly. Forward, and her arm would rip from its socket. But she could not let this monster cut off Ronan's hand.

Shifting her eyes sideways, she spotted the gilded hilt of a dagger that caught the sun from its place in Hrolgar's belt. But she couldn't reach it unless she freed herself.

Arienh gathered her remaining strength, took a deep breath. With a fierce yell, she lunged forward, away from her captor, as lightning pain jagged through her shoulder and muscle and tendon tore. The Viking that held her stumbled and dropped his hold. Throwing herself against Hrolgar's legs as she rolled onto her mangled shoulder, she snatched the dagger free from its sheath. She slashed upward. Hrolgar yelled as blood spewed.

Above her, the world burst into tumult. In the cloud of red and purple pain, legs and iron all jumbled with harsh sounds of the scuffle. Feet pummeled her, stepped on her, tripped and stumbled, and bodies tumbled atop her. Silence dark as pain shot through her head and ebbed to oblivion.

The instant Arienh dove away from her captor, Ronan leaped. His sword split through the raider who had held her, and the marauder crumpled to the sand.

He swung at Hrolgar. Startled from Arienh's slice across his side, Hrolgar fell away from Ronan's first blow, rolled, and jumped to his feet. The short stump of his left arm swung about as if an arm were still attached, groping for the gash. Fury doubled in his eyes as he lunged with a scream, sword high to slash down.

Ronan caught the blow on his shield and swept his sword around. Hrolgar dodged. The blades clanged, vibrated from the blow. Hrolgar, eyes darting side to side, swiped again as he retreated over the rise.

From behind the dune, a hail of arrows flew, catching raiders in the back, chest, face. Olav!

Olav's men rushed from the cover of trees, slashing with their swords, and arrows flying.

Distracted and tiring, Hrolgar staggered back and swung again. Ronan blocked and sliced, a lifetime's fury rallying in his blood.

With a double-handed stroke, his blade caught Hrolgar at the neck. Hrolgar's head flew free from his body and plopped in the soft sand of the dune.

Silence. Not even a bird peeped.

Arienh. Where was she?

A bloody raider's body stretched across her limp figure. Ronan tossed the body aside and knelt. He lifted Arienh into his arms. "Arienh. Arienh."

As he rolled her to her back, she mumbled. How badly was she hurt?

"Come on, love, wake up."

Her eyes rolled. "Light hurts." She closed her eyes again.

"Nay, love, wake up."

Egil bent over her, checking her head and the open cut surrounded by blood-matted hair. "Shallow. Not bad, Ronan. A lump on the head. Most of the blood isn't hers. I'd say her arm's out of joint. Better to fix it while she's still dazed."

That would hurt, but Egil was right. "Aye. Olav, help us hold her down. Olav?"

Egil frowned. "He's run down to the shore where the other women are."

"Oh." He'd forgotten about them. "They're all right, aren't they?"

"Aye. Bjorn's not, though."

Somebody else would have to worry about Bjorn. Tanni, too, was busy, with one of Selma's little cousins crying in his arms.

With two men holding Arienh firmly, Ronan probed around the dislocated shoulder, determining which way it had to go. He'd never done this before, himself, but he'd seen it done. It was almost like a reverse of the way the joint had come undone. And no matter how kindly he meant to be, it would hurt. Badly.

With an exasperated sigh, he wrenched the shoulder back into place. When she screamed, tears flooded his eyes. Once again, she fell unconscious. He scooped her into his arms to carry her to the *Black Swan*.

On the pebbly beach, the women he had brought comforted the rescued hostages. Men knelt beside the stretched-out figure of the blacksmith, who flailed about, raised his head, then slowly sat up, coughing. Elli, her blonde braid dripping and her soaked kirtle clinging to her body, loomed over him, hands on hips.

"How is he?" Ronan asked.

"Stupid fool," Elli said, her eyes blazing. "Can't swim, and he dives into the water after me."

"She had to pull him out," Mildread added.

Ronan tried to imagine the girl tugging the red-bearded blacksmith's huge body through the water. Another time, he would have laughed. "Bjorn? What did you do that for, Bjorn? You know you can't swim."

Bjorn hacked and spit out salt water. "Thought maybe I'd learn quick."

Bjorn would be all right. Ronan carried Arienh to the *Black Swan*, feeling her head toss feebly against his chest. When the other women had climbed aboard, he passed Arienh to Mildread and the clutch of women.

"You did well," he told Mildread. "Without you, we would have lost them."

She nodded and turned her attention back to Arienh, her brown eyes awash with worry.

Ronan joined Egil and Olav to release the grapples and set sail. This time, there would be enough men to row.

"What will we do with Hrolgar's ship?" Egil asked as the *Black Swan* pitched through the surf to deeper water. "It would make good firewood for our hearths."

"I want no reminder of him in our village," Ronan retorted.

There were no jokes today, the way it would be after an ordinary battle. Not even Tanni, who was rarely at a loss for humor. This time Hrolgar had struck too deeply. In his vicious demand for vengeance, he had threatened their very hearts.

Tanni, his jaw still hard-set, carefully watched Selma and the younger girls as if they might disappear if he looked away. "But every stick of wood burned would be a piece of vengeance," he said. "And think of the trees we would not have to cut down."

"Then give it to Bjorn to make charcoal for his forge," Ronan said. "That would be fitting enough."

Bjorn huddled in the far corner of the prow, neither rowing nor complaining, looking pale, his head bowed. Perhaps he was sick from the salt water he had swallowed.

With its sail turned, the *Black Swan* caught the wind. Ronan tacked across deep water until they turned again into the estuary. Repeatedly, Ronan's covert gaze roamed to where Arienh lay, cradled in Mildread's arms, then quickly back to Bjorn. He paused to puzzle over the blacksmith's strange behavior, then fixed his concentration back on the sailing ship.

The men lowered the sail to row against the departing tide and river current, and followed the central channel until they reached the junction with the stream that centered on their valley.

Their valley. It was theirs. Somehow, he had to meld these two opposing peoples. But he didn't know how to overcome all the hatred of the past. Vikings who were not Vikings, but men who wanted only the good life of the good earth. Fierce Celtic women, Loki's daughters, who would have made any man proud to lead them, but who despised men who were not of their kind.

They had done their part exactly as he had commanded. They shot their volley then turned to rescue the captives, leaving the sword fight to the men.

Only Arienh had been injured. Because of him, because of Hrolgar's vengeful hatred.

He beached the *Black Swan* and heeled it over on its side to ease the departure of the women. Arienh's injured arm, tied in a sling, rested across her as he carried her from the ship and up the hill.

The silent procession trudged up the hill behind him to Arienh's cottage, Egil walking by his side. Standing in the doorway, Birgit watched with her strange green eyes, with the intensity a hawk gives to its prey, as he carried Arienh inside their stone cottage and laid her on her bed. Could she really not see and yet stare that way? Nay, she had to have some vision. But how much?

He stepped back away from the bed, leaving the caretaking to Birgit and Elli, with Egil behind him. Egil, he noticed, took great care to avoid Birgit's eyes, and Birgit, who normally stared almost with ferocity, looked anywhere but at Egil.

Birgit tucked the wool blanket around her sister, who soon dozed from the dose of willow bark and lettuce Birgit gave her. Ronan lingered, Egil behind him, but soon it was obvious they could do nothing and were only in the way. They both sighed and turned toward the gaping door.

"Birgit, come out for a moment," Ronan asked as they stepped out into the bright afternoon sun.

Resignation thinned her lips. She nodded and followed them.

"How much can you see?" he asked, leaving the door ajar so he could see Arienh where she lay.

She squared her shoulders, lifting her chin. Yet in her eyes, hidden beneath fierce Celtic pride, lurked deep humiliation. A curious frown wrinkled her brow, and she held out her hand before her until it almost touched him, studying her fingertips as if she wondered if they were there. Again, she looked up, staring in that strange way of hers.

"I can see you, for you are directly in front of me, though I see you poorly. Your brother stands to your side, but I cannot see him. There are other things that tell me he is there."

"But how can you weave if you cannot see?"

"By touch. I memorize the patterns and count the rows."

"And the shooting?"

"She imitated her sister," Egil said. "I thought it strange at the time. I should have guessed."

Birgit nodded, and her lower lip thinned. "It was luck. You do not understand, do you?"

Nay, they did not. Ronan shook his head. "I confess, I do not understand you or your sister at all."

"She did it all for me. They all did."

"But why, Birgit?"

It was as if she drew back, thrusting up a barrier of pride between them. "They were afraid for me. Many things have been said about men from the north, and we have seen so many evils, it was far easier to believe them than to take a chance. We have always known Northmen had no compassion for the weak and helpless."

"The way you believe we eat children," Egil guessed. His voice held a bitter tone Ronan had never heard before.

What would Egil do now? He had been infatuated with Birgit from the beginning, but how could he make a wife of a woman who could not see?

Birgit's gaze roamed far beyond them as if she studied the ash grove beyond the village green, and Ronan realized how few clues she gave to her blindness. "We never believed that," she said, "but there is so much more. We had no way of knowing."

Egil opened his mouth to speak, but Ronan shook his head. Birgit was of a mind to divulge everything now.

"I am glad it is done," she said. Ronan's heart lurched at the sad catch in Birgit's voice. "It is best this way. Arienh would not agree, but this time it is best taken from her hands. She would die before giving up.

"She was so young when our last brother was killed, and she became our father's son, so to speak. She has always taken care of me. Then, in one day, about three years ago, we lost all our men. In our grief and loss, we all would also have laid down and died, but Arienh would not let us."

"Because she will never give up," Ronan said.

Birgit sighed with a resigned nod. "Aye, and that is your doing. Since the day you saved her, she has never surrendered, for she learned one can never tell what the next moment will bring.

"Since then, she has bullied us to do what we must to survive. And when we would not, she did what needed to be done for us. She has plowed the fields, hunted down bees for their honey, trapped hares. Whatever she had needed to do, she has done. She was always the last into the cavern, always the one who saw those she loved fall to the Viking ax. It is a wonder she has not been killed." The sheen of tears danced in Birgit's eyes.

"We can take care of her now."

Birgit smiled, a sadly wise smile. "But that is my point. What I have lost is easy for others to understand, but Arienh has lost far more. I do not think even Arienh understands this. Wonderful though she is, she should never have had this burden. She should have had the life of a normal woman. But she has not. She accepted her task willingly, but in time, the task itself became who she is. And now you have come, and you take that from her. She fears her people no longer need her. We do, of course, but in different ways."

"But it is no longer necessary. I can take care of her now."

Birgit shook her head. "You do not hear me. I know you can take care of her. But necessity has made her who she is, and I do not think she knows how to be anything else. If you do not accept this, you cannot accept her."

"Do you suggest I submit to her will, then? Where we come from, men make the decisions."

"A Viking submit to a woman? I could not imagine it, even though you are not where you came from anymore. But you have come here with your minds set on what we need. You did not ask us. Just as you did not ask Arienh's consent to wed her."

Ronan frowned. "It was she who made the offer."

"But she had no other choice, for you held Elli's life in your hand. She could no more let her die than she could you, on the day you came here, and you know that. Nay, you forced her consent, no matter how you say it. And among Celts, only willingness makes a marriage valid."

There had been nothing forced about the passion between them. Yet had that alone made it a marriage? He glanced through the open door, yearning to take Arienh in his arms and hold her, tenderly soothing her pain, patiently loving her as she recovered. Keeping her safe from all the horrors, wiping away the pain of the past.

But what if she really did not want him at all, what if she never had? Had he let his dream so encompass him that he had blotted out all her wishes? Believed hers to be the same as his merely because he wanted it that way?

"I have been fooling myself, then," he said. "She has made it clear all along she does not find me good enough for her."

Birgit almost smiled. "Ah, Viking, you only hear her words. Listen to her heart instead."

She raised her clasped hands to her lips and continued. "It is true, we learned you are not like those monstrous marauders. It was hard for us to accept, but we learned you are men, worthy men, men to be admired. But then there was Liam. Arienh would have never let you take him from me, no matter what it cost her. But I am resigned to that now. You are right, he needs a man, not his mother. It is best for him, so I will let him go."

"Let him go?" Ronan and Egil echoed each other. Their eyes met, exchanging confusion.

Birgit focused her pale, determined gaze on Ronan, almost as if she did not know Egil stood there. "Aye. I know I can trust Egil to foster him well. Arienh will not understand, but it is Liam's need that must be met. Nothing else matters. I want most of all that my son will become a worthy man."

Angry frustration boiled up in Egil's face, and he grabbed Birgit by her arms. "You expect me to take your child and not you? Nay, I will have you as well."

Even face-to-face with him, Birgit would not meet Egil's eyes. Her lids closed, fluttering. "I will be no man's wife."

"Why?"

"I have nothing to give." Birgit chewed at her lip and turned away. She stepped over the threshold and quietly shut the door behind her.

Through a horrible, strained moment, Egil watched the old oak door as if he expected it to open again and Birgit burst out of it, into his arms. Anguish deepened in his eyes.

Ronan touched Egil's arm, feeling his brother's devastation. Now that Birgit's secret was out, Arienh might come around. But Birgit? What could anyone do about her eyes?

Birgit was right. From the beginning, Egil had pursued his love with the greatest gentleness, but he'd had no idea just how badly Birgit had been damaged. How could she live the life of a normal wife? What if she had more children? How would she manage them?

And if Egil did not marry her, then Arienh would never leave her sister.

They walked in silence, the two brothers alone, following the path that led through the ash grove and the oak tree where Birgit had collided with the low-hanging branch.

"She never even saw it," Egil said, testing the sturdiness of the limb. "How did she manage to fool us for so long?"

"Because we did not expect it. Because she does not put herself in places where her secret would be betrayed. Because she weaves. Who would have thought anyone could weave so wonderfully if she could not see?"

Egil gave a mirthless laugh and nodded, as they turned back to the path toward the Bride's Well, their pace brutally slow.

"Or to hit the center of a target on her first shot? It must truly have been luck. But now I understand the look I saw on her face. She was afraid her shot was wild and her secret was about to be revealed." The slow shake of his head seemed laced with pain. "But Ronan, I still cannot imagine that they thought we might actually hurt her."

Ronan knew. "But how could they know that is not our way? They have never been anywhere but here. Every Northman they have ever seen has been a murderer, men like Hrolgar. What will you do now, Brother?"

"I don't know. I just don't know. I cannot give her up."

Ronan understood. They were very much alike, he and Egil, brothers in many ways, even if they did not share the same blood. And Egil would find a solution, just as he would.

With a clap to his brother's back, he encouraged Egil back to their tasks, and as they turned in the path, they heard the little brass bell Wynne used to announce supper.

The Northmen filled the cottage, murmuring quietly, eating in silence, and hanging about as if they expected something but had no notion what it might be. The gloom in the cottage hovered like a starving kestrel over an empty field.

Egil sat at the slab table, silently quaffing ale.

Wynne placed a gentle hand on his shoulder. "Mildread said it was an injury to her head, caused by the man who raped her. Her sight has faded slowly, but no one knows if she will go completely blind."

Ronan had already heard that. It didn't make the problem any simpler.

"You could find another woman, Egil," Tanni suggested. "There are plenty of others."

"No, there aren't." Egil's retort was as near to a snarl as Ronan had ever heard from his usually mellow brother.

From the corner where his bed was built into the wall, Gunnar rose slowly, edging his thinning legs over the side and forcing himself to his feet. He had been weak for several days, and the trip to the cavern earlier in the day had exhausted him. But Ronan knew his second father could not let his sons suffer without trying to comfort them. He shuffled painful steps through the throng of men, resting here or there with a hand to someone's shoulder, and finally reaching Egil at the table.

"Son, you are right, there is no other woman. Else you would not have chosen her in the first place."

Egil found a smile for his father. "Aye, Father. I just do not know how to persuade her. You should rest."

"Time enough to rest in eternity. We cannot solve our problems by resting. We will solve it by working together, the way we always have. Have you noticed, that is the way these Celtic women do it too?" With a slowness that betrayed the intense pain in his body, Gunnar eased himself down on the bench beside his son.

Ronan remembered the time when Gunnar had been as tall as Egil, and his bones bulky and strong. One of the many things Ronan loved about Egil was his close resemblance to Gunnar. He had wished many times that he also shared it. But they shared so much else, it was of little real importance.

"We will find a way," Gunnar said. "You cannot doubt, any of you, that you have won their hearts. But there is something else that bothers me. The girl, Elli."

Ronan knew where Gunnar was leading. "Aye, I agree. Vengeance or no, she is not the kind to risk her own folk without reason."

All eyes turned on Bjorn, who had tucked himself into a corner, nursing a horn of ale that he had already refilled several times. The blacksmith was not just feeling the effects of salt water.

Ronan strode across the hard-packed dirt floor and stood over the man, his arms folded. He folded his arms. "All right, Bjorn, out with it."

"Out...?" Bjorn stared, bleary-eyed, confused. But he had not had enough time to get that drunk.

"You know what I mean. The truth."

Bjorn swiped his hand across his mouth, and the foam along his bright red mustache disappeared. "That's the trouble."

Ronan let out an exasperated growl. "What?" he demanded.

"She's telling the truth," Bjorn said.

"She's what?"

"She's telling the truth. I think."

"By Odin's ugly face," grumbled Egil. "Don't you think you could've told us sooner?"

"Well, I can't remember. I've been trying to, but I just can't. So I think it must be true."

Ronan balled his fists, silently wishing he held Bjorn's neck between them. "You told me you never left the Green Isle."

"I didn't think it would matter. But I wasn't even from there. You remember Ivar the Bald?"

"Ivar the Berserker, you mean?" Ronan had heard of him. And this was sounding worse by the moment. Every man in the cottage jumped to his feet, surrounding Ronan.

"Well, aye, and it fits better. I was just an itinerant smith when I met him, and he took me on."

"Wait a moment," Olav insisted. "You must remember what you did, though."

Bjorn shook his head, and his rounded shoulders hunched like a beaten slave's. "I don't remember much of anything. We used to drink this brew when we went raiding. Something was added to the ale. I think aconite and nightshade and some other things. It made me feel like I was bigger than a house, like nothing could conquer me. But I don't remember anything I did very clearly, for that whole time. We raided and killed, and I don't even know what else. But this place—from the beginning, I've had the feeling I'd been here before. But that's all I knew."

"Hel's tits!" Egil's voice was as fierce as a growl. "Just what we needed. No wonder they hate our kind so much. They must have known all along who we had with us."

Wynne shook her head. "Nay, 'tis your black mood speaking, Son. The others didn't know what Elli intended. Nor do they hate you. But you have stirred frightening things in them that they do not know how to handle."

Ronan could see that more easily than Egil. Not even Arienh in all her rage had ever really hated them. Something in his heart had known that all along.

But they needed to focus on the problem of Bjorn.

"Ivar's dead," he said to the blacksmith. "Is that when you quit raiding?"

Bjorn nodded, miserably swirling his horn for the last dregs of ale. "I killed him. Found my woman with him. That was enough for me. I had to get out of that life, and I left and went to the Green Isle, where I took up smithing again. I never told anybody where I'd been. Thought maybe if I came with you, the ghosts would leave me alone. But they don't."

"Ghosts?"

"They come at night, unless I'm drunk enough. That's why I sleep in the forge. Alone. Scares people sometimes."

Ronan let out a disgusted snort. "The least you're going to do is apologize to Elli."

"Can't. Don't deserve her forgiveness."

"Maybe not. I didn't say you did. But there'll be at least a confession. We can't change what you did, but we'll do what's right, anyway. She has the right to choose what is to be done."

Egil rubbed a fist over his chin. "She can't hate him too much, Ronan. She pulled him out of the sea."

"Aye," said Olav. "I agree with Wynne. This thing hasn't gone beyond Elli, I'm sure. It's not too late tonight. Let's seek out the women and settle this now."

It was not like Olav to be so impatient. But Olav had secured his love with Mildread, and all that stood between them was Mildread's loyalty to the other women, whose fates were unresolved. Perhaps Mildread waited even now in some secluded glen, some secret bower for her lover.

Perhaps that was all any of them still wanted. Ronan studied the blacksmith, red-nosed and bleary-eyed in his cup, in the misery of the most painful part of love. Why Elli had bothered to save him, he could hardly imagine, if it wasn't love.

All around him, men hovered expectantly, ready to dash out the door at his command. He hesitated.

*Ah, Viking, you only hear her words. Listen to her heart.*

What had Birgit meant?

*I do not think she knows how to be anything else. If you do not accept this, you cannot accept her.*

He had come looking for a docile, submissive, sweet-natured girl and found instead a Celtic warrior woman, ferocious in her protectiveness of those she loved. Yet he had expected she would become the girl of his dreams simply because he dreamed it. Perhaps it was not just that Celts had trouble accepting Northmen. Perhaps Northmen, and one in particular, needed to accept Celts for who, what, they were.

Ronan almost laughed aloud. All these years, he'd had the wrong dream. It was the fierce warrior woman who excited him.

"Nay," he responded at last, feeling the slyness of a plan come upon him. "There's a better way."

A disconcerted grumble spread through the men.

Egil cocked his head in curiosity. "A better way?"

"Aye, and much depends on you. You mean to win Birgit over, don't you?"

"Aye." Curiosity doubled to anticipation.

The grin stretched broadly over Ronan's face as the idea expanded in his mind. "Loki's daughters have met their match. They think we're Vikings. We'll give them Vikings."

# CHAPTER TWENTY-FOUR

———✠———

Birgit didn't know much about Arienh's herbs, but she knew which ones would keep her sister quiet, and quiet was what Arienh needed to recover from the torn shoulder. Through the long night she had sat beside Arienh's bed to keep her from rolling, and her effort had not been wasted. Arienh had been a fidget, despite the wild lettuce.

But now her sister slept soundly. Leaving Elli to watch, Birgit left the cottage and the stale, somber air. Feeling the warmth of the bright sun on her head, she ambled down the path through the green as if she had no particular purpose. The Northmen did not seem to be about. But then, how would she know?

Birgit smiled and spoke of Arienh to all who asked, and told them she just needed to stroll alone in the sunlight for a while before going back to her vigil in the cottage. No one objected. They were used to her occasional rambling, which she used to do before the Vikings came. She followed the path into the ash grove, up the valley, and turned off at the narrow trail to the Bride's Well. She knew it so well, she had no need to see it.

Her saint's place, named for her patron saint, special to Birgit as long as she could remember. She found her peace there in the same way Arienh found hers in the stone circle.

She reached the crystal pool, a dark, cool blur before her, and dredged up memories from her childhood of the sparkle of warm sun upon its waters. The frolic of the Northmen played in her memory, more for what she heard of their merriment than the little she had been able to see. Once she had played like that with Arienh and their brothers. So long ago. Now only Beltane, when the old ones came back to dance, brought Trevor back.

She wasn't sure about Niall, if he was alive or dead. If he was dead, had he come back to the land of his birth and the spirits of his ancestors, from that faraway place where he had been taken? No one had ever explained that to her.

The path forked to circle the pool, and she chose the one that ascended over rising dark rock toward the cascading falls, to the high bluff that overlooked the pool and forested valley. From memory, she found her footing and climbed, heading toward the top. Halfway up, she paused, not from weariness but to reflect, and sat near the edge of the bluff, looking out, remembering the magnificent view.

Like Arienh, she wanted desperately for her people to live here forever. She wanted to come back and dance within the circle and know Celts still walked this land. Without the Northmen, this would not happen, for there would be no Celts, save those who were dead.

They were wonderful, these Northmen. Not just Egil. Ronan's tenderness tore at Birgit's heart, even more than Arienh's yearning for him. He was an unusual man, even for a Viking.

Northman. What sort of boy had he been back then, that he had risked his life for a girl he did not know? Not the same as those who had come to thieve and kill. And he had come back, not merely to pick out a valley and take it over. He had searched for Arienh and found her. And wanted her to care about him as he cared about her.

Ten years. A long time for a young man. They needed each other, deserved each other. How good it would be for Arienh to have such a man.

And Birgit stood between them.

She wished she could have the same sort of love from Egil, but that was really too much to ask. But for Liam...

From the day Liam was born, she had despaired of how to provide for him, a child lost between two worlds, perhaps hated in both. The Celts had comforted and sheltered the child, but he had always known he was different. But now his heritage had come to him, and Egil was showing him the way to be a good man in a harsh world. Liam must have Egil.

She stood between them as well. She alone stood between her people and their happiness, their very survival.

Was there an answer in the Viking way? Might the unforgivable sin be one at least God could understand? But what if He did not? Perhaps she would even be forbidden to come back to the circle to dance. She could not bear to face eternity without that.

She sighed and renewed her climb. The rock face steepened, becoming nearly vertical, but she knew the way. Many times, even since losing most of her sight, she had come here. Soon, at the very top, the plateau was as level as the ground near the seashore. She picked her way to the edge of the bluff, easily negotiating its deep cracks, and stopped at its edge, overlooking the stream that fed the falls and the deep, clear pool it made.

The sun warmed her hair, while an airy breeze cooled her face. The curly red strands that blew before her eyes were close enough for her to see the brilliant rainbow colors of sunset and gold that hid in those strands. She had forgotten how the sun could do that.

Years ago, she would have been awed by the view of dark, sparkling water, and its memory still made her heart beat faster.

Now it looked like the fluff of a dark ewe's newly sheared wool. Soft, springy. Like the wonderful down blanket Egil described.

She could fall, fall, fall, and not know the danger until it was too late.

Nay, she knew the rocks were there.

Strange, that for so many years she had just wanted to die. Only the love for Liam and Arienh had kept her from this. Now, she wanted so much to live. She wanted...

She wanted Egil. She wanted what she could never have, could never take. How had he become so dear to her?

Nay, that was no surprise.

Even at a fair distance, she could always recognize him by the way his blurred image moved and by the red slash of the leather sling for his sword. But not until she was close enough to actually touch him did his blue eyes become beautifully distinguishable.

For a moment, she paused, suddenly grateful that she was still able to see how wonderfully handsome he was. Perhaps long years hence, long after her eyes had failed, she would still be able to remember how she had savored all that there was about him. But what if she would not be there, long years from now?

Did she love him enough to do this?

She could make everything all right again.

Once again she peered over the edge, searching, for what she could not see, for the rocks that were there, yet not. Tightness gathered in her throat as she blinked at hot tears.

Nay.

Aye. She must. She loved them. She could not let them suffer for her sake.

Birgit swiped at the tears on her cheeks with her hand and took a deep breath.

Nay. She could not. She was too selfish. She could not help wanting to live.

"What are you doing, Birgit?"

She should have known. Of course he would follow her. His presence behind her was like the warmth of the sun. It sparkled in her like the memory of the clear water below.

"Come away, Birgit. You will get hurt."

He knew. As if he had read her mind. Why hadn't he let her go, then? Didn't he realize how much better things would be?

Egil's gentle hands touched her waist. He stood behind her, barely, just barely, touching with his body. His scent was warm and clean and sweet to her as newly cut hay. She remembered. He didn't like heights.

"You frighten me, Birgit. Come, let's move away."

Once more, she peered over the edge. "It's like a cloud below," she said.

"It isn't a cloud. The rocks would break you in pieces."

"There is no good way to die. You do not understand, do you?"

His arms slid around her waist, and his warm breath stirred her hair. "Nay. And I will not allow it."

"I have thought of it for a very long time. I keep everyone from what is best for them. You do not need a wife who cannot do her duties, nor does Liam need such a mother. You are right, he needs a man to teach him to be a man. My sister cannot be a wife when she must take care of me. The others, too, wait because of me."

"Do you Celts think of nothing but sacrifice? Do you all imagine yourselves as Christian martyrs? Do you not realize how much pain you would cause?"

"We have all suffered many losses. It would pass."

His arms tightened around her, and he bent his head to lay a cheek against hers. The warm moisture of his tears slid onto her cheek. "Nay, this would be the worst of all. Arienh would never recover from it. To lose all she has fought for, Birgit? How could you do that to her? Liam would never get over it. He would always blame himself, for he would know you did it for him. And I would not. If I must lose you some other way, I would have to accept it. But not like this. I love you, Birgit."

She shook her head. "You don't want a blind wife, Egil."

In a disgruntled huff, he lifted her up and carried her back several paces. He turned her to face him, cradling her face forcefully between his huge hands. "I don't want anything bad for you, Birgit. Not blind or deaf, not to lose a child, nor die in childbirth. I would not want to leave you a widow. But some things we cannot help, and who knows what the future will bring? We will have to work harder, but I will not live without you."

"It is not fair to you." Hot tears stung her eyes and rolled shamelessly down her cheeks. Birgit buried her face into his chest, her arms encircling him as if she clung to him.

"Ah, love, I do not care about fairness," he said, tucking hot kisses about her face, bending to catch the lobe of her ear gently between his lips. "Only that I want you and no other. We have everyone to help us, and you have much to give, far more than you realize."

"But there would be babes, and I could not look after them properly. Without Arienh, I could not have handled Liam."

"But we have her still, and my mother. Gunnar will soon be gone, and Wynne will need grandchildren then, to help her through her grief. Will you give her that comfort, love? And for Gunnar, a child of his blood, before he dies?"

Could she? Was it possible? Did he truly love her so much? Slowly, she lifted her head to search his eyes and saw his anguish, those wondrously beautiful eyes as blue as bright bluebells, stung with pain and longing. Could she fill him with happiness? She could not recall when she had thought of herself as anything but a burden.

"Be my love, Birgit. Be my wife."

His lips found hers, fiery passion fitting them together perfectly, every inch of their bodies molded to each other. So many
times, she had wanted to explore the feel of him, to feel powerful
muscles tauten beneath her fingertips, to test for passion rippling
through his body and hers.

A flicker of fear crept up her spine, remembrance of that
long-ago horror, and she had to break the kiss to look again at his
face, study his blue eyes, and run her palm over the bristling flesh
of his cheeks. This was Egil, and she was safe. Safe to let the past
go, free her passion just for him.

A silly smile sneaked onto her face. "You lied to me, Egil.
Before when you kissed me, you told me it would be the sweetest
kiss I ever got. And it wasn't. This one was."

His chuckle was like the gentle hum of honeybees. "There
will be many sweeter even than that. We will find a way, love, I
promise you."

She smiled. "Aye. Aye, my love, I'll be your wife. At Beltane,
you will be mine."

He laughed, startling her, as he suddenly sported a wide and
wicked grin. "Glad you mentioned that. We're going to need your
help. And Liam's."

Arienh woke to an odd collection of indistinct memories that
seemed to throb in her head like a muffled drum. Vague ones of
being carried, with her arm fierily aching, and burying her face
in Ronan's strong chest. Memories of Birgit dosing her with her
own tonics to make her sleep. Memories of waking, reaching out
for Ronan, and learning he was gone.

Of course. She had forgotten how she had chased him
away.

Once again he had come to her aid. He had even offered to give up his hand to that malicious uncle of his for her life.

What had happened after that? Her mind felt like it was full of fog. Was Ronan safe? Or had the Viking chopped off his hand? But he'd carried her back. He could not have done that without his hand, could he?

Arienh shook her cobwebby head and forced herself to rise.

"Wait," said Birgit, and Birgit's arm slipped gently beneath her to ease her up and slip pillows behind her. Arienh didn't remember having so many pillows.

Birgit reached for the tonic.

"No more," she said, waving Birgit away. "Where is Ronan?"

"Gone. With the other men."

"Is he all right?"

"Aye. Are you?"

Was she? Her shoulder ached and burned like fire. "Aye. I think so. Do you know what happened?"

"Egil told me some. Ronan forced the Vikings back to shore with his longship, then there was a fight. He took the women to fight with him, Arienh. It must have been something to see. Egil said you tore your shoulder escaping. They killed all the Vikings."

Familiar flickers of scenes floated through her mind, of Ronan walking like a god out of the sea, of a sharp blade pricking her nape. She wished she could have seen the rest.

"When is Beltane?" That would tell her how long she had been asleep.

"Tomorrow. Arienh, it could wait, couldn't it?"

"Tomorrow. I've lost two days. Why didn't you wake me? There is so much to do."

Birgit gently pushed her back as she started to rise. "Nay, it is done. We have not failed you."

"And the Vikings?"

"Who knows? They stay on their side of the stream. They know, Arienh."

"Know? About you? But how?"

"When Liam and I had to run back to the village. It was hard for them not to notice when I ran into a tree and knocked myself senseless."

Arienh studied Birgit's face carefully, but her sister had already shuttered down whatever it was she felt. "What did they say?"

"Nothing, really. They were too busy trying to figure out how to rescue you. I had to explain later."

"What about Liam?"

"They have not said. But I am resigned to it."

"Well, I am not."

"It is not for you to say." Birgit had an uncharacteristic deepness to her voice that resembled a growl. This time, Arienh suspected, Birgit would not tolerate interference.

What would they do now? She would help Birgit, as she always had, but their failures would be obvious. It would not be long, then, before the men stepped in and took Liam.

And they stayed away, on the far side of the stream. So Ronan had had enough. This time, she had made him so angry that he would never want to take her back.

# CHAPTER TWENTY-FIVE

—⊞—

IN THE STONE CIRCLE, THE BONFIRES WAITED TO BE LIT, AND AN ox was already roasted for the feast.

The Northmen kept their word and gathered all the herd animals to drive between the fires. But they kept to the far side of the stream as if they feared they might contract leprosy.

Arienh had always loved Beltane, the time when bright summer was ushered in with the joy of dancing and singing, the time when men and women came together and formed the bond that would be solemnized at midsummer. Not this time. She wished the whole thing were over.

Never had she felt so helpless or unneeded.

The truth was, the Vikings had won. But they no longer seemed to care. So perhaps the women had won. Now that they no longer wanted to.

Perhaps for the others there would be some reconciliation, but it was clear Ronan didn't want her anymore. Nor did Egil show interest in Birgit. She tried to imagine what that would mean, a future village in which she and Birgit had no place, for who would want a woman to plow and hunt when she had men to do it for her?

Just as she had the past three years, Arienh led the Beltane procession. Women and children, draped in spring garlands, walked in pairs along the stream that led to the Bride's Well, singing ancient tunes with archaic words. Arienh sang, too, trying to recapture the joy she had felt in years past. She felt only aching loneliness.

At the pool, they stopped, circling around its bank. Birgit stepped forward and tied a rag on the branch of the beech tree that overhung the pool. This place was named, as Birgit was, for the saint, so Birgit had always gone first. Everyone, down to the youngest who could understand its purpose, tied a rag onto a branch and made a secret wish, as people had always done.

The day's brightness faded, blue sky turning to dusky silver, the way a Viking's blue eyes softened with coming night. The little procession once again entered the forest, followed the stream bank, then ascended through groves of ashes behind the crescent of cliffs that marked the ancient pool of wishes. Across the grassy plateau stretched parallel rows of low standing stones, like guardians of the past, leading to the taller stones of the circle. Arienh led the Celts between the lines of stones, Birgit and Liam beside her, and Elli close on the other side, along a lane worn deep by the passing of people and time. The spirits of the past began to merge and walk with the living.

Ahead, the sounds of cattle lowing, the whinny of horses and bleat of sheep heralded the arrival of the animals from the pastures of the upper valley. Dogs and men worked the herded creatures within tight, flowing circles.

In the west, beyond the hills, the sky reddened in streaks and darkened. All the fires in the village were extinguished, and on this night a new fire would be started.

Mildread, the oldest among them, since Old Ferris still pouted and refused to come, assembled her tinder and kindling and knelt close to the gathered heaps of wood. Just as well. Arienh doubted if the old man had enough left in him to make a spark.

Mildread rubbed the spindle in her hands. The smell of smoldering wood scented the air. She rubbed faster. Smoke rose from the wood as the tinder glowed and Mildread teased the coals with her breath. The smoky aroma tickled Arienh's nostrils. It sparked, then burst into flame.

A cooing admiration rumbled through the crowd. The new fire. The kindling caught, then ignited a rush torch soaked in fat. Arienh held the torch to the old leaves and twigs at the base of the first pile of brush until it roared to life. Then the other.

In the deepening night, a new song rose to mingle with the fires. Joining hands, the women circled one fire then the other, chanting and skipping they way it had always been done. When they finished, they looked to the Northmen.

Garlanded oxen came first, patiently accepting the goading of the men. Behind them, cows with their calves.

The rams followed, then ewes and lambs, harried by the dogs, which nipped and circled, forcing the reluctant animals between the flames. On the opposite side, they were released to graze. The sheep took it all in as if it were only one more ridiculous thing the humans expected of them.

The horses balked. Their eyes flared like huge round disks, and the beasts bucked and snorted as two men forced each animal through separately. Some reared and flailed hooves in the air, fought to turn. But each was driven between the fires, until the last of the hoofed beasts had passed through the flames of Beltane once again. Protected yet another year.

Then the men left. Gone as if they had never been there at all. Vanished into the hills, returning their herds to their pens or loose into the higher summer pasture. They did not come back. Hardly surprising, since they had not been asked.

The world, the cool night air, all felt empty. It was not like things had been in the past. Beltane was once again theirs alone.

Silence replaced the accustomed revelry and joy, and the women sat down on pallets to watch the fires blaze.

All theirs. Alone. Lonely.

Stars scattered like jewels in the dark side of the sky, and the full moon shone from the south like brilliant silver over the ocean, coating the dancing crests of a quiet sea. Liam wandered off to play with Mildread's girls.

A lone pipe whistled the mournful tune of the Celtic dance, faint, hollowly echoing. Arienh glanced at Elli, for only she still piped the tunes. But Elli watched the fires as if she were lost in happier times, her reed pipe resting on the ground beside her. Arienh scanned the darkness behind them. But the music didn't come from there.

The echoing strands of a harp joined. No harp had played in this valley since her childhood. Arienh strained her eyes to see if the sound came from the tall hills behind the circle.

The flames danced where now there were no men. Nay, she saw them. The old ones. The spirits.

Didn't she? Arienh focused her eyes on the flames. It was an illusion. Shadowy and vague, undulating like the will-o-the-wisps in the bogs.

A young man leapt over the flames, a powerful, graceful leap, skimming just at the edge of danger. Admiring gasps hissed and skimmed across the crowd. Startled, Arienh, glanced behind her. Nay, not from this crowd, which was absorbed in its own doings. She turned back. The shadow figure leapt again, soaring over the licking flames. Niall. Beautiful Niall, who had been swept away in a Viking raid. Vanished forever.

"Niall. It's Niall!" she whispered. "He's come back!"

Interrupted from a sad reverie, Birgit jumped. She squinted hard. "Where?"

"Don't you see him?" Arienh's heart raced.

The figure of a young man, a different one, leaped and swirled before her, clear, yet oddly indistinct.

"Trevor!"

"Arienh, are you mad? Trevor's dead."

"Aye, I know." But they were there, spirits, yet somehow real. Ungarmented, faces without form, yet she knew them. It was Trevor's gentle, caring smile, the way she remembered the older brother who had thrown her into the air and ridden her on his shoulders, who had pulled her from the stream. She remembered the time when the rushing waters had suddenly frightened her, and she had stood stock-still in her terror, certain she would be swept off her feet and battered by the raging waters against the huge boulders. It was Trevor who rushed to her aid that day, as he had many times. She saw him now, the loving brother she adored, not as he had died, crushed, in agony, in her arms.

Tears collected in the corners of her eyes.

Was it vision? Memory? Or was it real?

She saw her father, his arms laced over the shoulders of uncles, cousins, as the shadowy dancers circled. A heavy sob lodged like a wad in her throat, choking her, then burst forth, shuddering through her. His loving eyes beckoned her. She ached to run into the circle and throw herself into his arms. To dance, arm in arm, swinging wildly.

She was not a man. Women did not dance with men. She did not belong. Yet she felt their pull as if they tugged her hand. Weylin, her cousin. Grandfather. She had been so very little when he had died. Great-grandfather, who had outlived them all. All of them, not as they had been when they died, neither old nor young, but without age.

The circle widened, spinning in a slow turn about the stones, around the fires. Arienh rose to her feet, drawn by the compelling force. Closer, closer. Stepping into the circle, she raised her arms, to touch, yet not, upon the shoulders of the dancers. Daringly, she raised her foot to begin a dance that had been reserved for men since time began. The spirits drew her in, enclosing her with an aching, welcoming warmth. Of their own accord, her feet began the steps, surefooted, in complicated patterns that were both familiar and untried.

The circle expanded as if it meant to fill the earth.

Women. Her mother, gone so long she could not even remember mourning her. Aunts, children she had not known, yet knew. Forms of those gone before her birth. She saw them clearly now, ethereally real, the old ones, who had always come at Beltane, who had been coming since long before her birth. Celt, Not-Celt, even the ancient ones. She knew them all by the way they touched her soul, knew the feel of their ancient blood still coursing through her veins.

She danced, danced with all of them, man, woman, child, Celt, and Not-Celt. The pace quickened, whirled around the circle. Hands clasped living and spirit, the eternal living thread of time that had no beginning nor end. In the dance, she embraced them all, spinning back to a time when everything was whole.

Tears streamed down her cheeks in hot, stinging trails, and still she danced, caught each ghostly partner by the arm, swinging round, took the next, knowing each, loving, aching, hungering, mourning each one she had lost. Remembering the wonder that had been their lives, that she could never have again. Her feet flew through the rapid steps known to her only from watching, understanding now what she had never under-stood before, the true meaning of a ritual begun in time so ancient there were no words to explain it. It was as if she had been born knowing the dance, had somehow forgotten it, and it was reborn in her. Her throat ached from the pain of her sobs.

But here, in the bosom of the dance, among those she loved, it was as if they wrapped her in loving arms and shared her suffering.

The pipe wailed its sadness; the harp plucked its joy. The dancers spun away into lines and pairs, changing, dipping, and swaying, a rhythm like the restless sea. Arienh spun around, taking each new partner in turn by hand, or perhaps by soul. Tears poured from her eyes, and she let them flow freely.

Once again, the circle tightened, even though it seemed that all were still there. Across from her, she saw the Viking. Ronan. Drawn, perhaps, by the Celtic part of him, standing motionless within the circle as the spirits swirled around him.

He did not belong. The interloper. She ached for him. Yet had not the Celts once been interlopers? Had not the stone circle been built by the old ones, long in the distant past before there were Celts?

They swarmed about him, these old ones, whirled him in. The Viking melded with the spirits, joining the frenzied steps of the dance as if he, too, had been born with the knowledge.

As the Celts before him had done, as those before the Celts had done, the Viking joined the circle. For the circle was shared by all.

Arienh raised her hands, and the Viking's palms touched hers. His eyes darkened, smoldering with hungry longing as they danced, palm to palm, in the middle of the circle of swirling spirits.

Then would it be true that Vikings would dance with Celts? For surely, the circle would never end. Just as Arienh knew the blood of these ancient ones still flowed in her veins, so the Celts and Vikings would be remembered and revered by those still to come.

She was part of both past and present. And future. The Viking was a part of it all.

Life would go on. And the dead would always return for Beltane. They would never be lost.

She blinked at her fading tears and through them saw the circle of dancers dwindle into shadows. The Viking was gone. The spirits departed. Niall. Trevor. Father. Mother. Grandfather. All of them, one by one, slipped back beyond the mystical veil.

Clean, cold air rushed into her lungs with each new breath. How glorious it was to be a Celt. To be alive, and know one's world was filled with those beloved departed ones.

The circle of dancers was gone.

Had she seen it? Or imagined they were here? Was the Viking really a part, or had she merely wanted him to be there?

Arienh looked back at the women who sat, transfixed, on their blankets. Had they seen what she had? Or had they decided she had suddenly gone demented from that bump on her head?

"Did you see them?" she asked Birgit as she sat again.

"The spirits? Of course not. I could not even see you."

"They were there," Arienh said, but her voice sounded foolishly weak.

"One doesn't have to see them to know that."

"Nay, I mean it. Truly. I wish just this once you could have seen."

Birgit smiled, wide and dreamily. "Niall, too?"

"Aye. I told you."

"I wondered if he would come back. Once he died, I mean." Birgit swallowed a big, visible lump and smiled. Arienh thought about how close Birgit and Niall had always been. "I thought he must be dead. Do you think you can let them go now, Arienh?"

Go? Had she been holding them here? Never had she cried for the dead, until the Vikings had come. She had always feared, if she ever began to cry, she would lie down and mourn so deeply she would never be able to get up again. Then the last of the Celts in this valley would have died out, for no one would have been strong enough to keep them alive.

But she understood now: she could not keep her grief buried forever. Perhaps those who were gone had needed for her to grieve for them. And sooner or later, she had to let it loose, and with it, let go of that terrible, possessive fear for all those who remained. Aye, she would lose them all someday, if they did not lose her first. She could not stop what was meant to be. But none were truly lost.

"Aye," she answered at last. "They will be back next year."

She sat in silence beside her sister, studying the flames, cherishing the moments past. The ancients, the vision of the Viking dancing with them. "Where are the Vikings?" she asked.

"I don't think they're coming back," said Birgit.

"I suppose not."

"We haven't been very nice, have we?"

She didn't answer. It was all such a tangle.

Birgit's pale eyes, almost golden by the firelight, stared at her demandingly. "He deserves better than this, Arienh. You wouldn't be alive if it weren't for him."

"I know. But I don't think he wants me anymore. I can't blame him for not understanding what I can't say."

"We were better off starving than we are with this kind of misery. Go to him, Arienh. You can think of something."

She shook her head, feeling a surge of moisture in her eyes.

"Nay, it's all right, Arienh. I am resigned. Their hearts are kind, you know that. And no mother can keep her son forever. If you don't do something, I will."

Arienh sighed. "If only they had found some other place to settle, someplace where Vikings have never been."

"Do you know what you just said?"

And it slowly came to her. That was what the dance was telling her. Ronan was right. It was only his Viking blood that kept them apart. Only what men of his kind had done before, what was said about them, none of it true of the man she had come to know and love. Nay, they would not harm Birgit, any more than they would eat children.

But they would take Liam, believing that they must. And no matter what Birgit said, it would destroy her.

From the dark edge of the bonfire, Mildread strolled in their direction, her hands clutching her heavy shawl about her shoulders. "Arienh, have you seen the girls?" Arienh caught Birgit's gaze, puzzled. Birgit answered, frowning. "I thought they were with you. Liam went to play with them."

"Aye, he came. But they said they were coming back here. I do not see them anywhere."

"They can't be far," Arienh said. "I think they were dancing around the stones just a moment ago."

But only silence came from the stones.

Together, she and Birgit rose from their blanket, shaking out their clothes. None of the children were in sight. And no childish giggles emanated from hidden places. She knew exactly where they would find them, clustered behind the stones, up to no good. She just hoped Liam wasn't playing with fire again, like he had last year.

With quieted steps, the women sneaked up on the far stones, pointing and signaling in hushed voices. Birgit took the left, Arienh circled to the right, each step careful and silent as they sneaked around the tallest upright stone, prepared to snatch children from certain devilment.

Nothing. Arienh fumbled about in the stone's shadow but found no sign that the children had been there. Looking up, she caught Mildread's anxious frown from where she stood, next to the neighboring stone.

"Bring a torch," she said. Elli nodded and returned to the bonfire. Arienh pictured Liam stealing a spark of fire with a twig, sneaking off with the girls to light their own fire. Sometimes the boy's curiosity and mischief were beyond bearing.

A father would have contained him. Channeled his curiosity.

Birgit rubbed her hands, but smiled. "They can't be far. They just don't mean for us to catch them at their mischief."

Taking a torch from Elli, Arienh circled the outer perimeter of the stones. Of the seven children, none could be seen or heard.

"Maybe they got bored and went home," Elli suggested.

Mildread huffed. "They live all year for Beltane."

"Well, down the valley, then."

"The stream," cried Mildread suddenly. "Oh, not the stream. They're playing in the water!"

"Nay, we'd hear them," Birgit replied.

Arienh grabbed Birgit's hand and ran down the path toward the little rill that rushed out of the hills and joined the stream just above the Bride's Well. No sign of children.

"What could they be up to?" Terror trembled in Birgit's voice.

Beneath their feet, the ground vibrated, then rumbled, like the roar of floodwater broken loose from an earthen dam.

Horses? Horses with riders. Out of the depth of forest darkness came riders, barreling down on the clutch of women.

"Vikings!"

"Run!" Shrieking women scattered up the narrow valley sides. Riders thundered through, snatching up women. Arienh grabbed Birgit's hand, tugging her toward shadows and safety. Birgit screamed, suddenly wrenched away from her grasp.

"Help! Arienh, help me!"

"Birgit!" Arienh ran screaming after the rider.

Birgit's voice suddenly muffled as the rider, with his horse and his awkward prize, rushed on, up the hill, and plunged through the circle.

Arienh sped up the steep trail of the small gorge and ran into the stone circle toward the Beltane fire, hoping the horse would shy from it. She was too late. No sign of them remained.

If she could just get away, get help…

Wait. Something wasn't quite right.

Pounding hooves grew louder. Louder, closer. She glanced over her shoulder just as the dark rider leaned from his saddle and swooped her off her feet. As a jolt of pain jabbed through her injured shoulder, she bit back a scream.

Kicking, squirming against the iron-hard band of muscle that pinned her arms to her side, she fought helplessly. The rider's opposite hand found the dagger in her sash and tossed it away.

"Give it up," the rider shouted. "You're my prisoner now. I've caught you fairly."

She knew his voice, knew his scent. Knew the very feel of his arms around her.

Ronan. Up to more mischief than the children.

That would have been Egil, then, who had grabbed Birgit. Help me, indeed. Birgit had lied to her. Deliberately deceived her.

And glancing back over Ronan's shoulder, she saw the red-bearded blacksmith down on his knees before Elli as she stood beside the glow of the bonfire.

The little horse struggled under its double burden as Ronan goaded it across the circle and into the forest gloom beyond.

"Put me down. Ronan, stop this!"

"Nay, my sweet. You're my captive. What sort of Viking would release his captive? We'll be there soon."

"Where?"

"My secret lair. Vikings have lairs, you know."

If he kept going this direction, it would take them to the high knoll overlooking the stone circle and the Irish Sea. She supposed it was a good place for a lair, knowing his most likely purpose. She smiled. He cared, after all.

"What are you doing?" She laughed to herself at her deliberate tone of irritation. "The children. What did you do with the children?"

"Captives, every one. Wynne and Gunnar are holding them for ransom."

"Captives? What is this?"

"Simple, love. You expect us to act like Vikings. We're giving you what you ask for."

"What's the ransom?"

"Wives. Submit to us and be our wives, or never have your children back. Wynne and Gunnar will keep them forever."

The little horse whuffed as it climbed the slope, struggling against the steepness. Ronan halted the beast at the top of the knoll where the forest bordered the grassy plateau. He leapt down and lifted Arienh to the ground.

"What if I escape?" She caught herself rubbing her sore shoulder, and stopped. He hadn't meant to bump it.

He laughed. "You won't. You're much too curious."

Aye, she was that. "What about Birgit?"

"You're too late to rescue her this time. I'm sorry to tell you, but she has already surrendered. They are no doubt already handfast."

She gasped. "Married? But she's…"

Even in the darkness of the forest, she could see his angled brows flipping wickedly. "Egil doesn't care. She is his captive forever. She will be forced to accept Wynne's pampering and the assistance of Viking as well as Celt."

Arienh hid her grin. Even if Ronan couldn't see it in the darkness, she knew it would infect her speech.

"And you, my haughty prize, will submit to me."

She could grow to like this game. "Submit to a Viking? Never."

At the edge of the forest, she spotted a bower of bent branches trimmed gaily with spring flowers and floored with the fur of the great white bear. So that's what the men had been doing that had kept them away from the village all day. Someone had snitched about the Celtic tradition of lovers. Most likely Birgit. If not Mildread. Or Selma. Liam, without question.

It was no wonder everyone had been rebelling. She was still treating them like they were her children, needing her to decide everything for them. But her children were growing up. And they knew this time, she was wrong.

The moon just before morning, full and bright, bathed even the grassy slopes with its silver. His arm slid about her waist, and she leaned into him, standing by the bower he had built at the crest of the knoll. The sky opened to sparkling darkness surrounding the brilliant moon. The dark sea, humming its eternal music, sent crests of rolling whitecaps skimming over its surface like little boats seeking the shore.

He wrapped his arms around her, unwittingly catching her injured shoulder that had been jarred by the rough ride.

"Ow!"

"Your shoulder? Oh, I'm sorry. I forgot."

"Some Viking you are. A Viking would never apologize."

"I suppose I don't make a very good one. But then I've been trying to tell you that."

She had to laugh. He was her Viking, always would be, in her heart. How odd it was that when he made her dream come true, she had refused to accept it.

He stood behind her, massaging her sore shoulder gently, a tender, loving touch. Yet when she had expected him to toss her onto the furs in his naturally exuberant way, he held back. For what?

"I dreamed for years of coming back here," he said, "but you are not at all the woman I expected to find."

Was he disappointed in her? She was not much of a woman. Too harsh and abrupt. Not particularly good at the things a woman ought to be doing. She leaned back against him, turning her cheek to rest against his shoulder, wishing she could be more like the woman of his dreams.

He turned her in his arms to face him and let his huge, gentle fingers brush back the loose strands of her hair, a hopeless struggle of power against the early morning wind.

"But that girl would never be enough for me now," he said.

He cupped her cheeks in his hands. "You are the wind and fire. You are the stones. You are my magnificent Celtic warrior woman. You are my dreams as I never dared dream them. Be my wife, my love."

He was so beautiful. Never had he been so beautiful as he was this moment. She let her fingers trace the edge between moonlight and shadow on his face, newly discovering the wonder.

There was a time for surrender, after all.

She felt released. Giddiness came over her, and she giggled like a young girl. "My Viking. Even if you don't make a very good one."

He laughed, and great, smoky wickedness rapidly darkened his eyes. "Blood will tell."

With a swift arm behind her back he swept her down onto soft furs so quickly that the breath was almost knocked from her. Just as quickly, he threw his huge body atop her, pinning her down from her lips to her toes. His knee slid between her knees as his hands laced into her hair and wound it through his fingers. "I'm going to make love to you until you are silly with passion and pleasure."

His lips descended to capture hers, slanting across her mouth and gently forcing access. She savored the lush, sensual pleasure. "You're going to ravish me?"

"Won't be necessary," he retorted. "You'll give me everything I want."

That was the truth.

The dark fringe of his eyelids shuttered down over his eyes as he lowered his lips to capture hers. Above her head, the early morning sky lightened and flickered through the bower of bent branches. She wiggled her arm around his waist beneath his tunic. He stiffened and groaned.

Once again his lips found hers but did not linger long before blazing a searing trail down her throat while his fingers caught the hem of her kirtle and raised it.

A shiver fluttered up her skin from the cool air and his fingers that skimmed along her hips and up her sides as the garment lifted, momentarily blocking her view of him.

Both of his big hands shaped over the curve of her shoulders, then descended to cup and lift her breasts. Dizzy with the sensation, Arienh wanted just to stop and feel his touch, yet wanted as badly to touch him. She ran her fingers beneath his tunic and wriggled it over his head as he had done her kirtle. His hands stopped their exploring as he lifted himself away and sought the knot of the cord at his waist. His breeches dropped, exposing the stout length of manhood among thick, dark curls.

She pushed the breeches free of his thighs and, remembering the tingling of his passing fingers on her flesh, slid hers along his bulky, hard muscles in the same fashion, meaning to give to him all the pleasure she could find to give. A passionate hum rumbled from deep in his chest. He kicked the breeches free.

Traces of first sunlight cast a dappling of elongated spots across his shoulder and chest as it passed through the leafy bower. The dark sprinkling of hair had a faint glow of gold where the light struck it. She followed its track downward with her touch, where it skipped across his belly, then began again in a narrow line and spread out to encompass his swollen organ. As she traced its length from base to tip, his entire body jerked into rigid agony.

A groan turned to a growl as he crushed her against him, his mouth hunting down hers and forcing it to his will.

"Don't you dare," he said, his words tinged with threat and desperation. "I want this to last."

"You didn't like it?"

He took several ragged breaths before answering. "Aye. But you'll send me to the stars long before I take you there. This time, this is for both of us."

He caught the tip of her breast with his tongue and nuzzled it between his teeth. Lightning jolted through her, down to that magic center of her that he controlled.

"You see?" he whispered, mingling his husky words with nips and tugs against her sensitized flesh. "Don't you want your share, too?"

She couldn't form a word in her mouth. Only moans escaped, blending with his whispered pleadings, so that she did not know his voice from hers. Hazy, frantic desire flooded her as she ran her hands over the iron-hard muscles that coursed and surged over his back like ripples on the open sea. She found the glorious curve of his spine and followed it down to strong, hard buttocks. She cupped them the way he did her breasts.

Sounds of lovemaking tangled with his heated breath and tingled her skin. His hands sought and found all the places she wanted them to be, in the creases and folds that had hidden the secrets of her womanhood from her, so recently awakened by him. Knowing, not knowing, wanting, he compelled her body to join his in its craving for completion.

He nudged his knee and then his thigh between her legs, and eagerly she wrapped herself around him, enclosing him, enticing him to enter. Moisture beaded on his brow. He pushed his way inside, and a great cry of victory burst from him.

She tightened her hold on him as he nuzzled at her ear with whispered, secret sounds. She sought his mouth with hers, wanting a complete joining, and pursued his tongue to mate with hers.

Slowly the rhythm of his body took over hers, slow and deep, filling her to endless depths, lingering, withdrawing, with each stroke leaving her to fear irrationally that it might be the last, when she was not ready for it to end. He lifted himself higher, away from her, joining only in the one place, yet coming deeper, faster, and their pace grew frenzied, as feral as wolves tangling for supremacy. She lost all thought, felt only the primeval power, need overwhelming them in its desperate rush for perfection.

The rhythm suddenly changed to urgent, violent thrusting, as if he could not go deeper, yet somehow did, his body rigid, straining.

The wave overwhelmed her, engulfed her, and washed her away. Washed away everything but Arienh and her Viking. Her beautiful, wonderful Viking.

Slowly, the world found her again. She opened her eyes to the dappled brightness playing through the bower on his golden skin and the feel of his fingers threading lazily through her hair. The heavy fringe of his eyelashes traced a streak of charcoal just above his cheeks, hiding those wondrously blue eyes. Did he sleep? Had she? She didn't think so.

Yet it was as if eternity had passed and the world had been reformed. She closed her eyes, soaking in the pleasure of lying in his arms. And this time, slept.

She woke again to a warm sunbeam penetrating through the bower's canopy and catching her in the eye. The scratchy wool of the blanket tickled her bare skin, reminding her of how she lay, flesh to flesh beside him. Twice he had awakened her and sought her body, and she had given it freely, happily. Once she had been dreaming of a feather and woke to find his fingers stroking her cheek, the feather of her dreams.

His eyes opened and lazily surveyed her, as if she were his raider's booty.

"You're mine," Ronan said.

"Aye." It seemed it was her heart smiling.

But the morning was in full bloom, and there was much to do. The Beltane was not over. Perhaps the men could join them now. She stretched lazily, reveling in the silken feel of the great white bear rug against her back.

"We have no Maypole. I did not want to ask you. But we could teach you the dances if we had a Maypole."

"Now?"

"It is still the Beltane. We have not had a pole for several years."

His eyes narrowed with a hint of suspicion.

"Just a pole. It is not all that hard. Except that it must be made of beech. The pole is the symbol of all the lovers of the night before. And the dance symbolizes their life together."

"Hmm. And you'll teach us the dances?"

It must have been delight lighting her eyes, for it seemed the Vikings were doing most of the teaching. "Of course. I danced with you last night, in a dream."

His face became suddenly solemn. "It was no dream."

Arienh bolted up to sitting. "You were there? When I danced with the old ones?"

He nodded.

"Did you see them, too?"

It was not quite a smile that quirked at the corner of his mouth. "I am a Celt, too."

"But did you see them?"

"Well, no. I saw you dancing and went to dance with you. But Egil was afraid I would mess up the plan and called me back."

Arienh snickered, mostly at herself. Whatever everyone thought of her strange dance the night before, he had been there, and the old ones had accepted him. They had told her so. "I'm glad you came," she said.

He stretched as he rose, revealing interesting, languid curves and cords of muscles she meant to investigate further, later.

But they had many things to decide today. For everything had changed. Reluctantly, she rose to her knees, pulled her kirtle over her head, and fastened her cord belt as she watched him pull on his buckskin breeches.

A high-pitched scream pierced the morning air.

"Birgit!"

She glanced at Ronan's startled face. She jumped to her feet, dashed across the high meadow, and scrambled through the forest down the steep slope of the knoll.

Behind her, Ronan crashed through the forest, making as much noise as a boar as he caught up with her.

"You said she'd be safe with him."

"She would. She is—"

Another scream. A high-pitched shriek.

"From the Bride's Well," he shouted, and dashed ahead of her.

Terror seized Arienh as she sped through the ash grove after him. They should have gone the other way and taken the horse.

Past the trees, across the open plateau, they ran, along the straight cut of the stream to the waterfall, as the shrieks grew wilder.

Not screams of terror. No, there was something oddly familiar about them. Something more like the Birgit of their childhood.

Ahead of her, Ronan stopped short at the edge of the cliff, staring down where the stream plunged over the cliff, bracing balled fists on his hips. Screams and splashes echoed from the pool below.

Gasping for breath, Arienh caught up to him.

Below, two heads bobbed to the surface of the pool, and ripples in rings spread out from them. Birgit shrieked again, laughter rippling like the rings, her arms wrapped around Egil as he pitched her upward, to splash, shrieking, back into the water. Egil dove after her, scooping her up again. They paddled about, cavorting like otters.

Ronan peered down at the two water imps, his nostrils flaring with disgust. "That's your sister?"

Arienh nodded. She'd thought Birgit had forgotten how to laugh. "With your brother. They jumped, I'd say. He doesn't make a very good Viking, either."

"Jumped?"

"From the falls. We used to do that when we were children. But Birgit hasn't done that since...She can't because she can't see the rocks. Egil must have helped her. You have to jump way out, beyond where they're standing to the deep water, where it's darker. If you ball your legs up right before you hit, you'll make a big splash."

Ronan studied the splashing, screeching scene below, then turned back to Arienh. That smoky look of wicked mischief crossed his face again.

"You realize they're having so much fun they don't know we're here," he whispered.

"I do."

The wickedness broadened into an evil grin. "They wouldn't see us coming until it was too late. It would serve them right."

"Aye. It would."

His eyebrows arched wickedly, and the corners of his eyes crinkled. "Shall we?"

She pointed to the jumping-off stone, the traditional spot from which Celtic children pretended, for long, exhilarating moments, that they could fly.

Stealthily, they crept up onto the stone like slinking foxes while the otter-like inhabitants of the pool below frolicked, unsuspecting of the coming attack.

Standing on the platform stone, they grasped hands and flung themselves into the air. Arienh's wild screech echoed off the canyon walls and mingled with the Viking's roar as they plummeted downward and smacked the water.

They popped back to the surface, water streaming down their faces. Egil and Birgit stared, open mouthed. But not for long. Egil lunged at Ronan, knocking him under the surface. Birgit splashed at Arienh, but Arienh was now far too wet to do anything more than laugh.

As Ronan came back up, Arienh pushed Egil aside. With a squeal, she climbed up Ronan's big body, legs wrapped around him, high enough to throw her arms around his neck and plant a passionate kiss on his lips.

Ronan leaned them both into the water and eased them back to where he could stand. He laughed and squeezed her in a Viking's tight embrace. She rested her head against his shoulder and sighed.

Life was good.

THE END

# A FEW LAST WORDS...

$L$OKI'S DAUGHTERS WAS MY FIRST GOLDEN HEART FINALIST, back in 1998, and it went on to be published and garner many fine reviews. But a lot has changed since then. Today, I would write the story differently, and hopefully with more skill, for what kind of writer cannot improve with years of practice? So I've chosen to go on with other books and leave this one much like it was back then.

I did not realize until I finished the book just how much Arienh was like my dear friend Jan Shaffer, who was just as stubborn, just as determined never to give up. Jan survived four battles of cancer before finally succumbing to brain cancer not long before the book came out in print. I know she would have loved it. She read everything I wrote and never failed to love every word. Every author, published or not, needs to have a friend like her.

*Loki's Daughters* is historical romance. As a romance, it is more true to the genre conventions than to actual history, but I have done my best to reconcile the two. I have studied the Viking English and the Celts extensively—they are my ancestors, after all, and they deserve to be portrayed well. They were fierce and raw, yes. But they were also people who loved and lived rich lives. They didn't know much about their own ancient past, for much of that history was lost to raids and the ravages of time. They based their lives more on faith in their religions, perhaps not really realizing how they mixed Christian beliefs with the pagan leftovers. I've tried to capture the flavor of people who live by faith sincerely, not having the tremendous store of knowledge we have today.

"Viking" has become an accepted name for the people who left the Scandinavian countries to raid. Whether they were so called in that day, we can't really tell, and some say the term was not coined until the nineteenth century. However, a similar term, *vikingr*, is known in the Icelandic literature of 1000 AD, at a time when that language was not so different from the Norse language of the day. In fact, there was so little difference in all the Germanic languages of the time that the Scandinavians could easily communicate with the Angles and Saxons of the British Isles.

Vikings did more than raid. Probably more were interested in moving on to new homes than in get-rich-quick raiding. They became a dominant fixture in the British Isles, especially in Ireland, Scotland, and eastern England.

If you'd like to know more about the Viking cultures in England, or the Celts, contact me through my website or blog and ask questions. I don't know everything, of course, but I dearly love researching and am always looking for an excuse. But please don't try to tell me "a Viking would NEVER surrender his sword." That may be a convention in romance novels, but the truth is nobody knows, one way or the other. And from what I can see, Vikings had a very realistic approach on when to fight and when to exit rapidly, with or without the weapons.

See me on my website/blog IN SEARCH OF HEROES:
www.dellejacobs.blogspot.com

## ABOUT THE AUTHOR

A NATIVE OF ILLINOIS, DELLE Jacobs has been crafting stories since the tender age of four. She earned a degree in geography from the University of Oklahoma and worked as a cartographer until eventually becoming a social worker specializing in troubled teens and families. Everything changed, however, once she began writing books in 1993, and by 2004, literary success convinced her to quit her day job and focus full time on writing. She is a seven-time finalist for the Romance Writers of America's Golden Heart Award, which she has won an unprecedented three times, in addition to numerous other writing awards for her novels, including *His Majesty, the Prince of Toads, Lady Wicked, Sins of the Heart,* and *Aphrodite's Brew.* Along the way she discovered a knack for designing e-book covers, which is a great way to get her creative juices flowing when her book characters are being particularly uncooperative. She lives today in southwest Washington State with her family.

Made in the USA
Charleston, SC
07 November 2012